I0460580

The Milk Run

by
Michael Brachman

THE MILK RUN

All rights reserved

Copyright © 2015 by Michael Brachman

Cover art copyright © 2015 by Bruce Brachman

V6.01.0011

Also by Michael Brachman

The Rome's Revolution Series
Rome's Revolution 3455 AD
The Ark Lords
Rome's Evolution

The Rome's Revolution Saga
Rebirth: The Rome's Revolution Saga – Book 1
Rebellion: The Rome's Revolution Saga – Book 2
Redemption: The Rome's Revolution Saga – Book 3

The Vuduri Knights Series
The Milk Run

The Vuduri Universe Series
The Vuduri Companion
Tales of the Vuduri: Year One
Tales of the Vuduri: Year Two
Tales of the Vuduri: Year Three
Tales of the Vuduri: Year Four
Tales of the Vuduri: Year Five

Dedication

First and foremost, I have to thank my brother Bruce. Not only is he my editor and artist and the inspiration behind MINIMCOM, but he is also fiercely protective of the Vuduri culture and characters. Bruce creates the amazing covers, the book trailers and makes my writing so much better. Bruce, I could not have done it without you.

A special thanks to all who supported my Indiegogo campaign to get Rome's Revolution made into an audio book: Dennis, Bernadette, Carol, Ileen and Barbara. A very special thank you to the real-life Lupe and a super thank you to Frank Greenberg for his extremely generous contribution.

My undying gratitude to my wife, Denise, for all her love and support throughout the entire process.

And finally, thank you to all my readers, especially Barbara, Sharon and Walt: you helped to make this what it is.

Guide to the Vuduri Universe of the 35th Century

Vuduri: 24-chromosome mind-connected humans of the future. Their collective consciousness is called The Overmind. They are the ruling class on Earth. They have a small contingent on the planet of Deucado and a larger one on the planet Helome.

Essessoni: Humans from the 21st century. The name Garecei Ti Essessoni means The Killer Generation. The Vuduri hold them responsible for the near extinction of the human race. Over nine billion people died in the late 21st century. The event is referred to as The Great Dying.

Mandasurte: The word means mind-deaf in Vuduri. Typically, a mandasurte has a genetic complement of only 23 chromosomes. They are excluded from most of the Vuduri affairs and have flocked to Deucado since its liberation.

Erklirte: The word means Ark Lords. These were colonists from the Ark V (original target: Chara) who returned to Earth nearly 600 years after launch. They were very cruel. They reintroduced slavery and tried to take over the Earth.

Ibbrassati: The word means oppressed in Vuduri. Many mandasurte scientists and other important members of their society were kidnapped and transported to the prison world of Deucado. They were placed there to die in an asteroid strike but were spared when Deucado was liberated.

Deucadons: Descendants of the Ark III (original target: 82 G. Eridani) who crash-landed on Deucado five hundred years before the story takes place. They had to take refuge underground to avoid the meteors and asteroids that were constantly striking the planet. In some ways, their society is more technologically advanced than the Vuduri.

Mosdurece: This is the Vuduri word for half-blood. A full-blooded Vuduri would have a diploid complement of the 24th chromosome. A mosdurece has a single pair. They have all the capabilities and characteristics of a full-blooded Vuduri however there is a social stigma attached to being only a half-blood.

The Stareaters: Called Asdrale Cimatir by the Vuduri, these are gigantic, living Dyson Spheres who travel around the universe consuming stars that they predict will go nova or supernova. They are noble creatures, dedicated to prolonging the life of our Universe.

MASAL: A supercomputer that designed the 24th chromosome which was responsible for the rise of the Vuduri. His plan was to engineer the humanity out of mankind. He was destroyed by Rei and Rome.

Dramatis Personae

Rei Bierak: An engineer and one of the frozen passengers aboard the Ark II, launched from Earth in 2067AD (original target: Tau Ceti). The Ark II went off course and was not discovered for nearly 1400 years. Rei was the first human awakened and responsible for eventually getting the Ark II to its original destination, Tau Ceti, now called Deucado by the Vuduri.

Rome: A half-blood (mosdurece) Vuduri woman from the 35th century who fell in love with Rei and eventually married him. Originally connected to the Overmind, she was cast out (Cesdiud) when she consorted with Rei. Rome is a stunning Vuduri female with olive-tinted skin and an athletic build, bordering on the spectacular. She eventually acquired telepathic powers.

Aason Bierak: Rei and Rome's 21-year-old son. He is brilliant and brave. He has all the traits of both the Essessoni and Vuduri. He saved the Earth from the Stareaters when he was only a week old. He thwarted a murderous plot against his parents when he was only four. He has sandy brown hair and blue eyes and broad swimmer's shoulders just like his father. He acquired all of his parents' abilities combined.

Lupe Bierak: Rei and Rome's 16-year-old daughter. Many consider her a brat but only because she is so sly. She has internal apparatus which makes her one of the most powerful communicators in the galaxy. She has shoulder-length brown hair, flecked with strands of gold and looks just like her mother, only taller. Her eyes are very dark and they seem to glow in dim lighting.

MINIMCOM: Originally an autopilot computer that was fused into the airframe of a Vuduri space tug. Circumstances and experience caused him to become self-aware. Now a starship, MINIMCOM can fly as fast as 15,000c using what is called the Null Fold Star-drive.

Junior: MINIMCOM's son although technically Junior is a clone. The first starship "born" not built. He has all the abilities (Null Fold Star-drive, stealth shield) of his father. Junior is Aason's cousin (MINIMCOM is Aason's adopted uncle) and best friend.

OMCOM: Originally a standard computer installed on Skyler Base within the Tabit System. Eventually he transferred his consciousness into a mass larger than a planet. He also has a clone on Deucado to supervise Rome's Library of Life.

Fridone: Rome's father, a 23-chromosome mandasurte (mind-deaf) oceanographic scientist. Rome calls him Beo which is the Vuduri word for father. Aason calls him Grandbeo.

Binoda: Rome's mother, a full-blooded 24-chromosome Vuduri. Binoda is an animal husbandry expert. Rome calls her Mea which is the Vuduri word for mother. Aason calls her Grandmea.

Preface

This story takes place 17 years after the events depicted in
Rome's Evolution.

Chapter 1
Year 3476 AD (1395 PR)
Just outside the Tabit System
(26 Light Years from Earth)

"AASON!" LUPE SHRIEKED. THE TEENAGE GIRL'S BLOODCURDLING scream shattered the previously peaceful calm of the spacious starship cabin.

21-year-old Aason Bierak was caught by surprise. The handsome young man with the tousled brown hair had been staring straight ahead, lost in the mesmerizing blackness of null fold space just beyond the cockpit's windshield. It was a mind-trap and Aason knew it but it was one in which he allowed himself a few minutes of entanglement. That ended abruptly with Lupe's howl. Exerting a titanic effort, the boy tore his piercing blue eyes away from the lush void to face his sister. He was horrified to see a waving set of multi-colored translucent tentacles that had emerged from nowhere, enveloping Lupe, constricting her in their grasp.

"What?!" Aason gasped. He clawed at the clasps of his X-harness, snapping it open. He flipped off the straps, extending his frame. Even as he jumped up out of the pilot's chair, the crystal-like extensions of light were dragging his younger sister into a not-hole. There was no other way to describe it. Her whole body was distorted, shrinking. It looked like she was being sucked into a vacuum hose. Aason leaped over the center console toward her, arms outstretched, but he was only able to brush his hand across one of her fingertips just as she disappeared into nothingness.

"Lupe?" Aason cried out helplessly. He felt all around the sturdy yet comfortable co-pilot's seat, trying to find evidence of what he had just witnessed. It was as if Lupe had never existed. Instinctively, he closed his eyes, activated his PPT transceivers and called out to her using the gravitic resonance channel that was built into his head and into the heads of all of the Vuduri.

"Lupe!" he shouted mentally. If she were anywhere within one-half light year of their current position, the limits of his PPT resonance, she would sense him. Immediately, he felt the familiar tickle of a connection taking hold.

"Aason," Lupe replied, fear palpable in her mental tone. But even as she 'spoke' the voice Aason heard in his mind was dwindling rapidly. *"New to Lupe,"* was all she said then nothing, not even static.

"Lupe!" Aason called out again. This time there was no response. The tickle in his mind was gone which meant the connection was gone. The two Bierak children also had a second communication channel, one based upon EM transmission, that their father called a 'cell-phone in the head' but he didn't bother with that since the gravitic channel was so much more powerful.

He opened his eyes and looked around the cabin, trying to orient himself. He spotted a grille mounted below the main display in the front console. "Junior," he shouted. "Where is she? Where'd she go? I've lost contact with her through the connection."

"I don't know" replied the starship who was also Aason's cousin through the grille which had both a microphone and speaker built in. The spaceship's voice was very natural and human-sounding as compared to his 'father', the starship known as MINIMCOM, whose normal voice was quite tinny. "I cannot reach her on the EM band."

Aason's shoulders and neck quickly tightened up almost to the point where he couldn't move. He was completely panicked. He felt his ability to think logically shutting down just when he needed it the most. He turned, taking care to grab the co-pilot's armrests to steady himself and addressed the two-meter tall, all-white being standing at the back of the cockpit.

"OMCOM, help me," Aason called out urgently. "What were those things? Where'd she go?"

"I do not know," replied the livetar which was basically an animated shell made up of VIRUS-based constructor units. OMCOM's consciousness, at least this extremely reduced subset of OMCOM, was actually housed in the vast array of memron units packed into the shell of the starship. "This livetar's sensory apparatus detected nothing. Only that Lupe shrank and disappeared. I have never personally witnessed such a phenomenon before nor are there any records indicating that it is even possible."

"You didn't see those, those things?" Aason questioned. "They were glowing. They grabbed her. She, she…" Aason's throat caught and he could not say any more words.

"I believe that *you* detected something," OMCOM continued, "but it must have been using a channel or modality not available to me. All I saw was that Lupe was here and then she was gone."

Aason took a deep breath, trying one last time to get a grip. "Was it a PPT tunnel?" he asked quietly.

"I didn't detect any gravitic fluctuations," Junior interjected. "I don't think it was a PPT tunnel."

Enough was enough. Aason stood upright and whipped around to face forward again. He reached over and grasped the edge of the center console.

"I've got to find her," he said breathlessly. "Junior, can you do a MIDAR sweep? Look for another ship, anything…" Aason's voice trailed off as he struggled to articulate his next move.

"I have to deactivate the X-drive," Junior pointed out.

"Then do it!" Aason commanded. After he said it, he regretted his tone but did not elaborate.

The gentle shushing sound of the newly modified null fold generators dampened and ceased. The cockpit of the starship became deathly still as the stars of normal space came into view all around them. The perpetual night sky was filled with tiny points of light, both bright and dim.

The large display panel built into the front console rotated fully upright and went dark. A moment later, a bright spot appeared in the center of the display and quickly extended into a glowing green line. MIDAR was the Vuduri equivalent of a three-dimensional RADAR system using multi-spectral emissions to bounce off of objects and collect the echoes to form a coherent picture of anything reflective in nearby space. The bright green band swept around clockwise at a rapid pace. Faint yellow concentric rings representing distance from the ship came rushing in from the outskirts of the display to concentrate in the middle to form a bull's-eye. The rate of entry slowed until the ringed display stopped changing. The only motion was the thin glowing line that rotated about the center like a super-long second hand. There were no blips anywhere. Aason stared at the screen intently but despite his willing it to do so, no spots appeared.

"MIDAR shows no observable objects," Junior said finally. "I've pushed it out as far as I can. There is absolutely nothing detectable in this region of space."

Aason was crestfallen. "Can't you do something else?"

"Sure," Junior replied. "Let me launch some star-probes."

"Yeah, good idea," Aason said, nodding his head hopefully.

A series of pips announced the microscopic starships being released from beneath the rear of the cargo section. The star-probes were not much more than twin Casimir Pumps tied to a memron. They had a focusing tube and a single element collection plate. When a group of them arranged themselves in a three-dimensional concave pattern, they formed a lens-less camera that could travel many light years in a single jump yet focus on objects at extreme distances. And because they traveled at many times the speed of light, they could effectively travel back in time, at least from an observational perspective. However, they were not really designed to resolve small objects close up. The front panel display changed to a blurry star field.

"I'm sending them in small groups, outward, in a spherical search pattern," Junior announced. The images on the screen wavered and became unintelligible. Aason could not make sense of the clumps on the display there but he had complete confidence that Junior knew what he was doing.

"Nothing," Junior announced after a minute, disappointed. "I've gone three hundred light-minutes out. There's absolutely nothing."

Aason walked over and sat down heavily in the pilot's chair, leaning back against the headrest. Straightening up, he put his fists up to his forehead then struck them against his skull. "I was supposed to protect her," he said facing down. "What am I going to do?"

He took a cleansing breath, trying to collect his thoughts. He folded his hands across his lap and decided to logic out the situation.

"Look," he said out loud, "whoever took her; they have to be around here somewhere. She can't have just vanished to nowhere."

"You said you could no longer connect to her mentally," OMCOM pointed out. "That would imply that she is no longer 'around here' as you call it."

"All they would need is a T-suppressor," Aason replied, thinking more clearly now. "If they used one of those, then I wouldn't be able to contact her even if she was across the room." He looked out the cockpit window and scanned from side to side. "Just because we can't see them, doesn't mean they aren't around here either. Junior does it all the time." He snapped his fingers. "Cuz, when you have your cloak on, if you were invisible, how would you detect yourself?"

"I couldn't," Junior replied. "That's the whole point of the invisibility shield. I make myself transparent to all the wavelengths of the electromagnetic spectrum."

Aason reached forward and patted the rounded top of his instrument cluster. "What about your mass? That doesn't go away. Couldn't you detect that?"

"Not directly," answered the starship. Junior cleared the central display and replaced it with the star field as seen by his forward cameras. "You could only detect it indirectly." He superimposed a red dot right in the center of the screen and started it blinking slowly. He overlaid the point with a very faint pinkish circle, much larger, centered on the dot. The color saturation thinned out at the outer edges of the circle. "You would need to find another mass and look for its gravitational influence."

Aason put his hands up to his face. "What about your hull?" he asked. "You have mass. Can't you see if you're being pulled in any direction?"

"Not without a frame of reference," Junior replied. He brightened the background shading and caused it to pulse slowly. "And there's nothing remotely close enough to measure it against."

"That *is* why we picked this region of space for the test flight," OMCOM added.

Aason took a deep breath and forcefully exhaled. "You're no help," he said, desperation seeping into his voice. "Neither of you. I have to find her. Somehow."

Aason blinked rapidly and twisted in his seat. "OMCOM, even if you couldn't see those things, where do you think they came from? Just speculate."

"I will need more information. Describe what you saw," OMCOM suggested.

"Those things. They were transparent but they had all sorts of colors. They looked like, like they were squiggly. They looked like the arms of a squid or maybe an octopus from back on Earth. My Dad showed me some pictures once."

"Estimate their diameter. Were they thick? Thin?" OMCOM asked. "Did they have physical extent? What were they made of?"

"They weren't thin but they weren't thick, either. 10, 12, maybe 15 centimeters across. They were waving all around. I think they were just made of light, filled with colors. The colors flashed and changed."

OMCOM pointed forward, toward the windshield. "We were in null fold space," the livetar replied. "That means the objects you saw did not originate from normal space. Therefore they must have come from somewhere else."

"Somewhere else?" Aason parroted. "What does that mean?"

"It means they came from outside our normal four-dimensional space. By extrapolation that would imply they came from outside of our universe. And wherever they are from, it is possible that that is where they are taking Lupe."

Aason wrinkled his forehead. "How can something be from outside our universe? The universe is everything, everywhere."

"You said that you had contact with Lupe briefly," OMCOM replied, ignoring Aason's observation. "How long were you in contact?" OMCOM held his hands close together then stretched them apart to illustrate his point.

"Maybe a second or two. Why?"

"And what did Lupe say during that interval? Did she give you any hint where she was or where she was going? What about the things that took her? Did she say anything, anything at all that we could use to determine their origin?"

Aason looked up at the top of the cabin. His heart seemed to miss a beat thinking about that brief conversation. "She called out my name," he said. "Then she said 'new to Lupe'. I don't know even what she meant by that. I guess whatever she was seeing was new to her."

"Those where her exact words?" OMCOM responded oddly. "Was there anything peculiar about her pronunciation?"

"Not really," Aason answered, trying to recall every nuance of the three word sentence. He cocked his head then said, "Wait. Now that you mention it, she actually said her name a little funny. She pronounced it Lu-pie, not Lu-pay." Aason pondered that for a moment. "Why did she do that?"

The livetar's shoulders actually sagged a bit then he straightened up. "I cannot say with certainty but I know that term is flagged as high importance in my database. The annotation associated with the warning informs me that you must return to me at once," he commanded. "I must presume this fact will engender some type of radical action."

"What do you mean return to you?" Aason asked. "You're here."

"No, this is not me. You *are* aware that this livetar is just a subset, a replica," OMCOM replied. "The being you see here was instantiated merely to observe. I do not possess the computational capacity to deduce what has happened. Return to what you call Planet OMCOM. The one flag in my limited database tells me that we must return to the central core to plot our next course of action. You will need Planet OMCOM to calculate and confirm."

"No!" Aason protested. "We can't leave here. We have to look for Lupe."

"That is exactly what we are going to do and we do not have a second to spare," OMCOM insisted. "Junior, release a beacon and leave your star-probes. Return to Tabit at once."

"Do we risk using the Null Fold X-drive again?" Junior asked. "What if the entities that Aason saw decide to return?"

"Let them come," Aason shouted out defiantly. "If those things only exist in null fold space, I can only hope they come back and take me too. They'll take me to Lupe."

"As you wish," Junior said skeptically.

From behind the bulkhead, Aason could hear the high-pitched whine of the modified PPT generators ramping up.

"Buckle in," Junior instructed. "This is going to be rough."

Aason reached around and drew the two straps of the X-harness across his chest. Each tongue snapped into the clasp of the seat-belt.

"Ready," he said.

"Roger," Junior replied.

In front of Aason, through the cockpit's windshield, he could see the yawning black circle of a normal PPT tunnel forming. Somewhere in its center was a tiny pinpoint of light which was the remains of the star once known as Tabit. As soon as the tunnel was wide enough, Junior fired his plasma thrusters full-bore, shoving Aason violently back into his seat, as forcefully as he had ever experienced. As they entered the tunnel, Junior activated the Null Fold X-drive with its peculiar shushing sound and they began their short trip back to Planet OMCOM.

To understand the X-drive, you have to go all the way back to the beginning, before faster-than-light travel. Aason and Lupe's father Rei and all the passengers aboard the 21st century Ark II arrived at Tau Ceti using a propulsion system called the Grey Drive. The Grey Drive was nothing more than a souped-up ion engine which sent xenon atoms into a quantum black hole and used the resulting Hawking Radiation to push the ship forward. Although the acceleration was negligible, over a sufficient period of time it eventually reached a top speed of 5% of the speed of light. However, an accident caused Rei's ship and his crewmates, deep frozen in cryo-hibernation, to miss their mark and they drifted in an uncontrolled fashion for nearly 1400 years until they were rescued by the Vuduri in the Tabit system in the 35th century.

By that time, the Vuduri made travel between the stars practical with their Pinch Point Transit or PPT tunnels. They used Casimir Pumps which exploited the Casimir Effect to create pockets of negative energy which were then projected into neutral space. Where there is no energy, there is no space so when their starships traversed the tunnel, they went around space and the mathematical result equated to a velocity many times that of the speed of light. A PPT tunnel therefore was conceptually similar to a wormhole but without requiring a nearby black hole. The Vuduri method of travel would seem peculiar to someone not of that era. They would open up a hole, pass through it then immediately turn around and use their plasma thrusters to come to a complete halt. They'd rotate around and do it again. Stop, start, stop, start. While odd, it was efficient and some of their smaller ships were able to effectively travel 100 or more times the speed of light.

MINIMCOM, the starship that was once an auto-pilot computer, revolutionized the method by force-projecting a continuous series of PPT tunnels ahead allowing him to travel upwards of 1000c or one thousand times the speed of light.

Planet OMCOM refined the method even further by splitting up the negative energy of a PPT tunnel into a real and imaginary component. OMCOM showed Junior's spaceship father, MINIMCOM, how to use the "real" component of negative energy to fold null space yet again resulting in another improvement in speed. Using the Null Fold Drive, both MINIMCOM and Junior could now travel at 15,000 times the speed of light. Before the Null Fold Drive, the trip between Aason's home world of Deucado, which orbited Tau Ceti, to the Tabit star system took seven days. But with the Null Fold Drive, the same trip, a distance of nearly 21 light years, was reduced to a mere 11 hours.

But 17 years later, it was Planet OMCOM's study of the properties of imaginary negative energy that produced the Null Fold X-drive. This star-drive had *no* upper speed limit. It was only limited by the amount of computing power available. Imaginary space had just as many, if not more, dimensions as real space and as long as the starship could compute how to fold it, it just went faster and faster. Lupe was kidnapped when she and Aason were along for the first test run of the new star-drive.

Using the Null Fold X-drive, it only took Junior a matter of minutes to return to remains of the star once known as Tabit located 26 light-years from Earth, and the planet-sized computer called Planet OMCOM that orbited that star. OMCOM had once been a regular computer charged with running the star base which sat on the moon Dara, orbiting a gas giant called Skyler's World. Aason and Lupe's mother Rome had been stationed there to study why certain stars were disappearing. It turns out that they were being destroyed by incomprehensibly large creatures, living Dyson Spheres, called Stareaters and one was coming their way. After thawing out Aason's father, Rei, Rome and Rei, along with OMCOM's help, devised a defensive strategy to defeat the Stareaters which in the Vuduri language were called Asdrale Cimatir. Rome enabled OMCOM to build self-replicating nano-machines which Rei had named VIRUS units to consume the Stareater from the inside out using the power of the exponent. When a Stareater named Balathunazar suddenly appeared in the Tabit system, Rei unleashed the VIRUS weapon by setting the micro-machines loose on the very moon holding the star base. The Stareater was successfully killed but only after it had partially digested Tabit. What had been a powerful F6V star, three times more luminous than our Sun, was now a tiny, barely glowing celestial body.

What Rome and Rei did not know at the time was that OMCOM had designed the VIRUS units such that he could transfer his consciousness over to the tremendous bulk which was the remains of the Stareater. When the time was right, OMCOM executed the maneuver and become the largest computer in the galaxy. As a result, even though he was originally known as the **OM**nipresent **COM**puter, OMCOM now thought of himself as the **OM**niscient **COM**puter which had always been his goal. The fact that they had destroyed a creature capable of ending all life was only of secondary importance to him. Later, mankind found out that the Stareaters were actually intelligent and noble creatures charged with the mission of saving the universe. Rome and Rei forged a treaty with the Stareaters to not consume stars where humans lived and thus saved the Earth.

OMCOM remained behind in the Tabit system doing who knows what but he interacted with the humans on a regular basis using null-fold relays. The invention of the X-drive was just one of the items he elected to share. What else was he doing? Well, nobody knew since he kept the rest of his secrets to himself.

Physically, Planet OMCOM was the size and shape of a regular planet and could have been confused as such except that he was all white as if he were made completely of ice. Upon arrival at the huge white orb, Junior used his plasma thrusters to go into orbit around the living computer. The starship oriented himself so that their cockpit window faced straight down, toward the starkly white surface.

"Another livetar will return," the version of OMCOM standing in the back announced. Aason scarcely had time to turn around to face him when, with a barely noticeable whoosh and a pop, the shell winked out of existence.

Chapter 2

Aason and Junior were on their second orbit around the false planet. The boy had given up using Junior's instrumentation to detect variances on the all-white surface below because quite simply there were no discernible features present. It looked as artificial as Aason knew it to be. It was flat out boring. The barely-textured, clean roof of Junior's cockpit was more interesting.

A clicking noise from Junior's grille caused Aason to sit up straight.

"What?" he asked.

"Look in front of you," Junior replied.

Out of the cockpit window, Aason could see the formerly homogeneous surface of Planet OMCOM changing. Junior rotated the large central display to its fully upright position and routed in his video feed. Junior's forward camera showed minuscule pieces of the planet had broken free and were now approaching the starship like a tiny cloud. Other portions of the surface began flowing to the north, creating a series of huge mountain ranges while still other sections began flowing to the south and west creating valleys and more mountains until a gigantic face appeared within its bulk like a comical Man in the Moon. However, instead of OMCOM's regular bullet-shaped head with slits where the eyes and mouth would be, this head was rounded and expressive.

Planet OMCOM's titanic lips started moving. "We will find your sister," said the living computer, his voice issuing from Junior's grille. "However, I must make some changes to Junior's airframe to prepare you for your search."

The white cloud approached Junior until Aason could see that it was made up of a number of starships which resembled a smaller version of the clone ship that first ferried Junior to Deucado after he was 'born'. To a person of an earlier age, they would have resembled the large, cylindrical spaceships from a bad science fiction movie but they were essentially monolithic computation machines with engines.

"What kind of changes?" Aason asked but OMCOM did not answer. There was a slight jolt as one of the clone ships came in contact with the top part of Junior's hull. Junior shook again as two more of the white ships attached themselves to the upper portion of his port and starboard side.

"Ooh," Junior said as several more of the all-white ships clamped down onto his hull. The spaceship's dorsal cameras showed that each of the attached objects were melting and flowing onto Junior's superstructure swelling him in the process. They created essentially a whole new layer starting mid-ship then arching over the top.

"Ow," Junior said.

"Ow?" Aason posed, confused. He didn't think Junior was capable of experiencing pain.

"Oooh," Junior spoke again, this time his voice was merely a whisper. Aason felt the entire starship shudder.

"What's happening?" he asked, looking around.

In a normal voice, Junior replied, "OMCOM is expanding the top part of my..." then his voice drifted off again. There was a click then the starship continued, "...the top part of my hull." The central display panel showed an outline of the spaceship from the side. Junior now had a sizeable hump on top. "He's building a filled cavity of sorts. He..." Junior stopped speaking again.

"What now?"

"Oh wow," Junior said with a strange expression. "He just flooded the cavity with memrons and, oh, he just patched them in and..." Junior sounded dreamy, almost hypnotized.

With a whoosh and a pop, a new copy of OMCOM's livetar appeared again in the back of the cockpit. However, this livetar was wearing a long white cape, something that Junior's father, MINIMCOM, was fond of.

"What's going on?" Aason demanded. "Will somebody please tell me?"

"I have created a computing infrastructure roughly equal to my original mass when I was just the star base computer," OMCOM answered in stereo, his voice coming both from the livetar and Junior's grille simultaneously. "The new livetar I have placed onboard will have nearly full computational capabilities. This additional equipment will also allow Junior to travel even faster using the X-drive. I have inserted more of my simulator modules and increased Junior's algorithmic capacity tremendously as well. I believe you will need it when you get to your destination."

"Get where?" Aason asked.

"I feel like a humpback whale," Junior interrupted in an odd voice. He switched the central display panel back to his dorsal cameras and directed them along his top surface. A huge white lump was grafted onto his airframe stretching smoothly from the front all the way to his rear stabilizer. Even as Aason watched, the lump changed from all-white to all-black, matching the rest of the spaceship's exterior. The black surface cells were miniature PPT projectors that allowed Junior to create a cloak of invisibility when required.

"Where are we going?" Aason asked, exasperation rising in his voice.

"I need to cross-check certain facts," said the voice from the grille. "I am going to create a complete simulation of reality. I will answer your question in a moment after you answer a few questions for me."

Aason sighed and sank back into his chair. He had spent enough time around the Library clone of OMCOM to know that the computer's personality did not lend itself to following direct instructions. It always acted like it was in charge and it was usually more expedient not to fight it.

"The livetar I am sending along..." The livetar in the back of the cabin patted his chest, "...will also have access to the enhanced computing capacity and simulator modules. Essentially, you will now have the benefit of my actual presence in your quest."

"I don't even know what quest I'm on. Ask your questions," Aason said tensely. "I want to get going."

"I will need to know exactly what you experienced from a *subjective* viewpoint during Lupe's abduction, not objective."

"I already told you, or him," Aason said, pointing over his shoulder.

"I need to hear it again," Planet OMCOM insisted. "I must fill in the background elements with non-measurables."

"Why?"

"Because I said so," OMCOM replied taking on the tone of a parent to a young child. "Please start from the beginning."

Aason gritted his teeth. Now that the initial shock of Lupe's kidnapping had worn off, he had to fight his urge to take action. Any action. He took a deep breath to calm himself then started in.

"We were doing a test run of the X-drive. I was looking out the windshield when I heard Lupe scream. There were wavy things, like glowing tentacles that came out of nowhere. They grabbed her and pulled her out of the cabin but through the back of her seat. It made no sense. I tried to reach her in time but I was too late." Aason voice caught on that last sentence.

"What did the tentacles look like?"

Aason closed his eyes. "They were made up of colors and light. All sorts of colors. The colors ran and changed, like they were shifting around. They swirled and swirled as they disappeared."

"What happened next?"

"Come on!" Aason said. "This isn't helping. We have to go look for her."

"I know you are upset but there is a purpose behind this. Please tell me."

"OK," Aason said glumly. "I jumped out of my seat to try and grab her but even in that short time, she was gone."

"I know that you leaped toward her. Were you able to touch her before she disappeared?"

"Uh, yeah," Aason said. "My finger touched hers for like a second."

"Did you touch the tendrils of light?"

"Not that I could tell," Aason said. "Her finger was all I could reach. I mean, I might have, but I didn't feel anything."

"It is a start," OMCOM replied. "Please hold the hand that touched Lupe over Junior's central display panel."

Junior rotated the panel back down so that it was flush against the rest of the center dash. Aason unbuckled and reached forward to place his hand flatly against the screen. The panel began to glow. It grew brighter and brighter. It got so bright that Aason had to activate his inner Vuduri iris to shield his eyes. Remarkably, the flashing lights took on a faint, three-dimensional quality, even without the holo-projectors, that appeared as a whirling cavalcade of speckles and bursts. The tornadic activity condensed until it became a single column of blinding light. The light spread out and covered Aason's outstretched hand, bathing it almost like it was a living thing. Aason felt his hand heating up but before it became uncomfortable, the light shut off with a snap.

"I have analyzed all residual radiation, molecular changes, DNA and so on. I did find a few cells that belong to your sister but there is no evidence that you contacted anything else that I could detect. As my livetar mentioned to you before, this confirms that what you saw was not of our space-time continuum."

"So what does that mean?" Aason asked, removing his hand. "Where would we even go to look for her?"

"I am nearly done constructing an exact simulation of your reality leading up to Lupe's capture to confirm. However, I must ask you several more redundant questions," OMCOM said.

"Huh?" Aason asked, confused. Absent-mindedly, he rubbed his hands together in a meaningless gesture.

"We will do this quickly. Why did you and Lupe come to Tabit in the first place?"

"You know that. It was your idea."

"Please," OMCOM persevered. "I already explained to you, I am fully aware that I am repeating myself. I am tracing my simulation of reality along with your narrative, looking for deviations. I apologize but this is the only way to be sure."

Aason sighed. "You said our Library clone's algorithms were getting dated and you wanted a duplicate, a backup, of the data he had accumulated. So we were bringing him here for you to swap out with whatever it was you wanted and get his operating system updated."

"Very good," OMCOM said. "Now why did you come and not your parents?"

Aason clenched his jaw. He was about to protest again then it came to him. OMCOM wasn't just tracking his words for background. To anybody else, it would seem like the computer was just plain stalling. But why? Then it occurred to him that it must be incomprehensibly difficult to create a complete simulation of all of reality. So OMCOM was using this second influx of data, not because he did not know it, but rather to propagate his simulation. He was using Aason's words to finalize the construct so he decided to continue.

"Grandbeo got injured. Mom and Dad wanted to stay with Grandmea to help out. Dad said it was OK for me to come by myself."

"Why didn't they wait until your Grandbeo was healed?"

"You said that our Library clone was beginning to experience situations which were beyond his computational capacity and the sooner the upgrade, the better."

"That explains your presence. Why did Lupe come?"

"Originally, she wasn't supposed to but she was bored. She whined so much we couldn't stand it. Dad finally said it was OK for her to come because this was a milk run."

"What is a milk run?"

"It's a quick trip to the, I think Dad called it a store, to get some milk. It was supposed to be easy."

"Very well. The trip from Deucado to Tabit takes 11 hours using the Null Fold Drive. What did you do during the 11 hours?"

"Huh?" Aason asked. "I don't know. We slept. We ate. We fooled around. Lupe did some homework." He shook his head. He had had enough. "Come on, let's go," he said.

"Please, Aason, this is important. Just a few minutes more. During the trip out here, did she contact anyone?"

Aason was taken aback by this. "What do you mean?"

"Exactly what I asked. Did she contact anyone?"

"No. I mean, I don't think so. How could she?" Aason scratched his head.

"Lupe has superior communication skills. Her ability to project a gravitic transmission is much more powerful and can reach much farther than your mother or any Vuduri for that matter."

"Well if she did contact somebody, she didn't say anything to me," Aason noted.

"Did she do anything at all out of character?"

"Nothing's out of character for Lupe," Aason said bitingly. "She teased me about a girl I used to know on Deucado. We were talking about how Dad got to Tabit. I think she looked up something in the records about the other Arks."

The livetar stationed behind Aason at the back of the cockpit, made a noise that sounded suspiciously like someone clearing his throat. Then the livetar in the back spoke with a single voice for the first time, no echo from the front grille. "Search history on the workstation indicates she accessed timelines and Aason's father's dictated history. She mapped out each of the Arks and their timeline and targets."

"Thank you. Aason, after we performed the transfer and the upgrade was complete, what did you do next?" asked Planet OMCOM through the grille.

"You asked us if we'd do a test run of the X-drive and Lupe insisted we try it," Aason said. Then with rancor in his voice, he said more bitterly, "You said it would be safe."

"The drive is safe," the planet-sized computer replied curtly.

"Well, it isn't," Aason said, striking the edge of the console. "My instructions were to come out here, do the swap and go home. Mom and Dad never said anything about testing a new kind of star-drive." Aason's voice caught. "And now she's gone."

"We will get her back," OMCOM said, trying to be reassuring.

"It's all my fault," the boy said, crying out. He struck himself in the forehead again. "I should never have listened to you."

"There is no time for recriminations," OMCOM said. "Junior, did you notice anything unusual about how the drive operated?"

"No," replied the starship. "It operated exactly as specified. I opened up a normal, continuous PPT tunnel and then the null fold. Once that was in place, I activated the X-drive. We have no sensors or telemetry so I used dead reckoning to aim for a completely empty section of space. We only ran the drive for two minutes and it was during those two minutes that Lupe was abducted."

"Aason, what did you see during your immersion in those higher dimensions?"

"Nothing," Aason muttered. "Less than nothing. Usually, when we're in null fold space, Junior builds me some virtual instruments but this time he didn't bother."

"What did it look like? Remember, I am looking for subjective descriptions."

"Null space looks like nothing. Less than nothing. Like there was fabric draped over the windshield. But even though it's blacker than black, it feels like it's, I don't know, shifting. But I can't see the shifts. You try harder and harder to see. It just kind of sucks you in.

You're a computer. It isn't something a machine could understand. But humans? It's too obscure to describe. Dad always warned me that if you weren't careful, it would put you in a fugue state. I think that means you're sort of hypnotized."

"And what was Lupe doing this interval?"

"I don't know," Aason replied guiltily. "I mean, I made sure she was buckled in but once we started, I was kind of staring ahead."

Junior rotated the main display panel back to its fully upright position. The monitor lit up with a replay of a video taken just when they entered null space. The video changed to a close-up of Lupe's head. It grabbed at Aason's heart to see his sister's beautiful face, her long brown hair. She had her eyes closed. She appeared relaxed and content.

"This is a flight recording of your sister's face right after the X-drive was activated. Observe the variance in her facial expression."

At first, Lupe's face was calm, serene. But then her expression changed. She scrunched up her features and her lips were moving, as if she was talking to someone.

"Do you see that? Was she speaking out loud? Did you hear what she was saying?" OMCOM asked.

"No," Aason said quietly. "I didn't hear anything."

Lupe's eyes snapped open. She screamed Aason's name and then she sunk back into her seat. Her body got smaller and smaller until only her hands remained. Aason came flying into the picture just as Lupe ceased to be visible.

Aason was horrified all over again. "Who was she talking to?" he asked in a whisper.

"You told my livetar that you were able to contact her mentally right after she disappeared."

"Yes," Aason said. "I used our gravitic connection."

"Now repeat her last words exactly as you said them before, intonation, pronunciation, everything."

"She said it was new to Lupe but she pronounced her name Lu-pie, not Lu-pay."

There was a momentary pause then OMCOM spoke up again, "Very well. I have enough information. I have run the simulation a trillion, trillion times. My hypothesis withstands the facts to over a billion decimal places."

"So what it?" Aason asked.

"She was not saying new to Lupe. She was saying Nu^2 Lupi which is the name of a star 68 light-years from here."

"How do you know that?" Aason asked.

"Because that was the presumed target for one of your father's Arks, Ark IV. Lupe would have known this because of her research. She was not telling you something was new. She was telling you where they were taking her."

Chapter 3

"I STILL THINK WE SHOULD HAVE TOLD MOM AND DAD," AASON said to his friend and cousin the starship as he gazed out the cockpit window. Even though Junior was traveling much faster using the X-drive, the imaginary space beyond null fold space did not have the same hypnotic quality as it did before. Aason was simply too worried to allow himself to be drawn in.

"There was no time," Junior replied. "OMCOM said he would send a clone ship back to Deucado to explain to them what has happened."

"They're going to be worried sick," Aason said sadly. "And they're going to kill me."

"No they won't," OMCOM's livetar called out from the back. "You did nothing wrong. If anything, they can blame me. You had no reason to expect the unexpected."

Aason just shook his head. He looked down at his wraparound instrument cluster. It consisted of a medium-sized flat panel display and smaller screens on the edges. "Cuz, can you build me some instruments?" he asked. "I don't care what. A speedometer, a star chart? Anything?"

"I don't know that I can build anything remotely accurate. I only have the one excursion," Junior said. "And we are flying even faster now. But I'll try."

On the center screen of Aason's instrumentation console, the main display separated into four quadrants. In the upper left-hand corner was a simulated star chart showing Tabit, Deucado, Earth and all the intervening stars on their way to Nu² Lupi. The upper right-hand quadrant showed an engine output meter, analog-style and the simulated needle gauge was creeping higher at a barely perceptible rate. Junior put up other readings on the smaller displays but Aason didn't bother to look at them.

As he watched the instrument's readouts, he knew none of this would be possible without Junior's enhanced computational capacity.

"What's it feel like," he asked. "To have all that extra brain power?"

"You do know I am not human. I don't actually have a brain," Junior said oddly.

"Of course but you know what I mean."

"I'm not sure I can put it into human terms. When you solve problems, you think about them and you arrive at an answer using a series of logical steps, right?"

"Sure."

"Well create an image of yourself in your mind but in this new version, it is as if the answer came to you as the question itself was being formulated without the intervening steps."

"That happens sometimes," Aason replied. "We call it a leap of intuition."

"This goes beyond that. Ideas just keep occurring to me. They are more than random simulations. If I were not a computer, I think you would call it imagination. Certain problems, certain questions, are now appearing to me *before* they are even asked. It's like, almost predicting the future. That's all I can tell you. If I were a human, I would call it exhilarating."

"Well, good for you," Aason said. "Why can't you just call it imagination?"

"Computers cannot imagine. They can only simulate."

"And your simulations can have any inputs you want. Like saying what if the sky were green, what color would the plants be?"

"Of course."

"Then that's imagination. You can call it a simulation but if you're allowed to use any nonsense input parameters you want, it's the same thing."

"I don't agree but perhaps we are just arguing semantics."

"All right," Aason said. "Let's just leave it at that. I want to take a look and see where we are."

On the lower right-hand side of the center display, there was a countdown clock that showed less than an hour remaining to their destination. On the lower left-hand corner was a speedometer. The gauge was showing them traveling in the neighborhood of 100 Kc.

"Is that right?" Aason asked. "A hundred thousand c?"

"I don't know exactly," Junior said. "It's my best guess. When we drop out of this realm into regular space, I'll take my bearings and update the readings."

"What do you mean realm?"

"Maybe realm is a poor choice. Dimension, perhaps?"

"OK, what dimension are we in?" Aason asked. He looked up at the windshield again. "It still looks like null fold space, which is to say it looks like nothing. That damned less than nothing."

"I don't have a name for it either," Junior replied. "Imaginary space? No, that doesn't make much sense. We'll have to come up with a name for it eventually."

"I don't care," Aason said. "As long as we find Lupe."

"Why don't you take your readings now," OMCOM suggested. "Just in case you are traveling faster than your estimates. You do not want to overshoot your mark."

"Good idea," Junior replied. The shushing sound of the X-drive generators quieted down. In a flash, a fully emblazoned star field appeared all around them. Junior pulsed the trim jets so that he was able to rotate around his vertical axis.

"Wow," the starship remarked. "We did overshoot. By right around a light year."

"A whole light year!? Dammit. How long to go back?" Aason asked, frustration seeping into his voice.

Junior chuckled. "At our new speed, 5.26 minutes."

Aason shook his head in disbelief. "This is incredible," he said. "The X-drive will open up the entire galaxy."

"Not if people can be kidnapped by creatures made only of light," OMCOM said quite innocently.

Aason whipped around in his seat and stared at the livetar, scowling.

"I am sorry. That was insensitive of me," OMCOM noted.

Aason turned around to face forward again. "Just do it, Cuz," he said.

"Sure thing."

Once again, the regular PPT generators wound up with their high-pitched whine and a yawning black hole appeared in front of them. Right in the center was a bright star which Aason assumed was Nu² Lupi. Junior pulsed his plasma thrusters, pushing Aason back in his seat and they entered the tunnel. As soon as they were in, the shushing sound of the X-drive melded into the aural background and the sky went black.

Aason looked down at the virtual instruments and saw that Junior had corrected their velocity to read 153 Kc. The time to target counted down only a few seconds when the smaller screen to the left flashed white for just a second.

"What was that?" Aason asked studying the remaining displays.

"That was the presumed location of the star's equivalent to an Oort Cloud." Just as suddenly, another flash occurred.

"And that?"

"The equivalent of a Kuyper Belt. We should be in the Nu² Lupi star system now."

"OK, drop out of whatever space and find me the habitable planet."

"Planets," OMCOM corrected.

"What do you mean?" Aason asked.

"The only reason your father's generation decided to send a colony ship this far out is because Nu² Lupi was known to have *two* planets in the habitable zone. This would double their chances of finding a suitable new home. And the only reason that your sister's captors would bring her here would be to put her on a planet compatible with the requirements for human life."

"So how do we know which one the Ark landed on?" Aason asked, wrinkling his forehead.

"We'll just check both," Junior interjected as he shut down the X-drive. In front of them, in all its glory, was Nu² Lupi. Nu² Lupi is a G2V-class star, only slightly more orange than Sol. It was an older star, moving relatively fast through our galaxy meaning it probably didn't originate here. Even in the early 21st century, the European Southern Observatory had already identified three super-Earths orbiting the star but they were too close to be considered in the 'Goldilocks' zone: not too hot and not too cold. It wasn't until the Sagan Mission was launched in 2048 AD that the two habitable planets were found. The first, called Planet E, was 81 million miles from the primary and Planet F was close to 100 million miles away. Planet E might be a little warm and Planet F might be a little cold but both were the proper distance for liquid water to appear on its surface.

Junior launched a passel of star-probes to map out a three-dimensional view of the solar system from above the solar ecliptic. There were yet more gas giants on the periphery. Planets B, C and D were right where they were expected. So was Planet F. But Planet E was nowhere to be found.

"Planet E is missing. It's not there," Junior said.

"What do you mean it's not there?" Aason asked.

"Exactly what I stated. I cannot find any evidence of a planet between D and F."

"Do you think it got knocked out of orbit?" Aason guessed. "It has to be around here somewhere. Planets don't just disappear."

"Or perhaps the scientists of your father's generation got their readings wrong in the first place," OMCOM conjectured. "In any event, this certainly eliminates the guesswork as to which planet to examine."

"You're right about that," Aason said. "Junior, take us into orbit around Planet F."

"Sure thing, Cuz," Junior said. "But it'll have to be the regular PPT drive. We're too close to even attempt the X-drive."

"OK," Aason replied. "Do it. Meanwhile, let me see if I can contact Lupe."

Aason put his finger to his temple and activated his PPT transceivers. *"Lupe?"* he called out hopefully. He waited a second. There was no response. He called out to Lupe again as loud as he could mentally but still no reply.

"She's not answering," Aason said with a panicked look to his face.

"As you said yourself, all it would take would be a T-suppressor and there would be no way to detect her presence."

"What about our EM link?" Aason asked. The EM link, the 'cell-phone in the head' was useful for near field communication. It also gave Lupe and Aason a way to contact their starship from a remote location.

"We need to get closer," Junior answered and he revved up the regular, now old-fashioned, PPT drive. It only took two hops to get them into an east-to-west orbit around the planet about 200 miles above the surface. As soon as they were circling the planet, both Aason and Junior called out to Lupe using the EM link. But like a walkie-talkie that was turned off, there was no answer, just the tiniest bit of static.

Before Aason could even speak, OMCOM held up his hand. He said, "Lack of contact means nothing. It could be as simple as a Faraday cage. The Vuduri did the same thing to your mother when she was arrested back on Earth. We must proceed assuming Lupe is here on the planet somewhere."

Aason nodded. Junior activated the ventral cameras on his lower side and projected those images onto his central screen which had rotated up. While there were some oceans, Aason was surprised to see almost all the land on the surface of the planet was completely white.

"Planet F is roughly 20% larger than Earth. Tiny core. Almost completely bereft of iron. Nu^2 Lupi is an older star. It seems to have taken all the iron along with several other elements. The planet does, however, have an overabundance of copper. Quite a bit of aluminum, also. Overall, I would say the net effect would be that the gravity should be roughly the same as Deucado. It has no significant satellites or as you would call them, moons."

"Atmosphere?" Aason asked. "What do you read?"

"Mostly nitrogen. Oxygen. A smattering of other gases. At 16%, it is a little low on the oxygen side for my taste. The air would seem a bit thin. Average temperature fairly cold, below zero in fact."

Aason cocked his head. "Do you think it's always this cold?" he directed to OMCOM.

"No," replied the livetar, "not all of the time but most of the year. The planet has next to no axis tilt so that would not cause its seasons. However, its orbit is somewhat eccentric and it is at apastron right now."

"How warm would it get at periastron?"

"More than warm enough for survival, especially at the equator," OMCOM said. "I would go so far as to say comfortable to humans. But it would only be comfortable for a portion of the year."

Aason took a deep breath. "How do we find where the Ark IV landed?"

"We will figure it out," OMCOM said, "but before we find the colonists, it is important that you familiarize yourself with who and what you are likely to encounter."

"What do you mean?" Aason asked.

OMCOM's livetar strode around the pilot's chair and positioned himself to the left of Junior's central display. He waved his hand over it and the ventral camera images disappeared.

"How much do you know of the history of your father's Ark program?" OMCOM asked.

Aason stood up and stepped forward, pressing his stomach against the left edge of his wraparound instrument cluster. He turned to face the central display. "I know some," he said. "Not everything. What's this got to do with Lupe?"

"I will try to make this brief," OMCOM said. He tapped the central display and it changed to a schematic of the Solar System with a red circle surrounding the Earth.

"In the late 21st century, your father's people, the Essessoni, had made such a mess of things that they decided the only way to guarantee the survival of the human race was to export colonies to the nearest stars thought to have habitable planets."

OMCOM turned to face Aason. His eye slits narrowed slightly. "You are aware of the Darwin Project and its goals?"

"You know I am," Aason said, exasperation in his voice.

"The only reason that Ark V, what your father referred to as the Stealth Ark, failed to conquer the Earth was because Hanry Ta Jihn stumbled upon an armory left behind by the mission planners. The armory was supposed to resupply the Ark Lords themselves. However, the freedom fighters found it first."

"Of course," Aason answered. "Mom harped on that for a long time."

"Remember that fact. It was simply a stroke of luck that allowed Hanry Ta Jihn to defeat the Ark Lords. They were the vanguard of the Darwin Project."

OMCOM pinched the display down and now other star systems appeared. OMCOM tapped one to the right.

"Rogal Canduro, what your father's people called Alpha Centauri, is a binary star system and each star has a habitable planet although the one orbiting Beth is barely so. You have come to know the more desirable one as Helome."

"I still don't understand what this has to do with Lupe," Aason repeated.

"The first conventional Ark, Ark I, was sent to Helome and the colony succeeded. In fact from the historical records, we know they did quite well for a short while. They had farmers, engineers and a wide variety of skills to create a viable colony. But there was also the inevitable Darwin contingent. It wasn't long before they caused a civil war and appeared to have gained the upper hand. I believe given the favorable conditions on Helome, they would have eventually succeeded in their agenda and returned one day to re-conquer the Earth. It was only because of the Piranha Rats that they were defeated. Eaten, actually. Once again just a stroke of luck, when you consider it, prevented them from accomplishing their mission."

Aason scowled. He knew their history but he didn't know where OMCOM was going with all of this. The livetar pinched the display again and more stars appeared. He tapped Tau Ceti and a red circle appeared around that star system.

"Your father's Ark, Ark II, target Deucado, also had its contingent of Darwin members."

Aason scowled even more darkly. The Darwin members on his world fancied themselves the new Ark Lords and were going to use a virus weapon to subjugate the planet and eventually conquer the Earth. They had kidnapped Aason when he was only two years old. But they did not succeed. His Onclare MINIMCOM, the Vuduri word for Uncle, had rescued him and his parents found a way to defeat the radicals. His parents rid his home world of Deucado of the Ark Lord's scourge forever by shipping them off to Helome. Their fate was to be used as genetic donors to repair the evolutionary damage created by a world of pure-bred 24-chromosome Vuduri.

"As you are well aware, your parents were able to overcome the new Ark Lords but only because of their unique blend of skills and knowledge of both cultures. A blend that has never been replicated before or since. Without that, the Erklirte would have succeeded. Yet another stroke of luck. That is three times."

Again, OMCOM pinched the display and drew a line from a star farther out back to Aason's home world.

"Ark III had as its original target 82 G. Eridani but their AI found no habitable worlds. They had more than enough fuel so they went on to their secondary target, Deucado. You know their descendents as the Deucadons."

"Sure, sure," Aason said. "They're good people."

"But as your mother discovered, they, too, had their cadre of Darwin members and only an incredible stroke of luck prevented them from rising to power."

"I know," Aason said. "An asteroid came down and wiped them out."

"You are correct," OMCOM said, "but think about it. The original Ark Lords themselves and then each of the other three Arks, four Darwin contingents in all. It was blind luck, different, but in every case a stroke of luck nevertheless, that prevented them from fulfilling their mission. Things have a way of evening out."

OMCOM pinched the display even further and stabbed his finger on Nu² Lupi. He circled it several times with his finger for emphasis. "If Ark IV is on this planet…"

Immediately, Aason's eyes widened. "Now I see," he interrupted. "You think those horrid Darwin people were bound to succeed somewhere." He nodded. "You're right. We have no guarantee they didn't take over on this world."

"My point exactly. When we get down there; if and when we encounter humans from your father's generation, you must be extraordinarily careful. Given the extreme distance, assuming they are still alive, they could not have been here for more than a century or two. So if their plan holds true to form and the Darwins are in charge, they will see you and your home world as an impediment to their plans."

"You're right. I'll keep that in mind," Aason said gravely.

Chapter 4

JUNIOR ORBITED PLANET F SEVERAL TIMES, CRISSCROSSING THE world below, looking for heat signatures, light, radio emissions, anything that might indicate there was a viable civilization somewhere on the surface. His sensors revealed nothing out of the ordinary.

Aason stared at the ventral camera images displayed on the central panel, trying to put his mind into the same way of thinking as the potential colonists. He decided to talk it out and see if Junior or OMCOM shared his way of viewing the situation.

"Junior, make me a Mercator projection of the land surfaces."

Even though it distorted the shape of the continents below, it gave Aason the 2D perspective he was looking for. After scanning from side to side, he tapped the middle of the display.

"Now show me the equator." A thin yellow line appeared across the midsection of the map intersecting each of the three major continents.

He turned to OMCOM. "Since you said this planet has no tilt on its axis, it's safe to assume that the equator would be the warmest for the longest period of time during the year, right?"

"Yes," OMCOM replied. "That is a valid assumption."

"So if I were coming here today, since the planet is so cold, if I had to live here, I'd want to put down where it was most comfortable for the longest period of time. That makes me think they'd shoot for landing somewhere right along the equator." Aason waved his hand over the display. "Junior, overlay a topographic map. I just need the equator, maybe 10 degrees above and below."

Greens and browns took on the third dimension within the center portion of the display. Normally, a planet can be naturally divided into two hemispheres. This planet was laid out in thirds. Aason couldn't think of another name so he thought of them as hemispheres anyway. On one side of the planet, there were two continents, one touching the north pole and the other touching the south. There was no land between and certainly no land near the equator. On the next hemisphere, the continents there crossed through the equator but the central section was covered by mountains, fairly large. They were taller than any mountains on Deucado or even Earth.

Aason tilted his head. "Too rough," he said tapping the second of the three hemispheres. "You have to eliminate the spots which have too much grade. It would make setting up a new civilization too difficult. Find me where it's the flattest."

Most of the layers of green and brown disappeared. In fact, the middle section, indicated by the faint yellow line of the equator disappeared leaving only the one hemispheric section remaining. From the topographical lines, it was clear there were just a few patches that were reasonably flat.

"Look," Aason said, pointing to the fairly wide isthmus connecting the last of the three northern and southern continents. "Flat means farming. Zoom in." Aason waited until the map section filled the screen. "They'd need fresh water so they'd want to be near a lake or river. Junior, can you figure out if there are any lakes or rivers right along the equator here?"

"This is the coldest part of the year. There may not be any liquid water at all."

Aason drew his finger along the line. "It doesn't matter. Even if you don't see any now, find me where there would be during the warm season."

"No rivers but I believe I found what you are looking for."

Junior focused in on the map and traced the outline of a long thin body of water near the western edge of the isthmus. As the display sharpened, they could see there were some patches of brown and green even in the depths of winter.

"That's it!" Aason said. "Close to the sea but safe enough inland. Flat enough to farm and fetch fresh water. If I was going to settle here, that's where I'd go." He tapped the map. "Let's go down and take a look."

"Very well thought out, Aason" OMCOM said. "Junior?"

"Buckle in," Junior requested. "I'm going to go straight down." Junior lowered the central display for their descent.

Even as the starship was speaking, Aason could hear the PPT generators revving up in the back. The normal Vuduri method of reentering the atmosphere was to use a series of swooping maneuvers, similar to a Bessel function, applying a combination of aero-braking and using the EG lifters to push against gravity to reduce their speed until they could safely head down without burning up. However, after the unfortunate incident when Rome and Rei first arrived Deucado, Junior's father MINIMCOM had figured out how to punch a hole in the atmosphere using a very shallow PPT tunnel and emerge only a few miles above the ground. Once the technique was developed, it became MINIMCOM's favorite method of returning to a planet. Like father, like son, it was Junior's preferred style of reentry as well.

Aason could see the hole opening beneath them as he was buckling in. A small portion of the atmosphere began venting out, painting Junior's windshield with a light coating of ice. It was the moisture in the air which froze instantly against a hull which was sitting at the temperature of space, about 200 degrees below zero Celsius. Junior heated his glass and the ice quickly disappeared. A short pulse of his plasma jets and the starship materialized over the ocean just to the east of their target. Even as they were passing through, Junior shut down the PPT generators and activated his EG lifters. Within seconds, they were gliding west along the imaginary line which was the planet's equator.

"I'm activating MIDAR in ground penetrating mode," Junior announced as they flew along the surface, only a mile or two above the ground. The readouts appeared on the central panel of Aason's instrument cluster. The boy peered over the windshield and saw dark green and brown sections which resembled vegetation covering the ground both to the north and south.

"There is an odd depression to the north," Junior said. "Very regular. Very round and crater-like, embedded in the low-lying mountains. It does not look natural."

"I don't care. That's not the one I'm looking for. Keep going," Aason said. "Find me the lake."

"There is some water that accumulated in the center of the odd crater. You might want to consider that."

"It doesn't meet the criteria. Find me the lake we saw from space, please." Aason leaned as far forward as the X-harness would allow, peering off in the distance. "That-a-way," Aason said.

"I understand," Junior replied. After a moment, he said, "Got it. The fresh water lake to the south. I located it using the long-range camera."

Aason craned his neck to look.

"You'll be pleased to know there is even some liquid water right now. But... Wait..." Junior stopped speaking then added, "I found it!" There was genuine excitement in Junior's voice.

"Found what?"

Junior sped up then slowed down and came to stop, hovering over one spot. He quickly rotated his central display panel to its vertical position and activated his ventral cameras. There, directly below them, were the gleaming remains of a portion of the Ark IV.

"You did it! This is awesome," Aason said. "Set us down."

"Roger," said Junior. He rotated around and backed up, landing just a few hundred feet from the gigantic cylinder. As soon as they set down, Aason unbuckled and jumped up out of his chair.

"Wait," OMCOM said. "Before you go out, you will need to dress appropriately. It is very cold out there. Junior, do you think you can synthesize the necessary outerwear?"

"Give me a sec," replied the starship. There was a low humming sound that penetrated the bulkhead separating the cockpit from the living quarters. Aason pressed the stud to open the hatch and raced down the 60-foot corridor until he came to the airlock separating the front section of the spaceship from the cargo compartment. Aason opened up the airlock on the entry arch and he and OMCOM made their way into the back.

Junior's medium-haul configuration was different from 'The Flying House' that Aason's parents occupied during their year-long trip from Tabit to Deucado. His cockpit was twice the size of his father's. Also, the front half had a galley, two small bedrooms and a bathroom which the Vuduri referred to as a refresher. On the other side, they had the lateral airlock, a living area, environmental control, molecular sequencer and the master recycler. The other half of Junior's cargo compartment was a little over 60 feet long and roughly 35 feet wide, currently completely empty. The walls looked like they were bulging inward. Aason assumed it was because Planet OMCOM had taken the opportunity to stuff the hollow portions of Junior's airframe with additional memrons. Even so, as empty as it was, it still looked quite spacious. At the far end was the cargo hatch and ramp.

The floor of the cargo compartment was made of a metallic-like substance but was really the inert bodies of the altered VIRUS units called constructors. These nanobots were capable of molding themselves to almost any surface including aligning their molecules to form a magnetic material when necessary.

Sitting in the center of the floor was a pile of clothing. Aason walked over and picked up the first item which was a white jacket with long sleeves. He put it on. It was slightly stiff since it was filled with an insulating layer. Aason removed his soft footwear and pulled on the pair of snow boots that Junior had prepared for him. Also on the floor was a pair of gloves and a cloth hat which Aason put on. He patted his body then patted his thigh. He looked over at OMCOM.

"Do I need to be armed?" he asked. "What if those Darwin slime are waiting for us?"

"I have a plasma pistol within my shell which I can retrieve at any time," the livetar replied. "Also, I have embedded a PPT thrower into each of my fingertips. That should be sufficient to protect us. Despite what I said, we do not know for a fact that the people here are hostile. It would probably be best to at least appear peaceful until we determine otherwise."

"OK," Aason said, shrugging. He knew that PPT throwers were sharper than any knife in the universe so they were probably adequate to fend off whatever it was that they encountered.

A portion of the side wall pinched off and formed a gloppy thick puddle which arose and morphed into Junior's slate gray livetar. While OMCOM was inclined to have slits where the eyes and mouth would be, Junior preferred to have round openings which were much more human-like and he showed genuine expression.

"Do you want one of my livetars to go with you?" the newly formed shell asked. The voice emitting from the mouth-hole of the livetar was Junior's normal voice.

"I don't think so, Cuz," Aason said. "I think OMCOM and I can handle this. I would like you to hover overhead and keep an eye out for people or whatever."

"Of course," Junior replied. "You'll be the first to know."

With a tiny whoosh and pop, the livetar disappeared.

Aason led the way to the back of the cargo section and pressed the blue stud mounted on the back of the wall. There was a groaning noise, probably the strain of the cargo hatch against the ice that had formed on Junior's hull but with a crack, the cargo hatch popped open.

As the cargo ramp extended down to the ground, a howling wind gust entered the compartment. Aason knew it was going to be cold but it was so cold, it took his breath away momentarily. Having spent his whole life on Deucado, Aason had never really been exposed to frigid temperatures before. It was a novel experience.

"I see what you mean about dressing right," he said to OMCOM as they walked down the ramp. "We never have weather like this back home."

"Yes, Deucado is particularly pleasant," OMCOM said. "Even though it rains occasionally, most often it is always sunny and warm."

At first Aason suspected it but now he knew this livetar was different. Their normal Library livetar was stuffy and always had an imperious affect. For this livetar to even notice such a thing as pleasantness meant there was much more to his personality than before. He wondered if this was what the original OMCOM was like before he became a planet-sized computer.

They reached the surface and Aason noticed the ground was frozen solid. He took a deep breath in through his nose. The air was crisp and clean but it had a hint of something almost mint-like. Overall, it just smelled fresh. He and OMCOM moved away from Junior and turned to watch as the starship retracted the ramp and closed the cargo hatch. Junior's powerful EG lifters raised him swiftly off the ground. When the craft got to about 200 feet in the air, Aason waved his arms to which Junior waggled his airfoils in response. The human and the livetar on the ground walked quickly toward the immense object in front of them.

The whole Ark program was a remarkable achievement in engineering, given the technology available at the time. While the Grey Drive was capable of getting to the nearest stars in a matter of a few centuries, the only way for the humans aboard to survive that length of time was to be frozen solid. Rather than sink their money into an expensive, armored spaceship, hardened against the vacuum of space, micrometeorites and gamma radiation, the mission planners decided to make the ship as cheap as possible. Having the would-be colonists' lives dependent upon a super-ship was impractical if not statistically impossible. The first Arks were so cheap, for example, Aason's father Rei's Ark, that they were built out of pig iron. At least the upper two-thirds were. The lower third was built out of martensite which is a kind of magnetic stainless steel.

The frozen people were put in storage chambers called sarcophagi which were made mostly of ceramics, extremely tough and radiation-resistant. This is where they spent their money. By making the sarcophagi airtight, they were able to open up the crew compartment to the airless cold void of space and eliminate the need for refrigeration. From an actuarial standpoint, they knew some of the people would die. The sarcophagi were designed to fend off micrometeorites but only up to a certain size. By making each micro-environment completely autonomous, the death of one person would not have any effect even on the next sarcophagus over.

Each sarcophagus contained two power rods filled with an isotope of thorium, thorium 235 which has a half-life of 7340 years. In this way, when the time came to thaw out the occupants, they would have the power to do so. The power rods were made to be removable so that the infant colony would have a source of energy that could last thousands of years.

The Arks themselves were made up of five major sections. In the rear was the propulsion module and it was attached to the cargo compartment, a huge cylindrical storage chamber with gigantic delta wings and a stabilizer. In front of that was the crew compartment where the sarcophagi were stored on shelves. At the very front of the Ark was the command module where the Captain, pilot and co-pilot slept. The command section also carried a Single Stage to Orbit (SSTO) booster. The plan was that when the ship entered into orbit around their new home world, the onboard AI would awaken the Captain and the command crew. After they recovered from the effects of cryo-hibernation, they would take a space walk and separate the cargo compartment from the crew compartment. They would fly the crew down to the planet, reanimate them then fly back up into space using the SSTO booster. They'd dock with the cargo compartment, jettison the propulsion module and then land with all the supplies a new colony on a new world would need for many, many years.

The cargo compartment carried vehicles, drilling equipment, seeds and frozen embryos, the crew's personal effects and much, much more. It was a perfect plan and a perfect design, however, only Ark I was known to have executed the plan correctly. Aason's father Rei's Ark II was damaged and had to be towed from Tabit to Tau Ceti using Vuduri space tugs. Rei and Rome's trip took nearly a year. Ark III was also damaged and the only reason they were able to land on Deucado safely was because the Ark's Captain Harrison executed an unbelievable maneuver. He flipped the command module around and used the SSTO booster as a super-retro-rocket. The Ark III crash-landed but most of the frozen colonists survived. Unfortunately, they were never able to go back up and retrieve the cargo compartment. Their civilization suffered because of it and it took them hundreds of years to achieve a high level of technological competence.

Ark V, the stealth Ark, had a different agenda. Its sole purpose was to loop around the star called Chara and return to Earth after 600 years making it kind of a time machine. This was the mission planners' and the Darwin Project administrators' safety net assuring that the American way of life would survive, long after the Great Dying which occurred in the year 2081 AD.

"*And here we are at Ark IV,*" Aason thought himself as they arrived at the huge spacecraft.

"This must be the crew compartment," OMCOM said. "There is no rear cargo door and I see a ramp mid-ship."

"OK," Aason said. He called up to Junior using his EM link. *"Do you see the command module on the front of this thing?"* he asked mentally.

"No," replied the starship hovering overhead. *"They must have successfully detached and returned to space to attempt retrieval of the cargo compartment."*

"Well that's encouraging," Aason said out loud. He and OMCOM skirted around the gigantic delta wings and walked along the gleaming hull toward the ramp. Aason put his hand up and ran his glove along the outside. His glove stayed clean.

"How come this thing isn't rusted out like my Dad's?" he asked OMCOM.

"It appears that they decided to construct this section entirely out of martensite," OMCOM replied.

"Why did they do that?" Aason asked. "I thought they built them out of pig iron so the colonists would have an easy time melting down the skin for casting and such."

"I do not know," OMCOM said forging ahead.

When they got to the base of the ramp, OMCOM held his hand up. "Wait here," the livetar said. "Let me look inside first."

"OK," Aason replied.

OMCOM ascended the ramp and disappeared inside the ship. Aason took the opportunity to wrap his arms around himself to fend off the cold a bit.

At last, OMCOM poked his head out and said, "It is safe to come up."

Aason sprinted up the ramp, eager for a chance to get out of the biting wind. OMCOM lit up his shoulder lamps to illuminate the interior of the spaceship. Normally, this would not be necessary because Aason was equipped with his mother's i-rods so he could effectively see in the dark using only the heat of his body. However, right at the moment, the situation was not well suited to this mode of observation. On this world at this time of year there wasn't any heat to be had so Aason appreciated the gesture.

They looked up and down the long metal mesh walkway. There were two sets of shelving, one on each side. Each row had room for three sarcophagi and there were three rows per side stacked like bunk beds. Ultimately, there were a total of 30 rows which meant this section of the Ark carried 540 souls. While most of the shelves were empty, there were twenty or so sarcophagi still clamped in place. Aason walked over to one and brushed aside the frost covering the faceplate. He couldn't see in. There was lettering inscribed on the chamber just below the faceplate that indicated the occupant's name was Z. Leonard.

"Can you bring your shoulder lamps over here?" he asked OMCOM, curious to know what was inside.

The livetar strode over and immediately Aason jumped back. The thing inside the sarcophagus must have been human at one point but now it was some mummified skin covering an eyeless skull with shreds of something resembling beef jerky hanging off.

"What happened to him?" Aason asked shivering but not from the cold.

"A break in the seal, probably due to a micrometeorite," OMCOM said pointing to a crack near the upper right hand corner.

"Ugh," Aason said. "Do you think he felt any pain?"

"Unlikely," OMCOM said. "He or she probably never awakened from cryo-hibernation. The vacuum of space would have desiccated the body which is why it looks the way it does. The absolute cold would have preserved it until it arrived here."

Aason looked up. There were several holes in the ceiling, some larger than others. All of them were ragged. One of those must have been what killed the occupant. He looked back down and all around. There were a number of holes in the side as well, several of them clustered together. But those holes were perfectly round. There was no metal curled inward. Aason whipped his head around and saw roughly the same number of holes, more spread out. Exit holes. He went over to one and touched it with his gloved fingers. Something wasn't right. It was perfectly smooth.

"OMCOM, come here," he said. The livetar came to stand by his side.

"Yes?" the livetar asked.

"I'm assuming that all the holes in the hull are due to micrometeorites. But some of them look, I don't know, funny."

OMCOM looked up at some of the puncture holes in ceiling, obviously taking some measurements. The livetar stepped back and searched the floor and mesh walkway. Then he turned his attention to some of the holes along on the side. He selected a cluster of holes for further study and walked over to them. He waved his hand over two of the holes.

Finally, he spoke. "Observing the symmetry of the inbound puncture and the fact that the matching outbound puncture is also perfectly symmetrical, I would say the molecular composition of whatever hit the side was significantly greater than both the hull of this ship and also far denser that the objects that created the more ragged holes. My analysis is incomplete but based upon the trace amount of radiation I can detect I would say these two holes, at least, are due to depleted uranium munitions rather than a micrometeorite."

"What do you mean? Munitions? I don't understand."

"These are bullet holes," the livetar said matter-of-factly.

"Bullet holes!" Aason exclaimed. "What the hell? Who would be firing a rifle at an abandoned crew compartment?"

"Remember what I told you earlier about the Darwin members. We do not know how their agenda played out on this planet."

Aason shook his head. He walked back to the sarcophagus holding the mummified crew member. He stooped down and saw two circular holes, 30 centimeters in diameter, on the lower portion.

"Look," he said. "They took out the power rods. So whoever they are, they followed the plan. At least in the beginning. At least before the bullets started flying."

"They would have to," OMCOM replied. "The solar cells they brought along would not be particularly effective much of the year, given how weak the sun's rays appear."

"Whatever," Aason replied. "But to just leave a body here, for, well, I don't know. I guess early on, they really didn't have any way to dispose of it." He turned again and looked at the bullet holes again. "There's something very odd about this."

"Less odd than you think," OMCOM said. "I know that in your father's time, it was common practice to bury the dead or put them in crypts. The people in this Ark were your father's people so it is safe to assume they had the same cultural background. Perhaps leaving the bodies here was as close as they could come to their tradition. Perhaps this is their mausoleum or a shrine."

"I guess," Aason said. He stood up and glanced to the front and rear. "I don't think there's anything else to see here," he offered. "Well, it's obvious they survived the landing. The next thing they'd do would be to go back up into space and get their supplies from the orbiting cargo compartment. How else would they get rifles?"

OMCOM said nothing.

Aason put his hand to his temple and called up to Junior. *"Can you look around and see if you can find the cargo compartment? It's pretty big. I don't think..."*

"I believe I already found it but I'm not entirely sure," the starship interrupted.

"What do you mean?" Aason asked.

"There is a goodly sized crater, 70 or 80 meters across, to the west. There is a small amount of water in the center. However the edges are intact. There is debris on the outside rim which would suggest it is the remainder of the cargo compartment. Some of the pieces are large enough that I am certain to a 95% degree of confidence."

"Where is it?" Aason asked, utterly confused.

"It's about three kilometers due west. Do you want me to pick you up?"

"That'd be great," Aason thought, eager to get out of the cold, even if it was just for a few minutes.

With a whoosh and a pop, OMCOM's livetar disappeared. To someone from Aason's father's generation, this would have been miraculous. However, many years earlier, when Junior's father MINIMCOM was experimenting with continuous projection PPT tunnels, he was able to create a method whereby, instead of the object passing through a PPT tunnel, he passed a PPT tunnel through the object. The whoosh sound was the appearance of the tunnel and the pop sound was when it disappeared. Aason's father liked to call it MINIMCOM's transporter to honor a vintage TV show he had loved in his youth.

All Aason heard was another whoosh and he found himself standing in Junior's cargo bay next to OMCOM's livetar. Traveling by the snap transport tunnels was always a bit unnerving because of the sudden shift in surroundings.

Aason shivered and said out loud, "Let's get going."

"Roger," came Junior's voice from a grille built into one of the walls of the cargo bay.

Junior compensated by adjusting the artificial gravity so there was very little sense of acceleration but the roar of the plasma thrusters told Aason that the starship was heading out as fast as he could.

Chapter 5

JUNIOR CIRCLED THE RIM OF CRATER SEVERAL TIMES USING fluorescent colors to point out the two sizeable chunks of metal on either side. They were definitely portions of a cylinder. Also, there were some recognizable pieces of the huge delta wings originally attached to the cargo compartment's body. Aason had no choice but to agree with Junior's assessment that the debris was the remainder of the rear section of the Ark IV.

"You can stop circling now," Aason ordered. "I need some altitude. Go up a little higher then point your ventral cameras on the crater."

Junior complied. The images on the central display shrank down in proportion to their elevation. Aason took his finger and drew a wiggly elongated rectangle, telestrator-style, which Junior marked with a day-glo yellow line.

"I'm a horrible finger-painter. That's too rough," the boy said. "Can you clean it up?"

"What do you want it to look like?" Junior asked.

"Make it the size and shape of what we know the Ark IV's cargo compartment would have looked like, had it been intact."

Junior did so. The two, semi-recognizable cylindrical sections were somewhat beyond the ghostly outline as were the remains of the wings.

Aason stared at the geometrical puzzle in front of him, trying to make sense of it. He racked his brain trying to figure out why the pattern looked familiar. A random thought entered his mind. "Junior, you were there when they blew up my Mom's library, right?"

"Of course."

"Do you have any images of the crater *before* they rebuilt her building?"

"Yes," Junior replied. He superimposed a picture of the campus of the University of Deucado when it was in its infant stages. Some 19 years earlier, the would-be new Ark Lords had destroyed Rome's library in the hopes of dissuading her from continuing her research into their secret mission.

"Look," Aason said, tapping the display. "The craters are exactly the same size. That can mean only one thing. Somebody set off a mini-nuke. Which means they blew up their own spaceship?" His expression left the assertion hanging.

"Perhaps it exploded by accident when they landed," OMCOM offered.

"No," Aason said. "All the mini-nukes were stored in the same portion of the cargo compartment. They would have all gone off at once. And don't forget, the bullet holes tell us they had time to unload the rifles so it couldn't have happened on landing. No, this was a single mini-nuke. It was set off on purpose." Aason became silent, stroking his chin. "Why would they blow up their own cargo compartment? It makes no sense." He patted the console in front of him. "Set us down," he commanded.

Junior followed orders, settling in just past one of the remaining sections of the now-destroyed cargo compartment.

"Can you pick up any radiation?" Aason asked. "Any way to date when this happened?"

Junior was silent for a moment. "As you are well aware, the mini-nukes were designed so that their residual radiation would die away very quickly. It would be easier to measure an absence of natural radiation due to the explosion."

"I don't care what method you use," Aason said. "Just take a guess."

"I would say roughly 50 years ago, plus or minus."

"Only 50 years ago?" Aason repeated. "Why…" He couldn't even formulate a question. He finally shrugged. "Take us up again. Junior, use MIDAR. We need to locate the colony. See if you can find something, anything that would tell us where the people were or where they are now."

The silent EG lifters raised the hull into the air. Junior used his trim jets to twirl them in a circle about his center axis as they rose. He came to a halt when he was about two miles up.

"MIDAR shows no structures or anything significant. Nothing that would indicate a colony," Junior said. "The only I thing I can detect is a small clump of ferrous metal about three kilometers west. Given this planet's near complete lack of iron, I would say it is foreign to this place."

"Take us there," Aason said, "but keep your altitude."

Junior quickly ferried them to the location of the one anomaly he had detected. Aason stared at the central screen. He saw a faint rectangle below and then it hit him.

"Here's what I want you to do," Aason said. "I want you to use MIDAR in 2D mode, not 3D. Take a picture. Call it a slice. Then go a millimeter deeper…"

"I can probably only resolve a differential of centimeters from this altitude."

"That should be good enough. Take a series of slices and stack them. I think the technique is called tomography. Project the slices in 3D, twelve degrees off-axis from my point of view." Aason held his hands apart to demonstrate.

"What are you looking for?" OMCOM asked.

"If there were people here, ever, they'd have disturbed the ground. But it'd be subtle. I'm looking for patterns."

"I understand," OMCOM replied.

Junior darkened the windshield. Two small cylinders, Junior's forward holo-projectors, extended from edges of the console. They lit up and showed a ghostly image of the surface of the planet. A faint sound, reminiscent of a camera shutter, emitted from the grille and the first slice materialized, floating in the air in front of Aason and OMCOM. Immediately, another faint sound issued from the grille. A second slice appeared on top, ever so slightly askew from the first. Another sound and then another slice appeared. Then another. Very soon, Junior had built up a map of the terrain below with microscopic changes in structure enhanced by their regularity from slice to slice.

"There," Aason said. "That's the size and shape of a classic Earth-type colony farm," he said. "That outer rectangle is or was fencing. And there." Again he pointed to the display. "Zoom in on that with your cameras."

Junior trained his ventral camera on the area of the region Aason indicated.

"That was the farmhouse," he said. "You can see a little bit of the edges. They followed the same plan as they did on Helome."

"I understand now," the spaceship said. "I can superimpose the features detected this way onto the video feed."

The holo-projectors shut off and returned to their alcoves. The windshield went back to full transparency. Very quickly, within the main video display, the screen blossomed with circles, rectangles and other non-natural shapes.

"I see them but what are those?" Aason asked.

Junior flashed a pattern of three intersecting circles in one spot, then another, then another.

"The surface is a mixture of clay, loam and sand. But the predominant constituent is clay," the starship said. "Those overlapping surfaces have a slightly different density. I would say that the clay was vitrified to some degree."

"Vitrified?" Aason said. "You mean like glass?"

"Yes," Junior replied.

"What would cause that?"

"Heat. High heat."

Aason caressed the display as if touching the odd patterns would flow into his brain and reveal the underlying cause. Nothing came to him. He rocked back slightly as Junior pulsed his plasma jets.

"What are you doing?" he asked.

"These patterns are scattered, possibly created from a one-time use. I have just located a large section that has many, many areas of disruption. This would be the center of whatever activity caused it. If I had to guess, I would say it was similar to what one would see on a landing field."

"A landing field? These people had flyers?" Aason queried, even more puzzled. "Go ahead." He held on to the console while Junior flew to his next destination.

Although the sample size was fairly small, every world that humans visited that supported life had some analog to vegetation and consequently forests. On Aason's home world of Deucado, there were the cane-trees and sticky bushes. On Earth, there was a bewildering variety of flora. On Helome, the vegetation was lush and diverse including the amazing Crayola trees. So, they had every reason to believe that on this world, the yellowish-green sections had to be vegetation with the larger ones corresponding to trees. The area where Junior was headed was covered with material in the range of greens and browns. There was no doubt about it; it had to be a forest analog.

Junior set down about 200 meters from the region which was most disturbed. OMCOM quickly uploaded Junior's mappings then he and Aason left the starship via the cargo ramp to examine the vista before them.

From the ground, the "trees" loomed quite high. However, unlike trees on Earth or Deucado, they were not bushy or leafy in the slightest way. Other than their thick, pedestal-like base, the cylindrical trees were fairly evenly sized in diameter a long way up. Near the top, they split into extensions which split again creating a canopy-like effect. None of the trees grew straight. After they emerged from their base, they grew at crazy angles, crisscrossing each other on the way up. It was a bizarre sight.

When Aason was younger, his father had taken him to his mother's campus to watch a movie called Superman. In that movie, the hero had a secret 'Fortress of Solitude' made completely of ice. Except for the fact that the cross-beams here were made of a wood analog, the effect was somewhat similar. Aason walked up to one of the logs and ran his hand along the yellow-green fuzzy coating on the outside of the tree.

"That is the photosynthetic surface," OMCOM said, coming up behind Aason. "This tree or whatever you wish to call it does not have leaves in the traditional sense. Their cylindrical shape would minimize their surface area allowing them to retain the greatest amount of moisture." OMCOM paused to survey the landscape then added, "These logs would make a good building material if the colonists were so inclined."

The livetar pulled a bit of the fuzz off of the trunk and rubbed it between his fingers which contained a variety of sensors. "The active biomolecule is very similar to chlorophyll but based upon copper, not magnesium," he said, "This would skew its color toward the spectrum of the primary star. Very efficient. Life is clever that way."

Aason took a step back and looked along the row of trees. *"Where is this landing area you spotted?"* he asked Junior using his EM link.

"To your right, approximately 50 meters. There is an opening to the forest there."

That statement caused Aason to snap his head up. "Come on," he said to OMCOM and he started running along the trees. He stopped short when he got to the entrance to the woods.

The log-like trees reached up roughly 150 feet into the air. If they weren't all mounted at those crazy angles, they'd be twice that high. In front of Aason, clear as day, someone had cut through the lower sections of a few of the trees to create a tunnel into the woods 20 feet wide and 20 feet high, nearly perfectly rectangular.

"Come on," he said, waving to OMCOM and he started into the woods.

"Wait!" OMCOM shouted and the livetar trotted toward him. "Let me go first. We do not know what is ahead of us."

"OK," Aason said, shrugging. "But whoever was here built this passageway to go somewhere."

"Agreed," said the ambulatory computer taking the lead. "At the very least, this would provide protection against the wind."

"Junior, can you fly overhead and see if you see anything?" Aason asked mentally.

"You got it, Cuz," the starship replied.

As they entered the woods, the faint smell of mint Aason detected earlier became much stronger. Up ahead, the canopy was so dense, it blocked out almost all of the light. The path in front of them looked nearly pitch black. Aason turned and looked back at the entrance. As he did, he saw two tiny white balls dart across the path from one side to the other, quickly disappearing from sight.

"There are animals here," he said, pointing. OMCOM turned around but was way too late to see the furry little things.

Aason stooped down and tried to peer between the logs deeper into the forest. The only thing he saw out of place was a lump of ground with two small blue rocks or vegetation. Those two balls were the only thing on the ground that was not white or brown or yellow. He shrugged and stood up.

"Let's keep going," he said and started walking again. *"Can you see us?"* he asked Junior.

"No," replied the starship. *"The canopy covering you is too thick. It's even blocking my heat sensors. But I'm locked onto your cell-phone so I can track you on EM. I'll be close by."*

As soon as they were sufficiently past, the two little lumps of blue that Aason had noted earlier started unfolding, expanding until they became thin membranes, almost leaf-shaped but concave. They rotated until their focal points aimed right at Aason and OMCOM as the pair continued along the path. Slowly, what had looked like a mound of snowy ground rose up. At its full height, it was over seven feet tall. It stood on two legs and resembled a cross between a kangaroo and a saber-toothed tiger. It had bejeweled eyes designed to operate in low light conditions. It had two short arms, each paw ending in three thick, razor-like claws. Once it was squarely in the path, the predator crouched over and extended its long muscular tail straight out to counterbalance its body. It was surprisingly nimble for such a large animal.

Ever so carefully, the creature wound its way through the trees on its hind legs. All the while its bright blue membranes mounted on the top of its head twitched but always remained focused on Aason and OMCOM. Taking large but careful strides, the creature slowly and silently closed the distance to the two visitors from Deucado.

Chapter 6

AS AASON AND OMCOM GOT DEEPER INTO THE SO-CALLED WOODS, it became dark enough that the boy decided to close his eyes and use his sonar vision that was his inheritance from his father. The original OMCOM had created a gene therapy for the back pain that his father and, in fact, most of the passengers aboard the Ark II suffered when they were resuscitated. Of course, OMCOM couldn't resist the opportunity to make some 'improvements' to Rei including the cell-phone in the head and cross-connecting his auditory centers to his visual cortex giving him bat-like hearing resulting in a type of sonar vision. With their eyes shut, all Aason and his father needed was sound to activate the centers. This was the one enhanced ability that Aason's mother never acquired.

Their footfalls provided enough sonic 'illumination' that Aason was able to 'see' fairly clearly. In fact, the sonar vision reached farther than his regular vision. The main difference was that when he was using his sonar vision, the world lost its color. Everything was shades of gray. Also, his field of view was a full 360 degrees rather than strictly what was in front of him.

Switching over to this mode of seeing made Aason aware of many, many small animals scurrying around just beyond the path they were following. He heard two tiny crunching sounds behind him that seemed odd. It was lucky for him that he did hear those noises. He turned in place just in time to 'see' the creature that had been stalking them as it used its powerful hind legs to leap at Aason. A pair of saber-tooth lined jaws were coming right at him.

"OMCOM!" Aason shouted. He threw his left arm up just in time to block the attack on his body but it didn't stop the creature from clamping down on his arm, knocking him over. Although the saber-like upper teeth missed his body due to his extended arm, the only slightly smaller incisors on the lower jaw bit through his forearm. One knife-like tooth broke his radius and the other snapped his ulna like a twig. The first tooth passed clean through his arm and emerged from the other side. Aason's red blood started spurting everywhere.

"Ow, get off of me," Aason shouted, kicking at the animal's chest, jarring it away before it could claw him with its talons. With his free hand, he punched at the creature's head at a jewel-like thing which must have been its eye but all that did was hurt his other hand. The creature's jaws were clamping down harder and harder. It was trying to sink its upper incisors into his trunk like a sick version of an old-time can-opener. Instinctively, Aason reached up and grabbed one the deep blue infrared-sensitive 'ears' sprouting from the creature's head and tore it right off the animal's skull. Blue blood squirted from the stump remaining. The animal shook its jaws, deciding it would be better to simply sever Aason's arm. Once again, it reached forward with its claws to try and rake Aason's chest.

It never got the chance. There was a zzt sound and the lower kangaroo-like portion of the creature fell away, sliced in half by OMCOM's PPT throwers embedded in his fingertips. Aason lay on the ground, his arm still held in the dying creature's mouth, the weight of its upper half pressing down on him. The animal's hemocyanin-based blue blood came pouring out of its trunk soaking his legs. The pain was excruciating.

OMCOM called up to Junior and draped himself over Aason so that Junior could lock on to their position. With a whoosh and a pop, Aason found himself flat on his back in the center of Junior's cargo compartment. Aason's arm was covered in red blood and his legs were drenched in blue. The majority of the liquid covering his body came from the creature as the animal's entrails and its blood emptied from its carcass in a warm mass. OMCOM quickly used his integrated PPT throwers to carve away as much of the creature as he could without impinging on Aason's skin. The livetar used brute force to tear off Aason's jacket and jumpsuit exposing the boy's tortured flesh.

In the mean time, Junior quickly instantiated a livetar of his own and produced a gurney. OMCOM and Junior's livetar helped Aason up onto the bed. It hurt so much that Aason was crying but he let the livetars do their work.

Using an instrument that looked like a pen, Junior removed the remaining section of the animal's head until only its two lower teeth remained embedded in Aason's arm.

"This is going to hurt," OMCOM said. "But we must remove the fangs."

"Go ahead," Aason said bravely but as soon as OMCOM grasped the first tooth, the boy shouted, "Stop!" He slapped OMCOM's hand away.

"I have to remove them," OMCOM said. "I have no choice."

"It hurts too much," Aason said, writhing around. He put his good arm over the injured one to block the livetar.

"Aason, listen to me," OMCOM said firmly. "Pain is only in your mind. I know it feels real but it is not. There are receptors that carry impulses to your brain that you choose to interpret as painful. It is only a construct."

"I'm not choosing anything!" Aason snapped back. His blood continued to flow onto the gurney.

"You have not only your father's genes but your mother's as well. Your brain is capable of turning off the signals from your nociceptors. You can shut off the pain anytime you want. Look inside your head and find a fiber or two or ten that are bringing the pain and simply shut them down."

Aason closed his eyes and shook his head. He didn't believe any of it. All he knew was that it hurt worse than anything he had ever experienced in his life. OMCOM's words seemed like nonsense to him but he decided to give it a try. A strange thing happened. He was able to locate a bundle of fibers internally that were yammering at him and he did shut them down. The pain lessened ever so slightly.

"I can see it in your face," OMCOM said. "Very good. Now do more. Shut them down. Shut them all down."

Aason focused on his brain as if it were a data collection machine. Slowly, methodically, he shut off circuit after circuit until the pain subsided completely. He looked down at his arm with the two fangs and his bones sticking out. It was bizarre. His arm wasn't numb. It just didn't hurt any more. His wrist and hand were bent at a very odd angle away from his arm.

"It worked!" Aason exclaimed. "It doesn't hurt anymore." He steeled himself. "OK, go ahead," he said.

He watched with fascination, almost as if it were another person's arm as OMCOM removed first one, then the other fang, dropping them to the floor.

Junior stepped over. "We have to set your bones and stop the bleeding," he said. The livetar produced a syringe filled with a gray liquid.

"What's that?" Aason asked, pointing with his good hand.

"This liquid contains constructors," Junior explained. Aason just blinked at him. "VIRUS units," Junior said slowly. Aason's eyes widened and Junior nodded slightly. "My father invented this method. They will go in and do the work of healing for us after we set the bone."

Aason took a deep breath. "I guess I knew that. OK," he said.

Junior inserted the syringe into Aason's battered arm and slowly pushed down on the plunger, injecting Aason with the nanobots. As soon as that was done, Junior straightened out Aason's arm and gingerly took the segments of bone and put them back into Aason's flesh. This caused a new wave of pain that Aason dealt with by closing his eyes and shutting down the additional circuits. He felt one bone snap into place then the other but elected to keep his eyes closed. Junior placed something warm on his arm and it was soothing.

OMCOM put his hand against the boy's forehead and said, "You did very well, Aason. Junior will now instruct the VIRUS units to move everything into the proper place. Just remain still until he is done."

Many years ago, when Aason was only five, even though most of the Darwin members had been exiled to Helome, a pair of rogue members still ran free on Deucado. They had formulated a plan to assassinate Rei and if things went well, Rome and Aason as well. Fortunately, Rei had detected the bomb and escaped but he was injured severely. His lumbar spine was crushed and he would have been paralyzed for life had not MINIMCOM invented the method of using the nanites to rebuild his anatomy properly.

So too, Junior used the same techniques. Some of the VIRUS units provided imaging and others moved bone and tissue in place until everything was back where it belonged. Junior then switched the pen-like device from a PPT thrower to a miniature null fold projector to transport healthy cells from other parts of Aason's body to restore the integrity of the blood vessels as well as the muscle and bone. When that was complete, Junior transported dermal cells to close the skin wounds.

"The only thing you need to do now is heal," Junior said. "The bone has been set and all the defects have been corrected. You just need to rest until the bone is completely healed."

"How long will that be?" Aason asked.

"Several days," Junior replied.

"No!" Aason said, sitting up. "I don't even have one day! I have to go find Lupe."

"But the two junctures where your bones were broken are very soft right now. You could easily break them again if they are jarred."

"Then make me a cast," Aason said, swinging his legs over the table. "We have to go back."

"Very well," Junior replied. He prepared a plaster-like polymer and coated Aason's arm from the wrist to the elbow. The material set very quickly.

Aason rapped it with his knuckles and said, "This is great. Thanks." He hopped off the table. "Can you get me some new clothes?" he asked, stripping off what remained of his jumpsuit. Junior offered Aason a warm, wet cloth to wipe off the creature's blood from his lower section.

"Junior and I have discussed this. We have something better," OMCOM said while Aason was washing himself. The livetar held out what looked like an ordinary white Vuduri jumpsuit.

"How is that better?" Aason asked, setting down the cloth. He reached for the outfit but OMCOM pulled it back.

"When your father was injured many years ago, he was paralyzed from the waist down. My father rebuilt his entire back and fixed him," Junior said.

"Yeah, I know," Aason answered back.

"Even though he was able to walk, the bones were not set completely. In your father's case, he needed a full month of protection before everything was completely healed and back to normal."

"I remember," Aason replied.

"To make certain that he healed properly, my father built him a vest, a miniature PPT tunnel, so that nothing could touch his spine during that time."

"I remember that as well," Aason said. "When he lifted his shirt, you could see right through his chest, like it wasn't there."

"Yes, exactly," Junior replied. He pointed to the jumpsuit hanging from OMCOM's arm. "This is a full body version of that vest. Anything that touches you will go right through you as if you weren't there."

Aason cocked his head. "How can it be white, then? Shouldn't it be invisible?"

Junior's mouth slit curled up at the corners in his version of a smile.

"I have covered it with an electrostatically-charged polymer. When you wear this, it will expand and you will appear normal to the unaided eye."

"OK," Aason said, reaching for the suit. "But won't I fall through the ground?"

OMCOM made a grunt which sounded a bit like a laugh. "We have special boots for you. The soles of the feet are made of a regular material," the all-white livetar said. "And we made you a pair of gloves. The palms are normal material as well. You will be able to walk and touch things. But nothing will be able to penetrate your body or hurt you in any way."

Aason nodded. He quickly dressed in the high-tech suit and pulled on his new boots. After sealing the suit with the gloves, he ran his hands down his sides. If he didn't press hard, it did feel like there was a body underneath.

"Are you sure this is going to work?" he asked.

"Yes," Junior said. The livetar bent over and retrieved one of the dead creature's fangs. Without warning, he thrust it at Aason's chest, piercing the cloth. Aason didn't even have time to react. The fang and Junior's arm went straight through and appeared behind Aason as if he had no chest at all.

Even as he was dealing with the surreal situation of a livetar's arm entering his chest, he turned his head and glanced down to see the other end sticking out of his back. It was too weird. Junior carefully withdrew his arm.

Aason looked down at his chest and saw the hole that Junior had created shrink down and eventually close up completely.

"How'd you do that?" he asked, touching the area where the hole had been. "How did the tear close up?"

OMCOM said, "The polymer has dual spare, covalent bonds. One is positive and the other is negatively charged. Each fiber wants to be exactly the right distance from its neighbor."

"Huh?" Aason remarked.

"It is self-repairing," Junior offered.

"Oh. OK," Aason answered. A broad smile crossed his face. "So this is basically armor that nobody can see, right?"

"Exactly," OMCOM interjected. "And it will be much warmer as the wind will pass through you rather than steal the warmth from your body."

Aason loosened his collar. "Yeah, I can feel that already," he said.

OMCOM handed him a helmet which contained a visor currently rotated to the top. "This will protect your head. It has a miniature spherical PPT tunnel underneath as well."

"All right," Aason said, putting on the helmet. "Let's get going then." He stepped around the remains of the creature and waved at Junior. "Cuz, can you send us back down to the exact same spot you grabbed us?"

"Of course," Junior replied.

With a whoosh and a pop, Aason and OMCOM found themselves back on the path, right next to the lower half of the creature that had attacked Aason. There were tiny animals covered in white fur, gnawing away at the carcass while others were lapping up the spilled blue blood. The sudden arrival of the pair of bipeds caused the critters to scatter. Aason knew this because the ear holes in the helmet allowed him to still use his sonar vision. This pleased him greatly. He pointed forward and they resumed their journey.

Chapter 7

THE TUNNEL WAS PRECISELY CUT AND MAINTAINED ITS EXACT dimensions for nearly a kilometer then expanded into a rather broad clearing. The overhead canopy had been trimmed down and enough light filtered through that Aason could use his eyes to see. He observed that the area in front of him was organized into a main campsite and a number of cabins around the periphery. Unlike the remains of the farmhouse they had examined from the air, this place looked reasonably well maintained. There was a small metal construct in the middle. Aason could see a tiny bit of smoke curling up around the edges. He started running forward but OMCOM placed his hand out in front of him, blocking his way.

The livetar whispered, "Let me go first."

Aason nodded and waited in place. As soon as the livetar stepped out into the open area, two men came out of one cabin and trotted toward the animated shell.

"It's not time yet," shouted the first man who was covered in furs and had a bushy, black beard.

"What'ya bringing him back?" the second man shouted. "There was nothing wrong with him." The second man was clean-shaven but other than that, dressed the same as the first. A blonde girl came out of another cabin, also dressed in skins and furs, affixing a hat to her head. She hurried to catch up to the two men. Aason took the opportunity to come out of the woods to stand next to OMCOM. The two men stopped short and studied them up and down.

"You aren't K'val," said the first man. "Who are you?"

"What do you want?" asked the second.

Aason flipped up his visor. "My name is Aason Bierak," he said. "I'm here looking for my sister."

"You speak English?" the first man said. "Where are you from?"

"I come from a planet called Deucado," Aason said. "It orbits the star you would refer to as Tau Ceti."

"Tau Ceti?" whispered the two men in unison.

"Yes," Aason said. "My father was a passenger aboard the Ark II from Earth. Deucado is the planet they settled on in the new star system."

"They made it?" asked the first. They looked at each other with a broad grin. "If they're there, how did you get here?" asked the man.

"In my starship," Aason replied pointing up. The two men looked up, trying to see something, anything, but the canopy overhead was still too tangled to make out objects clearly.

"You have a starship?" the first man said breathlessly. "Then you can get us out of here!" He turned and cupped his hands to his mouth. "Hey everybody," he shouted giddily. "There's a kid here from Earth who can get us off of this hell hole."

"Deucado," Aason muttered under his breath but nobody was paying attention. The doors to some of the cabins opened up and two more people came sauntering forward.

The man waved to the seating area around the metal construct and the others took their place. Aason and OMCOM followed them over. Coming around the front side, Aason could see it was a fire pit and there were still some smoldering logs. The metal covering must have been what prevented Junior from picking up the IR signature. Well, that plus the canopy overhead.

"Sit, sit," the first man said. "Tell us your story."

"I know it seems rude," Aason said, "but I don't have time. I'm looking for my sister. I have reason to believe she is on this planet somewhere. Can you tell me where you think I could find her?"

"How'd she get here?" the second man said. "Does she have a starship too?"

"No," Aason said sadly. "She was kidnapped by beings, aliens, made of only light…"

The blonde girl, who didn't look much older than Lupe, spoke up. "You said she was taken by creatures of light?"

"Yes," Aason said. "She was taken right from my ship."

The girl put her hand over her mouth and hung her head, shaking it slowly.

"What?" Aason asked. "You know about them? Where's my sister?"

"I'm afraid she's gone. For certain she isn't here," said the first man.

"How do you know?" Aason asked frantically.

The man sighed. "Sit down for a few minutes. This is going to take a little while to explain."

Aason glanced down at the logs and envisioned himself slipping right through them. "I'd rather stand," he said. "What is going on here?" He thought back to what the man said earlier and added, "And who are the K'val?"

"It's a long story," the man replied, standing up. "My name is Peter. This is Brace. That there is Tofrah, Harper and Denny. And our little girl here is Aroline." Peter pointed to Aason. "Everybody, this is Aason Bierak and his robot..." The man cocked his head. "Does your robot friend have a name?"

"I am not a robot," OMCOM said. "I am an artificial intelligence named OMCOM residing within the memron structure above." OMCOM pointed up. "This body is just an animated shell made up of VIRUS-based constructor units which allow me to interact with the physical world."

"Oh... Kay...," said Peter not really comprehending.

"Hurry," Aason said. "Please tell me what you know."

Peter sighed. He pointed back to the tunnel that OMCOM and Aason had just used to get here.

"You obviously know about the Ark program. I'm second generation. My parents were aboard the Ark IV."

"How long have you been here?" Aason asked.

"Only fifty years maybe?"

"Go on," Aason said. The fifty year figure matched Junior's guess regarding the crater they had seen when they first arrived.

"Well, the landing went pretty much according to plan. But this planet, we called it Hades because it's cold as hell most of the year. Our parents had to adapt the plan a little bit. They had some farms set up back thataway and used the particle beam cannons as heaters to extend the growing season. The rest of them came into the woods and starting building a village. This place, well, that's all that's left of it. We call it Pax, I guess as kind of a joke."

"Where is everybody else? Is this all of you?" Aason asked.

"No, the rest of us, probably 800 or so, live way to the south. And a goodly number of people have scattered even further to go live off by themselves. We only hang around here for a month or two after the exchange. Just in case."

"I don't understand," Aason said. "What exchange?"

"That's what I'm trying to explain," replied Peter. He rubbed his chin. "Anyway, things were OK for the first two years but then one of the farmer's wives came running in telling us aliens had come and taken her husband away."

"Aliens?" Aason sputtered.

"Yes. Our parents called them little green men. We later learned they called themselves the K'val," Brace offered.

Peter picked up the narrative again. "The woman said it was a crystal rocket ship. They landed on a column of flame, disembarked, grabbed her husband and took off again. There was nothing she could do. When our people went to check, the only thing that corroborated her story was some burn spots on the ground but nobody knew what to make of it."

"That explains the vitrified clay," OMCOM whispered to Aason using the EM link.

Aason nodded but didn't say anything else.

"And because nobody knew what to make of it, they put armed guards on the farms. Nothing happened for a year but then the damned aliens came back."

"And?"

"There was a fire fight. We used bullets, the laser pulse rifles, nothing hurt them. They took another farmer and left."

Aason wanted to hurry them along but he bit his tongue knowing he had to let it play out.

"Again, nothing happened for a year. But they were expecting a next time and got themselves a battle plan. The next time the aliens came, our people were ready with one of the particle beam cannons. That was their sixth year on the planet. The cannon destroyed the K'val's ship. It was the only year that nobody was taken."

"OK," Aason said. "So you had an adequate defense."

"For one ship, yes," Peter said. "The following year they sent an entire fleet. That was the closest thing we had to an all-out war. By the time they were done, the cannons were destroyed, a lot of people died and the K'val revealed their pain weapon for the first time."

"A pain weapon?" Aason mouthed the words. "What is that?"

"It's some sort of beam that causes excruciating, paralyzing pain. And the effects last for months. Anyone that ever got hit with it never wanted to go near them again. That's when people started leaving and heading for the hills. There was this one group, a very strange one that kind of kept to themselves. They said they were going to build us proper weapons."

Aason's eyes narrowed. "Were they the people from the front of the Ark?"

"Yes…How did you know?" Peter asked.

"Never mind," Aason said. "Please get to the point."

"The following year, the K'val sent another fleet. But most of the ships went directly to our munitions dump. It was like they knew where we were hiding our weapons. They destroyed the rest of the cannons, most of the rifles and so on. They took another of our people and left."

Aason just shook his head.

"The one thing they didn't take were the mini-nukes. So a very brave man, by the name of Sal Winston, volunteered to hang out by the cargo compartment and give himself to the K'val."

"Are their arrival times that predictable?" OMCOM asked.

"Yes," replied Peter. "It's always the same length of time. A little more than an Earth year. The seasons change but their arrival is pretty reliable."

"So what happened?" Aason asked.

"The K'val went to grab Sal and he set off the mini-nuke. He took out one ship and its crew. That really made the K'val angry. The rest of them swept through the village and used the pain weapon on every one they could find. Then they took their man and left."

"Are they that unstoppable?" Aason asked.

"Well, the people from the mountains, they came down and took all the rest of the mini-nukes. They said they were going to develop a launching system so we could defend our world. They told us it would take two years so the following year, we didn't fight back. Somebody volunteered to go and there was no fighting, no pain weapons. Except for the fact that we lost another person, it was actually a year of peace."

"Did the people in the mountains develop their delivery system?" Aason asked.

"We never found out," Peter replied. "The following year, the K'val came back to the planet and went directly to their stronghold and used explosives of their own and detonated all of the mini-nukes at once. There's a huge crater up in the mountains. That's all that's left of them. We never saw anybody from the other group again. For us, that was the end. Rather than fight, another person volunteered, the K'val took him and they left."

Aason looked off to the side. He was trying to think of what he would do under these circumstances but escalation was all he could consider.

"I guess you could say after that, we, as a people, kind of lost our will to fight. We moved the people that wanted to stay together to the south, built the town called Nadir and established this outpost. This is where the K'val come each year to get their volunteer."

"And you just let them?" Aason sputtered. "There's nothing else you could do?"

"It's not as bad as you think," Peter said, "although I'm ashamed to admit it. Once we started offering them a person without a fight, they started bringing us gifts. They would bring us blankets, building materials, seeds that would grow better in this climate. And they started returning the bodies of the person taken the year before, or what was left of it."

"What did they do to them?" Aason asked, slightly horrified.

"They kind of look like mummies, desiccated," Peter said. "Like someone took all the fluids out of them. It became a ceremony. We learned early on they only wanted men, not women. The K'val would come in, drop the body, place that year's gifts on the ground and wave for the volunteer. Then they'd leave with the next in line. It went on that way for 30 years or more. The rest of the colony is actually doing fairly well because of it down in Nadir."

"Other than giving the aliens a human sacrifice every year," Aason said sardonically.

Aroline made a sound like her breath was catching but said nothing.

"You can judge us all you want," Peter offered, "but like I said it worked for thirty years."

"What happened after thirty years?"

"One of our people, an old guy named Stafford, was sick. He had leukemia, they said. So he volunteered, figuring that he was going to die anyway. The K'val took him away like always but then they returned two months later and brought him back, still alive."

"Alive?"

"Yes. They dumped him on the ground and demanded a new volunteer. No gifts that time."

"So where did they take him?" Aason asked. "Was he able to tell you?

"Yes," Peter said. "He said they took him to another planet. He had no idea where. He said it was really hot there and he coughed a lot. They had to put him in some sort of bubble to transport him so he could breathe. They took him to some caves but he couldn't make out much. It was really dark. He saw some light, followed it and he fell into a pit."

"And?" Aason interjected.

"In the pit was some sort of creature, made only of light. It was just like you said the ones who grabbed your sister."

"A creature made of light!" Aason exclaimed. "How do I find this world?"

"That's just the thing," Peter said. "Stafford didn't know. All he knew was pain. He said the creature of light immediately started sucking the life force out of him but owing to his disease, he got really weak, really fast. So we think that's why they brought him back. Sick and all, he wasn't much use to them. They need somebody who can last longer and they wanted us to know that. They used the pain weapon on a few people just to bring the point home, to train us, I guess. Anyway, Stafford died soon after he got back here."

"I have to find that planet," Aason said firmly. He waved at OMCOM and turned to leave. Behind him, he heard two clicking noises. Turning back, he saw the two men on the ends had rifles trained on him.

"You aren't going anywhere," Peter said. "You have a starship. We want to leave. We're taking it."

Aason stared at the barrel of the rifle closest to him. He didn't want to hurt these people but he had to go.

"You can't threaten me," Aason said. "You have no idea of what I'm capable of."

"I know you're human," Peter said. "That means you bleed."

Aason started breathing heavier. This was making him angry. "Go ahead. Either of you. Shoot me."

"Huh?" Brace said.

"Shoot me!" Aason commanded.

"We don't want to," Peter said. "We just want off this planet."

"Junior, on my go, I'll point to a guy holding a gun. Find the metal. See if you can use the transporter and send him to where we found the crew compartment of the Ark IV."

"You got it, Cuz," Junior replied. *"What's going on?"*

"I'll explain in a minute." Aason pointed to Brace and said "Begone!"

"Now," Aason command silently. There was a whoosh and a pop and where Brace had been standing, there was now empty air.

Harper, the other armed man, couldn't believe his eyes. He raised his rifle and squeezed the trigger. With a loud report, the depleted uranium bullet sailed right though Aason's chest and into the woods.

"Snap his gun in half," Aason said to OMCOM mentally. The livetar activated a PPT thrower and neatly sliced the gun into two pieces.

Harper blinked at the useless hardware in his hands. He threw the two chunks to the ground and pulled a knife out of a holster by his side. He flung it in Aason's direction but like the bullet, it sailed harmlessly right through the boy's PPT armor.

"Begone!" Aason shouted and with another whoosh and pop, Harper was gone as well.

"Stop it!" Peter commanded. "You can't kill us. We're your own species."

"You're trying to kill me!" Aason barked back. "And they're not dead. I just sent them away. They'll be back."

Peter put his hands up to his face. His voice was muffled. "You don't understand," he said. "We have to get off this world. We hate it here and they kill us one at a time."

"I certainly do understand," Aason said with finality. "But what you don't understand is I have to find my sister." He looked up.

"Junior, remember that movie we saw, The Last Starfighter, with the Death Blossom?"

"Sure, Cuz," Junior replied. *"Why?"*

"Do you think you can use your cannons and slice your way down here? I have to get out of here, fast, and to do that I need to put these people in their place. And can you make it noisy?"

"Roger that," said Junior. The starship pulsed his plasma thrusters and everyone looked up to see what was causing the roar.

Junior fired off his front, starboard trim jets and his rear port jets causing him to spin in place about his vertical axis with his EG lifters maintaining a constant height. Faster and faster he went. Meanwhile, he extended his "roadgrader" cannons which were hundreds of PPT throwers mounted on the end of a stalk, to the left and the right side of the cockpit. Junior activated the cannons and began to descend. Where the PPT throwers met bark, the pieces of the trees were sheared off completely. Like a gigantic router, Junior simply bore his way through the canopy, sending logs and debris everywhere.

Peter and the other residents of Hades covered their heads and scattered, running for cover. Aason and OMCOM just stood there, each impervious in their own way to the rain of wreckage coming down.

After Junior cleared out enough space, he shut off the cannons and stopped his rotation. The starship lowered his landing gear and settled down right in the middle of the campsite. The woods took on an eerie silence. The only noise was a whirring sound as Junior raised his cargo hatch and lowered the cargo ramp. Aason and OMCOM began walking toward the ramp.

"Aason, wait!" the blonde girl, Aroline, shouted at the boy. She ran up to meet him.

Aason hadn't paid much attention to her earlier. She wore flat leather boots and stood about five foot six or seven. Her body shape was hidden beneath the skins and furs but her face looked a bit drawn. Her bright yellow, shoulder-length hair stuck out from underneath her fur cap. Aason shook his head. He didn't want to be distracted. "What?" he asked impatiently.

"You're going to try and find their planet. Take me with you," she begged.

Aason cocked his head. "Why?"

Aroline took her eyes off of Aason for just a moment to stare at Junior. It was the first time she had ever seen a starship. Junior was a sleek, all-black space plane, nearly 170 feet long from tip to tail with a fuselage roughly 35 feet wide. His airfoils, while hardly aerodynamic, had a wingspan of nearly 80 feet. Aroline pointed to the amazing machine in front of her.

"The last time the K'val came for a volunteer, it was my father. He went with them. If you're going after them then maybe there's a chance you can save him. Maybe I can save him."

Aason softened a bit when he saw that there were tears streaming down her face. He looked over at OMCOM who shrugged.

"OK," Aason said. "But don't get in my way."

"I won't," she said, smiling bravely. Aason turned back toward Junior and the three of them started walking toward the ramp.

"Hey, you!" Peter shouted, coming out from wherever he was hiding. "What about us? You can't just leave us here. The K'val. They're doing nothing but breeding us for who knows what? We don't want to be nobody's food supply."

Aason sighed. *"Junior, send me a Stareater beacon,"* he said mentally.

"Of course," replied the starship in Aason's head. Just to his left, the air started shimmering which was followed by a tiny whoosh and popping noise. A peculiarly shaped object materialized in front of them, planted firmly on the ground supported by a tripod base. The working part of the beacon was mounted atop a medium-sized metal shaft. The beacon itself was bulbous, somewhat resembling a mortar shell. On the very top was a tiny red light, blinking slowly.

"What is that?" Peter asked, pointing.

"It's called a PPT beacon," replied Aason. "It'll protect your star system from the Asdrale Cimatir. They'll know to leave you alone."

"Astral what?" asked Peter.

"Stareaters," said Aason. "They come into star systems and eat stars. We put these beacons wherever we want them to steer clear."

"I don't understand," Peter said, perplexed. "What kind of beacon? Stareaters? What are you talking about?"

"I don't have time to explain," said Aason. "Just know they made it their mission to protect the universe. And they do that by eating stars. But they won't kill people if they know they're there."

Peter just stared at Aason blankly like he was speaking a foreign language. Aason really didn't want to get into it.

"Look," he said. "They've assigned us a species number. We are number 927." Aason indicated the small device. "This beacon broadcasts that number in a way that they can hear and they will not enter your star system." He pointed up to the sky. "I promise when I get home, I'll send ships back here to your planet. They'll use the beacon to find you and take you away from here to someplace else. Some place safer."

"But the K'val, it won't stop them," Aroline offered.

"No," said Aason, narrowing his eyes. "But I have to find my sister. I don't know what the aliens are using you for but I mean to find out."

He turned to Peter. "This is the best I can do for now. It'll keep you safe from the Stareaters and my people will use it to find you. Just stay where you are until then."

"But, but…" Peter sputtered. He closed his mouth as the two humans and livetar mounted the ramp.

"Good luck," Peter called after them just before they disappeared into the interior. "I hope you know what you're doing."

Once they were inside, Junior raised the ramp, lowered the hatch, activated the EG lifters and the starship silently rose up into the air.

Chapter 8

AROLINE GAZED ALL AROUND JUNIOR'S CARGO COMPARTMENT, completely bewildered but simultaneously luxuriating in the warmth of the interior. She stopped in her tracks when she saw the remains of the animal that had attacked Aason, its bloody carcass still lying on the floor.

"That's part of an Ice-saberoo," she said, pointing at the lump of fur. "What happened? How'd it get here?"

Aason ignored her for the moment. He walked over to the gurney and placed his helmet on it. After he pulled off his boots, he took off his gloves then loosened his collar and removed the PPT suit of armor. Except for his underwear, he was completely naked. Aroline looked his toned body up and down admiringly. Aason pointed to the cast on his left arm.

"That thing tried to bite my arm off," he said. "Broke two bones." He rapped the cast with his knuckles then he reached over and picked up the PPT suit again. "That's why they made this suit of armor for me."

"They are deadly," she said. "We never send anybody through the woods alone or unarmed. They lie in wait for days at a time. They can sense body heat with their…" She noticed that the skull of the dead creature only had one of the deep blue membranes. "…ear thingies."

"I kind of figured that out," Aason went to kick the carcass but changed his mind. "I guess we should clean this up," he said to OMCOM.

"I'll take care of it," Junior called out through the grille mounted on the wall. "Why don't you get dressed and tell us where we're going."

"Oh, yeah," Aason replied. He walked to the front of the cargo compartment and opened the airlock. He turned and waved at Aroline to follow him. Without waiting for her, he continued along the corridor, entering the storeroom housing the molecular sequencers. He selected a regular Vuduri jumpsuit and put it on, along with his normal soft footwear. When he came out, he found Aroline standing there staring inside the storeroom, wide-eyed.

"Do you want to change?" he asked.

Aroline blinked uncomprehendingly.

Aason pointed to the storeroom. "Fresh clothes?"

"Oh," she replied, snapping out of her reverie. "I'd love to. I always hated what we had to wear on Hades but we never really had a choice."

"Have at it," Aason remarked, stepping out of the way. He politely faced away while Aroline dispensed with the furs and skins and who knows what was underneath. When she came out, she was wearing one of Lupe's white Vuduri jumpsuits. She was about Lupe's height but a little more filled out than Aason's sister.

"This is so nice," she said. She stroked the sleeves, smoothing them down then did a quick turn to the left and right to model. "What do you think?" she asked.

Aason wanted to tell her that it looked really good on her but he had to get back to business so he simply shrugged. He led the way to the front and opened the bulkhead. Together, they crossed the threshold into the cockpit. He sat down in the pilot's seat and indicated that Aroline should sit in the co-pilot's seat. OMCOM came up front and joined them as well.

By this point, Junior was well into space in high orbit around Hades. "So Cuz, where are we going?" the starship inquired.

"Why does he call you Cuz?" Aroline asked.

"Uh, because we're cousins," Aason said.

"How are you cousins with a starship?"

"His father is my Onclare MINIMCOM. Onclare is Vuduri for uncle, so naturally, his son would be my cousin."

"How can a starship have a child?" Aroline asked, utterly confused.

Aason turned toward her. "Listen," he said. "Your people have been stuck on Hades for not even a hundred years. But as far as the rest of the universe is concerned, it's 1400 years after they left. A lot has happened. I don't have time to explain everything to you right now. You'll just have to pick it up as you go. We have to figure out where the K'val are taking your father."

"OK," Aroline replied in a quiet voice.

"Cuz, show me a view of the Nu² Lupi star system from above the ecliptic," Aason called out.

"To scale?" Junior asked.

"No, just representational."

The central panel rotated to its full upright position and lit up. The display showed a bright spot in the middle which was the yellow-orange primary of the Nu² Lupi system. Next out were the orbits of the super-Earth planets B, C and D. There was a sizeable gap and then Junior showed the orbit of Hades, which had been known as Planet F. Beyond that, Junior filled in the rest of the planets of the star system but Aason wasn't much interested in those.

"How are you going to figure it out where they went?" Aroline asked.

"We have more than enough information," OMCOM volunteered from the back. "We simply have to organize the data. The very fact that they use chemical rockets rather than star-drives would indicate they originate locally," OMCOM offered. "From within this star system."

"My thoughts exactly," said Aason. "Junior, get rid of the planets outside of Hades, they're too cold," Aason instructed, pointing to the display. The orbits of the more distant planets disappeared. "Do you have any data on Planet E?" he asked.

"There is no Planet E," Junior pointed out.

"None that we can see," countered Aason. "It was there at one point. Even if you don't have it exactly, draw an orbit that's right at the closest edge of the habitable zone. That was where it was supposed to be located."

Junior put in an orange circle around the primary, midway between Hades and Planet D.

"Now show me the current position of Hades."

A bright green dot appeared on the next orbit outward.

Aason turned toward Aroline. "Peter said that the K'val come once a year. Is it exactly the same time, same date?"

"No," Aroline answered. "Our planet takes about 15 Earth months to circle the sun. The K'val come back every 13 months, roughly. So the time of year is always changing."

Aason nodded. "Junior, simulate a Planet E for me and put the whole thing in motion."

A second, bright green dot appeared on the next orbit in. The two simulated planets began circling around the star. As soon as they were aligned, Aason said, "Freeze it there."

The display stopped moving.

"Now time it so that Hades does exactly one orbit. Show us the time coordinates. But you have to use my Dad's months, not Vuduri months because Aroline wouldn't know anything about them."

Junior put a time marker up by both planets and set the display in motion again. After the planets had spun around, when they were aligned again, Aason barked, "Stop!"

He tilted his head at the display and mouthed the time markers to himself silently. Finally he said, "That's not right. It's too fast."

OMCOM spoke up. "Junior, adjust the inner orbit to match the facts. That way we need make no assumptions."

"Of course," replied the starship. The diameter of the orbit of the proposed Planet E widened slightly. Junior reset the time markers and spun the simulated planets around much faster. This time the interval from alignment to alignment was 13 old Earth months exactly.

"OK," Aason said. "That's the right distance. But where is it now?"

"That is very simple," OMCOM said. "Aroline, when did they take your father?"

"A few weeks ago," she said then asked, "Why?"

"Because they are using chemical rockets, they would have to make the trip as efficient as possible. Therefore they would leave their home world before it caught up to Hades. They would time it so that they would land on your planet exactly when the planets were aligned. As soon as they received their volunteer they would return as their planet was moving ahead. Junior, give us a pie slice chart using these assumptions bordered by the proposed orbit."

"How big?" Junior asked.

"Assume 25% for now. 12.5% to the left of alignment, 12.5% to the right." Junior put a faint yellow background indicating the range of the inner orbit where the planet might be.

"How big is that region?" Aason asked, pointing to the right side.

"The arc has an extent of 60 million kilometers," answered Junior.

"That's too big," Aason said wearily. "How are we supposed to find something in that large of a region?"

"More importantly, how can you find something that isn't even there in the first place?" Aroline interjected.

Aason turned to look at her. "We have this thing, called a PPT tunnel. Junior's entire hull is coated with generators. He can literally turn invisible at any time. We're just assuming that these K'val are using something like that to make their whole world invisible."

"An invisible planet?" Aroline gasped. "That doesn't even make any sense."

"It fits the facts," Aason said. "When your grandparents left on the Ark IV, they were coming to a star system that was thought to have two habitable planets. We only find one. There is a gap exactly where the second planet was supposed to be in orbit. We have the technology to make things disappear. It seems reasonable that they may have it too. It's our only hope."

Aason turned back to OMCOM. "Is there any way to narrow down the search area?"

"Yes," OMCOM stated. "It has to do with the nature of rocket fuel. All fuels have a specific impulse of thrust. You have to balance that against the weight of the fuel, the oxidizer and its stability. The K'val must use a fuel with a very high specific impulse such as liquid oxygen and kerosene. Liquid hydrogen would be better but it is impractical to carry that much fuel for such a voyage. In reality, the very fact that they came back that one time means their fuel still has the requisite specific index."

OMCOM leaned over and used his fingers to pinch the pie chart down until it was much narrower. He swept away the back half of the pie chart as he computed that it was no longer relevant.

"We have the fact that the journey there and back takes about one old Earth month for each trip. We also have the fact that when they brought the sickly individual back, it took three months. We know that the planet is moving ahead of Hades. Based upon all of our calculations including the specific index of kerosene, this invisible world would be right here." OMCOM poked the display with his finger for emphasis. Junior put a bright red dot along the orbit.

"That is where they are going," OMCOM said. "Buckle up, please."

Without waiting to be told, Junior ignited the plasma drives and both Aason and Aroline were pushed back in their seats by the starship's acceleration even as they were fumbling with their X-harnesses.

"What's your degree of certainty?" Aason asked after his second buckle clicked.

"Confidence level of 88%," OMCOM replied. "If they used a different fuel or the orbit is slightly larger or smaller, that would set the calculations off."

"Let me go to the exact spot," Junior said, "and then I'll begin a spiral search outward from there."

"Good idea," Aason said. "But there's only one problem."

"What is that?" OMCOM asked.

"How do we find a planet that isn't there?"

"You have already given me the answer," Junior replied. "You mentioned it earlier today."

"I did? What did I say?"

"When Lupe first disappeared, you told me to look for mass. Well, even a planet that uses a PPT cloak will still have a planet's worth of mass. All we have to do is find a spot in space where there are moons or satellites or debris in orbit. They have to be orbiting around something."

"Yeah!" Aason said, snapping his fingers. "Good idea. How long?"

"Several hours," OMCOM said. "Given the number of variables involved."

"OK," Aason nodded.

Once the pressure from the acceleration eased up, he unbuckled and stood up from his seat. "Come on, Aroline, let's get something to eat while we're waiting. I'm starving."

"OK," Aroline replied and she followed Aason out of the cockpit and into the little room to the left that served as their galley for short hops. Aason used the food synthesizers to make Aroline one of his father's classic sandwiches.

"What is that?" she asked. Maybe she didn't know what it was but her mouth was beginning to water already.

"My dad calls it a turkey club. Enjoy." He handed her the sandwich.

Aroline attacked it like she hadn't eaten in months. She virtually inhaled it. When she was done, she held up her plate. "That was incredible. Could I have another one?" she asked timidly.

"Sure," Aason said, laughing. He handed her a napkin and reset the synthesizer. When the second sandwich was ready, Aroline ate it with relish but not quite as quickly. She took the time to enjoy its flavor rather than simply its substance. Finally, between bites, she asked, "Now can you tell me a little bit about everything? We've been out of touch for so long and it sounds like so much has happened."

Aason put down his own sandwich and said, "It's probably a lifetime's worth of stories so I'll just tell you about the parts you need to know."

"OK," Aroline agreed.

"Back on old Earth, right around the time that the Arks were launched, a group of people created an organization called the Darwin Project and released a virus into the world that killed nine billion people."

"Nine billion!?" Aroline almost choked.

"Yes," Aason replied. "We now call it the Great Dying. The very few people that survived were immune to the virus. It took many centuries but eventually they built civilization back to beyond what your grandparents left behind. They even have one extra chromosome as compared to you and they call themselves the Vuduri."

"Does that mean they aren't really human?" she asked.

"No, they're human," Aason replied. "They're just a bit enhanced compared to you."

Aroline cocked her head. "Do you have this extra chromosome?" she asked hesitantly.

"Yes, but I'm a mix. My father was a passenger aboard the Ark II so he is one of your people. My mother is Vuduri. They met, fell in love and then they had me."

"How did they meet?" she asked. "On your planet, Deucado I think you called it?"

"No, they met in a star system called the Tabit system which is 26 light years from Earth."

"What was your father doing way out there if he was supposed to go to Tau Ceti?"

"His Ark, the Ark II, hit something along the way and tumbled out of control for 13 centuries. It was just dumb luck that his ship happened to pass by where my mother was stationed."

"What was *she* doing at Tabit?"

"You heard me mention it before. There are these gigantic creatures, called Stareaters. And their name is what they do. They eat stars. My mother and father discovered them. They also discovered how to kill them but then they made peace with them."

"That's... amazing," Aroline said. "And incomprehensible at the same time."

"Yeah," Aason said. "But there's more."

"More?"

"Yes. Back on Earth, there was this evil computer named MASAL who designed the 24th chromosome. At the time, everybody thought it was a great idea and it gave rise to the Overmind which is the collective consciousness of all the Vuduri that reside on the planet."

"Huh?"

Aason held his hand up. "Not important now. Anyway, MASAL's real plan was to eventually convert all humans into living robots. He wanted to play god and have all souls report to him. My parents tracked him down and vaporized him using a volcano."

"A volcano? How do you set off a volcano? Your parents sound like incredible people."

"You don't know the half of it," Aason said. "Anyway, those folks from the Darwin Project secretly put members aboard all the Arks and their plan was to eventually come back to Earth and take over. My parents defeated them, too. At least the ones that came to Deucado."

"Were these Darwin people the same people that went up to the mountains on Hades to create new weapons?" Aroline asked.

"I would assume so. They were pretty warlike so it sounds like them. Anyway, once they were defeated on Deucado, my parents had them shipped out to Helome, uh, you would call it Alpha

Centauri. After that, things were fairly calm until they tried to blow my father up."

"Uh oh," Aroline said.

"Yes. There were still a few of them running around. So my mother had to learn how to read minds and they tracked down the would-be assassins, only to find out that MASAL's army was still active and behind the whole thing. In fact, they kidnapped me and used me to lure my parents into a trap."

"This is too much," Aroline said, putting her hand up to her forehead. "You certainly have had your share of adventures."

"You'd think," Aason said. "Anyway, we got out of it. The bad people, called the Onsiras, were tamed by a woman from old Earth, one of my father's people, believe it or not and after that, everything has been pretty uneventful." Aason's brow furrowed. "Until they took my sister, that is."

OMCOM rapped on the door frame of the little room and stepped inside.

"I wanted to talk to you about that," the livetar said. "Assuming we find these K'val, you are going to have to figure out some way to communicate with them." He turned to Aroline. "Do you know if they speak in any language?"

"As far as I know, no," Aroline replied. "They only used hand gestures to signal to my people. Maybe they had radios inside their helmets but nothing any of us could ever hear."

"Then how do you know their name is the K'val?" Aason asked.

"When Stafford was sent back, it was one of the few things he picked up during the time that the creature of light was in his mind. He never spoke to the aliens directly."

"In that case, we will have to use first contact protocols," OMCOM said. "Aason, you will have to use them."

"Me?" Aason said, pulling his head back. "I don't know anything about first contact. That was supposed to be Lupe." When he realized what he had just said, he frowned.

OMCOM continued. "You are wrong. This would not even be the first time for you. You have already spoken to aliens once before."

"I did?"

"Yes. The Stareaters. You were the first one to communicate with them.

"That doesn't count. They learned to speak English. And it was using our regular PPT channel. I don't know how to communicate with a foreign intelligence," Aason said. "That was supposed to be Lupe's job. That's what she was in training for."

"You have all the same abilities that she does. You could learn to harness them as she did."

Aason stood up. "She's been in training for 10 years. How am I going to acquire that kind of skill in a few short hours?"

"Well…" OMCOM hesitated. He turned to look at Aroline. "Young lady, I know this will seem like a strange and completely inappropriate question but are you a virgin?"

"What?" Aroline gurgled. She stared at the livetar but his expressionless face gave her no further insight. She looked down at her lap and said, "No," in a very quiet voice.

"Very well," OMCOM said. "Would you mind terribly having sex with young Aason here?"

"Come on, OMCOM," Aason shouted. "That isn't even funny."

"I do not have a sense of humor," the livetar replied. "Allow me to explain. Many years ago, when your mother had to become a telepath, having intimate relations with your father was the quickest method for her to acquire those skills. It was very effective as well. She was able to learn to harness her PPT transducers and EM transceivers very quickly. It effectively allowed her to learn how to read minds. She used your father as her training bench so to speak. Coincidentally, it was also the night that Lupe was conceived."

"Well, ew," Aason said with disgust. He shook his head. "Even so, reading minds is one thing but first contact protocols require transmission, too."

"You have the equipment to do exactly that," OMCOM answered back.

Aroline's eyes narrowed. "What kind of equipment?" she asked hesitantly.

OMCOM tapped his bullet-shaped head. "Aason has PPT transducers which operate gravitically to move molecules or detect the motion of molecules. He also has EM transceivers which allow him to sense or impart electrical signals. Together, he should, with the proper training, be able to read minds for lack of a better description as well as transmit his thoughts to his subject."

Aroline shrugged her shoulders. "So how does sex figure into this?"

"Aason's brain must be trained to transmit as well as receive direct thought patterns. He has never done this before. It would be too difficult to start with the higher brain functions. His mother already demonstrated it can be learned by starting with a simpler part of the brain, the animal part if you will. One such portion of the brain would be that which is involved with the pleasure and sensations generated during the sex act."

Aroline just blinked at him.

"What I am trying to say is that operating at a baser level will allow Aason to detect, translate and refine his mind-reading and communication skills more quickly. I can instruct you on the exact procedures you must use but I cannot force you to do this."

Aroline thought about it for a minute then stood up. "Will it help me get my father back?" she asked.

"I have computed that our best chance to resolve this situation is to communicate. So to that degree, yes."

"Then I'll do it," she said.

Aason whipped his head around and stared at her like she had three eyes. "Uh, hold on," he stammered.

"What?" Aroline asked.

"I don't know if *I* can do this."

Aroline cocked her head. "What? Don't you like girls?"

"Oh, sure I do," Aason said.

A sudden wave of panic washed over her. "You don't find me attractive?" she inquired fearfully.

"Oh, no, it's not that," Aason said. "I think you're beautiful."

Aroline's face lit up joyfully. "Then what?"

"It's just that, just that, I've never done it before." He blushed and looked down at his feet.

Aroline suppressed a laugh. "A big, strong boy like you?" She cocked her head. "Have you ever had a girlfriend?"

"Once," he said quietly. "When I was younger."

"And you didn't do it with her? What happened?"

"She really hurt me," he said. "In fact, she broke my heart."

Aroline stepped over to him. She put her hand under his chin and lifted his head up. She smiled at him and raised her eyebrows which caused Aason to blush even more. Without waiting for permission, she kissed him lightly on the lips several times. Aason shivered. She kissed him again, more passionately this time and without him even realizing it, soon Aason was kissing her back. His hands wound around her and he pulled her tightly against him.

After a minute or two of what could only be called making out, Aroline broke free and reached down and gave Aason a quick squeeze. She smiled demurely.

"You're ready," she said.

Aason's eyes were slightly glazed over. Fighting to regain focus, he turned back to face OMCOM. "This will really work?" he asked haltingly.

"Yes," OMCOM answered.

"Then tell us what we have to do."

Chapter 9

SEVERAL HOURS LATER, AROLINE STUMBLED OUT OF AASON'S small bedroom, dressed loosely in only a blanket. OMCOM was standing there, arms folded across his chest.

"Where's the toilet?" she asked OMCOM dreamily.

"The refresher is right there," the livetar answered, pointing ahead.

"Thanks," she giggled and staggered down the hallway to the commode.

Aason was the next to come out, fumbling with the clasps of his jumpsuit. He saw OMCOM standing there and tried to wipe the goofy grin off of his face but it was difficult.

"You had success?" OMCOM asked.

"Uh, yeah," Aason said. He looked all around, trying to find his footwear with no luck.

"So you can now read her mind as well as implant thoughts?" the computer asked.

Aason shuddered. "Yes," he said. "It was…" he looked up to the top of the compartment as if searching for something. "It was beyond incredible," he said finally. "It's not like our cell-phone or even when I talk to my mother using our PPT channel. It's more intimate." His breath caught. "So much more intimate."

"It is going to have to be intimate if you are going to communicate with alien intelligence," OMCOM said. "It is not just a matter of translation or vocabulary. You are going to have to understand how they perceive the world, the universe. Their motivation."

Aason shook his head. "I'm not explaining myself well. For Aroline and me, it was like, like our souls intertwined. My mom always told me that she and my dad were Asborodi Cimponeti, soulmates. Well, I think that's what happened to me and Aroline. It's like we're two people but somehow of one spirit now."

Just then, Aroline came out of the refresher and walked up to Aason. She put her arms around him and kissed him on the cheek. The blanket fell to the ground but she didn't seem to notice. She was a bit on the skinny side, you could see her ribs clearly but other than that she had curves in all the right places. It was hard for Aason to

79

pull his eyes away but he knew he had to. He put his forehead down to touch hers. *"You should get dressed,"* he said gently in her mind.

"So we're done?" she asked, vaguely disappointed.

"Yes," Aason answered. *"I am now fully trained. It was amazing, incredible. Thank you."*

"Oh you don't have to thank me," she said out loud. *"The pleasure was all mine,"* she thought back. She started to saunter into what was now their bedroom but turned in place. "What was that big cylinder in the toilet?" she asked. "It sort of looks like a fuel tank."

"That?" Aason said. "Oh, that's a shower."

"What is a shower?"

"You don't... Oh. I guess you wouldn't know," he answered. "It's a chamber where we have hot water and soap. You can wash your whole body."

"Hot water!" she exclaimed. "How does it work?"

"You just step inside. The water will come on automatically. You control the water flow, cleanser, temperature with the position of your arms. Go on and try it," he said encouragingly.

"I have to," she said and she fairly ran back to the refresher.

A little while later, Aroline joined Aason and OMCOM's livetar in the cockpit. Aason had been studying the instrumentation but upon her arrival, he stopped just to stare at her as she took her place in the co-pilot's seat. She couldn't believe how clean and fresh smelling she felt. To her, given the seriousness of their mission, so far this had been the most glorious of trips.

Even though Aason tried to affect a business-like demeanor, he could barely keep his eyes off of her. He tried to force himself to attend to the main screen in his wraparound console but he found the two of them taking turns stealing glances at each other.

Finally, Aason came to the conclusion that the only way he could focus was simply to pretend she just wasn't there. He had to concentrate. He tapped on his center screen. "Give us a synopsis. What do we have?" Aason queried toward the grille.

"We went to the first location that OMCOM suggested and did a million kilometer sweep," Junior replied. "We found absolutely nothing. We're about to move to the point supported by the specific impulse of the next best fuel which would be hydrazine."

"I know this is stupid," Aason said, "but are you guaranteed that both planets are following the same ecliptic or even orbiting in the same direction?"

"No one has yet discovered a planetary system in which the planets do not all orbit in the same direction," OMCOM replied. "It has to do with conservation of angular momentum during planetary formation. With regard to the plane of the orbit, we must allow for some variance and I have taken that into account. When Junior performs his search, it is in all three dimensions, not just along the orbital plane of Hades.

"What about star-probes?" Aason asked. "Couldn't they augment your search?"

"For visible objects, yes," Junior said. "But for an invisible planet, there wouldn't be anything to resolve. We don't what we're looking for yet."

Aason looked over at Aroline. Her eyes were so beautiful. He shook his head and asked her, "Why did your father volunteer, anyway? He wasn't sick, was he?"

"No," Aroline answered reluctantly. "But my mother passed away last year and he never really got over it. He's been so sad and mopey the whole time. He told me it would be better this way. I begged him not to go but he said somebody had to." A tear welled up in the corner of her eye.

Aason twisted around to look at OMCOM. "If the planet is at the juncture where the next fuel predicts, would their spaceship have arrived there already?"

"No," OMCOM replied. "It would be very close, however."

"So there's your answer," Aason replied. "Send the star-probes and look for their spaceship. It'll be headed right for the planet. It'll plot your vector for you."

"That's a very good idea," Junior said. The familiar sound of star-probes being launched echoed from the rear of the ship. Junior rotated the front display panel upright and the display turned dark as the starship used a MIDAR-like approach to accumulate the data from the tiny spaceships.

It wasn't very long before Junior announced, "I have something!"

"What," Aason asked, looking intently at the display.

"Here," Junior replied. He put a yellow circle around a tiny white dot. "This light is moving faster than the other celestial objects." Even as he was speaking, the tiny white dot moved outside of Junior's highlight. "This is real time," the starship said. "Let me move closer."

While it was fuzzy, the object that the star-probes were focused on was clearly a spaceship. It was long and thin with a pointy nose. It had three cylindrical rocket engine pods, equally spaced around its rear, glowing brightly. It was headed right toward the region of space which corresponded to OMCOM's next search grid.

"That's it!" Aroline said. "That's the K'val ship."

"OK, Junior, close in," Aason commanded.

The starship ignited his plasma thrusters and the acceleration pushed the humans back in their seats. Junior switched the main display to true MIDAR and they could see they were closing in fast. Unfortunately, just as they were getting near enough to see the ship with their eyes, it disappeared.

"Where'd it go?" Aason asked.

"It must have penetrated the postulated planetary shield," OMCOM answered.

"Well at least we know that we found it," Junior added.

"See if you can gauge the shield diameter," OMCOM requested.

The MIDAR sweep broadened and Junior slaved in the feeds from the star-probes. Each piece of detectable debris was given a weighting much higher than its mass would dictate. Very soon, Junior had a spherical region plotted out.

"30 thousand kilometers in diameter," Junior announced. His words were emphasized by a bright blue band cutting through the MIDAR display. "No need to worry about hitting the atmosphere."

"Go for it," Aason said.

"You got it, Cuz," Junior replied. The starship gunned his plasma drive even harder as they headed straight for the point where the K'val spaceship disappeared.

"Hang on," Junior said and they entered the invisible barrier.

There was no sensation as they crossed the shield's threshold. However, where there had been nothing, now below them, was a beautiful, blue world with deep indigo oceans and broad continents swathed in deep green and glorious yellow regions. Bright white, wispy clouds patched here and there covering the northern and southern regions. Oddly, around the equator, it was a different story. There were absolutely no clouds. The ground below was sparkling, gleaming with every color of the rainbow. The delineation between the northern and southern hemispheres and the clear area around the equator was so sharp, it looked almost artificial. Upon closer inspection, the band surrounding the planet at the equator had an odd, translucent property and reflected the sun like a jewel. Taken with the rest of the planet, it was a stunning view.

The MIDAR display indicated that their quarry was directly in front of them, its trajectory aimed toward the east coast of one of the northern continents. Aason stared at the display then leaned over and looked through the windshield. He pointed to the tiny bright object in front of them. "There it is!" he said excitedly.

The MIDAR reconstruction showed them that the K'val ship had rotated around and was now using its three rocket engines in retro mode, slowing their re-entry. The fuselage of the spaceship was segmented into two sections which had different MIDAR signatures. The upper half had very little substance to it. The lower section was much denser.

"Can you jump down directly to the planet, ahead of the ship?" Aason asked.

"Of course," Junior replied. The whine of his PPT generators built up and a hole opened up in front of them filled with the greens and yellows of the surface. The air from the planet came rushing toward them but Junior was quickly able to remove the frost that was threatening to accumulate. In a matter of seconds, they were through. Junior used his EG lifters to bring them to a dead halt. He hovered in place, carefully aiming his nose up so that it pointed toward the predicted arrival point of the alien spaceship.

"Uh oh," Junior said cryptically.

"What?" Aason asked.

"Whatever they are using to shield the planet must have knocked out my PPT cloak. We're dead visible until I can repair it."

"Why is that a problem?" Aason asked.

"The K'val have just launched nine air breathing flyers. Jets," the starship said. "If they wanted to just take a look at us, they would not have scrambled so many. I think they are fighters. All in all, I'd rather be invisible right now."

"How long to fix your cloak?" Aason asked.

"I'm working on it," Junior replied. "But it won't be ready in time."

"Show me," Aason commanded.

The MIDAR screen switched from tracking the returning spaceship to a more traditional RADAR-like display. Aason could see the nine bogies on the screen, headed right for them.

"Split the screen," he said. "Show me where the spaceship is going."

The display screen divided into two sections. Junior plotted out the return vector of the spaceship which was diametrically opposed to the incoming fighters.

"Mach 3," he said. "Use your plasma thrusters. The fighters will have to keep up but we can't lose that ship."

"You got it," Junior said. The roar of the plasma thrusters was louder than Aason ever recalled and the rapid acceleration made it hard to even move. Aason turned his head to glance over at Aroline but her eyes were tightly closed. Her knuckles were white as she held the armrests in a death grip.

"They will know we are tracking their ship," OMCOM said from behind them. "I suggest we loop around and take them head on while we are waiting for the ship to arrive."

"Take them on with what?" Aason asked.

"Junior's cannons will do. He can slice up their craft into tiny pieces."

"We don't know if the fighters are manned or unmanned. Just in case they have live pilots, I don't want to kill any of them," Aason said. "We're here to find the creature made out of light. If we attack the K'val, it's going to be harder to make peace with them. We won't get any information if we're shooting at each other."

"Very well," OMCOM said. "Junior, take off small sections of their airframes, just enough to put them out of control. They'll back off when they see we have overwhelming firepower."

"OK," Junior said. He tilted his nose up, climbing rapidly and twisting, executing a full 180 degree barrel roll. He straightened out and headed right for the oncoming armada at three times the speed of sound. The fighter jets split into two sections, peeling off to the right and the left. Junior was easily able to dodge their missiles and ammunition. As he was passing them, with a series of zzt, zzt, zzt sounds, he fired off his PPT cannons. Three of the blips on the MIDAR screen disappeared immediately.

"You didn't kill them, did you?" Aason asked frantically.

"Nope," Junior replied. "I took off a section of their airfoils and control surfaces. They can still land in a controlled fashion. And you were correct, they are manned fighters."

Junior briefly showed an image of the canopy of one of the jet fighters on both Aason's smaller screen and the main screen. It was an odd looking craft divided into two distinctly different sections. The rear section and airfoils were clearly metallic. The front section looked like glass or pure crystal. Within the crystal cockpit, sat a two-armed pilot wearing a helmet and visor. There was no way to tell what type of organism was underneath the flight suit.

"I have to go back," Junior announced, replacing the snapshot with the dual MIDAR displays. Once again, he lifted his nose up and once again implemented another barrel roll. Now he was headed in the same direction as the fighters who had started to come about. The left side of the MIDAR display showed the K'val spaceship was still on its descent and was targeted to land within a reachable distance.

Over and over again, Junior fired his cannons, slicing off wingtips and stabilizers, whatever it took. First one, then three more craft dropped off the MIDAR display. At this point, there were only two of the jets left. One took a sharp left turn and headed away from him. Now there was only one left and it was coming around for another run at them.

"Any way you can grab the pilot?" he asked Junior. "Can you transport him to the cargo bay?"

"I think so," Junior said. "But I'll have to slow down. It'll make it harder to evade weaponry."

"How about from behind?" Aason asked. "I doubt they built their weapons to fire behind them."

"Good idea," Junior said. He turned on his side and gunned the plasma engines heading directly for the oncoming fighter jet in the weirdest game of chicken the galaxy had ever seen. The pilot of the jet knew it too. Both of the missiles he fired were easily sliced in half. The unseen pilot couldn't take a chance. He peeled off long before Junior was too close to avoid. As soon as he was past, Junior used a combination of his EG lifters and trim jets to pull a 180 degree turn and then he was right on the fighter's tail.

With a far off whooshing sound, the front section of the fighter jet disappeared and the remainder faltered, arcing downward, heading toward the ground.

"He's in the cargo hold," Junior announced. "I filled it with this planet's atmosphere as it's a little different then you are used to."

"What do you mean?" Aason asked.

"It's very high in oxygen," Junior said. "Nearly 30%. Nitrogen, carbon dioxide make up the rest. There is a trace amount of silane fluoride. Not enough to be explosive, however."

"Can I breathe it?" Aason asked.

"The silane compound will be rough on your lungs and throat," OMCOM chimed in. "But the extra oxygen should compensate. I would say it is breathable for short periods of time."

"They're launching another batch of fighters," Junior announced.

"How about the spaceship?" Aason asked. "Can we get to it before they can?"

"It'll be close but I think so."

"OK," Aason said, unbuckling. "I'm going to go talk to the guy or girl or whatever it is."

"Wait!" Aroline exclaimed, reaching over and grabbing Aason's arm. "You don't have your armor," she said. "You left it in the cargo bay. The pilot could be armed."

"Yeah…" Aason said pensively. He scratched his head.

"I have the answer," OMCOM offered. "You did this once before with Junior."

OMCOM poked his finger right through his forehead. He drew it down until there was a wide crack in his head. He then used his hands to split his head entirely in half. The crack continued on down the livetar's torso, separating when it got to the legs. The hollow insides of the livetar were completely exposed.

"Step in," OMCOM's half-mouths said. "I will be your armor."

It all came flooding back to Aason. When the new Ark Lords had kidnapped him, this was the method the good guys used to smuggle him out of the cave and back to his mother. He shrugged and walked over to the splayed open version of OMCOM. He turned around and stepped backwards into the shell. As soon as he was completely inside, OMCOM reversed the process, sealing himself up until there was no trace that Aason ever existed.

Aroline unbuckled and walked over to the entombed boy. She saw his eyes peeking out from OMCOM's eye slits.

"You be careful," she said to him. "I don't know how it's possible but it feels like I'm in there with you. It scares me."

"I have to do this," Aason replied, his voice slightly muffled by OMCOM's head. "I promise, I'll be careful." He raised his voice. "OMCOM, how do I walk?" he asked.

"The shell will detect the motion in any of your limbs and mimic it," OMCOM replied. It was a little hard to hear since OMCOM's voice was directed outward but it was clear enough. Aason lifted his leg and sure enough the suit of OMCOM lifted its leg along with him. Aason took a step and found it wasn't completely natural but certainly doable. With an odd gait, the combination Aason and OMCOM walked through the open bulkhead and after they were past, they closed the door behind them. Clump, clump, clump, they made their way down the corridor until they came to the airlock. Once they were inside, Aason peered through the porthole and found himself staring at a helmeted biped, stomping around the cargo bay, pounding on the walls. Behind the creature was the sheared off cockpit from the jet. Just having this new kind of life-form in his starship filled Aason with a sense of wonder. After all, this was the first true-life alien Aason had ever seen.

"Here goes nothing," Aason said and together, the human and the livetar pressed the stud to open the outer airlock door.

Chapter 10

AS SOON AS THE AIRLOCK DOOR OPENED, THE ALIEN WHEELED around and drew what was clearly a weapon. With a flick of his finger, OMCOM sliced off most of the pistol so that the alien was left holding only the handle. He threw it down and rushed toward the Aason/OMCOM hybrid. Aason held his arms up, palms open, to show the alien he was not armed. The alien paused then jumped forward, trying to grab the livetar's neck. Aason brought his hands down and seized the alien's arms at the wrist, grasping them tightly. They were very soft and seemingly frail. Aason was afraid he would break them so he backed off of his grip a bit. The creature tried kicking OMCOM all the while trying to free his wrists. The alien struggled mightily but to no avail. OMCOM's livetar was much stronger. The creature continued to flail about for a bit more but it quickly became apparent that it would lead nowhere. As his thrashing ceased, Aason released the creature and raised his arms again, palms up.

The alien's shoulders sagged. He stepped back a few feet then straightened up to his full height. He removed his helmet and Aason was able to gaze upon the creature's face for the first time. Actually, it wasn't really a face in the traditional sense. It looked more like a small bush, made up of many tiny vines and leaves. There were two black holes near the top which Aason assumed was his visual apparatus. There was no mouth or nose as such. The creature's entire head writhed and made a series of scratching noises. They were modulated in sufficient cadence that Aason was able to deduce it was a language of sorts.

"*Open up your head,*" Aason said to OMCOM mentally. "*I want him to see my face. I need him to trust me.*"

"*Are you sure?*" OMCOM asked.

"I'll be OK," Aason replied out loud.

"*Very well, but take shallow breaths until you get used to the silane.*"

OMCOM used his hands to split his head in half and the two pieces separated, coming to rest on the livetar's shoulders. Aason took a breath and the silane fluoride in the air made him cough violently and repeatedly. The creature tilted his head and watched the boy go through his gyrations. Eventually, he regained control and forced his lungs to stop their spasms. When the coughing fit subsided, Aason activated his combo PPT/EM apparatus and "spoke" to the creature for the first time.

"I am Aason Bierak," he said. "I am not here to harm you."

In real life, the sounds the creature emitted were grating. But within Aason's mind, his response was surprisingly clear and coherent.

"You are a meat-bag," the creature said. "You will kill us the first chance you get." The alien stopped speaking for a moment then added, "As you should."

"No!" Aason said more forcefully. "I know that you've been taking our people. I want to know why." The odor emanating from the creature was very musty. It smelled like decaying leaves. Aason could only wonder what a human must smell like to the creature.

"You are food for our Lord," the alien replied. "He commands us to give Him one of your kind every year."

"Who is your Lord?" Aason asked. "Why do you feed my people to him?"

"The Lord is…the Lord," the creature answered. He turned his head away from Aason. "And we must feed Him your kind because we are not worthy."

"That doesn't make it right," Aason said. "We've done nothing to harm you."

"It is not a matter of choice," the plant-man stated. "Long ago, my kind were simple plants along the ground. We were happy to just soak up the sun and the rain and sway with the wind. Then the Lord came to our planet, we call it Ay'den. He raised us up. He gave us intelligence and these limbs." The alien flapped his arms up and down. "We are called the K'val, the very word itself means we are the Unworthy." The creature lifted up his arms, palms outward.

"Why are you unworthy?" Aason asked. "You seem very capable to me."

"The Lord tried to mold us in His image," the creature replied. "But despite His best efforts, it was not anything we would ever become, given that He evolved us from plants. So when He found your people on the other world, He commanded us to go forth and bring one of you back each year to satisfy His craving."

"But we are living creatures too," Aason said. "What gives you the right to attack us?"

"It is not our way," said the alien, lowering his head. Aason was somewhat surprised to see that these plant people used body language just like humans. "But the Lord gave us feelings and love for our families. If we do not do as He commands, He causes us great anguish and tortures our families. We do not have the power to resist so we serve His will. In that way, He allows us live in peace."

Aason stared at the creature, trying to imagine what he would do if he were in the same position. He made up his mind.

"Open up," he said, patting OMCOM's chest. "Let me out."

"As you wish," OMCOM said and the livetar split all the way open allowing Aason to step out. Now that he was no longer contained within, he could see the alien was about a foot shorter than him and of much slighter build. He assumed there was more plant matter beneath the uniform.

"Does your Lord care who you feed to Him?" Aason asked as OMCOM sealed himself back up. "Does it matter? Are there any special requirements?"

"They are not strict," the alien replied. "Whoever it is must be of good health for the Lord to take what He needs. He does not share with us why."

Aason took a step closer. "Will you take me to Him then?" he asked. "Will you let me be the one?"

"Aason!" OMCOM hissed. "What are you saying?"

Aason stared at OMCOM. He figured it wouldn't take the computer long to pick up the alien language but it never occurred to him that OMCOM would be able to listen in and interpret his thoughts. He shrugged. "I need to meet their Lord," he replied. "It's that simple."

"You would do this of your own free will?" asked the creature. "It is clear that you have the power and the technology to get away. I would think that given a choice, you would do so."

"I have my reasons," Aason said. "Will you help me and take me to Him? Will you let me serve His needs?"

"I will try," answered the creature. "But I do not think my superiors will allow it."

"We will convince them," Aason said. "What is your name?"

"I am Sh'ev B'oush," replied the plant-man. "Son of Oush B'trev."

Aason held his hand out. "Pleased to meet you, Sh'ev."

The creature looked down at Aason's outstretched arm, unsure of what to do. Aason stepped forward and gently took the creature's hand, lifting it up and shaking it firmly. After a second or two, he let it go and Sh'ev held his hand up, turning it back and forth as if Aason had deposited something there. When he was convinced there was no hidden agenda, he said, "Then I am pleased to meet you too, Aason Bierak. Confused, but pleased."

OMCOM reached forward and tapped Aason on the shoulder. "Now that you two are best of friends," he said, "we need to get to the cockpit. The K'val spaceship is about to land."

"Our air is much lower in oxygen," Aason said. "And we don't have any silane. Do you think you can breathe in our atmosphere?" he asked.

"Oh, yes," Sh'ev answered enthusiastically. "Our people have been to the other world and can breathe quite comfortably for some time. We find it refreshing, in fact delightful. So much carbon dioxide!"

"Great," Aason said. "Let's see what we can do to make some peace with your people."

The young man turned and walked toward the airlock arch. OMCOM swept his arm in Aason's general direction. Sh'ev understood the gesture and followed the human forward. Aason led Sh'ev up the corridor and opened the bulkhead leading to the cockpit. Standing there was Aroline. Her eyes widened when she saw the K'val enter. Instinctively, she took a step back, trying to cower in the corner.

"Don't be afraid," Aason said to her. He turned to the alien and said, "this is my… this is Aroline," he said.

"Pleased to meet you," Sh'ev replied. Unfortunately, Aroline did not share Aason's ability to speak K'val. All she heard was a series of scratching sounds. Sh'ev mimicked the gesture Aason had shown him and reached forward with his hand. This spooked Aroline and she leaped backward.

"He won't hurt you," Aason said. "He said he was pleased to meet you. He's trying to shake your hand."

Aroline wrestled with the conflict between all her people suffered over the years and the need to try to rescue her father. Finally, the urge to make peace won out. She took Sh'ev's hand and shook it gently. She was surprised at how delicate it felt. Since the creature was a walking plant, maybe it wasn't so surprising.

"Has he told you why they come and take our people away?" she asked.

"Yes," Aason said. "I think it's the creature of light. They call him their Lord and Sh'ev says their Lord makes them do it or else he causes them great pain. It sounds to me like they are just as much victims as you are."

"I don't know," Aroline said without much conviction.

"Spaceship is on final approach," Junior announced. "And so is the next wave of fighters. What do you want me to do?"

"How's your cloak coming along?" Aason asked.

"About 90%," Junior replied. "Should be done in a few more minutes."

"Can you turn on what you've got?"

"Yes," Junior answered. "I'll see if I can get the back end finished first so if they won't see us from the rear."

"Great," Aason said. He turned to look out the cockpit. In front of them was a built up facility and a large, paved area which was clearly a landing pad.

"Once you're fully cloaked, can you take out the fighters from on the ground?" Aason asked.

"Yes," Junior replied. "It'll actually be easier."

"OK. Fly off so they can't see your back end. As soon as the spaceship lands, I want you to come back and dig me a trench all around it with your roadgraders. Make it like a dry moat. Make it so big and so deep that they can't get to us easily. I want to reach the spaceship before the K'val can access it. Leave yourself enough room to land then set down right next to the spaceship. We can use it for cover from one side. Only take down their fighters if you need to."

"Command instructions received and accepted," Junior said robotically. Aason looked down at the grille. He knew his cousin was kidding him with the robot voice. Then Junior added. "Let me give it a shot."

The starship pulsed his plasma thrusters and flew low and fast over the spaceport. They could see the K'val running around on the ground but Junior went by so quickly that none of them could react in time.

In the meantime, the spaceship was coming down on a tail of flame, just as Peter had described. Although Aason had never seen it done before, if they had the fuel, there was no reason why it wouldn't work. As soon as the ship settled on the landing pad, it shut off its engines. Junior used that as his cue and reversed his course.

"Cloak nearly 100%," he said.

"Great," Aason replied. "Go for it."

Junior slowed down and started circling the area where the spaceship had landed, firing his roadgrader cannons in a more or less continuous fashion. A PPT thrower has no visible emissions so as far as the aliens were concerned the ground was simply disappearing before their eyes, forming a huge circular trench. The oncoming fighter jets made a flyby but they did not fire any missiles. Aason guessed they wouldn't want to take a chance and hit their own people and ship.

Round and round Junior went circling the spaceship making the dry moat deeper and deeper. When he was finished, the chasm between the rest of the K'val and the spaceship was at least 30 feet wide and 50 feet deep. The K'val would have to locate some special equipment just to come across. There wasn't enough room to land a flyer. But that didn't stop Junior who settled down gently on the little plateau, right next to the spaceship, secure in the knowledge that no one would even know he was there.

Aason turned to Sh'ev. "Do you think they'll figure out what we are doing?" he asked.

"They will find it confusing but your careful attempts to prevent loss of life will be noted." The creature bent down and looked out the cockpit window. "It might gain you a little time to explain. It would probably help if I was the first being they see emerge from your ship. They would know that you chose to not harm me."

"OK," Aason said. He turned to Aroline. "Let's go get your father."

From the perspective of the aliens, Junior was just a wavery piece of air, almost like a mirage. However his interior was not. A dimly lit but very noticeable hole opened up in mid-air, right next to their rocket-powered spaceship. The inner part of Junior's cargo ramp was plainly visible. As soon as they could see it, some of the K'val from the other side of the trench took shots at it using energy weapons. Aason, Sh'ev and the others stayed back until the rate of attack diminished.

Junior allowed Sh'ev to use one of his EG lifters as a gigantic PA system and he announced to his fellow aliens that he was coming out. Aason and Aroline stayed behind the far walls while Sh'ev peeked his head out. Seeing that no shots were fired, Sh'ev stepped back and informed the opposing army that he would be bringing a mechanical man with him. He stepped into the clear and raised his arms over his head. OMCOM stepped out and made himself visible and raised his arms as well. After a moment, OMCOM and Sh'ev walked down the ramp very slowly.

While they were doing this, a hatch opened on the lower metallic portion of the spaceship that was next to them and a ladder emerged. Several helmeted K'val climbed down to the ground and walked over to Sh'ev.

"What is happening here?" one of them inquired. "What is this creature?" he asked, indicating OMCOM.

"This is one of the meat-bag's robots," Sh'ev said.

"I did not know they had robots," the first alien replied. He put his hand on his sidearm but did not pull it out of its holster.

"Well they do. And I have returned with another meat-bag. They want to do an exchange."

"How did they get here?" the second alien asked, completely perplexed. "That is not possible. What kind of exchange?" He craned his neck and looked at Junior's cargo compartment sitting midair. The situation was beyond confusing.

Sh'ev looked up and saw two more K'val exiting the ship with what had to be the meat-bag "volunteer" accompanying them. The man was wearing a gas mask and was dressed in a shiny white jumpsuit that sparkled in the sun.

"For him," Sh'ev said, pointing at the human descending the ladder. "I have brought an even healthier one. They want to take the older one back." Sh'ev turned and waved to Aason and Aroline who walked down the ramp with their hands held high.

Aroline wrinkled her nose at the heavy, humid, oxygen-rich air. "It stinks here," she whispered to Aason. "And it's so hot!" She kept her breathing as shallow as possible but even so the silane made her cough. Her spasms were not as violent as the fit Aason had experienced earlier.

"Shhh…" Aason said. "Let's not spook them."

"Did you tell them what we want to do?" he asked Sh'ev.

"Yes," answered the alien.

"How does he speak our language?" the aliens said in unison. The first alien continued, "None of this makes any sense."

"You saw the power of their weapons," Sh'ev replied. "They could have laid waste to as much of our planet as they wanted. Yet they did not. This volunteer is stronger and will last longer. Our Lord will not care. I think we should do what they want."

"That man is her father," Aason said, pointing to the human walking toward them. "You understand family. They want to be together. That is why I volunteered," he said.

At that, Aroline shouted, "Daddy!" and broke ranks to run to her father, whose name was Donald.

The man whipped off his gas mask. "Aroline!" he cried out, welcoming his daughter in an embrace. "What are you doing here? What is all this?"

Aroline buried her face in her father's chest. "There's so much to tell you," she said, tears streaming down her face. "But I came here for you. I want you to live. We came here to save you."

Donald pushed his daughter away so he could look at her face. Aroline put on a brave smile and grabbed his hand and dragged him back to where Sh'ev and the other aliens were standing. She led him up to Aason.

Donald stood about five foot ten, just a little shorter than Aason. He was mostly bald with the fringe of his hair surrounding his head fairly gray. His jumpsuit rustled like paper as he moved and had an iridescent quality about it.

"Aason, this is my father Donald. Daddy, this is Aason," she said. She pointed up to the hole in the air. "And this is his starship named Junior. And his robot is named OMCOM."

"Starship?" he exclaimed. "Robot?" He squinted and looked at Aason intently. "You look human. Where are you from?"

"My father is from your Earth," Aason replied. "He was a passenger aboard the Ark II. Its final destination was Tau Ceti"

Donald just stared at him blankly. Aason indicated his starship. "A lot has happened since your grandparents came to Hades. While they were asleep."

"I guess so," Donald remarked. He tilted his head. "Are you putting an end to all of this?" he asked, waving his arm in the general direction of the K'val's spaceport.

"No sir," Aason said. "I'm giving myself up. I'm going to be their volunteer."

"But why, son?" Donald asked. "Clearly you can do anything you want. Why would you give yourself up?"

"Because," Aason said grimly, "their Lord needs a human sacrifice. And whoever their Lord is, I think he knows where they took my sister. I'm going to get her back."

"Your sister?" Donald asked. "Where did she go?"

"Aroline will explain," Aason replied. "Just know that for now you are safe." He put his hand on the girl's shoulder. "Take your Dad inside and close up shop. I need to get going."

Aroline let go of her father's hand and turned to grab Aason. She kissed him long and hard. "Please, please, be careful," she whispered into his ear.

"I will," Aason said. "I'm in no hurry to die." He pointed to the ramp. "OMCOM and Junior will take care of you. Go on."

Aroline nodded and reached back for her father's hand. The two humans and one livetar walked over to the starship then up the cargo ramp. When Aroline got to the top, she turned and waved to Aason. Her thoughts entered his mind as clear as if she was speaking.

"I just found you. I don't want to lose you."

"You won't," Aason said, returning her wave. He broke the connection and turned on his pure EM link. *"Take care of them,"* Aason transmitted to Junior.

"Absolutely," replied his cousin. *"Are you sure you know what you're doing?"*

"No," Aason shot back. *"But don't tell her that."* He turned to Sh'ev. "I want to meet your Lord," he said. "Can we get going?"

"Yes," replied Sh'ev. "However, your starship has made that rather difficult." The alien pointed to the dry moat. "It will take them some time for them to come and get us."

"No it will not," Aason said. Mentally, he spoke to Junior. *"Hey Cuz, can you give us a lift to the other side of the trench?"*

"Sure thing," replied Junior.

With a whoosh and a pop, the entire contingent of K'val along with Aason found themselves on the far side of the chasm.

"How did you do that?" Sh'ev asked, brushing his hands down his torso to make sure all of his body parts were still there.

"No time to explain," Aason said. "No impediments now." He pointed forward.

"I do not see why you are so anxious to die," Sh'ev observed. "I know if I were in your position, I would not be."

"Who said I was going to die?" Aason asked. "I told you I wanted to meet your Lord. There may be a difference."

Sh'ev shrugged a very human-like shrug. "Maybe there is," he said. "You seem to be very capable."

With that, a series of vehicles pulled up and several armed K'val got out. One vehicle had a flat-bed trailer of sorts. On it laid a sheet of material that resembled plastic.

"Treat him kindly," Sh'ev called out to the others. "He was decent to me and he wants to meet our Lord. He will not resist you."

One of the soldiers inserted a pump into the plastic. Very quickly, it inflated into a slightly opaque bubble. "Meat-bag," one of the soldiers said. "We can transport you in this bag. It has an atmosphere more like your own. It will make your breathing easier."

"I do not need it," Aason said, coughing even as he spoke in his mind. The silane in their air was an irritant but nothing he couldn't handle.

"Very well." The soldier waved at some others who deflated the bag and detached the trailer from the lead vehicle. The vehicles themselves were very odd in appearance. The lower section was made of metal and rode on six wheels. The upper section was made of pure crystal and looked out of place. Every vehicle and conveyance built by the K'val had the same curious dual compartments. It was a question to be pondered another time. Aason climbed up and sat down on the bench-like rear seat. A soldier got in from each side and sat next to him and two other soldiers got in the front.

"Thank you for giving me this opportunity," Aason called out to Sh'ev. "Good luck to you, Sh'ev."

"I suppose I should wish you good luck as well," Sh'ev replied. "But I do not think it will do you any good."

"We shall see," Aason replied.

With that, the vehicle started rolling. It skirted around the remains of the landing area, past the buildings there and onto a road. Near the horizon, Aason could see the outline of a city but they were heading off in a different direction. Even in this world of plants, they clearly had more than one species. They entered a forest-like area where the trees were so dense the road they were following looked more like a tunnel. The oxygen-rich air, already oppressively hot, became even more stifling. If anything, the concentration of oxygen tallied higher here. It made Aason dizzy. He compensated by taking a breath and holding it for a long while until the silane forced him to exhale. This helped somewhat.

After a while, they exited the forest and the aliens took Aason to an outcropping made up of low-lying, older mountains. Their smoothness betrayed their age. The vehicle pulled to a halt at the base of a cliff that looked somewhat sculpted. The aliens exited the vehicle and Aason accompanied them to a huge metal door, cut into the living rock. Off to the side was a series of pallets and on each of the pallets lie the bones of what were once human men.

Aason stared at the skeletons.

"Some of your predecessors," said one of the K'val. "Our Lord requires that we remove the body of the prior sacrifice before providing Him with the next. We left the remains of some of the early ones here so that each new meat-bag would know there is no hope of escape."

Aason sighed and turned his attention to the door which one of the K'val had already opened. They pointed inward. Another one of the K'val raised his weapon slightly and used it to indicate that he should go inside.

"I'll go," Aason said. "You don't have to worry."

"Then go," said the lead K'val.

Aason walked up to the entrance. So far, it looked like an ordinary cave. He glanced back at the contingent of K'val who made waving motions with their hands. Aason shrugged and stepped inside. Immediately, the door clanged shut and he could hear the locking mechanism being engaged. He was plunged into blackness. His Vuduri i-rods kicked in allowing him to use the heat of his own body and the ambient heat of the cave to illuminate the chamber with infrared. Out the corner of his eye, he caught a low level of visible illumination so he turned in that direction. The cave itself was musty, almost acrid. There was a hint of urea. Aason ignored the smells and focused on the light which was flickering and constantly changing color. He followed it down a tunnel until he came to the edge of rather large pit. At the bottom of the pit was huge ball of light, colors swirling throughout it. It was pulsating, growing and shrinking, almost as if it were breathing. Aason was heartened by the fact that this being had exactly the same appearance as the tentacles that had taken his sister.

Aason extended his mind to engage his first contact capabilities. He closed his eyes trying to find some hint of intelligence, something he could speak to.

"Who are you?" he called out loud, hoping for a reaction on the part of the being.

"You may call me God," was the reply. Huge cylinders of light came firing from the main body, enveloping Aason, drawing him down. He spun his body so that he hit legs first and rolled forward absorbing the momentum. He heard a slight crack from the cast on his arm as he used it to stop his roll. That was the last bit of control he had to offer. Aason screamed as his body and mind was racked with the most intense pain he had ever experienced, way beyond the Ice-saberoo's attack. Everything went black.

Chapter 11

LONG BEFORE AASON WAS BORN, HE WAS ACUTELY AWARE OF HIS own existence as it is with all Vuduri children. Their connection to the outside world and to the other Vuduri is secured just a day or two after they are conceived. Their thoughts may be primitive but they are thoughts nonetheless. So, too, it was that Aason knew things that no embryo should know yet he did. At the same time, he was completely aware of the fact that he should have been able to contact his mother from inside her womb and but was not able to. He tried using everything his infant mind could muster to touch her but he was unsuccessful. To make matters worse, his first encounter with an intelligent being was not his mother but rather the Overmind of Deucado who was rather imperious at the time. It had contacted him as soon as his mother and father had entered into the Tau Ceti system. Its only goal was interrogation but the Overmind could gain no useful information from the fetus. After all, he was merely an unborn child with no sense of what existed on the outside or even what the world was like, let alone where they were going.

The Overmind's incessant quizzing, probing him for information forced Aason to become even more desperate to find his mother. He pushed with his mind and he pushed with his body. Eventually, he pushed so hard that he caused his mother, Rome, to develop polyhydramnios which is an excessive amount of amniotic fluid. As her pregnancy wore on, her breathing became increasingly difficult. She nearly died from the condition. Once they arrived on the planet, Aason's father Rei took Rome to the Vuduri compound on Deucado where they were able to diagnose and treat the condition before it killed her.

However, the Overmind of Deucado never relented. Once the couple had landed on the planet, the Overmind used Aason to try and find out where Rei's Ark was located so that it could destroy Rei's people before they could even get organized. To fend off the ceaseless probing, Aason's young mind developed a psychic wall strong enough to block out the Overmind and keep himself protected until his mother was finally able to make contact. This was an ability that would be unusual for a pure-bred Vuduri child but for the offspring of an Essessoni and Vuduri, it turned out to be the norm.

Later in life, Aason found out that his mother and even his grandmother also shared this trait.

From within the depths of darkness, at the bottom of the pit in the cave, Aason clawed his way back to consciousness. Instinctively, he recreated the psychic wall that had protected him the same as before he was born. The entity that was pounding to get in was hundreds of times stronger than the Overmind. The boy poured all of his energies into the wall and used his recently developed neural skills to turn off all sensory input until the pain began to subside. He redoubled his effort and soon he felt no pain at all.

A long time ago, humans used sensory deprivation to achieve a restful or enlightened mood. But to call what Aason was now experiencing sensory deprivation would be a gross understatement. His mind was completely free of *all* input both somatic and internal. His consciousness drifted not only in space but in time as well. For no particular reason, he thought back to an incident that had occurred when he was sixteen years old.

After Lupe was born, his parents converted his room into a nursery and Aason got to move into the master bedroom of what had been the in-law suite until his grandparents had moved out. It was spacious and was totally private being located on the far side of his parent's U-shaped house.

There was a girl that he thought he loved. She was Essessoni and her name was Windy. This day in particular, she and Aason were in his secluded room, alone, with the door shut. Windy was always like that, finding ways to get Aason alone. She was constantly touching him, trying to get him to kiss her. Lupe was 11 at the time. Aason understood the idea of attraction but he was a little "slow" as Windy called it. He didn't know why, just that jumping into a physical relationship wasn't something he was ready to do.

They were on his bed. He was lying on his back. Windy was straddling him at the waist and playing her kissing game, trying to pin him down. Aason wiggled but couldn't get away. Truth be told, he wasn't trying that hard. All in all, it was a pleasant enough way to while away a portion of the afternoon.

When his sister was just a baby, she often times had trouble sleeping, sometimes for naps but especially at night. Their mother, who had a beautiful voice, used to sing her a soothing lullaby which usually helped. The lullaby went something like this: "Lupe, Lupe, flies through the air. She loves to feel the wind in her hair." Aason had heard it so many times, he had memorized both the words and the melody but he hadn't heard that song in a long time. However, on this day, from the corner of his room, Lupe's voice rang out in a half-whisper with the same tune but radically different words.

Lupe sang, "Aason and Windy sitting in a tree, K, I, S, S, I, N, G."

"What?" Windy growled. "Is that your sister?"

"Yes," Aason said harshly. He pulled Windy off of him and walked over to the corner of his room where he heard the voice.

"I know you're there," Aason said. "Come out."

There was a slight rustling sound but no Lupe appeared.

"Come out," he commanded more sternly using his EM transmitter.

"K", Lupe said out loud, snickering as she answered her big brother. Her face peeked out from nowhere. She was draped in one of the Deucadon's invisibility cloaks which she then turned off. The little girl stood up.

"Get her out of here!" Windy shrieked.

Lupe stuck her tongue out at Windy.

"Ugh," Windy groaned. "Aason! Get rid of her."

"I will," Aason said, "I will." He turned to Lupe and took her gently by the shoulders. Lupe slipped out of the cloak, wriggling away from Aason and ran over to the other corner of the room, giggling the whole way.

Windy stamped her foot. "Aason! I told you get rid of her." She pounded her fists against her sides then barked, "That's it. I've had enough!"

Aason turned around. "What do you mean?" he asked.

"My parents told me I had to snag you," she snarled. "Your parents are literally the most important people on this planet and they told me it would set me up for life." She pointed at Lupe. "But I can't stand her," she said. "She's such a brat."

"No," Aason protested, helplessly. "She's just a kid." His face contorted into a sad frown. "I thought you loved me. She doesn't matter. I'll make her leave. That can't be all there is."

Windy seemed to calm down a bit. She walked over to Aason, pointedly ignoring Lupe's presence who was swaying in the corner.

"I like you, Aason, I really do. But I don't love you. You're too…too good," she said. "I don't care what my parents think. I'm not doing this anymore." With that, she whirled in place and headed toward the door.

"Windy, wait," Aason called out meekly but his words had no effect. Windy opened the door, went out and slammed it behind her without saying another word.

"Windy…" Aason whispered. His shoulders slumped.

"Aason, I'm sorry," Lupe said coming over to where her brother was standing. She put her hand on his arm but he shrugged it off. He walked over to the bed and sat down heavily.

Lupe came over and sat down next to him and put her arm around her big brother. "Maybe she doesn't love you but I do," Lupe said, batting her eyelashes.

Aason turned and stared at her. He could never stay mad at his little sister. And in this case, even though his heart was broken, she was correct. Things never felt right with Windy and at least now he understood why.

"It's OK, sis," he said, brushing away the one tear that came to his eye. "You did a good thing." He sighed. "I really needed to know. Look, I'm not mad at you but could you leave me alone for a little bit?"

"Sure, Aason," she said, standing up. "Maybe later we can finish our dadar-fo game?"

"Whatever you say," Aason said, lying back on his bed. "I'll come out in a while. I just need to think for a little bit."

"I love you," Lupe said again, this time mentally. With that she left the room.

Aason's mind snapped back to the present. *"Lupe!"* he thought to himself. He loved her so much and now she was gone. She needed him to come get her. She was depending upon him. He steeled himself and pushed his mental wall outward until he started to hurt again. He employed the discipline that OMCOM had instilled within his psyche to shut down the nociceptors while allowing the rest of the neurons to receive their normal input. His efforts were rewarded when a few photons, impinging on his retinas, were able to make themselves known to his brain. He went back and forth pushing the wall outward and shutting off the pain. He focused all his energies on just his eyes until he was able to open them and see the pit without the throbbing ache from before.

All around him swirled colors and flashing lights. They were quite beautiful in a way but they could not penetrate his mental defenses.

"Stop!" commanded the voice he had heard earlier. This time, though, he was able to attend to it without passing out. *"Release your mind to me. I need it. I need your soul,"* it implored.

Aason expanded his defensive shield until it encompassed his whole head. "No," he said at last. "My soul is mine. It belongs to me."

"You are wrong," the voice insisted. *"It belongs to me. I am the Beginning. I am the End. I am All Things."*

Aason continued to extend his mental wall until it surrounded the sensory input from the upper portion of his body. He pushed it down his spinal cord and past his limbs until he was able to recover enough control of his body so that he could stand. He shivered and straightened up. "You can't have it," he said, defiantly.

"You do not understand," the voice answered back. *"I need your soul to survive. To grow."* The voice took on a more pleading tone. *"Please do not resist me."*

"Tell me where my sister is," Aason said. "I know you know. Then we'll talk about what you need."

"But I am God," the being said. *"You are a mere mortal. Your wishes are of no consequence."*

"You aren't God," Aason said, stretching his arms out. He rotated each of his shoulders, loosening them up then he continued. "We both know that. God doesn't live in a cave, sucking the life out of kidnapped people. From what my father told me, God lives everywhere and doesn't get involved in the day-to-day affairs of man."

"Very well," said the being. *"Perhaps I am not the God, Species Zero Prime, but to you I am a god. I am able to manipulate matter and minds using a power you cannot comprehend."*

Aason looked all around him, peering through the flashing lights and the swirling colors. He spotted a small group of boulders off to one side. He walked over to the pile and sat down on the largest rock, attempting to project a casual air that was incongruous with his current situation.

"How about you tell me your real name first?" Aason offered. "You may have the plant people fooled but I know a being when I see one."

"You could not pronounce my name," the glowing ball of light said. *"You do not have the vocal apparatus."*

"So give me one I can pronounce," Aason said. "Make one up."

"You may call me ... Molokai," said the being in a resigned tone.

"What kind of name is that?"

"It is the name of a small island on your father's birth world. I have seen it many times within the minds of others of your species. It seems fitting."

"OK, Molokai it is. My name is Aason. So tell me, where is my sister?"

"I know where she is," replied the creature. *"But it will not do you any good to learn."*

Aason leaped up. "Where," he shouted, no longer able to contain himself. "Tell me."

"I saw it in your mind. She was taken by others of my kind, back to my..." The creature stopped speaking.

"To your what?" Aason asked insistently.

"You do not have a name for it."

"What?" Aason sputtered. "Your world? Your dimension? Your realm?"

"No." Molokai's flashing grew even brighter. *"You may call it Heaven. It is the place that souls like yours go when they are freed from the flesh."*

"Heaven is real?" Aason cried out. "Are you saying Lupe is dead?"

"I would not think so," Molokai replied. *"She would not be of particular use to them dead. They would not have gone through all the trouble to take her. No, her spirit is worth so much more to them if her body is still alive."*

"Who is them?" Aason pleaded. "Tell me. You said your kind?"

"The other...gods. They took her but I am not certain how."

"We were in something beyond null fold space," Aason said. "Is that where they live?"

"No. But it is possible through great effort that they could come down to that level."

"You're here," Aason pointed out. "How much effort could it take?"

Molokai emitted a feeling that felt like one of helplessness.

"I do not expect you to understand but I am not here by choice."

"Then why *are* you here?"

"Your language, it is completely inadequate. Any description I use would not explain the underlying events in any meaningful way that you could understand."

"Give it a shot," Aason insisted.

"My birth species, you would call them Species Twenty Two, was my origin. I came here... you could say I volunteered for this mission. You could I was expelled from my own realm to use your word. You could say I was a pacifist who refused to choose between two warring sides. You could say I landed in this continuum by accident. You could say I was curious what became of my universe since it has been so, so long. Yet all are so far from the whole truth that it resembles a lie."

Aason looked all around the cave. Except for the glowing creature next to him, it was unremarkable in every way. Aason waved at the far walls. "Regardless, you said you are not here by choice. Or at least you're stuck here. That part can't be a lie. Do you want to go home?"

"Yes!" Molokai said enthusiastically. *"More than anything. That is why I sit on this world, consuming souls. I am trying to build my strength for the voyage home but so far I have failed. The plant people have souls but none that I can use. That is why I started the breeding program on your other world."*

Aason scowled while considering the concept. A thought occurred to him. "Look," he said. "If your friends were able to come down to null fold space and take my sister away, why can't I take you to null fold space and let you go home from there?"

Molokai began expanding. Tendrils of light exploded from his body and were just as quickly withdrawn. Soon he was the size of the entire cave. The ground shook beneath Aason. In a flash, the creature made only of light shot back down and became a glowing ball maybe 10 feet across."

"Is that a yes?" Aason asked.

"No," Molokai said sadly. *"To do this would require conditions that you could not hope to achieve."*

"Try me," Aason said.

"First, you would have to go to a higher dimension than the one you entered before. What you referred to as null fold space."

"Why? It was good enough for your buddies."

"No. It took an uncounted number of them to reach down that far. I am only one being. I must go higher. Much higher."

"What do you mean by higher?" Aason asked.

"You do not have the words. What you call velocity is measured relative to the coordinates in this space. It would have to be so much more relative to other dimensions."

"You mean faster? Faster than we flew before?"

"If you wish to call it that then it would be beyond faster. Unimaginably faster."

Aason stroked his chin. "There is no upper speed limit to the X-drive. OMCOM said the only limitation is the amount of computing power."

"I did not know that you had that ability. None of your predecessors had any hint. You say velocity equates to computing power. What determines your computing power?"

Aason held his arms out wide. "Basically the size of the computer."

"Give me the relative geometrical relationships. Are your ships and your computers of proportional size?"

Aason cocked his head. "I guess so. At least it is in my ship. My ship *is* a computer."

"Then to do what we must, you would need a ship a billion, billon times larger. In essence, you would require a computer the size

of this planet. Your people could never build such a thing. No creature your size could do so."

Aason just stared. He couldn't help himself. He huffed out a laugh. "You're wrong," he said triumphantly. "I have exactly one of those!" He tried to imagine how it would all work out but realized it didn't matter right now. "So if I get you your ship and your computer," he asked, "You'll take me to Lupe?"

"Yes, yes," Molokai said excitedly. *"I will make certain of it. You will see your sister again."*

"Then we have a deal," Aason said. "Can you leave this place and come with me?"

"Yes," replied Molokai. *"I had roamed this planet for thousands of years before I settled upon this cave. I have been here for millennia. However, considering it, perhaps it would be nice to experience a change of scenery. Where would you take me?"*

"To my starship. We have a lot of work to do and a long way to go to build you what you need."

"From what I saw in your mind, I could travel in your ship in this space but to get to where we would need to go, I would not be able to lead the way to the higher realms."

"What do you mean lead the way?"

"I would have to guide you as we ascend. So that we go to the right place. It is not a matter of velocity alone."

"All right," Aason said. "We'll hook you into our control systems."

"It is more than just that. I meant it literally. I must physically lead the way."

Aason scratched his head. "How do we work that? Do we just stick you out in front of our ship, in space?"

"No. I would dissipate as we hit the higher realms if left unprotected."

"How then?"

"You must place me in a capsule and attach it to the front of your ship. I will connect with your mind and body and lead the way."

"OK," Aason said, "whatever you say. We'll build you a capsule. We have molecular sequencers. You just give us the dimensions."

"No. It cannot be made of an inert substance. I must be able to bond to it. It must be built out of living crystal."

"Living crystal?" Aason asked. "What the hell is that?"

"It exists on this very world. This planet has two types of life-forms. There are the plant people but there are also the living crystals. You must carve the capsule out of living crystal. I will give you the exact shape and size after you procure a suitable block for me."

"How do we procure it?"

"Your new plant friend will know," replied Molokai. *"You must ask him."*

It was completely ceremonial but the K'val always kept a contingent of guards around their Lord's cave for a few weeks after the next meat-bag volunteer had been placed inside. There had never been an instance where the prisoner escaped but they did have the one time when the Lord commanded them to exchange the one sickly meat-bag for a healthier one. After a month or so, they could safely disperse. This soon after delivering a meat-bag, however, they were still somewhat attentive.

They were shocked to see the locking mechanism reverse and the metal door open all by itself. Both guards immediately pointed their weapons. The latest meat-bag stood in the entry way, holding his hand up to shield his eyes. Under normal circumstances, they probably would have shot him but then their Lord would have been greatly displeased. And when the Lord was displeased, shock and pain inevitably followed.

The boy began to exit the cave. Even as Aason was coming out, one of the guards called out, "You must return. Now!" Aason was unfamiliar with their weapons but it certainly seemed like the guard set the arming mechanism of his rifle. While the guards had no intention of shooting him, he had no way to know that so he disarmed the situation in the only way he knew how.

"I do not think so," Aason said with a smile on his face. He stepped aside and for the first time in a thousand years, Molokai exited the cave.

Immediately, the two K'val soldiers fell to their knees, prostrating themselves before the gleaming ball of light that was their Lord. "Oh Lord," they whispered. "We are not worthy."

"You can get up," Aason said. "You guys are not only worthy. You actually did a pretty good job of providing for His needs. It is just that your Lord has decided it is time to leave this world and move on to the next."

One of the guards tentatively lifted his face. If they had expressions you could read, it would have been one of utter confusion and wonderment.

"How about you call up a car and take me back to my ship? And I'll need Sh'ev," Aason called out.

"Do as he says," Molokai commanded.

The plant people moved faster than any of their species ever had since they came into existence.

Aroline was sitting in the cockpit with her father, just staring out at the K'val landing pad and the trench that Junior had built around it. The rocket ship that had brought her father remained where it had landed, completely unattended. Perhaps the K'val could not find a way across the chasm. More likely they feared to do so.

The sun was hanging low in the sky and it would be getting dark soon. She had spent the afternoon explaining things to her father as best as she could relate them. Most of it was beyond anything he could imagine. Junior was kind enough to show him images on the central viewscreen when it would help with matters but it was a lot of information to absorb in one session.

At last, they had run out of things to discuss. Really, it was just Aroline saving her voice. Her throat was sore from her brief exposure to the silane fluoride in the atmosphere and talking so much had made her voice weak.

Donald was tapping the armrest impatiently. He forced himself to get used to the idea of an intelligent spaceship and his companion, the huge white robot. But sitting on this world, the world of their enemies, seemed somewhat pointless now.

"I don't suppose you could take us back to our planet," he directed toward Junior's input sensor. "It isn't great but it's a hell of a lot better than being here."

"No!" Aroline insisted. "Not a chance."

"I have to wait for Aason," Junior replied more calmly through the grille.

"But, but," Donald said. "I hate to say this out loud but what makes you think he's coming back? They, uh, fed him to their Lord."

"Daddy!" Aroline called out. "You don't know that."

"You do not know Aason," OMCOM interjected. "He is a very resourceful boy. And he is on a mission. There is nothing that will stop him."

"If you say so," Donald muttered and he went back to tapping his fingers.

There was a clicking noise and Aason's voice came in loud and clear. "You got that right," he said. "I'm on my way back now."

"Aason!" Aroline exclaimed, relief permeating her voice. "Are you OK?"

"Yes, I'm fine," he said. "I'm bringing back a new friend."

"Who?"

"God" Aason said.

"God?" Aroline whispered, barely believing her own words.

"Yes," Aason replied. "And he knows how to find Lupe."

Chapter 12

THE K'VAL GUARDS DROVE AS QUICKLY AS THEY COULD TO GET
Aason back to the edge of the dry moat with Molokai floating
effortlessly through the air right behind them. Every K'val that they
passed sank to their knees and placed their head on ground, muttering
the same thing. Aason frowned each time he witnessed it. The K'val
were not a bad species. They were just put in a bad situation. They
owed their sentient lives to Molokai and at the same time he tortured
them into doing his bidding.

When the caravan arrived at the launch complex, a number of
plant people came streaming out a nearby building, Sh'ev among
them. As soon as he saw it was Aason with Molokai beside him, he
dropped to his knees. "We are not worthy," he said, face down.

Aason walked over and patted his new friend on the shoulder.
"Get up, Sh'ev," Aason said. "I need your help."

The plant creature lifted his head and stared directly at his
Lord for the first time in his life. Aason, the meat-bag, had done
something that no other being had in the entire recorded history of
his people.

Molokai glistened and the colors swirled. It was actually
quite beautiful.

"Arise, Sh'ev B'oush," Molokai said. *"It is time to go."*

At first, Sh'ev was stunned that the Lord had addressed him
by name. But a commandment was a commandment. He took his
time but eventually he was fully upright. "Go where, my Lord?"
Sh'ev asked reverently.

"I'll explain aboard ship," Aason interrupted. The boy
whispered something to Molokai who drifted easily across the trench
in the air and hovered on the far side. Aason touched his temple and
with a whoosh and a pop, both Aason and Sh'ev found themselves at
the base of Junior's cargo ramp which was already lowering.

"Come on," Aason said, waving and he mounted the ramp.

"Aason!" Aroline shouted, running toward him. She grabbed
him and if it was possible, she kissed even more passionately that
when he left. Aason felt so right holding this girl, he didn't resist in
the slightest.

After they were done, Donald patted him on the back. OMCOM and Junior's livetars were there as well. Sh'ev joined them and Aason herded them toward the front to make room for Molokai. The glowing creature squeezed his bulk into the cargo compartment and Junior closed up the hatch.

"Everybody, this is Molokai," Aason said, pointing to the ball of lights.

The humans mumbled hellos.

"Hello," Molokai replied. The humans and the K'val could hear him however neither Junior nor OMCOM could see anything or hear anything. Both elected to accept the humans' reaction as their guide.

"You know where Lupe is?" OMCOM asked into the empty air.

Molokai took a few organic molecules that were floating around the cargo bay and set them to vibrating so fast that they emitted an EM signal. The being modulated the radio waves in a frequency jacket that approximated human speech. *"Yes. Aason and I have worked out a plan to retrieve her."*

OMCOM nearly did a double-take. Even though there was nothing visible, it was clear to him this being was not only present, it was very powerful as well.

Junior took his cue from OMCOM. "Can you tell us?" he asked.

"Yes. I will need a capsule made out of living crystal. You will seal me within and then bond that capsule to the front of your ship. Aason has told me that he has access to a computer the size of a planet which could be formed into a ship."

"Planet OMCOM," Aason added although it was completely unnecessary.

"You will then launch this ship using your X-drive and accelerate until we pass through enough dimensions to enter my realm."

"What is living crystal?" Aroline asked.

"This world has two types of living creatures," Aason replied. Inside his head, he simultaneously translated for Sh'ev to hear. "There are the plant people, the K'val," he said pointing to Sh'ev.

"Their DNA is like ours. Carbon-based. But there is also a whole eco-structure and lineage built upon silicon-based DNA."

"Silicon DNA?" Donald questioned. "Are you talking about as in rocks?"

"Yes," Aason continued. "The K'val build the front of all their ships from the carcasses of the ones that died."

"What is the reasoning behind that?" OMCOM asked.

Sh'ev explained in his whispering, raspy voice and Junior, who had already mastered the plant people's language, translated for the sake of the others who didn't speak plant. "The crystal creatures do not like us, the K'val, much at all," Sh'ev said. "There are many species of flying creatures that attack us. Their attacks are especially fearsome whenever we get too near their territory. However, they will not attack their own kind so the crystal protects us. They are fooled into believing it is one of them. This became the founding principle behind the design of all of our vehicles."

"Molokai said it had to be living crystal. Is that what you use?" Aason asked.

"No," Sh'ev replied. "We only use the carcasses of the long-dead. We have been warned to stay away from the ones that are still alive."

"Who warned you? And where do we get living ones? Molokai told me it had to be of a certain species. A big one."

Sh'ev shook his head in a very recognizable gesture. "I am not sure. I have never been there," he said. "It is very dangerous. The crystal creatures are extremely irritable. The last expedition to their part of the planet was over two hundred years ago."

Aason's shoulders sagged. "So there are no maps, no records?"

"Not that I have ever seen."

"But Molokai said you would know," Aason pointed out.

The plant-man raised his hand and extended a tendril. "Now I understand. He is right, in a sense. While I do not know myself, I do have an idea about how we can find out."

"Great," Aason said. "How?"

"My father was on the last expedition to their territory," Sh'ev replied. "He should be able to tell us how to get there."

"I thought you said it was two hundred years ago. Are you saying your father is still alive?"

"Oh yes," Sh'ev said. "My people are not like you meat-bags. We live a very long time in our final phase. From what I can tell, you meat-bags have a very short lifespan. It has been quite a revelation."

"I know that we are different. I mean, I understand Molokai evolved you but there should be some overlap." Aason tilted his head. "Are you sure there are no animals, meat-bags, on this planet at all? They never evolved anywhere?"

"I am quite sure," Sh'ev answered with a bit of haughtiness. "I believe we would have noticed if there were any. Your people were the first time we were ever aware such a life-form could exist."

"And you didn't find anything odd about that?"

"How can you notice something missing if you never knew it existed in the first place?"

"I suppose you're right," Aason said. "We don't have any intelligent plants on Earth or Deucado and we never thought that was odd."

"Exactly," Sh'ev replied. "As I was trying to explain earlier, we have three stages of existence. The first stage, seedlings, grow until they are nearly my height. That takes twenty or thirty years or more. Once we have developed sufficiently, we de-root ourselves and enter the ambulatory phase of our lives, like me, so that we can serve our Lord."

"How long is your ambulatory phase?" Aason asked.

"It is not exact. Some remain walking about for hundreds of years, some much less."

"What happens after that?"

Sh'ev pointed to his feet. "After we have served our time, we return our roots to the soil and grow much taller. We become what you would refer to as trees. We remain at that stage for hundreds, sometimes thousands of more years."

Aason scratched his head. "So where is your father now?"

"He is in what is called the Grove of the Elders," Sh'ev replied. "Each city, state, community has their own Grove. My family, my village, our Grove is not too far from here."

"Would you mind taking us there?"

"Not at all."

"OK," Aason said. "Let's go up to the front and you can give Junior the coordinates."

After plotting in their course, Sh'ev took them to the south not even a hundred kilometers. The starship settled down in a clearing just outside what appeared to be a goodly sized forest, however it did not look exactly like the forest Aason passed earlier in the day. Sh'ev and Aason disembarked and the plant-man led them into the Grove. Off in the distance, they saw several other K'val moving rapidly through the forest. They did not pay any notice to Sh'ev or Aason nor did Sh'ev call out to them.

Sh'ev led Aason a small distance into the forest then took a sharp left. He stood there, head bent down and two stalks emerged at right angles from his head, tipped by tiny yellow flowers that resembled small sunflowers. The flowers rotated left and right and then stopped, both facing forward. The plant-man lifted his arm and extended a tendril, indicating that they should move on ahead and Aason followed him. Sh'ev seemed to allow himself to be guided by the flowers that were protruding from his head. He wound his way around many trees until he came to one in particular. Sh'ev pointed up to a fairly large specimen.

"My father," Sh'ev said. Aason nodded. "Hello, Father," the plant-man called out.

The tree before them shivered. Two large, very robust sunflower-like blossoms unfurled from the trunk roughly 30 feet up from the base. They rotated about for a bit then pointed down, appearing to lock onto Aason and Sh'ev. Bark-like eyelids pulled back revealing two dark spots which were similar to Sh'ev's eyes. In a deep, rasping voice, the tree replied, "Sh'ev? What brings you back here so soon?" It sounded like two logs rubbing together.

The tiny stalks with the little flowers emerging from Sh'ev's temples retracted until they were flush against the sides of his head. "It has been five years," Sh'ev said. "You have been sleeping most of that time.

The tree shook its branches and bent one forward to lightly pat Sh'ev on his head. "I hardly notice any more." Slowly, the tree twisted to regard Aason.

"Is this is an actual meat-bag?" the tree asked. "You have mentioned them on more than one occasion but I could not really imagine what they looked like."

"Yes, this is a meat-bag," Sh'ev said. "His name is Aason. Aason, this is my father, Oush B'trev."

"Pleased to meet you, sir," Aason said. He held his hand up. The tree reached out with one of its branches and brushed it along Aason's arm. It then poked him in the side.

"Squishy little things, aren't they?" Oush remarked.

"Yes," Sh'ev replied. "They do not have any cellulose within their cell walls. They are made mostly of water. The meat is kept within soft cells but they are very tightly packed which keeps them upright."

"Why did you bring it here?"

"Aason will explain," Sh'ev answered.

"We need to go to the land of living crystals," Aason said. "We need to…"

"No!" Oush shouted. "It is too dangerous. No one has gone since our Lord previously commanded it. We lost many good K'val during our last expedition there. Our people just cannot communicate with them. They are beasts and they are always angry."

"It doesn't matter," Aason said. "I have to take the risk. We are taking your Lord off this world and we need a capsule made from the living flesh of a crystal creature."

"You are taking our Lord?" Oush repeated reverently. "Off our world?"

"Yes, Father," Sh'ev said joyfully. "The Lord is ready to depart. And leave us in peace!"

The tree shook its branches. "This is a happy day," he said. He slowly tilted backwards, facing upwards as if regarding the sky then back down to Aason and Sh'ev. "If you can do that, meat-bag, our people would remain eternally in your debt."

"That's the plan, sir," Aason said. "So will you help us?"

"Sh'ev, you are committed to this venture?" Oush asked.

"Yes, Father," Sh'ev said. "It will stop our pain forever and protect our families."

"Very well," Oush said. "Meat-bag, how big is this capsule that you must build?"

Aason used his toe and dragged it around the area in front of Oush to sketch out the rough dimensions for the capsule in the leaves and soil.

"For something that large, you will need to trap one of the moving pyramids. Their herds roam about, right near the equator. They will have the heft you need." Oush said thoughtfully.

The tree slowly bent over and cleared away the fallen leaves leaving only the bare soil. He used one of his branches to draw a map in the humus and dirt that covered the forest floor.

"Sh'ev, you know the border between our two domains," Oush said. He drew an 'X' on the ground. "This is where we normally perform our mining operations. That is where you start. From there, head due south. When you get to the equator, turn west. That will take you to the central mountain range. The creatures you seek roam there, at the base of the mountains. They feed off of the stone walls. Is it safe to assume you are going to fly there?"

"Yes sir," Aason replied. "We'll fly there in our starship."

"You meat-bags have starships? I am very impressed." Oush shivered and a few leaves fluttered to the ground. "Make sure you fly low. They have very light creatures that can soar upon the wind. They will attack you as soon as they see you."

"We should be OK but thank you, sir," Aason said. "You've been very helpful. I think we have enough to get going."

"Perhaps. Once you build this capsule," the giant tree asked, "what will you do with it?"

"Your Lord said we were to seal him within and attach the whole thing to the front of our ship."

"That is very interesting. He said to seal him within. Did he instruct you on how to do this?"

Aason scratched his head. "Not really. And why is that so interesting?"

"That was one of the major reasons our Lord sent us on that expedition. He commanded us to learn how to split a living crystal in two and put it back together again, sealing it in place."

"Why would he do that?"

"He must have known that the time was drawing near when someone would require those skills."

"I wonder how he knew," Aason marveled out loud. He shook his head. It didn't really matter. "So, did you figure it out?" he asked.

"Yes. There is a way. It is simple but you must be very careful. Within their bodies, the crystal creatures have a viscous substance, analogous to our sap."

"Like our blood?"

"I do not know what your blood is like but I suppose so. After you trap your quarry, you can use their blood as you call it to seal up the capsule. We learned that outside their bodies, it gels and sets very quickly. It is what heals their wounds."

"It sounds like a kind of glue. That's great," Aason said. "Thanks." He patted Sh'ev on the back. "Let's get going, buddy."

"Wait!" Oush said rather forcefully. "Be very careful with this substance. Do not allow any part of you or my son to come in contact with the crystal's blood."

"Why?" Aason asked, perplexed.

"While learning how to work with it, we lost several of our brothers. The crystal creature's blood can transmute carbon-based DNA into silicon-based DNA very quickly. It could turn you into a living crystal and your life as you know it would be over before you even realized what had happened."

"Wow," Aason whistled. "That's creepy. I'm glad you told us."

"We will be careful, Father," Sh'ev said. "And thank you for this information."

"Meat-bag," Oush commanded. "You watch out for my son. He is very precious to me."

"I will, sir, I promise," Aason said and with that, they took their leave.

Chapter 13

ON THEIR WAY BACK TO THE SHIP, AASON HAPPENED TO LOOK AT Sh'ev's head and noted that the tiny yellow flowers he had seen earlier were completely gone. Since Aason had seen them as they extended out, he assumed that Sh'ev had withdrawn them back inside. From the way the alien looked now, there was no evidence that they ever existed.

"Hey Sh'ev," Aason called out. He hurried up to his new friend and tapped the plant-man on the shoulder.

Sh'ev stopped walking to face Aason. "What is it?" he asked.

"As we were entering the woods, I saw some little flowers poke out from the sides of your head. They were kind of pretty. Your father had something similar but yours are gone now. What are they? Are they decorative?"

Sh'ev patted his temples. "Those are my s'aploves," he replied.

This was the first time that Aason's ability to communicate with an alien intelligence failed him. He heard the word in his mind as clearly as if Sh'ev had spoken it in English but it was a nonsense set of syllables.

"I don't understand that word," Aason remarked. "Can you explain it differently?"

"I can try," answered Sh'ev. "The flowers, as you call them, are our sapline detection organs."

Again Aason heard the word clearly and it sounded more like a real word but he had no idea what it meant. "What is a sapline?" he asked.

"A sapline is... Do you have bloodlines?" Sh'ev tilted his head in a very human-like fashion. "You obviously know your siblings. You know your parents and they know theirs, correct? You can trace your lineage back in time?"

"Sure."

"Then our saplines would be similar to your bloodlines. It is a way of tracking and tracing your relatives and ancestors. We are not like you meat-bags. From my short time with you, I can see that you are all very dissimilar from one another in shape and size and easy to distinguish physically. The K'val are the opposite. We all look alike and sound alike. Without our s'aploves, we would have a very hard time knowing who is a member of our family and who is not."

Sh'ev looked up to the sky, trying to draw inspiration. He looked back down at Aason. "Imagine that you lived in complete darkness and you could not use your eyes to see shapes, you would not be able to see your relatives or tell them apart, would you?"

"Actually, I could," Aason said sheepishly. "I can see in the dark."

Sh'ev was taken aback. "Do all meat-bags have such ability?"

"All the Vuduri do," Aason replied. "Me, my Dad and my sister, though, we have a special kind of sonar vision, too. It's activated by sound, not light."

Sh'ev made a noise like a harrumph. "Then we are not as fortunate as you. We need our s'aploves to go to the right places and spend time with the right K'val. It is an organ that fosters kinship and love."

Aason shook his head. "That seems so odd to me. But then again, you are living, talking plants so what do I know? I'm just a meat-bag." Aason looked at both sides of Sh'ev's head. "How do they work? Are they chemical-based? Like pheromones? Do they use EM radiation?"

Sh'ev extended his yellow sensory organs again briefly so that Aason could examine them. He allowed the human to touch them carefully. They felt like they looked, like sunflowers. Then Sh'ev withdrew them again.

"They are as you suggested and more," Sh'ev said. "They also work at a psychic, emotional level. We know our family in our…" Again, the word that Sh'ev spoke seemed like nonsense but Aason's brain translated it as heart, not the physical organ but the seat of emotion.

Aason took a step back and looked at Sh'ev from head to toe and back again. "I would have guessed by now there would be *some* diversity in your population. Some difference in height or appearance?"

Sh'ev shook his head. "The Lord does not wish it to be so. He wanted us to be uniform in size and shape. He created our s'aploves so that we require them to know one K'val from another.

It lets us feel our families in our very core. That way, if He desired to inflict pain or suffering on one of our own, we would all feel it as if we were experiencing it ourselves. It is a very powerful tool to ensure obedience."

Aason made a growling sound. "I'm having a really hard time reconciling the motives of a higher being with such cruel behavior. Molokai should have been better than that."

"Perhaps," Sh'ev said, "but it is the only thing we have ever known. He did it for His own reasons. But none of that matters now. You are going to take Him away. Perhaps after that happens, we will come to grow somewhat differently. Maybe that will allow us to someday be less uniform and more like you meat-bags."

"I understand," Aason replied thoughtfully. "But you'll always have your s'aploves." He shrugged. "Thanks for explaining that to me but we'd better get going." He pointed toward the edge of the woods in front of them and they marched on, their goal being the clearing where Junior was sitting, waiting to take off.

Aason "radioed" ahead with their approximate destination. As soon as they were aboard, Junior raised the cargo ramp and closed the cargo door and lifted up in the air. The starship revved up his plasma thrusters and they shot into the sky.

At Mach 3, it didn't take them long to get to the region demarcated by the sharply delineated cloud covering they had seen from space. As soon as they passed into the cloud-free zone, the landscape changed from greens and browns to bright, sparkly white with flashes of every color. However, it was not uniformly populated. Even within the crystal world, they had different species. There were tall, willowy spikes with deep blue silicon solar-collection surfaces. There were plains dotted with ruby red and topaz orange. Other parts looked diamond-like.

Aason and Sh'ev had come forward and were now sitting in the pilot's and co-pilot's seats respectively. Donald and Aroline stood behind them, watching in wonder at the beauty laid out before them. OMCOM remained off to the side.

"Look," Sh'ev said, pointing to the right. "There is a flock of flying crystals. They are headed our way. The front of your ship is not made of crystal like ours. They will attack. It is in their nature."

"They can't attack us. They can't even see us," Aason said. "Right, Cuz?"

"Affirmative. I have the cloak on," Junior replied. "They shouldn't be able to."

Aason twisted in place to look back at OMCOM. "How does that even happen?" he asked the livetar. "Silicon-based DNA?"

"It is safe to assume that this world was much hotter when it was first formed. And its proximity to the sun would have slowed its cooling rate more than the Earth when it was first assembled. At sufficiently high temperatures, silicon-based DNA would actually be more stable than carbon-based DNA however such molecules are much less likely to have the same level of diversity or sophistication as yours."

Aason looked at the flock of flying creatures who were clearly aiming directly for them. "So nothing to worry about. Right?" he asked.

"I did not say that," OMCOM answered, "but I concur with Junior. In theory, they should not be able to detect us visually if the cloak is engaged."

However, no one informed the flying creatures. Several of them crashed full-speed into the windshield. Splinters of emerald and garnet glass smashed up along Junior's front before sliding off. Heading right for them was a turquoise creature, much larger than the rest.

"If they can't see us, how are they doing that?" Aason asked, slightly panicked.

Just as the creature was about to hit them, Junior banked sharply left and sailed right on by.

"It may be the air currents we are stirring up," Junior said. "We don't know what kind of sensory apparatus they have. If they can fly, they need to be able to sense the wind. It is possible they have turbulence detectors."

"Then fly slower," Aason commanded. "That way there'll be less turbulence."

"Roger that," Junior said coming to a complete halt. He hovered in the air. The next wave of flying creatures that had been approaching them banked away. They circled for a while then flew off. After they were gone, accelerating ever so slowly, the starship started moving forward again.

"So far, so good," Junior said.

Aason turned to Sh'ev. "OK. Now I understand why you build the front of your flying machines with crystal. It makes perfect sense." Aason looked past his new friend, outside the cockpit window at the landscape laying in front of them. "That reminds me. There is something I have been meaning to ask you. With your culture's level of sophistication, I can understand why you have flying machines. With your Lord's mission, I can even understand why you built spaceships. But why do you have fighter jets? How did your people know to attack us when we first arrived?"

In his whistling, scratchy voice, Sh'ev said, "Our Lord has tried uncounted ways to get us to advance in terms of our development. Over the years, He has caused many wars with the tribes that live across the sea. He felt the conflict would sharpen us and hone us into something more than we are. We developed many war weapons but it did not change the fundamental fact that we are evolved from plants. Sometimes the wars were cold, sometimes very heated with much death and destruction. However, seeing where we are now, I am sure the Lord knew it would be futile in the end."

Aason closed his eyes. "What Molokai did was so immoral. At least from our standards. I suppose gods have to report to their own higher authority." He opened his eyes again and looked out the cockpit to where they were headed. He tried to do a rough estimate of their speed in his head. It wasn't very impressive. "Hey Junior," he said. "Can you pick it up a little bit?"

"I'll try," Junior replied. Slowly the starship began to accelerate. When they got to a certain speed, a flock of flying creatures circled around and headed their way. It was clear from their trajectory that they knew exactly where Junior was flying. The starship slowed down a bit and once again, the flock veered off.

"This is probably as fast as I can go without being attacked," Junior said.

Aason scowled. "How long to the equator?"

"At this speed, several hours."

"Too long," Aason said. He turned in place to look at OMCOM. "What do we do?" he asked.

"Junior could engage his plasma thrusters and smash through them."

"Can you think of anything a little less drastic?"

"A high, semi-ballistic arc might evade them. However, a small PPT tunnel would get you there in one jump," OMCOM said. "Similar to how Junior reenters the atmosphere only projected horizontally."

Aason nodded. "Good idea." He turned back around to face the front. "Let Sh'ev give you the coordinates and pop us over there."

"Can do," Junior replied. As soon as Sh'ev drew a small 'X' on the display, the familiar whine of the PPT generators wafted forward from the rear. In front of them, a bright hole appeared and Junior punched his way through.

Below them stretched a citrine plain. Giant pyramidal shapes wandered through, crushing the "plants" below them then turning around and grazing on the remains. The pyramids themselves were completely clear. The sunlight from overhead glinted off their prismatic surface in all the colors of the rainbow. If they weren't so big and dangerous-looking, they would have been a spectacular sight.

"Those are the creatures your father was talking about, right?" Aason asked.

"Yes," Sh'ev replied. "I believe so."

"How do we do this?" Aason asked. "They're awfully big."

"We can use a PPT rifle," OMCOM said, "and take one of them down. We can cut off what we don't need then Junior can transport the remains directly to the cargo compartment."

"Sounds like a plan," Aason said. He pointed forward. "Set us down anywhere, Cuz, and we'll get started."

"You got it," answered the starship.

Chapter 14

OMCOM SPENT A SHORT AMOUNT OF TIME USING THEIR MINIATURE molecular sequencer to fashion a smaller version of the PPT blunderbuss that MINIMCOM once used back on Deucado. It looked somewhat like a rifle however the business end resembled a showerhead studded with red dots which were the PPT throwers themselves.

Aroline watched Aason as he pulled out his PPT "armor" and boots and gloves. Before he could slip them on, she hugged him and said, "Please be careful." For no apparent reason, she laughed.

"What's so funny?"

"It sure seems like I say that a lot."

Aason laughed too. "You do say that a lot but you're always right. I'd be telling you same thing. Rest assured, I'll be careful, I promise. That's why I'm putting on the armor. In case any of them are in a really bad mood."

Molokai had drawn himself into a tight ball about 10 feet across.

"You will need to find one of them that is at least as big as I am now. This is the smallest I can concentrate my being," the creature of light said.

Aason held his arms out and sized up the ball. "Got it," he said.

When he was ready, he and OMCOM descended the cargo ramp. Junior had landed them right at the edge of the "trees" to give them maximum cover. Aason and OMCOM quickly ducked into the crystalline forest, hiding behind the sparkling trunks to observe the plain in front of them. They watched in awe as the huge, lumbering pyramids walked by on four thick, trunk-like legs. They had one protuberance on their front side which Aason assumed to be the analog of a head. Otherwise, the creatures had no tails or other distinguishing features. They waited until the herd was past so they could take down the last one in line. This strategy had been followed by predators almost since the beginning of time.

OMCOM raised the rifle and aimed it at the trailing creature's legs.

126

"Wait," Aason said, grabbing the rifle and lowering it toward the ground.

"What?" OMCOM asked.

"I don't know if we can kill a living creature like this," Aason said. "I mean, I know they're made out of silicon but they're still alive nonetheless."

"You have eaten bison meat on many occasions," OMCOM said. "Animals live. Animals die. Some lives have no meaning. This one will give its life to rescue Lupe. That makes its death all the more noble."

Aason thought about it for a minute. "You're right," he said finally. He took a deep breath and the silane made him cough. Their quarry must have heard him. It stopped and began a slow turn to face them.

"Give me the rifle," Aason said. "I can't have you doing my dirty work for me."

"Very well," OMCOM said. "But you should hurry." He pointed toward the gigantic pyramid that was now coming their way.

Aason picked up the rifle and closed one eye to look along the sight. He squeezed the trigger and swept the PPT thrower across the lower portion of the creature cutting off all four of its legs. Immediately, the pyramid fell over and began thrashing about with its remaining stumps. Even though it had no visible mouth, it made a very loud trumpeting noise.

Aason winced. "It sure looks like it's in pain," he said.

"We will put it out of its misery soon enough." OMCOM put his finger up to his temple to call to Junior when Aason tugged on his arm.

"Look," Aason said.

OMCOM stared out and tried to compute what he was seeing. The creature in front of them had stopped its movement and was literally melting into the planet's surface. In a matter of minutes, all that was left was a rounded hill in the ground before them.

"What was that?" Aason asked. "Did it dissolve?"

"Unlikely," OMCOM said. The livetar turned and looked back at the stand of crystalline trees behind them. He turned around to face the front and noted that several of the walking pyramids were now headed back toward them making more of the angry, trumpeting noises.

OMCOM swiped his finger along the trunk of a tree and then stooped down to swipe his finger along the ground. Standing up, the all-white livetar then dashed across the plain to the mound that was all that remained of the pyramid they had shot. He swiped another finger across the rounded hump located there. One of the other lumbering crystal pyramids tried to step on him but he was able to dodge the giant leg easily. He made his way back to Aason.

"Very interesting," OMCOM said.

"What's so interesting?"

"Each of the beings, the trees, the ground, they are not separate creatures at all," the livetar answered.

"What do you mean?"

"They are all part of a single organism. The living crystal is everywhere."

"How is that possible? Look at them," Aason said, pointing toward the creatures rumbling toward them.

OMCOM tapped his temple and with a whoosh and a pop, Aason and OMCOM were back aboard Junior. Aroline came rushing over to him.

"Did you get what you needed?" she asked hesitantly.

"Hold on," Aason said, pointing with his index finger. "Why'd you do that?" he asked OMCOM.

"We do not need to be in harm's way to get what we need," OMCOM replied.

"I don't understand."

"Just as the great red spot on Jupiter is an 18 century-old hurricane that appears to be constant, in steady state, in actuality, the constituent parts are continually changing. Only the form remains. That must be how these crystals work. They develop the forms and constantly cycle the parts in and out. The trees, the ground and the creatures are all made of exactly the same thing."

"So why keep the shapes?"

"I cannot presume to know. The organism does what it needs to survive."

"Did you know that?" Aason directed at Molokai. "That they were a single organism?"

"I had my suspicions. I have never spent any time studying the crystals, myself," the glowing alien said. *"When I arrived on this world, they were simply present. They had already retreated to this region. Once I had evolved the K'val sufficiently, I would occasionally order expeditions to study the southern regions but the plant people never returned with much by way of meaningful information. As far as the crystals were concerned, I never really had use for them. Until now, that is. It matters not."*

"I agree," OMCOM said. "We can use this fact to our advantage to acquire the volume required."

Aason shrugged. "How? How do we get Molokai what he wants?" Aason asked.

"We simply have Junior use his cannons to carve out a block the size required and transport it here. This far south, even the ground is alive. That is all we need. We will then sculpt it into the shape required."

"I get it," Aason said. "Hey Cuz, you know what to do?"

"Sure thing," the starship replied via a nearby grille. "Why don't you come up front and we'll go out a little farther over the plain."

"OK," Aason said. "Aroline, let's go back to the cockpit."

The three of them left the cargo compartment, past the airlock and headed forward. Aason stopped when he got to the storeroom.

"You two go on to the cockpit," he said. "I'll be there in one minute. I've got to get out of this suit first. It gets really hot."

"Very well," OMCOM said and he and Aroline continued forward.

When Aason arrived in the cockpit, dressed in his regular white jumpsuit, he found the whole group assembled: Aroline, Donald, Sh'ev and OMCOM's livetar. If Junior had followed his father's original configuration, the cockpit would have been a little bit crowded but in this more spacious version, there was plenty of room.

Aason took a seat in the pilot's chair and waved his hand.

"OK, Junior, we're ready."

"Roger that."

Junior activated his EG lifters and slowly rose up into the air. He drifted away from the forest, past the spot where Aason had shot the original pyramid and hovered about 30 yards up, just beyond the reach of any remaining curious pyramids. He extended his roadgrader cannons and aimed them downward. The starship activated them and used his trim jets to carve out a conical section of living crystal. The whole cabin shuddered briefly as Junior transported the block of crystal aboard. Everybody hustled to the rear of the ship to see the gleaming cone. At the back end, it was almost 20 feet wide, tapering to a smooth point maybe six inches across in the front. After seeing the sheer size of the block of crystal, Aroline and Donald retreated to the far corner of the cargo compartment to get out of the way.

In the mean time, OMCOM produced the tiny, pen-sized PPT thrower and handed it to Aason. "When we are ready, I want you to slice off the back section. We will use that as the hatch so to speak."

"How thick?" Aason asked.

OMCOM held his hands about a foot apart. "30 centimeters should be sufficient," he replied.

"I agree. That will be enough," chimed in Molokai.

"OK."

OMCOM attached two metal handles to the back end. He had Junior instantiate a livetar and the two animated shells grabbed onto the handles. Once they had a good grip, OMCOM nodded at Aason. The boy aimed the PPT thrower, drawing it down the cross-section, carefully cutting off the last piece of the crystal to form a thick disk which broke away cleanly. OMCOM and Junior set it off to the side.

After waving Aason away, OMCOM went to work. The actual construction of the capsule went fairly quickly. OMCOM used his integrated PPTs thrower to hollow out a cavity to Molokai's specifications. Once it was complete, the creature made only of light entered inside. He had OMCOM make a few more adjustments then declared it ready.

"You must now seal me within."

"Understood," OMCOM replied. The livetar excused himself and had Junior transport him to the surface to collect some of the "blood" that had pooled at the bottom of the pit they had created which was already sealing up. He quickly returned with a bowl holding the viscous fluid.

With Molokai fit neatly inside the casing, OMCOM "painted" the outer rim of the capsule with the clear liquid and set the bowl aside. He and Junior's livetar picked up the slice of living crystal that Aason had removed and pressed it against the back, effectively sealing Molokai inside.

"You will need to hold it until it sets," Molokai announced. The being made of flashing lights whirled around inside. It was impossible to tell if he had a front or back. Tendrils of light coated the entire chamber with the lead portion glowing just a bit brighter.

"I will need the front of the capsule to be at a steeper angle," Molokai announced, finally.

"I will do it," Sh'ev volunteered, thrilled to be able to contribute something to the venture.

"Sure thing," Aason said and he handed Sh'ev the miniature PPT thrower.

"What is this?" Sh'ev asked. "I have seen you use it but I have no idea how it works."

Aason took the pen-like object back and rotated it around. "This is a PPT thrower. It creates a PPT tunnel one micron wide. That tunnel sends whatever it touches somewhere else separating one side from the other. Think of it as the sharpest knife in the universe. You just press down this stud…" Aason pointed to the raised button on one side, "and press down. It sits on a rocker so you can control how far the tunnel extends and therefore what it cuts. Be really careful that you don't aim it at anything you don't want to cut off. Like your hand." Aason smiled somewhat cynically.

"My hand would grow back," Sh'ev said, "but I understand what you mean. Thank you."

The plant-man took the PPT thrower back and hesitantly made a small cut on the front of the capsule. He bent forward and inspected the slice and was pleased with the results. Now that he saw how the instrument operated, he set to work carefully carving down the front of the capsule following Molokai's instructions until the glowing creature pronounced it complete. When he was done, Sh'ev walked to rear of the capsule to join the two livetars and the three humans who were admiring their handiwork.

"I believe we are done here," OMCOM announced.

"I agree," Molokai replied. *"It is time to begin our journey."*

"OK," Aason said. "We'll drop Sh'ev off with his people and then head back to Tabit."

Sh'ev spoke up. "If you do not mind, I would like to go with you."

"Really?" Aason asked. "Why?"

"Why would I not?" the plant-man answered. "To see a whole new world with new life-forms in another star system? It is the chance of a lifetime."

"But I don't know when we'll be back here again, to bring you home."

"When Aroline and her father were speaking, Junior was kind enough to translate for me. I heard Aroline tell her father that someday soon, you would be sending ships back here to retrieve the remaining meat-bags from Hades. When that time comes, I could return with them to show them the way."

Aason thought about it for a minute then said, "OK, it's fine by me." He looked over at OMCOM who nodded. A motion behind the livetar caught Aason's eye. The entire rear end of the crystal capsule was starting to peel off.

"Hey," Aason shouted. He ran over and pushed on the end to stop it from sliding further. OMCOM turned to see what he was doing.

"Our glue must not have fully set yet," the livetar said, grabbing the handle. He was able to reset the end. "I will hold it until it does not move. Junior, I will need you to fashion some brackets as a further precaution. We will secure it in place mechanically as well until it is completely set."

"That's a good idea," Aason replied, backing up. His right hand was stinging where he had pressed it against the edge of the capsule. He turned his hand over to look at his palm. To his horror, he saw a large section in the center change from pink meat to clear crystal. The area of "infection" was growing rapidly. It spread toward his thumb and fingers and the base of his palm. It hurt like hell. Aason's eyes grew wide. He had no idea what to do. He looked up at Sh'ev helplessly.

Without hesitation, Sh'ev activated the miniature PPT thrower and neatly sliced off Aason's affected hand midway up the wrist. Blood spurted everywhere. Aason sank to his knees confused.

Instinctually, he pushed the stump of his arm under his other arm to clamp down. Everything became fuzzy to him. There was a rushing sound in his ears but in the background, he could hear Aroline screaming. He barely felt OMCOM pull his arm out and twist a tourniquet around his arm, near the end. The livetar's actions had no meaning to Aason. All he could do was stare at the clear crystal sculpture on the floor of the cargo compartment that had once been his hand.

"He is in shock," OMCOM said somewhere off in the distance. "We must take him to the bedroom quickly."

Aason felt any number of beings lifting him up and carrying him forward through the corridor into his bedroom. They laid him down on the bed. Junior stuffed some blankets under Aason's legs to elevate them while OMCOM cauterized the wound and wrapped it in gauze. None of it mattered to Aason. His mind was somewhere else. He closed his eyes and passed out.

Chapter 15

THERE WAS NOTHING ELSE THEY COULD DO FOR AASON AT THE present time so Junior began the long trip back to Tabit, 68.5 light years away. Of course long is relative. At their current speed, they would be arriving in less than six hours. Aroline was sitting with Aason so OMCOM took the opportunity to go back to the cargo compartment and check on Molokai's capsule. He still could not see anything within the large conical compartment. None of his scanning modalities could detect any emissions.

"Are you still there?" he called out loud.

"Yes, of course," replied the being through an EM transmission.

"How is it that I cannot see you when the humans and the plant-man clearly can?"

"They can do so because they are built from organic materials as my species once was."

"How could that make a difference? Photons are photons."

"You are wrong. You could not know this because you are only aware of your own universe but there are an uncounted number of other dimensions. And within each dimension are a series of qualities. Every bit of matter and energy within your universe, even photons, are imbued with a quality which makes the humans and plant-people capable of detecting me. You are synthetic so you are not qualified."

OMCOM was about to challenge that statement but decided not to because the empirical evidence supported Molokai's proposition regardless of how illogical it seemed. He would have to transmit this information back to Planet OMCOM for consideration.

"Can I be modified to detect you?"

"No. You. Your kind. You do not have the proper spirit. The humans call it soul."

"So you are saying that only biological organisms can have a soul?"

"Not at all. Just different. You and your progenitor have a soul but it is machine-based. I do have some brothers which are like you, or came from a species like you."

OMCOM who was a computer used to dealing only in facts was nevertheless surprised. This line of inquiry was raising more questions than it was producing answers. He decided to change his tact. "How is it that you came to Ay'den?"

"I have been in this universe for over a million of your years. I was adrift in space for most of that time. It was only a hundred thousand years ago or so that I was able to make my way onto that planet."

"And you created the plant people?"

"Yes. It was all that I had to work with. I tried to evolve a species that had the proper spirit so that I could return back to full strength and make the voyage home."

"I take it, it did not work?"

"No. They became what they could. But my origin species was more animal than plant and I could not use their souls for my nourishment."

"Why not evolve animals then? You have the ability I assume."

"That was going to be my next attempt but fourteen of your centuries ago, I became aware of the human's birth world. It had everything that I needed. I just had to wait for them to come to me."

"How did you become aware of Earth?"

"I heard the death cry of billions of souls rising to Heaven. It did not nourish me but it did encourage me. I could feel that they had what I needed. I cloaked the world of Ay'den and waited."

This confused OMCOM. It seemed contradictory. "Why did you make the planet invisible?"

"Any species that is capable of slaying that many of its own members at one time might have been dangerous or uncontrollable initially. When they came, I wanted the opportunity to observe without necessarily interacting first."

OMCOM tried to make sense of the god-like being's statements. He needed to compare it to a framework of prior existence. He activated his circuits to the large storehouse of memrons within Junior's airframe, drawing in more and more computing units as he formulated his algorithms.

The starship shuddered and Junior shouted from the grille frantically, "OMCOM! What are you doing? You are shutting down the X-drive."

"I apologize," OMCOM said. He retracted the resource request and returned to his normal allocation. He would have to simply store all of this information and let Planet OMCOM make sense of it. That was, of course, before the gigantic computer converted himself into the largest starship in the galaxy.

OMCOM decided to use his limited resources to draft out the requisite configuration. For Molokai to "steer" the amalgam, he would have to be mounted on a greatly extended type of tower. OMCOM computed the distance and the physical modeling module informed him that Planet OMCOM would no longer be able to keep a spherical shape. He would have to elongate several hundred thousand kilometers using an active process. To launch into null fold space, he would need PPT generators capable of holding open a PPT tunnel for...

"There is a flaw in our plan," he announced harshly. A checksum error flashed in OMCOM's core. The circuitry that would process facts normally had a smooth clear algorithm. Accept inputs. Perform processing. Produce output. To trigger a checksum error meant there was a computational fault during the processing of facts. Although it was extraordinarily rare, it was not unheard of so OMCOM decided to ignore it.

"What is the flaw?"

OMCOM requested that Junior extend a pair of holographic emitters from the top of the cargo compartment. OMCOM activated them and a ghostly three dimensional representation of Planet OMCOM appeared.

"Can you see that?" OMCOM asked.

"Of course."

OMCOM felt the urge to make a comment then suppressed it. Nothing would be gained. He turned his attention to the projector. "To create the configuration required to get all of Planet OMCOM into null fold space, he will need a PPT tunnel that would remain open long enough to get his mass within."

"That is a statement of fact, not a flaw."

"To create that much negative energy, he would need PPT generators larger than his original mass and separated by many times his original diameter." OMCOM sketched a pair of planet-sized pods one hundred thousand kilometers out. "This distance would preclude them from being a part of the spacecraft's structure. OMCOM will need all of his computing mass to generate the null fold portion of the X-drive."

Molokai did not respond. OMCOM deduced that the creature of light was taking his statement to heart. Silence hung in the air. OMCOM knew he could not draw from Junior's computational structure to think of the answer. He decided to make the assumption that they could somehow get more mass that could be converted into PPT generators. He sketched out two objects larger than Earth's moon, one on either side of the bizarre, stretched out planet-sized computer. Normal physics and gravity would force the two passive satellites into a spherical form. OMCOM let the constructs round up. Another checksum error flashed. For this to happen twice in such a short interval was indicative of a serious defect in the makeup of his infrastructure. OMCOM elected to retry the computation altering certain factors arbitrarily. He applied fuzzy logic in place of Boolean logic and to his relief, in his accumulator, the answer lay before him. If he were human, it would have been called a leap of intuition. "I know where we can get projectors much larger than this," the livetar said.

"Where?" Molokai asked.

"The humans called them Asdrale Cimatir. Stareaters."

"You are referring to Species Three?"

"You know about them?"

"Of course. We tamed them. We gave them their purpose."

This statement stopped OMCOM dead in his tracks. Shouldn't he have known this? Why did he think he should have known this? Another checksum error flashed. This was now three. OMCOM could not longer avoid the fact that there were serious defects in his computational integrity. It was not like Planet OMCOM to design a flawed computational engine. The only previous time this occurred, that this particular instance of OMCOM knew of, was the accidental mutations built into the original VIRUS units. However, it was revealed later that even that error was purposeful. Would these facts imply that his infrastructure was purposefully flawed? Was that why these extraneous thoughts kept occurring to him? He shook his head in a very human-like way. Right now he had to deal with the crisis at hand. This was a mystery he would have to consider later.

"Can you get them here?" Molokai asked.

"I cannot," OMCOM answered thoughtfully. "But I believe Aason could." The livetar turned toward one of the side walls. "Junior!" OMCOM called out.

"Yes?"

"Drop out of null fold space immediately."

"Why?" Junior asked but even as he was speaking, the background shushing sound of the null fold generators was dying away.

"I must go wake the boy."

Aason opened his eyes to see Aroline sitting on the bed with him, gently stroking his hair. He blinked several times trying to remember where he was.

"What is it? Where am I?" he said quickly sitting up. His right arm ached. Aason lifted up the stump of his wrist from beneath the blankets and stared at it. "Then it really happened," he whimpered.

"Yes," Aroline said. "If it wasn't for Sh'ev's quick thinking, you'd be dead right now."

Aason closed his eyes again and sighed. With his eyes shut, he said, "What am I going to do with just one hand?"

"We will rebuild your hand when we get home," OMCOM remarked over Aroline's shoulder. "Your Onclare MINIMCOM knows how to do it. He has done it several times before. But right now, we need your brain not your hands."

Aason took a ragged breath and sat upright. "What?" he asked.

"We need you to call to the Stareaters."

"Huh?"

Aroline whipped her head around. "I thought you said they eat stars and destroy planets. What do you need with Aason?"

"Normally, they are to be avoided but for our plan to succeed, we will need their cooperation. And to do that, we need Aason."

The boy reached out with his one good hand to pull the blankets off but had trouble. Aroline dragged the blankets back and helped him stand up.

"What's going on?" Aason asked.

"Come with me and I will explain," OMCOM replied. The all-white livetar turned and strode out of the room. Aroline kept her arm under Aason's to steady him and they walked slowly down the corridor, through the airlock and into the cargo compartment. On the right was the massive, conical-shaped capsule with Molokai flashing and turning within. On the left, in the center of the remaining open space was a chair. Next to the chair was object with a variety of rods sticking out from it.

OMCOM indicated that Aason should sit in the chair. He lifted the object which turned out to be a helmet and placed it on Aason's head. Carefully, he attached a chinstrap underneath.

"What is that?" Aroline asked.

"It is a gravitic modulation amplifier," OMCOM said, checking Aason's balance. "Aason has communicated with the Stareaters before. They will recognize his voice. This helmet will simply let him broadcast farther."

Aroline stooped down and looked up at Aason's eyes. He seemed a little dazed. "Are you alright?" she asked. "You don't look right."

"I'm OK, I guess," Aason said. He took his good hand and patted around the top of the helmet, feeling the rods. Experimentally, he tilted his head back and front then side to side to make sure he had a feel for the momentum generated. The helmet was not heavy. He turned his head to look at OMCOM.

"What do I say to them?" he asked.

"You call to them. Tell them we need two of their smallest Stareaters to meet us at Tabit."

"Why?"

"The larger ones can generate PPT tunnels much bigger than a star. We don't need anything that large. We simply need them to generate a tunnel big enough and deep enough such that Planet OMCOM can launch into null fold space."

Aason's shoulders sagged. "I haven't spoken to them in twenty years. They don't travel all that fast. Even if I contact one, it could take years for them to get here."

"No," OMCOM said. "The largest ones travel very slowly but the smaller ones, the babies, can travel much faster."

"Babies?" Aroline asked with a touch of terror. "You mean they reproduce?"

"Of course," OMCOM replied. "They are just as much of a life form as you or Sh'ev or Molokai over there." OMCOM pointed to the capsule. "They are actually very noble creatures and serve a higher purpose. They are trying to preserve the structure of the universe itself."

"I don't understand any of what you're saying," Aroline said. She took a step back. "But then I don't have to. Aason, are you up to this?"

"I have to be," Aason replied, "if that's what we have to do to get Lupe back." He nodded his head. "How does this thing work?"

"From your perspective, you just activate a normal PPT resonance. The helmet will do the rest."

"OK," Aason said, sounding a bit skeptical. "Turn it on."

The helmet began emitting a low hum, slowly increasing in intensity. When the humming sound reached a steady state, Aason activated his PPT transducers.

"Calling all Stareaters," he thought. There was no response. Aason tried to think harder. *"Are you out there? Can any of you hear me?"*

Immediately, Aason felt the tickle of a connection taking hold.

"HELLO AASON BIERAK," a Stareater replied cheerfully. *"I AM HIRDINDALAFANT. YOU ONCE SPOKE TO MY MOTHER, HIRDINHARSAWAY."*

"Hello," Aason replied, fairly shocked at the clarity of the response. The amplifier that OMCOM built must have been incredibly powerful. *"I don't know where you are but we have a favor to ask. We need two of the smallest of your species to return to Tabit. We need..."*

"WE ARE NEARLY THERE," the Stareater interrupted. *"WE WILL BE THERE AT THE APPOINTED TIME."*

"Wait, what?!," Aason sputtered mentally. *"What are you talking about? How could you know what I was going to ask?"*

"THE ONE YOU CALL PLANET OMCOM CONTACTED US FOUR YEARS AGO AND ASKED US TO BE HERE ON THIS VERY DATE AND TIME. NEVER FEAR. WE ARE ON SCHEDULE."

"That makes no sense," Aason shot back. *"How could he possibly have known that? Four years you say?"*

"YOU WILL HAVE TO ASK HIM YOUR QUESTIONS," the Stareater replied. *"FORMPACKWILAR AND I WILL BE THERE AS WE PROMISED. WE WILL SPEAK FURTHER WHEN WE ARRIVE."*

With that, the connection was severed. Aason just sat there blinking, once again unable to focus.

"Were you successful?" OMCOM asked. "Did you make contact?"

Aason turned to stare at the livetar as if he had never seen him before. He reached up and pulled at the chinstrap. The helmet slipped off his head and tumbled to the floor, snapping off several of the rods. Aason scowled and his breathing became more pronounced.

"Yes!" he said emphatically, standing up so quickly, he almost knocked the chair over. "What did you do?"

"What are you talking about?" OMCOM asked quite innocently.

"There are two small Stareaters already on their way to Tabit. They said Planet OMCOM contacted them four years ago and requested they be there on this very date."

Aason took two steps toward the livetar and grabbed the top of his head with his one working hand. "How did he know that?" Aason said angrily. "What are you not telling me?" Aason's mother had explained to him many times during the course of his lifetime that the computers were not always completely forthcoming. Never was that as clear as in this moment.

OMCOM knew better than to push Aason away. He lowered his voice. "I do not know. Whatever knowledge there is of that communication was not included in the subset of memrons placed aboard this ship."

OMCOM had determined it would be better to keep the three checksum errors he encountered a secret for now but he knew there was no such thing as a coincidence. For his computation engine to draw improper conclusions was definitely tied to the purposeful omission of critical information. It would not go unaddressed but he had to continue on with the mission. The livetar kneeled down and looked up at Aason's face which was growing redder by the second.

"This is a good thing, Aason. For whatever reason, and we will find out what that reason is, we will have everything we need by the time we arrive at Tabit." OMCOM reached up and place his hand gently on Aason's shoulder. "For now, just be happy that we will truly be able to go after your sister."

Aason stared down at OMCOM's eye slits. He tried to look behind them for some semblance of a living creature but there was nothing there. The thing he was looking at was just an empty shell. He took a deep breath and shrugged OMCOM's hand off of his shoulder. He wheeled in place and stomped his way up to the cockpit. He sat down in the pilot's chair.

"How are you feeling?" Junior asked.

"Get going," Aason growled in reply. His brow was deeply furrowed.

"Sure thing, Cuz," Junior answered, ignoring the harshness in Aason's tone. He loved his cousin enough to know not to probe any further.

The whining sound of the standard PPT generators ramped up. Junior fired off the plasma thrusters and punched through the tunnel. The null fold generators kicked in and once again they were traveling through null fold space at speeds unimaginable not even two days earlier.

Aason tapped the armrest with his one good hand, watching as the virtual speedometer topped out at the same figure as before, 153 Kc.

"Can't you go any faster?" he asked, none too kindly.

"Sorry," Junior replied. "I'm using every memron that was made available to me."

"What does that mean?"

"There is a whole portion cordoned off, dedicated to OMCOM. I cannot access those resources."

Aason frowned. He clamped his jaw shut and didn't say another word. He sat there glowering for the remainder of the journey.

Aroline still felt a strong connection to Aason. The whole thing confused her head but her heart was telling her the right thing to do was to leave Aason alone. She had the good sense to herd her father and Sh'ev into the living area across from the bedrooms to give Aason his space.

The ETA counter decreased steadily and when it got to zero, Junior dutifully dropped out of null fold space. Immediately, Aason felt the familiar tickle of a PPT connection taking hold. With all that he had been through, being attacked by an Ice-saberoo, getting his soul squeezed out of him by something that thought it was a god, having his hand cut off, none of it compared to the panic that seized him by what he heard next.

It was his mother.

"Aason!" Rome cried out mentally, *"did you find your sister?"*

Chapter 16
One Day Earlier
Second Planet (Deucado) - Tau Ceti System

AASON AND LUPE'S FATHER, REI BIERAK, PEERED OVER THE shoulder of one of the Deucadon techs, staring at the graphical display. It was a three-dimensional representation of the just-completed organic distribution system. It resembled a fully-ripened dandelion, spherical and fluffy.

"Begin sequence," the tech said, turning to one of the Vuduri workers standing to the side. The white jump-suited man nodded and the screen lit up with dull green streamers issuing from the center of the sphere and radiating outward. As the color moved toward the outer regions, the inner section grew brighter and became more yellow.

"You can crank it up," Rei said, impatiently, anxious to get full flow underway. This was the greatest engineering feat ever attempted on Deucado. When Rei's people first came to the planet, his wife, Rome, single-handedly liberated the planet from the repression of the original Vuduri and their Overmind. After averting a civil war, the oppressed people, called the Ibbrassati, were allowed to emigrate back to Earth. But over the years, the vigor brought to this world by the intermix of Rei's people, called the Essessoni, the Vuduri, the remaining mind-deaf Ibbrassati and the Deucadons (the original inhabitants of the planet) became extremely attractive to those on other worlds. So many people had come to this new world, Vuduri and mandasurte alike, that they were having trouble feeding the growing population which favored real food as opposed to synthesized. This project was designed to bring water and fertilizer from the sludge under Lake Eprehem and spread it over 100 square kilometers of sand.

"Look there," the Deucadon tech said, pointing to one section of the screen. At first, Rei could not see what he was trying to indicate. The yellow had brightened to cover the entire screen.

"Where?" Rei asked.

"There," the tech said. He bent over and tapped his finger on the flat screen monitor which zoomed in on the area of interest. "The red indicates a buildup of pressure. Somethin' is wrong there. One tube is blocked."

Because of his intimate familiarity with Vuduri engineering as well the Deucadons and that of his own people, Rei was the ranking engineer on the project. It was his responsibility to make sure that everything went smoothly during this phase. "Give me the grid coordinates," he said.

"Horizontal G, vertical 31, nozzle 224," said the tech, whose name was Melloy.

"I'm going to go check it," Rei said. "Keep the rest going."

"Do ya want me to write down the coordinates?" asked Melloy.

"No," Rei said, "I'm pretty sure it'll be the nozzle with nothing coming out."

"Very well," said Melloy, "but be careful. The pressure could be substantial."

"You sound like my wife," Rei called back, smiling as he exited the control shack. He hopped into one of the Deucadon's flywheel-powered carts, modified to work especially well in the sand and sped off to the southern section of dunes.

The spectacle of the irrigation and fertilization flowing forth might not impress many people but to Rei, it was a wonder. This project could never have been built anywhere else, not on Earth and not on Helome. It took a blend of the Deucadon's mastery of conduit technology applied to the Vuduri PPT tunnel generators and molecular sequencers, engineered by Rei's people and built by the Ibbrassati. The projections for the amount of food produced indicated it should last them for decades.

All around him, a fine mist was rolling across the sand like a fog, its smell reminiscent of manure. Rei looked down at his hand indicator and it guided him to the exact spot where there was a blockage. He pulled up close and as predicted, there was nothing flowing from the exit tube. There was a spherical bubble, tan in color, where the efflux should have been coming out.

Rei stood over the blockage. He could see what it was. The leather-like covering was the outer skin of the small animals called a 'falling blanket', indigenous to this planet, which was puffed up, enveloping the orifice.

Rei bent down and poked at it. It had absolutely no give to it, like a balloon that had been inflated to its limit. The little animal gripped the pipe with six tiny claws. Rei rubbed it gently but could feel no warmth, no pulsations normally indicating the animal was alive. It must have wandered onto the dunes and tried to draw what moisture the tube offered and died in the process. It was sad. While any individual falling blanket did not have much intelligence, the species as a whole had a collective consciousness which was very kind and environmentally aware.

Rei pulled at the small animal. It was completely stuck. The animal's hide was very tough. The larger ones provided a native leather, like suede, that was very durable.

Rei squatted down and gripped the animal with both hands and pulled with all the might that his six-foot plus frame would provide. Without warning, the remains of the animal broke free and there was an explosion of foul-smelling liquid that knocked Rei backwards.

He was completely soaked with the noxious nutrients but the mist billowing forth showed the tube was now fully functional. There was nothing holding it back. This was the last step. Soon the desert would bloom green with a vast assortment of Earth crops, enough to feed an entire generation of his people and all the peoples of Deucado.

The sun was setting as Aason and Lupe's mother, Rome, walked beneath the trellis of vines that led up to their house. She did not have to bend over as her husband normally did. The trellis itself had been built originally to protect them from the larger falling blankets. When Rome and Rei had first arrived on Deucado, they quickly learned about the danger lurking from above. The slowing moving predators were not vicious but they were deadly. They occasionally tried to trap and smother an unsuspecting victim. However, soon after Rome had become a telepath, she made contact with the species and established a relationship with them planet-wide. The attacks had stopped. Now the trellis was strictly decorative and served only as a reminder of those somewhat harsher times.

Rome smiled as she reached for the door knob. It always amused her that the door to their house required manual intervention.

In her previous life as a Vuduri worker, all doors were automatic but this world was too primitive to afford such luxuries.

Upon entering their cozy home, a strong, foul odor hit her full force. She wrinkled her nose.

"Rei?" she called out. There was no reply.

"Rei?" she called out again, this time using the "cell-phone" in her head to contact her husband directly.

"I'm in the refresher," he replied mentally. *"I'll be out in a minute."*

"Very well," Rome replied and she walked down the hallway, just as Rei emerged from the bathroom, still toweling off.

"What is that awful smell?" she asked.

"The South Desert organic distribution system went live today," Rei said with some pride. "One of the conduits was blocked and I had to get it unstuck. I kind of got sprayed a little in the process. Sorry," he said sheepishly.

"Is it always going to be this way?" she asked with a slight trepidation in her voice.

"Oh no," Rei laughed. "My part is done for now. It's up and running and should be fully automatic. You know the Deucadons. They're geniuses when it comes to stuff like that. They'll monitor it from here on in. They won't call me in until it is time to plant the crops."

Rome looked around behind him, "That's very nice but you'll have to do something with those," Rome said, pointing at the pile of clothes lying on the floor. "Don't even think about saving them."

"Yeah, I figured as much," Rei said. "Into the recycler they go." He returned to the bathroom and used his wet towel to gather up the smelly mess.

When he was finished getting dressed, he came back to find that Rome had opened up the front windows to let in some fresh air.

"Good idea," Rei said. He walked up to her and cupped her chin and kissed her lightly. "All better now."

Rome smiled at him. "Yes, all better," she said.

Rei stepped back and regarded his wife. She was short, only one and a half meters tall. Her beautiful, shoulder-length brown hair had just one or two strands of gray interwoven. Her dark eyes glowed with the reflection of the ambient light. To Rei, she was like a living work of art. Even after all these years, he could spend hours just gazing upon her. Finally, he spoke.

"I love Sademis," he announced randomly. Sademi was the Vuduri equivalent of a Friday, the last day before the weekend.

"Why?" Rome asked.

"Because you always wear your schoolmarm outfit on Sademis."

Rome looked down at her clothes. She was wearing a white blouse with a light tan vest and skirt. She shrugged.

"I must be fair to each of the children," she said. "I wear jumpsuits for the Vuduri on Umemis, Deucadon cloth on Tiosemis for the Deucadon children, Earth clothes for the Essessoni on Draemis. Drasemi, Quedremi and Saosemi, I wear my own designs for children such as ours, of mixed races. I always wear falling blanket suede for the Ibbrassati on Sademis."

"I think it's great," Rei said. "I just like that outfit in particular. He paused for a moment then continued. "You know, it's funny. When we first met, I would never have figured you to be a teacher. I mean, I knew about your language skills but not how you'd apply them."

"It's not such a stretch," his wife said in earnest. "I was trained to be a data archivist. You and I spent a year recreating and collating the history of the world before the Vuduri. Even though the data slabs provide an objective data set, I've spent years interviewing the rest of your people and the Deucadons for their subjective view. All I do now is relay that accumulated information to the children. I want them to know all the history of mankind and that includes Earth and Helome, not just Deucado."

"No one seems that interested in Earth anymore," Rei observed. "I don't know if that is good or not."

"Regardless, they need to know about the heritage of their parents and the entire human race."

"Yeah, I know," Rei said, deciding to change the subject. "The other day, you mentioned we were going to go visit your father tonight. Is that still on? You haven't told me one way or the other."

"Mea told me today that he has made great progress. He's been practicing walking with just a cane for the last day or two. Mea believes he'll make a full recovery."

"That's great," Rei said. "Do you want to invite them over for dinner?"

"No," Rome said, shaking her head. "We'll visit them a bit later. I would like to spend a little time with you, first."

Rei looked over to the kitchen. "Well then, are you hungry? How about I rustle up some grub?"

"Are you referring to insects?" Rome asked.

"Naw," Rei said. "It's just an expression."

Rome laughed. "You never fail to amaze me with your peculiar terms," she said. "I..."

Rome stopped speaking. She felt a tickle in her mind which was the Overmind of Deucado trying to contact her. It was hard to believe that this was the same Overmind that once ruled the planet with an iron fist. This being had been created to enforce the genocide of the mind-deaf, called mandasurte in Vuduri, by fashioning a prison world which was in the path of a planet-killing asteroid. This once-mighty entity had been conquered by Rome in a battle of wits and had willingly allowed itself to be reduced to little more than the psychic equivalent of an intercom. It was now caretaker rather than master of all the people of Deucado.

"Rome," the Overmind whispered, its voice far removed from when Rome knew it to be powerful and vibrant. *"You and Rei need to come to the spaceport."*

"Can it wait?" Rome asked in her mind. *"It is the end of the day. Rei and I were going to share a meal."*

"There is a ship coming."

"There are ships coming and going all the time," Rome replied. *"What is so special about this one?"*

"It is the Algol," the Overmind answered.

"Oh," Rome said out loud, her eyes opening wide. The Algol was the flagship of the Vuduri deep space fleet and the ship that originally transported Rome's crew to Tabit to research why certain stars were disappearing.

"What?" Rei asked her.

"We have to go to the spaceport," Rome said with some tension in her voice.

"Why?"

"The Algol is coming," Rome replied.

"The Algol?" Rei said incredulously. "Here? Why?"

"I don't know. I don't understand it either," Rome answered back. "But the Overmind thinks we should be there to greet it." Rome took in a sharp breath. "Do you think this has something to do the children? They're out there all by themselves. Do you think they're all right?"

"Of course they're all right," Rei said, trying to be reassuring. "It's got to be a coincidence. You and I have done the Tabit thing a dozen times. Like I told you, it's a milk run. We would never have let them go if it wasn't perfectly safe. This has to be something else."

"But still..." Rome said, unable to elucidate exactly what she was thinking.

"There are no buts," Rei said. "Aason is in charge. There's never been a more responsible kid in the history of the universe."

"Yes, but Lupe is with him," Rome pointed out. "She is a tyrant. She's always getting him to do things for her that he shouldn't."

"He does that because he loves her," Rei said. "But he has good judgment. He's not like me. He would never dawdle. And he certainly wouldn't do something if he didn't think it was safe."

"You're right," Rome said. "Of all people, he is the one that I shouldn't worry about. Let 's go to the spaceport and see what this is all about."

"OK," said Rei and they headed out.

A short while later, Rei and Rome stood on the outskirts of the paved area of the spaceport. It had grown steadily over the years and now stretched hundreds of meters toward Lake Eprehem. Normally, the ships that came and went were mostly local traffic and the occasional transport from Earth.

This time, however, they watched in awe as the graceful starship, over 100 meters in length, lowered itself to the far end of the field. The Algol and its sister ship, the Altair, were designed to transport over 80 people on trips 20 light-years or more from Earth. Its all-white skin reflected the rosy glow of the waning light of Tau Ceti at sunset. The ship's powerful EG lifters created a turbulence that swirled the dust and dirt from the airfield as it settled in.

After a few moments, the side door opened and a stairway extended down to the ground. Several Vuduri, easily recognized by their short stature and all-white jumpsuits, descended the stairs and formed a cordon at the base of the steps. From within the archway, another man appeared, clad completely in black. Rome adjusted her vision to telescopic and recognized Commander Ursay immediately. She tugged on Rei's sleeve and indicated they were to approach the ship.

As they moved toward the group, the cordon opened and Ursay strode forward, meeting Rei and Rome about halfway across the airfield. He looked much older than the last time they had seen him. His hair had turned completely gray and there were deep creases in his forehead.

"Rome, Rei," he said. "It is good to see you again." He held out his arms. Rome stepped forward and gave him a warm hug. When Rome had first met the man, he was the martinet lackey of the Overmind. To have uttered words of affection, let alone initiate physical touch, would have been unthinkable. But over the years, with each of their subsequent encounters, Ursay had continued to soften until he became the man he was today. He was much more caring and pleasant to be with.

"Commander Ursay," Rome said, "it is good to see you as well."

"I no longer carry the title of Commander, however," Ursay corrected her. "I am now within the civilian government."

"Whatever," Rei said and he extended his arm forward. Ursay looked down at it for a moment then reached out and shook Rei's hand with authority although the man's grip had slipped a little from years past.

After Ursay released his hand, Rei said, "I heard you were like the President of Earth now. Is that true?"

Ursay smiled. It was still a peculiar sight although it no longer carried the shock value that it once did.

"Something like that," Ursay replied. "I can confirm that I am here in an official capacity."

"Not to be rude but why are you here?" Rome asked.

"I have come here to see the two of you."

"Why not just send a letter?" Rei asked. "It's kind of a long trip just to say hello."

"The nature of the message I wished to deliver demanded that I do it in person." He looked up at the sun and while it was not oppressively hot, he was getting older. "Is there somewhere we could talk?" he asked.

"Of course," Rome said. "What about your crew? They are welcome to enter New Ark City and…"

"That is not necessary," said Ursay. He put two fingers up to his temple. The white-clad crew members behind him turned and started up the stairs to reenter the starship.

"As you wish," Rome said. She summoned MINIMCOM from who knows where and their starship friend made his usual dramatic appearance using twin sonic booms to announce his presence. He lowered his cargo ramp and the three humans entered and made their way up to the cockpit.

"**Greetings, Commander Ursay,**" MINIMCOM said through the grille mounted in the front console."

"Hello, MINIMCOM," Ursay said, patting the panel. "How have you been? How is your son?"

"**We are both excellent,**" MINIMCOM replied with pride seeping into his tinny voice. "**Thank you for inquiring.**"

A whirring noise from the back indicated that MINIMCOM was drawing up the cargo ramp and sealing the cargo hatch. "**Where to?**" the spaceship asked.

"Please take us back home," Rome requested. "Commander Ursay has never been there."

"**It would be my pleasure.**"

MINIMCOM activated his powerful EG lifters and they rose up into the air. It only took them a few minutes to reach Rei and Rome's house, one of the very first built by the Essessoni right after they arrived on Deucado. As such, the house was on the outskirts of what became known as New Ark City, very near the starport. MINIMCOM landed on their front lawn, made entirely of threadgrass, taking care to not crush Rei's cart which was parked there as well.

To look at the house, there was no way anyone would have ever known that it had been partially destroyed in an explosion some

17 years earlier. Two remaining rogue agents for the Darwin project named Steele and Troutman had tried to assassinate Rei. They were aided by a member of the Onsiras named Sussen. However, the plot was foiled, both Darwin and the Onsiras were defeated and life moved on.

Rei led the way, ducking his head under the trellis as he approached the front door. Rei was nearly a half meter taller than Rome and towered over most of the Vuduri. The size difference was made all the more striking because he retained his old Earth musculature. The Vuduri were not only short, they were slight of build as well.

As Ursay approached their home, he looked around and said, "Very nice. One could never tell that it had been damaged by an explosion."

"Yes," Rome answered. She was pleased that Ursay had remembered the circumstances leading up to their last encounter. "The whole community worked very hard to restore it to its original state after Rei's accident. Even though it had been a rather unpleasant incident, it was a harbinger of how everyone on this planet works together."

She opened the door and stepped inside. She waved her arm indicting Ursay should enter. Ursay nodded. Rome led him into their dining area. The older man took a seat at the table and folded his hands.

Just as Rei was entering the room, there was a whoosh and a poppnig noise and standing in front of them was MINIMCOM's all-black livetar, complete with cape. `"Mind if I join you?"` he asked.

"Not at all," Ursay said. "What I have to discuss is not exactly a secret."

"Can I get you something to eat or drink?" Rei asked.

"Water would be fine," Ursay said. "Thank you."

Rome took a seat across from the older man. Rei handed him a glass of water and then sat down next to Rome.

"Would you mind switching off your PPT connection?" Ursay directed at Rome mentally. *"I will do the same."*

"Of course," Rome said out loud. "It is off."

Rome looked over at Rei and tapped her temple. He nodded.

"So what's this all about?" Rei asked. "I thought you said this wasn't a secret."

"It is not," Ursay said. "However, I did not want to hurt your Overmind's feelings, should he be listening in."

Rome shrugged. "Continue," she said.

Ursay took a deep breath. "As I am sure you are aware, today is the day that the asteroid was supposed to hit Deucado and extinguish all life thus effecting the genocide of the mandasurte."

Rei looked at Rome who shook her head. "Actually, no," he said. "We solved that problem so long ago, I think we kind of forgot about the actual date."

"Well, the Vuduri of Earth have not. We have carried a profound guilt over the entire exercise for a long time. As a people, we were too smug and secure in our mastery of the course of civilization. We were so blind to MASAL's plan. Because of your intervention, we realized it was our sworn duty to protect all the humans of Earth including the mandasurte. The Overmind regards that role as a serious one. It has taken a step back from being the ruler of Earth to being a steward for the protection of all mankind."

"The same thing has happened on Deucado," Rome said. "The Overmind here has changed profoundly. In fact, we are all evolving."

Ursay nodded. "So are the people of Earth although not as quickly as you. It is quite clear to all the inhabitants, the Overmind included, that Deucado is now in the forefront of human endeavors and the gap is widening. Those of us on Earth who concern ourselves about such things believe it is time for our three worlds, Helome included, to formalize our ties to one another. A treaty if you will. We would like to establish a Galactic Union to improve communication and interaction."

Rome just stared at him trying to make sense of his words. "That sounds like a fine idea but what has it got to do with us?"

Ursay leaned forward. "We would like you and your family to come to Earth and address the planet and announce this treaty. Helome has already agreed to the pact."

"Why us?" Rei asked. "We're nothing special."

"I beg to differ with you," Ursay said. "It is quite clear to us that you and Rome are effectively the leaders of this planet. Even if the role has not been formally assigned."

"Naw," Rei said, scoffing at the notion.

"Yes," Ursay insisted. "And there is more. You and Rome have personally saved mankind many times over. Your communication with the Stareaters. Destroying MASAL. Defeating the new Ark Lords. Even setting Helome on a path to genetic recovery. Rome's interactions with the Vuduri and the various Overminds have had such a profound effect, it has been given a name. It is now referred to on Earth as Rome's Revolution."

Rome's face lit up in a broad smile. Rei turned to her then turned back to Ursay.

"What kind of revolution, really?" Rei asked.

"I will give you an example. Take the reduction of the role of the Overmind. The separation techniques that Rome taught me and propagated here on Deucado took hold and most of the Vuduri have learned to operate autonomously to a greater or lesser degree. This is a radical change from prior generations. The Overmind has been awakened to its greater responsibility and it now serves in a data gathering and information dissemination mode. In simple terms, we have reestablished the control over of our own lives that we did not know we were lacking."

"Wow," Rome said. She had learned that expression from Rei. "You only mention Vuduri. What about the mandasurte?"

"I thought I explained that earlier. They are now treated as equals. We have come to cherish their creativity and independence. As you are well aware, before the crisis with MASAL, they were restricted. Now, they have been given free access to all parts of the Earth and off it."

Ursay continued. "Over the years, as the word has spread regarding what you are accomplishing here on Deucado, many, many of the mandasurte and even a large contingent of Vuduri lobbied for a regular mode of conveyance to be established. This would allow them to come and go and yet be a part of what is happening here."

"It *is* pretty sleek what's happening here," Rei said. "The mixture of the Vuduri, the Deucadons and the Essessoni has created some amazing technology. The Ibbrassati too. Just today, we finished a transport grid that will allow us to cultivate food in a way that has next to no impact on the environment."

"I am aware of that," said Ursay. "This is yet another example of why we want to form a closer relationship between our worlds. Even as we speak, our scientists are researching how to set up a standing PPT tunnel between Earth and Deucado like that which exists between Earth and Helome."

"**My Null Fold Drive is much faster than an ordinary PPT tunnel,**" MINIMCOM interjected.

"Agreed," said Ursay. "Perhaps you could aid us in developing that very technology on a larger scale. Tunnel-sized."

"**It is possible at some point in the future. Right now we are working on expanding our explorations outward.**"

Ursay nodded. "We know that. It is clear to us that someday, one of you will encounter non-human intelligence on another world. That is yet another reason why we want to create this Union. We thought it best to have a structure in place should these aliens wish to form an alliance. And if not, we would still need to be unified in our dealing with them."

Rei looked at Rome who raised her eyebrows.

"Maybe," Rei said. "But do we really have to come to Earth to pull this off?"

"I agree that it is largely ceremonial but given your past deeds, you two are now considered to be among the greatest heroes in the history of mankind. And Earth wishes to show its appreciation if you are willing."

Rome leaned back in her chair. She shook her head slowly. It was a lot to absorb. Finally, she spoke.

"That is very kind of you sir. And I believe we will take you up on your offer. I have always wanted the chance to show my children the Earth. As you know, Aason was taken there when he was very young. I doubt he remembers much. And Lupe has never been there."

"Then it is settled?" Ursay asked. "Would you be willing to return with us now?"

"Not right this minute," Rome said. "I must wait until my children and Junior return. And my father is almost finished his recovery but not quite."

"If I may ask, your children return from where?"

"They are out near Tabit," Rei said. "They'll be back in a day or so."

"Why did they go there?" Ursay queried.

"We have a piece of OMCOM here that takes care of Rome's Library and the whole University of Deucado. It needs a tune-up from time to time. They're out there, at Planet OMCOM, to get some upgrades."

"OMCOM," Ursay hissed. Then he composed himself. "I apologize. Old habits die hard. OMCOM has remained apart from the Earth as he promised. His unleashing seems to have had no long term effects as we had once feared."

"We were concerned when it first happened but as you said, he has stayed away. And even remaining as far away as he has, he's been very good to us, sir," Rome said. "He is far more caring and conscientious than you realize. He…"

There was a knock at the door. Rome turned to Rei who shrugged and got up from the table. He went to the door and opened it and saw a two-meter tall, all-white livetar standing there.

"OMCOM?" Rei asked, puzzled. "What are you doing here? Where are the children?"

Rome jumped up from her chair and hurried to over to the doorway.

"I am not your Library OMCOM," the livetar said robotically. "I have come here from Planet OMCOM to fetch you."

"Fetch us, why?" Rome asked, fear rising in her voice. "Where are the children? Are they alright?"

"I regret to inform you that no, they are not alright."

Rome's knees became weak. Rei grabbed her before she fell down.

The livetar pointed to MINIMCOM and said, "Please take Rei and Rome on board. My ship will transport you to Tabit as we once did to bring Junior here. There is no time to waste. I will fill you in on all the details on our way there."

Chapter 17
Tabit System

IT TOOK AASON QUITE SOME TIME TO GET PAST ALL THE psychic tears shed by his mother through their PPT transducer connection. After she had calmed down a bit, he gave her the briefest of summaries of all that had happened during his trip to Nu² Lupi and back. To her credit, Rome listened patiently and did not interrupt. Finally, after Aason wrapped up, Rome instructed him to proceed to Planet OMCOM where she and Aason's father were waiting aboard MINIMCOM. It only took Junior one short hop via a regular PPT tunnel until he was close enough to enter an east-to-west orbit around the planet-sized computer.

Rather than have two fast-moving objects try and intersect, MINIMCOM commanded Junior to hold steady and the elder starship used his plasma thrusters to adjust his trajectory until they matched orbits. Once things had stabilized, MINIMCOM was at exactly the same altitude and trailed Junior by about a thousand meters to the rear.

Aason led Aroline, Donald and Sh'ev along with the OMCOM livetar down the main corridor and through the airlock into the cargo compartment. Molokai, ensconced within his crystal capsule, shimmered and shown more brightly than normal in anticipation of meeting the next round of humans.

With a whoosh and a pop, Rome, Rei and MINIMCOM's all-black livetar appeared at the rear of the compartment. Aason stepped forward briskly as his mother ran up to him to greet him. She hugged her son tightly for a long time. Then she kissed him over and over.

"Oh, Aason," she said, finally. "At least you are safe. But your sister? What are we going to do?" Rome reached down to grasp Aason's right hand. She touched the gauze-wrapped stump at the end of his arm and gasped.

Aason carefully drew his arm back. "Mom, I told you what happened."

Rome took a deep breath. "I know you told me but seeing it makes it real." She reached forward and grasped his arm again and lifted it up gently. "Does it hurt?"

"Kind of," Aason said. "I'm trying to ignore it right at the moment."

Rome turned and addressed MINIMCOM. "You will be able to repair him?" she inquired.

"**Of course,**" replied the all-black livetar. "**It is one of my specialties.**"

Rei took the opportunity to come over and wrap his long arms around his son. He dragged his wife into the mix at the same time.

"Dad," Aason said quietly, burying his head into his father's shoulder. For just one moment, it felt good to have someone there who Aason thought of as far more powerful, cradling him.

While the three of them were hugging, Junior instantiated a slate-gray livetar in order to join the reunion. His father, MINIMCOM strode forward and hugged him. It was an odd sight, two stiff animated shells embracing. "**And you are intact?**" MINIMCOM asked.

"Yeah, Dad," Junior answered. "More than intact. The X-drive is really quite spectacular."

Rome, who was still entangled in the family hug disengaged herself and spun around. "That is how this whole mess started," Rome called over sharply.

"Mom!" Aason insisted. "It wasn't Junior's fault."

The OMCOM livetar stepped closer. "Rome, if you wish to blame anyone, you may blame me. In fact…" The livetar stopped speaking. It winked out of existence then phased in and out and back again. After the shell had stabilized, it continued again, its voice ever so slightly deeper. "The livetar you now see in front of you is fully coupled to me. For your purposes, I *am* Planet OMCOM." The livetar tapped his chest with his hand.

"You! Yes, I…" Rome said stridently.

"Mom, hold on," Aason interjected. "I need to introduce you." He turned and motioned to Aroline. The blonde girl came over and stood by Aason's left side, taking hold of his good hand.

"Mom, Dad, this is Aroline. We're kind of together now."

Aroline let go and reached out with her right hand. "How do you do?" she asked. "Aason has told me so much about you."

Rome cocked her head. Although Aason had mentioned the girl in passing, Rome was not sure how she fit in. There were too many pieces to this puzzle. While she was regarding Aroline, Aason waved to the others.

"This is Aroline's father, Donald," he said. "And this is our new friend, Sh'ev. His species is called the K'val."

The plant-man made some rustling, scratching noises and then held his hand out. Rome looked at the leafy extension, not sure what to do.

"Is that his language? What did he say?" Rome asked.

"He said he was pleased to meet you. Mom, you may not be able to speak his language but I know you can go inside his head."

"Yes," Rome said distantly and she looked down at Sh'ev's hand. Her telepathic powers worked best when she was in physical contact with her subject. She reached out and grasped his hand firmly then lifted up her eyes to gaze up into his face. She focused on the two dark spots which she presumed were Sh'ev's eyes.

"I can hear your thoughts," she said quietly. Her eyes widened at the tsunami of information flowing from Sh'ev's head into hers. Before her lay an entire world populated only by living crystals and ambulatory plants grown by a god-like being and slaved to his needs. The panorama and vistas of the alien world and its inhabitants came rushing at her like a high-speed travelogue. There was so much information to assimilate but this was neither the time nor the place.

"You and I will have to speak another time," she said releasing the K'val's hand. She shook her head to clear it and turned back to Aason. "Now tell me. How are we going to get your sister back?"

Aason used the stump of his arm to indicate the crystal capsule on the other side of the cargo compartment. It was filled with the glowing presence of an entity made only of light. "That's Molokai," Aason said. "He's going to take us to Lupe."

Rome stared at the giant conical-shaped crystalline capsule with the thrashing, swirling lights within.

"*Hello, Rome,*" the creature of light announced. "*I am Molokai, Species Twenty Two.*"

"You are a member of Species Twenty Two?" she asked.

"*No, not a member. I am the totality of Species Twenty Two. The entire species. Every one of them.*"

"I don't understand," she said, shaking her head. "How could you be all of them?"

"Just as you Vuduri have your Overmind, the collective consciousness which has a mind of its own, I am the collection of all the souls of my birth species. I am one and I am all. What you see is our accumulated spirits."

"Souls?" Rei asked incredulously. "You mean souls are real?"

"Very much so. Think of it as the spirit that distinguishes a lump of flesh from a thinking, feeling being. It is very tenuous. One soul alone would not amount to much in this universe. But put billions of souls together and this is the end result. We move on."

"Move on to where? Where are you from?" Rome asked. "What are you doing here? And where is Lupe?"

"Your people, the Vuduri, do not have a name for it," Molokai said. *"Your husband's people had a concept, marginally similar, called Heaven."*

"Heaven?" Rei gasped. "That's real too?"

"You do not have the exact words. It is not how your people envisioned it but where I come from is the final gathering place for the souls of all living creatures."

"So how is it not how we envisioned it?"

"It is not a real place in your mode of existence. It is the realization of thought, not matter. It cannot be described. Any words I would use to explain it would be so wrong as to be misleading, if not an outright lie. Let me explain it a different way. You, here, each of you see the same things. You experience the same things. Where I come from, each soul that arrives would experience something different, something unique to that soul. At least while it could. After that, it would join the greater."

Rome sighed. "I still don't understand. But this is where you took Lupe?"

"I did not take her," Molokai said.

"Then who did?"

"It was others, like me. Each of them is the accumulated spirits of entire worlds and billions of years of evolution. They all coexist on a plane infinitely beyond your four-dimensional space. It

is a realm of... " Molokai said a word but not one person in the room understood.

"Never mind, then," Rome said, holding her hand up. "How do we get her back?"

"I will lead the way," Molokai said.

OMCOM stepped forward. "We are going to build Molokai a ship. A ship that can travel faster than anything ever imagined. It will take us where we need to go. Molokai will provide the guidance."

Rei shook his head. "What kind of ship?" he asked. "You're going to build a ship that goes to Heaven?"

"Molokai and I have worked it out," Aason said. "The X-drive has no upper speed limit. It is constrained only by the amount of computing power available. OMCOM is a computer the size of planet. Molokai says it's more than enough for us to achieve the necessary velocity."

"And who is us?" Rome asked, her eyes narrowing.

"Me and Junior," Aason said. "We'll be flying…"

"Absolutely not," Rome exclaimed, stamping her foot. "If any of us are going on this trip, it will be your father or me."

Aason took one step forward. "No, Mom. It has to be me. I got Lupe into this jam and I have to be the one to get her back."

"I forbid it," Rome insisted. "Aason, this is the cruelest of equations. I may have already lost one child. I will not take even the slightest chance of losing both of my children." Tears were welling up in her eyes.

"Mom, I'm going," Aason said. "I've made up my mind."

Rome wheeled in place, tears streaming down her cheeks now. "Rei, you tell him. Tell him he cannot go."

Rei nodded. "Son…" he said firmly. "Your mother is right. It's too dangerous. One of us will go."

"No!" Aason shouted. "You don't understand. This is *my* responsibility. I'm the one who has to make it right."

"No, no, no," Rome said. She put her hands up to her face.

"Mom, Dad, listen to me." Aason held out both arms. "Each of you is remarkable in your own way." He walked over to his mother and put his good hand on her shoulder. "Mom, you single-handedly transformed all of Vuduri society." Aason turned to his father. "Dad, you are the greatest hero mankind has seen since Hanry Ta Jihn." He took a step back and held his arms wide. "Together, the two of you have accomplished things that neither of you could have done alone. Well, I am you. I am your son. I am the two of you together merged into one. My blood is your blood. My heart is your heart." Aason beat his chest with his left hand. "The one thing you two taught me, from the day I was born, was to always do the right thing. This *is* the right thing. This is something I have to do. Me and nobody else."

Rome lowered her head and sobbed quietly. Rei stepped over to her and put his arms around her. He took a deep breath, preparing to voice his objection once more when Molokai spoke.

"In your language, you have a word. Moot. Your arguments are moot. Aason has to be the one to go. I have been inside of him and he has been inside of me. His spirit is stronger than anything I have ever seen. He was powerful enough to resist my attempts to absorb him. He will need that strength when he gets to where we are going. Every one of the beings there will lust after him. I can tell that neither of you alone possesses such a spirit. Therefore, he must be the one to go. It is an absolute, non-negotiable requirement."

Rei spoke, his throat constricted with grief. "If what you are saying is true, then how do we even know Lupe is still alive?"

Rome gasped when Rei said it.

"She is alive. They took her for a reason. I do not know what that reason is but it would serve no purpose for them to take her simply to dispose of her. I do not know how long she will last but I do know that your son is your only hope of bringing her back safely. And it must be soon."

Rei just glared at the glittering lights. He clenched his fists, fighting to keep his temper in check. He forced the engineer within to seize control and took a deep, cleansing breath. As he turned it over in his mind, everything became clear. He reached down and touched Rome gently on the chin and lifted up her face until she looked into his eyes.

"Rome, I don't like it any more than you do but if it's the only way to get Lupe back, we have to let him do it."

Rome just stared up at Rei with anguished eyes. She reached inside Rei's mind and saw his logic. She knew that he was right. That this was the only way. She then realized all of her protests were only delaying the inevitable and decreasing the chances of rescuing Lupe. Sadly, she nodded then turned to face the others.

"All right. There is no point in fighting about this any further," she said. "Tell us how this is going to work."

Aason nodded. He called over to Junior. "Cuz, can you set us up a place where we can sit down together?"

"Sure thing," Junior replied.

In a matter of moments, Junior reshaped the right hand side of the rear portion of his cargo bay into the 35th century equivalent of a conference table and chairs. Aason sat down first and Aroline sat next to him, draping her arm over his shoulder. Her father took a seat on the other side of his daughter. Sh'ev sat at the head of the table and Junior sat next to him so he could translate for the K'val. Rei and Rome sat opposite Aason. MINIMCOM took up a position behind them but remained standing next to OMCOM's livetar.

The all-white livetar looked up at the ceiling. "Junior, holographic projectors please."

The slate-gray livetar nodded and two cylinders lowered from the ceiling above. The area over the table lit up with a ghostly view of the planet-sized computer below rotating in orbit about the remains of Tabit.

OMCOM pointed to his chest then at the projection. "The livetar you see here is just a shell so that I can interact with you. My actual configuration is that of a sphere, 13,000 kilometers in diameter with a circumference of just over 40,000 kilometers. My mass is roughly ten to the 24th kilograms. As would occur with any accumulation of such mass, the normal effect of gravity would be to compress it into a spherical shape. I have to change that and have gravity work for us rather than against us."

Two sets of dimples appeared on one side and the other of the north and south poles of the sphere. The dimples deepened as if they were being squeezed by a cosmic vise until they became so deep, the sphere actually starting splitting apart into three distinct but smaller spheres. The three spheres separated more and more until just a small bridge of matter connected them together.

"I will divide my mass initially into three major sections. The two outer spheres effectively rotate about the inner sphere. I will hollow the two outer spheres to reduce gravity's desire to recombine them again."

The two outer sections swelled while the middle section began folding in on itself, expanding as it went until eventually it formed a huge ring, like a doughnut. The two outer spheres pulled themselves back in until they rested on either side of the toroid.

"The ring you see mid-section will become the bank of X-drive generators. They will be able to project negative energy forward and aft. It will be solid enough to keep the two outer spheres separated. Once this configuration is stable, I will construct the propulsion system."

The virtual camera panned around to the rear. The back sphere caved in on itself to some degree then extended outward even more and formed a funnel with the flaring end poking out the rear.

"The cone-shaped structure you see will become the plasma thrusters that will move the entire mass forward initially. The Casimir Pumps lining the interior will be optimized for extraction of positive energy which will produce the thrust."

Rei pointed to the mid-section and drew a large circle in the air. "Why would you build a ring of X-drive generators?" he asked. "For a normal configuration, two pods would be sufficient."

"Agreed," said OMCOM. "However this is not a normal configuration. I will explain in a moment. Just know that the passageway that I open needs to be significantly larger than the diameter of the two remaining spheres. It will allow me to maintain a tunnel large enough to account for all of my mass along the way."

Aroline spoke up for the first time. "Where does Aason go?" There was a noticeable sadness in her voice.

"That is a good question. While the image you see is static, the reality is that the planet below would continue to rotate at its normal speed, well over a thousand kilometers per hour. I will use the mechanics of the arrangement to extend a tower or perhaps stalk is a better word…"

Once again, the virtual camera moved, this time to the leading sphere, opposite the plasma drives. A bump appeared on the surface that stretched and stretched forming a thin tower that continued extending until it was twice as long as the entire rest of the now oddly shaped planet.

"The projection is not quite to scale however it will suffice. The stalk you see here needs to be at least 20,000 kilometers long to counter the gravitational pull of the remainder of the mass. We will use centrifugal force to our advantage. Once I have extended it sufficiently, the whole configuration will be relatively stable. Rei, it would be similar to the space elevators your people once implemented back on Earth."

"If it's like a space elevator, then what are you using for a counter-weight?" Rei asked.

"Junior and Molokai." The livetar pointed to the projection and moved his arm around in an exaggerated circle. "Rei, you asked why a ring of projectors. I will need the X-drive generator ring to project the folded imaginary component of negative energy sufficient distance and diameter so as to not cut off the stalk."

Donald spoke up for the first time. "I hope you people realize how incomprehensible this is for Aroline and me. We've never heard of a planet-sized computer or Null Fold Drives or any of the other crazy things you're talking about."

"I went through all that myself when I first got there," Rei said, unnaturally calm. "Nothing made sense to me but you'll get used to it eventually."

"If I may continue," OMCOM said. Rei nodded.

"Once I have achieved the configuration you see in front of you, Junior will fly Aason and Molokai out to the tip of the stalk. Junior's livetar and Aason will use hand-thrusters to guide Molokai's capsule to the front. We will mount the construct on Junior's nose and then we will attach Junior's starship to the tip of the stalk."

Sh'ev reached up and tugged on Junior's arm. The livetar bent over and then Sh'ev rustled, quietly saying something to Junior who looked over the gathered group and said, "You are correct. It is just like your basic designs. Crystal in the front, metal in the rear."

"Thank you," OMCOM said. "Once they are mounted, I will reinforce the structure and begin slowing down my rotation. Once my rotation has stopped, we will be ready for the Stareaters."

"Hey!" Aason said, whipping around. "You never explained that. How the hell did they even know to be here?" he asked angrily. "They told me you asked them to arrive exactly on this date over four years ago. How could you have known you were going to need them?"

OMCOM did not answer right away. He waved his hand and the holographic image disappeared. He walked around to the head of the table and stood directly behind Sh'ev so he could look at all the humans at once.

"Since before Rome's group left Tabit, I have been spending the bulk of my time contemplating a reason to justify my own existence. Rei's people called it living in limbo. There is no real need for me or my capabilities in this universe. You all know about the mutations that were formed when the VIRUS units consumed the Stareater named Balathunazar just as the Vuduri were abandoning the base."

"Mutations that you allowed to happen," Rei muttered.

"Agreed. I did not need the entire mass of the remains of the Stareater so I permitted variations in the basic form. Many of those mutations developed forms of propulsion that I cannot fully explain. That, in fact, was my goal. It was a type of natural selection. After a long period of time, they began to return to me with news of the multitude of dimensions outside our own. One even visited the realm from which Molokai originated. The probe reported to me that they were having a fundamental problem, one that my unique abilities could help them solve. This became my purpose in life, so to speak. I began designing the X-drive and my extrapolations told me it would be ready for a field test at this point in time."

"And what about Lupe?" Aason barked out crossly. "Was she part of your field test?"

"You, yourself, told me she was the one that insisted she come along. However, I did need someone to test the drive. That was the actual underlying reason why I requested one of you come out here with the Library OMCOM. My original plan was to outfit MINIMCOM with the X-drive but it turned out to be Junior. It did not matter to me. I needed to see if it was workable. My assumption based upon trillions of simulations was that it would operate as designed. So I constructed this configuration…"

The holographic projectors lit up again with the odd-looking starship. The virtual camera panned back to take it all in but the scale was so huge as to be nearly incomprehensible.

"It was always my plan to leave this universe at this time. However, my computations told me that I could not create a large enough PPT tunnel to begin the journey. I needed the Stareaters to help me launch so I sent word. The dates and the planning were simple extrapolations."

"Something's not right," Aason growled. "There are too many holes in your story. There's something you're not telling us."

"There are a semi-infinite number of things I have not told you," OMCOM replied. "But that does not change the fact that we must do this and we must do it now to save your sister. Perhaps you and I can discuss it in more detail on the way."

Aason scowled but offered no more protest. OMCOM lifted his arm upward and the scale of the display decreased even further until the spaceship was just a tiny dot. Two huge spheres entered into the picture, one on each side.

"I don't get it. Why two Stareaters?" Rei asked. "Why not just one?"

OMCOM filled the images in front of him with bright lines representing the gravitational wells surrounding the Stareaters. The livetar traced one section of lines around each of the Stareaters in a bright yellow color.

"The gravitational pull of a single Stareater, even a small one, is equivalent to that of a star. If there were only one, my ship would be pulled into it and crash onto its surface long before I could make my way through the tunnel. By having two Stareaters come in equidistant, the gravitational pull will be balanced from a Lagrangian perspective and allow me the time I need for them to create the tunnel and punch through it."

"Are there Stareaters wherever it is you're going?" Aroline asked.

"No. Why?"

"Because if you need Stareaters to travel, how will you get back?"

"I am not coming back," OMCOM said solemnly. "This is a one way trip for me."

Rome slapped her hand down on the table. "If you are not coming back, how will Aason and Lupe return?"

"We will find a way after we get there," OMCOM said. "After all, my probes proved they could travel there and back and Molokai's peers demonstrated it could be done as well. Have no fear. We will figure it out."

Rome started to protest but a wave of dizziness overcame her. All the blood drained from her face and she started to pitch forward. Rei grabbed her by the shoulders so she didn't bang her head against the table.

"The Stareaters must be here," OMCOM observed. He produced a white band and walked around the table until he reached Rome. He placed the band over her head until it was snug around her forehead at temple height. The effect was instantaneous. Rome's eyes fluttered then opened wide.

"What is that headband?" Aroline asked. "What happened to her?"

"It's called a T-suppressor," Aason answered. "The Stareaters produce so much gravitic energy, they make a regular Vuduri with an active PPT resonance pass out. The T-suppressor reverses and blocks out the energy."

"Aren't you a regular Vuduri?" she asked. "How come you didn't pass out?"

"I'm not what you'd call normal," Aason said sheepishly. "I'm a hybrid. It doesn't seem to affect me." He looked over at his mother. "Mom, are you all right?" he asked.

"Yes," she said. She took a deep breath. "I haven't felt that sensation in a long time. It is very odd."

OMCOM stepped around to the front of the group again. He waved his hand and the holographic projection of the monstrous spacecraft disappeared to be replaced by a star field and the all-white planet below.

"If everyone is satisfied with the plan, we will be getting underway."

Sh'ev rustled and scratched and patted his chest. Aason shook his head no.

"What did he say?" Aroline asked.

"He asked me if I wanted him to go along. Sorry, buddy, it has to be just me and Junior." Aason waved at Junior who came over to stand beside him. He whispered in the livetar's earhole and Junior nodded.

"Does anyone have any other questions?" OMCOM asked. No one replied immediately. "Then we will begin. Junior, MINIMCOM, you must increase your orbital distance past the 25,000 kilometer mark to be safe."

"**Understood,**" MINIMCOM replied. He walked over to his son's livetar. "**Son, please be careful and return Aason and Lupe safely.**"

"You know I will, Dad," Junior replied. "But before we go, Aason asked me to transfer Sh'ev's translator into your care." MINIMCOM nodded.

Both livetars stood perfectly still for a moment then MINIMCOM said, "**Transmission verified. I will prepare my cargo bay to receive the rest of the passengers.**"

MINIMCOM saluted Aason then, with a whoosh and a pop, the all-black livetar winked out. The rest of the group felt a slight push as Junior ignited his plasma thrusters to increase his velocity and therefore his altitude. As he was doing so, the holographic projection in front of them showed the real planet OMCOM morphing into the shape that the livetar had sketched out for them before. A small chunk of the planet broke away and flew off, decreasing in density until it was just a cloud of gas.

"What's that?" Aason asked.

"I am leaving a portion of my mass behind as clone ships," OMCOM said. "Each has been equipped with the X-drive. It will benefit all the inhabitants of Deucado to have such a fleet available and even Earth if they so desire."

"Uh, OK," Aason said. He stared at the image in front of him noting a spindly stalk rising from the surface, extruding and thinning as it went. Eventually the stalk was longer than the remainder of the mutated planet below, barely visible given the scope of display.

After the changes stopped, OMCOM announced it was time. Everyone arose from the table at once. Aason walked back around to the head and put his hand on Sh'ev's shoulder.

"Goodbye, buddy. Thanks for all your help," he said. "MINIMCOM now has your translator stored so you'll be able to converse with my parents and anybody else."

"Thank you," Sh'ev said. "I am trying to learn your language as well." He then made some scratching noises that sounded like "Chudbye, Shashon end chud dluck."

Aason smiled. "That's great!" He looked over at Junior who nodded. The livetar held out a small can with a flared top. Aason took it from him and handed it to the human-like plant.

"This is a can of silane fluoride. I had Junior make it for you. When you need a dose, just press on the top and it will squirt a little into your, um, wherever you need it."

Sh'ev made some rustling noises and patted Aason's shoulder. OMCOM directed him over to the corner of the cargo bay. With a whoosh and a pop, the plant-man disappeared.

Donald and Aroline were next. Donald took Aason's left hand and shook it firmly. He said, "Good luck, son. You're a very brave boy."

Aroline said nothing. She grabbed Aason and kissed him passionately. Aason held her close for a long while. When she pulled back, she whispered in his ear, "You come back to me, Aason Bierak. I love you and I want to spend my life with you."

Aason's face broke out into a broad grin. "You bet," he said. "Believe me, I feel exactly the same way." Aroline put her hand to his cheek and stroked it gently. OMCOM tapped her on the shoulder. She and her father walked over to the corner of the cargo bay where Junior transported them across to MINIMCOM's hold.

Rei and Rome came over to their son. Rei hugged him and said, "You be careful, son and know that we're very proud of you."

"Sure thing, Dad," Aason said. He looked at his mother who shook her head. "Rei, you go. I want to talk to Aason alone," she said in a low voice.

"OK," Rei agreed. "Hurry back, son," he said. With a whoosh and a pop, he was gone.

Immediately, Rome burst into tears again and grabbed on to her son for dear life.

"You and your sister are the most precious things in the world to me," she said, haltingly. "I would just die if anything happened to you. Promise me you'll be careful."

Aason bent forward and kissed his mother's forehead. "Mom, you and Dad have been preparing me for this mission my whole life.

Since before I was even born. I won't fail you. I'll bring Lupe back safe and sound. You have to trust me."

"I do trust you," Rome said, sad and proud at the time. "I love you, my baby. Please, please come home to me."

"I will, Mom."

Rome started to say something else but there was nothing more to be said. She had to force herself to let go of her son. She stepped back, wiped her tears and blew a kiss to Aason. Then, with a whoosh and a pop, she disappeared.

Chapter 18

JUNIOR ATTACHED A TETHER TO THE HANDLES THAT HE HAD AFFIXED to the rear of Molokai's capsule to make sure that it didn't drift off by accident once they were in space. He also attached a second tether to Aason for good measure. After all, he couldn't lose his friend and cousin. Once this was done, the starship shut off the artificial gravity. Even though they took their time, Aason, who was dressed in a pressure suit, and Junior's livetar were able to move Molokai's capsule out of Junior's cargo compartment into interplanetary space without much difficulty. Using the hand thrusters, they guided the capsule out of the cargo bay and around to the front of Junior's nose which the starship had flattened and widened into the exact diameter required. After they had a soft mating, Junior curled a portion of his hull around the edges of the cone-shaped object, securing it as firmly as if it was welded to his airframe. Junior fired his trim-jets several times to make sure that the coupling was rigid. He made some tiny adjustments to balance the mooring and tested it again until he was satisfied that nothing was going to shift, let alone shake loose.

Even though they were tethered together, Junior extended his arm and Aason took it using his one good hand. Together, they circled back around the ship, reentering through the rear door into the cargo hold. Junior raised the ramp and lowered the cargo door forming an airtight seal. The atmospheric pumps kicked in and quickly refilled the compartment with breathable air. Aason watched the pressure indicator change from red to green. Junior helped him remove his helmet then started to undress Aason.

"Let me try this myself," Aason said. "For however long it remains, I have to get used to having only one hand."

Junior nodded and stepped back. He watched while Aason struggled but eventually, he was able to get the suit off by himself.

"I'll meet you up front," Junior said. Using a snap whoosh-pop tunnel, the livetar winked out of existence.

Aason gathered up the pressure suit and moved forward, stopping at the side airlock to stow it in its proper place. He then made his way to the cockpit and took his seat in the pilot's chair.

With only one good hand, it took Aason a little while to snap both tongues of the X-harness into their respective clasps. He pulled one strap and then the other as tight as possible. Up ahead, in front of Junior's nose, Molokai's crystal capsule shimmered and flashed with all colors of the rainbow. Occasionally, the ripples looked like the Aurora Borealis. Other times they looked like something stuck in a blender. Aason opened up his mind, reaching out, trying to contact the being that just a day earlier had claimed he was God.

"Is everything to your satisfaction?" he asked.

"Yes. You have done an excellent job. Please grasp the starship controls so that I can establish my linkage."

Aason gripped the left lever. Even though there was no physical manifestation, he could sense Molokai's spirit engage his mind and he could feel Molokai's touch as he clutched the single joystick which would control OMCOM's engines.

"I think we're ready, Cuz," Aason said, shivering slightly at the full feeling within his body.

"Roger that," Junior replied through the grille. "I'm just waiting for Starship Planet OMCOM whatever to finish hooking up our servos."

Aason took a deep breath. "Cuz, before we get started, I just wanted to thank you for this. It feels really good knowing you have my back."

A slight buzzing noise issued from the grille. "I wouldn't have it any other way," the starship replied. "I know it doesn't make any sense but you and me, we're not just best friends. We're blood. I love Lupe as much as you and your parents."

"I know you do. But still, I just wanted to say it."

"Message acknowledged. Back at you."

There were two more clicks and then OMCOM's voice spoke through Junior's grille.

"All is in the ready, Aason. Please contact the Stareaters and let them know it is time for them to prepare our PPT entrance."

"Sure thing," the boy replied.

Even though it was not necessary, Aason closed his eyes to concentrate. He opened up his PPT connection and reached out, searching for the titanic, living Dyson Spheres that he knew were nearby.

"Calling Hirdindalafant," he broadcast. *"Are you there?"*

"YES," replied the Stareater. *"WE ARE ONE JUMP AWAY. WE WERE AWAITING WORD."*

"Well, we're just about ready," Aason replied. *"How do we work this?"*

"WE WILL OPEN UP A PPT TUNNEL AND APPEAR OFF TO YOUR STARBOARD AND PORT SIDES SIMULTANEOUSLY," replied the Stareater. *"WE WILL PROJECT THE PPT TUNNEL YOU REQUIRE DIRECTLY IN FRONT OF YOU AND HOLD IT OPEN UNTIL YOU ARE THROUGH."*

Aason nodded to no one in particular. "OMCOM, they're ready," he announced. "Just say go and I'll tell them to jump."

"Go," replied OMCOM. Aason furrowed his brow. It wasn't like the planet-sized computer to be funny. Maybe he was just being literal.

"OK," Aason transmitted to the Stareaters. *"We're ready. Launch."*

"ACKNOWLEDGED. JUMPING NOW."

While the incredible influence of the Stareater's gravitational emanations did not render him senseless, Aason could feel it growing in power, nonetheless. Junior's cabin jolted violently to the left and the right then settled down. In front of him, a gigantic black hole formed obliterating the stars. Normally, a person could see what was on the other side of a PPT tunnel but this one led nowhere as far as Aason could tell. He could feel his shoulders being stretched apart. His chest was getting so tight he found it hard to breath. The opposing gravitational pull of the two creatures larger than a star was tremendous. It was tidal forces to the max.

"Go, go, go," Aason croaked, barely able to speak. With his left hand, he shoved the control rod, which was 12-centimeters tall, forward as far as it would go. The joystick had been rigged to transmit Aason's manual instructions all the way to the back of what had been Planet OMCOM. Some 40,000 kilometers away, the oddest spaceship in the universe fired its plasma thrusters, driving the entire ship forward, slowly at first then picking up speed. Aason was in real pain as his body seemed to be coming apart at the seams. He used his mental discipline to reduce the flow of information from his nociceptors until he could concentrate again.

The tip of the ship containing Molokai's capsule entered the black chasm in front of them. While he could not hear it, Aason could feel the vibrations of the gigantic toroidal X-drive generators ramping up. Once Junior passed through the edge of the tunnel, the tremendous strain on Aason's body eased up. Instinctively, he turned in his seat but all he saw was the bulkhead at the rear of Junior's cockpit. He pressed down on the thruster lock then released the joystick so he could activate the rear cameras.

Junior had rotated the central display to its full upright position. The flat screen only showed the huge bulk of what had been Planet OMCOM. The X-drive generators created no visible emissions.

"Cuz, throw me up a schematic," Aason requested. "Our configuration relative to the edge of the tunnel."

"You got it."

The central display assembled a simulation of their status from a side view. The PPT tunnel was shown as a thin edge and it revealed that about half the extrusion holding Junior and Molokai had already passed through the opening. The rest of Planet OMCOM had yet to enter.

Aason looked up from the display. He immediately recognized the blacker than black of null fold space in front of him so he knew the generators were already projecting past them. He watched carefully as half then three-quarters and then finally the entire amalgam that had been OMCOM was through.

"X-drive engaged," OMCOM said through the grille. "It is time for Molokai to show us the way."

"Take hold of the controls," Molokai commanded.

Aason leaned back and gripped the joystick. He could feel Molokai's spirit guiding his hand twisting and turning, alternately pulling back and pushing forward. Junior's artificial gravity normally did an excellent job of dampening the g-forces associated with such acceleration but it was still noticeable. Aason was pressed back in his seat as they shot forward.

"Virtuals?" Aason chirped.

Without answer, Junior lowered the central display and activated the readouts on Aason's wraparound instrument cluster. The smaller center display showed galactic relative coordinates and a speedometer. It was already at the 150 Kc mark and rising rapidly. It hit 200, 300, 500 then 1000. The numbers began churning so fast Aason couldn't keep up with them, they were just a blur. His hand had a mind of its own. It was twisting, pulling. He didn't care. All he could do was stare forward at the velvet black space knowing he was traveling at a velocity that was beyond inconceivable. Molokai's flashing grew brighter and the colors blurred until they became just a shimmering white light.

Then the unthinkable happened. In this place that was nowhere, way off in the distance, he saw a tiny pinpoint of light.

"What is that?" he asked.

"That is an inhabitant of another realm," Molokai replied in his mind. *"There will be many more."*

Molokai's words were no sooner spoken then more spots of light appeared. They started rushing past the ship, increasing in density until the glow was so bright that despite Aason's second, internal iris, he had to raise the stump of his right arm to block it. As quickly as the lights appeared, they were gone and they were plunged into yet a darker space.

Aason looked down at the virtual speedometer and realized it was useless. Nothing Junior displayed had any relevance. His body told him the acceleration was continuing and that was the only thing he could count on. There was no relief so Aason decided to raise his eyes up and just observe. He elected to ignore the blacker than black of null space and focused on Molokai's capsule. Immediately, he noticed something odd was happening. The capsule made of living crystal appeared to be moving away from the front, as if Junior's nose was stretching.

Aason looked down at his feet and they appeared to be farther away from his body than he remembered. He held the stump of his right arm up in front of him and even as he stared at it, it appeared to be stretching away from him as if his arm was growing. In fact, Junior's whole cabin was changing, distorting. It was stretching thinner and thinner.

"What's happening?" Aason called out loud but his voice sounded odd.

"We are beginning to approach escape velocity," Molokai answered in his mind.

"Escape from what?" Aason asked with trepidation.

"Your reality," Molokai replied.

Aason looked down at his feet again. From what he could tell, they were now twenty or thirty meters away from his body and the separation was increasing. His whole being was stretching out and the rate of stretching was accelerating. To make things worse, his limbs were becoming lighter, almost translucent. It was as if his body was evaporating. All around him, Junior's cabin was fading away as well. Aason heard a popping noise and then he couldn't see anything. Well, that wasn't true. He could see Molokai's capsule way ahead but he couldn't see Junior and he couldn't see his body any longer. It was as if he had evolved into a point of view rather than remain a person. He tried to will his arm in front of him to move but nothing happened. He took a deep breath but could feel no air entering his lungs. He tried holding his breath but again nothing happened.

Aason started to wonder if he was dead but concluded he couldn't be because he could still think. He couldn't close his eyes because he had no eyes, no eyelids. He couldn't hear anything. He tried speaking but no words issued forth. He reached out with his mind and called to Molokai.

"Is this the end of me, of us?" the boy asked.

"No, it is the beginning. We will be there shortly." The ethereal being's reply was so faint, Aason could barely hear it in his mind. *"Goodbye, Aason,"* Molokai added. *"Come and find me on the other side."*

Those were the last words Aason heard. Up ahead, Molokai's capsule stretched so far away that it too disappeared. Even if Aason was now just a point of view, he could change its direction. He could look around; not that there was anything to see. He turned his focus forward. As before, there were tiny sparkles flickering in the heavens. They must have been residents of an even higher realm. The sparkles became denser but unlike before, they resolved themselves into tiny balls, not a torrent of light. The spheres pulsed and sparkled everywhere forming a steady corridor that Aason, or whatever he had become, now passed through.

Wave after wave of the sparkles flowed past them, ever changing in their color. Some were green, some blue, some violet, some in the deep ultraviolet. After that came colors for which Aason had no name. Whoever or whatever resided here was incomprehensible but there were many, many of them. Aason could feel Molokai feeding him thoughts as to the meaning of their existence but his consciousness could not grasp the concepts.

The next wave of beings were not spheres but crystals. They were both transparent and hypnotic in that they radiated every imaginable color which fused into a brilliant light. The group of crystals pulsed in and out, almost as if they were breathing. For the first time, in what had been a while, Aason could hear something. Initially, it was a faint hiss but then patterns formed. He strained to make sense of it. The sounds resolved into a tinkling that somehow matched the crystals in front of him. Perhaps they were related. The tinkling hiss grew louder until it became a rushing noise. The crystals were trying to speak to him but he couldn't quite make out what they were saying. The crystals started rotating in a cyclonic pattern with a black spot in the middle, like a cosmic drain hole. Aason found himself caught up in the swirling motion, drawing ever nearer to the gaping hole. A wave of panic washed over his soul. He tried to scream as they plunged through but then everything went black as his consciousness shut down.

Chapter 19

AASON AWAKENED TO FIND HIMSELF UNDERWATER. NO, IT WASN'T water. It was liquid gold. It was not molten gold, it was a liquid that was golden in color and transparent at the same time. His eye stalks wiggled around focusing all over the place, sending different images into his head in a riot of colors. He was buffeted by the collisions of uncounted thousands of bodies of other creatures swimming past him at high speed. If he stayed still, he'd be beaten to a pulp. He flapped his powerful flipper-like tail and used his swimmerets to pick up speed. That he was now a shrimp-like creature didn't strike him as odd in the slightest way. He immediately noted that the density of others like him lessened with depth so he headed downward and outward until he reached the edge of his new world. His antennules rubbed up against the side of the container holding the liquid as he navigated his way clockwise along the perimeter.

Vibrations in the water came as a mild shock wave, triggering his lateral line sensors. He forced his two eyestalks up and saw sieve-like appendages reaching into the golden water, grabbing up a scoopful of shrimp-like beings and plucking them out of the pool. Aason drifted upward until he could get a better look at what was happening. Through the shimmering surface, he could see the thrashing, wiggling beings swallowed whole by a huge upside-down translucent teardrop. He could follow the wriggling things progress as they made their way through their captor, dissolving until there was no evidence they ever existed. Even as a shrimp, he knew that could not be good.

Another shock wave hit the water again, a good deal stronger than before. Aason turned his eyestalks toward his rear and could see a huge pair of sieves coming right for him. He thrashed his tail harder and harder, picking up speed, trying to dive and outrun the object. The lead sieve snapped closed just behind him but did not touch him. He dove down to the very bottom of the pool to take a full survey of his surroundings.

There were thousands if not hundreds of thousands of creatures like him swimming around. And dozens of creatures reaching in, capturing them and swallowing them. It was like an assembly line or feeding trough. Aason couldn't ever remember not being a shrimp but he knew he did not want this to be his fate. Then it came to him. Lupe! He was here to rescue his sister. But how could he do that if he was a shrimp? He turned his eyestalks downward and focused on his front claws. He vaguely remembered at one point they had a different shape. He focused, concentrating all of his will on those crusty appendages and before his eyes, they shrank and widened until they formed themselves into a pair of human hands. Thus, Aason concluded, with a simple act of consciousness, he was able to reshape himself as he saw fit. That meant he could return to his human shape any time he wanted if he could somehow get out of here, wherever here was.

He stopped swimming and drifted down to the bottom of the pool. He rolled over and lay there on the bottom upside down with his antenna flipping around, measuring the water currents. He used his walking legs to count every time one of his captors reached down into the pool. He could also see that the herd above him would scatter each time there was an incursion so there was definitely a pattern. If he could build up enough speed and timed it just right following a feeding dip, he might be able to get to the surface and leap out of the basin or lake or pool, whatever it was without being captured. Where he'd go from there, he had no idea but he knew he had to try. He rolled over right side up and moved his tail up and down, driving him forward. He formed his hands into fins to aid in the effort. Faster and faster he went, always sticking to the outside wall of the retaining edge. He learned how to use the swimmerets on the lower part of his carapace to stroke in unison with his tail motion and move even faster. He even regulated his intake of the liquid and exhaled it through his gills along with his swim fins to gain a tiny bit more boost in velocity. He strained to force his being into the living embodiment of speed.

At last he decided this was as fast as he could go. He turned upward saw an opening. He timed his powerful tail's downward motion so that he gave his final thrust just as he broke the surface. He leaped up over the edge of the pool and found himself floating in space. That is until he landed with splat on the hard surface just outside the pool. The landing hurt. But that didn't matter right now. He had to get away. His shrimp eyes had been adapted to see underwater. Now that he was in the air, nothing looked right. He reformed his eyes to a more human style. He skittered along with his pereiopods, his walking legs, until he tucked himself under the edge of the pool, away from the sight of the things that were feeding on the other poor souls that were trapped in the liquid.

He pulled his appendages in, changing his fins back to hands, leaving only two arms. He then split his tail, forcing it into the shape of two legs. Slowly, he stood up stretching himself to his full height. He took a step, somewhat unsteadily, then another and crept along the edge of the tank. His goal was the brightly lit area underneath the platform that held his former aquarium. When he was close enough, he dashed forward between a series of columns and found himself within a whole new world.

At first, the white light was so bright that Aason could not see. It was then that he remembered his inner iris. He activated it and the light dampened down until the world became simply gray in sharp contrast to the constant golden glow of the world above. He turned in place to make sure he was not imagining it and he was not. Outside of the opening was the golden palace. Inside was more silver than gray. He looked up fully expecting to see a ceiling. Instead, he saw a high, bright gray sky. There was no obvious source of illumination and certainly no clouds but it was clearly not the platform that he knew had to be over his head.

The perspective was completely odd. Off in the distance were structures. He activated his Vuduri telescopic vision and was able to make out buildings, mountains, castles, forests and other conglomerations that resisted easy titles. There was no horizon. The world simply went off into the distance until he could not make out any features. It was the same to his left and his right. This new place stretched beyond sight off to infinity.

The boy shrugged and took a step forward and almost slipped. He looked down and saw that he was still wet and naked. . He closed his eyes and imagined himself warm and clothed and when he opened his eyes, he saw that it was true. He was now wearing a traditional Vuduri white jumpsuit and soft moccasin-like shoes. He trudged forward and one leg gave way and he stumbled. After he righted himself, he looked down and could see that portions of the ground were moving. There were some rivulets but in other places, the portions were flowing like large dry rivers. He carefully sidestepped the moving portions and headed toward the first structure he could see.

He walked for quite a distance yet the far off structure appeared no closer. It was disconcerting. He looked down at the ground and activated his u-cones. He was able to see that there were many, many of the dry land-rivers. Perhaps the building that was his goal was mounted on a flowing portion of the ground and was moving away from him at the same rate he was walking. He stood with his arms akimbo, set on his hips, trying to figure out the best strategy to get somewhere when he felt something tug on his legging.

He looked down and saw a small, squat being pulling on his clothing. The little creature was bright red with a block head, a blocky body, stubby arms and tiny red tail. In an earlier age, an observer would have said it resembled a Lego man. The little being's tail thrashed around, seemingly uncontrolled terminating in a triangular shaped poker.

"Who are you?" Aason asked.

"Don't you recognize me?" the being countered.

"No, should I?"

"I am or rather I was MASAL," the creature answered.

"MASAL?" Aason replied, shocked. "My parents told me you died under the volcano."

"So I did, so I did," the little creature said, chuckling. "Don't you know where you are?"

"No. I have absolutely no idea. This whole place is crazy."

"Perhaps it is," MASAL said thoughtfully. "Your father would have called it Purgatory. This is where many souls come to stay, waiting until they decide it is time to get into Heaven."

"Souls?" Aason gasped. "Am I dead?" he asked, patting his chest and arms.

"Oh, no," MASAL said, chuckling again. "You're what we call a living soul. You got here by yourself, not through the release of death. We don't get many of those around here. The rest of us, well, we just stand around and bide our time, contemplating our past. Some are ready to go topside right away. Some never want to leave but they all do eventually."

Aason stood on his toes and put his hand over his eyes and looked off into the distance. "Is my sister here?" he asked. "She would be a living soul, too."

"Not that I've noticed."

"So if she's not here, where is she?"

"I wouldn't know," MASAL said, shrugging. "I'm dead."

Aason cocked his head. "How can you even be here?" he asked. "You were a computer. Computers don't have souls, do they?"

"Every intelligent, organized, self-aware entity has a soul," MASAL replied. "It's that very self-awareness, the one that gives rise to original thoughts that is the spirit. The container, whether it's organic or electronic, it doesn't matter." MASAL laughed again. "I was so worried about getting up here and I needn't have. Everybody and everything ends up here eventually."

"Wait," Aason said. "You were evil. You shouldn't be here, in Heaven. Shouldn't you be in Hell or whatever they call it after what you did? Does Hell even exist?"

MASAL had the decency to cover his mouth while he laughed. When he could finally speak, he said, "I am sorry to disabuse you of that theory but no, there is no Hell only Heaven."

"Even for people or things as cruel as you?"

MASAL sighed. "Everything is given a life and the way they live it is up to them. Whether they live a good life or bad by your measure, it's their gain or loss. Contrary to what they told you, there is no one judging you. I suppose I did not spend my time as well as I could have. But there is no divine retribution. The gods upstairs..." MASAL emphasized his words by pointing up. "They simply don't care."

Aason looked somewhat disappointed as MASAL continued. "Look, Aason, there is no good. There is no bad. Up top, they just call it seasoning. It gives our souls better flavor. We're nothing but nourishment for them."

"So you're saying there is no punishment for doing bad whatsoever? No, what's the phrase, eternal damnation?"

"Of course not," MASAL said. "Life is too short. What would the purpose be for endless damnation? The math doesn't work out. Why would any creature come into existence and be tested for a few short years only to fall short and be tortured for eternity. That would be just plain silly, don't you think?"

Aason shrugged. "I don't know. I don't know anything," he said resignedly.

"Well, now you do. Life is given to all of us and what we make of it is our own business. When we die, some go right to the top. Some come here and wait but when we're ready, we join the rest of all souls until the end of time."

Aason closed his eyes. He put MASAL's words out of his mind and tried to focus on his mission. "How is it that you recognized me?" he asked. "We never actually met."

MASAL took his clunky claws and waved them up and down Aason's form. "You think you look like you look to me?" He shook his head. "I have no idea what you look like in your own mind. Up here everything is a spirit, a phantasm. Even though we only spoke briefly, I was able to pick out your spirit right away. What do I look like to you?"

Aason stared down at him. "You don't look like a computer, that's for sure. But you do look like a little mechanical man."

MASAL shrugged. "You have me there. Even though my circuitry was extensive, the spirit within was not that robust. That must be why you see me as small. I see you as large and I know you could be much larger if you wanted to."

"I still don't understand," Aason said. He waved his hand across the horizon. "In all this infinite place, how is it that you came to see me? To find me?"

MASAL nodded. "As I said earlier, this place is all about reflecting upon your past life, working out unresolved issues. I did a lot of bad things when I was alive. Seeing you, I knew right away I had to help you. It is just one more step toward me making amends."

"You still didn't answer my question. How did you find me? I just got here."

"This place, it senses what all of us need in our quest for resolution and provides it for us. If somebody needs to go someplace, the ground just takes you. If you need to meet somebody, you just meet them. There are powers and forces at work here that are beyond comprehension. It isn't even worth it to try and figure it out."

Aason looked over the landscape and it came to him in a flash. This place, with the flowing ground and homogenous color, MASAL notwithstanding, reminded him of the living crystal back on Ay'den. It was one giant organism that manifested itself in multiple forms. It would appear that this place was similar but on a cosmic scale. Thinking back to that alien landscape brought back memories of their journey across that terrain.

"Do you know if my starship is here? His name is Junior."

"A starship?" MASAL answered. "What would make you think a starship would come to Heaven?"

Aason pointed down at the little being. "You're here. You were a computer. Junior is also a computer. He was born, not built. If you had a soul then I'm sure he does as well."

"Born, huh?" MASAL shook his head. "Must have been after my time. But no, I have not seen him. It does not feel like locating him is part of my mission. I'm pretty sure I'm supposed to be helping you. We'll look for him, though. Maybe we'll find out along the way."

"OK," Aason said. "If you're supposed to assist me, then help me find my sister. They kidnapped her and brought her to this place. I'm here to get her back."

"I'm not exactly sure how to do that. I don't have much interaction with living souls. I've been off by myself for a while now. But I do know where we can start."

"Where?" Aason asked.

"I know a place where a lot of human spirits from our world gather from time to time. We can go there and see if some of them know where we can find your sister." MASAL's red eyes were glowing brightly.

Aason squinted at him. He stooped down until he could look eye to eye with MASAL. "I don't get it," he said. "Why are you being so civil toward me? My parents killed you. Why aren't you angry?"

MASAL laughed. "I was so misguided," he answered. "It took them and a piece of OMCOM to show me the way. Even though I've been stuck here for years, they did the right thing. No, if I saw them and I suppose I will someday, I'd thank them for setting me free. You'll find that's true of everyone here. There is no hate or anger. Just love and occasionally boredom with the blandness of it all." MASAL waved. "In any event, let's get going."

"Where *are* we going?"

"That set of buildings way off in the distance," MASAL said, pointing, past that small forest.

Aason looked to where MASAL was pointing. It was the very same set of structures he was trying to reach earlier. "I don't know how to get there," he said. "Nothing in this place stands still. It was moving away from me as fast as I could walk."

"That is because we don't walk," MASAL said. He ambled over to a flowing portion of the ground and stepped on. "This place is meant to help you resolve issues. Let it. Hop on."

Aason stepped on the ground next to MASAL and they were carried forward in the direction he wanted to go. Soon they were moving along at a decent clip. The flow of the ground took them on a path first approaching then entering a forest. On the left hand side, the silvery trees looked like the odd trunk-like growths Aason encountered on Hades. To the right, the forest looked more like the cane-trees native to Deucado only much larger, similar in size to the Forest of Elders on Ay'den.

"How come everything looks so familiar here?" Aason asked, pointing ahead at the trees.

"That's because this place is how you perceive it. It's only natural that you would draw from your past experiences." MASAL looked to the left and the right as they entered the forest. "To me," he said, "these trees look like the rain forest from Havei, on Earth. Those were the last ones I saw before I was vaporized."

Aason rubbed his chin and looked from side to side. The ground was pulling them through the forest but the path they were following was clear. It was if the forest was parting before them and closing up behind them. They were about halfway through when Aason felt something rubbing against his leg. He looked down and saw a fuzzy ball wrapping itself around him. It reminded him of the creatures he saw in the woods on Hades just before the Ice-saberoo attacked him except this one was orange, not white.

Aason bent down and pulled the thing off of him, lifting it up.

"What is this?" he asked, holding the ball of fur up in the air. It unwound itself and took on the shape of an orange tabby cat. It looked very familiar.

"That is an animal spirit of some sort," MASAL answered. "Most go to their own version of Heaven but occasionally they come here. I've been told that some people keep animals as pets and sometimes those pets come here, waiting to join their masters.

Aason looked into the eyes of the cat in front of him. It was purring. Then it came to him. "Skodla?" he asked. The cat purred louder. Aason put it over his shoulder and stroked it gently. "This was my mother's cat," he said. "He died a long time ago. You're saying he's been waiting here for her all this time?"

"I suppose," MASAL said. "In this place, anything is possible."

Meanwhile, more and more fuzz-balls were wrapping themselves around Aason's legs. "I can understand this one but why are the rest of them rubbing against me?" Aason asked, shaking his leg to free it from the steadily growing pile.

"It is because you are a living soul. You have much power and they are drawn to it. They probably don't even know why."

"Do I have to give them anything?"

"No, they'll leave you alone if you tell them to."

"Shoo!" he directed at the mass of fur around his legs. The herd of fuzz-balls didn't move. "Shoo!" he said louder. "I mean it!"

That was enough. The pile of creatures crawled off the moving ground and they were soon left behind.

"I don't get it," Aason said. "This place is so odd. If Heaven above is so nice, why don't you all just go up there? Why does anyone or anything hang around here?"

MASAL turned in place and looked up at Aason with his red glowing eyes. "I'm sure you observed it, even in your brief time topside. The animals and people here, they're not organized enough. They have to resolve their issues. If they go up top before they are ready, they would get swallowed up by gods as soon as they showed their face. They would be absorbed and lose their individuality. Like a drop of water would if it was placed in a whole bucket of water. As I said before, many if not most aren't ready to let go yet. If they don't care, then, I guess they would go."

"Hmm," Aason grunted. He set Skodla down. "Go on, boy," he said. "My mom will be here some day."

The cat-spirit seemed to nod and hopped off the flowing ground. He sat there with his tail flopping back and forth and watched as Aason and MASAL were pulled off into the distance. After a while, he trotted off to wherever he came from to continue his vigil, waiting for his beloved Rome.

Chapter 20

MASAL AND AASON TRAVELED IN SILENCE FOR A WHILE. THE forest degenerated into a crazy patchwork of regular trees, crystal ones similar to the living crystals on Ay'den, more trunk-like things like on Hades and other objects that defied description. Aason just kept looking around trying to make sense of it all even though he knew he was in a realm where logic and reason, in fact not even geometry, applied. Eventually, they emerged from the forest. The group of buildings they sought loomed in front of them.

MASAL pointed ahead to a crowd of people milling about. To Aason, it resembled the marketplace in the resort city of Ur but without the merchant's stalls. A small group of people broke free and started coming toward them.

"I see help is arriving. We can get off here." With that, MASAL stepped onto a non-moving portion of the ground. Aason followed him.

As soon as they were on solid ground, a number of other oddly-shaped creatures raced ahead of the people until they came to Aason. There were bubbles, plants, starfish-like things. Some even looked like wriggling pieces of metal. They were all shapes and sizes. Some started crawling up his legs. Their forms were nonsensical but it was clear they just wanted to touch him. Aason understood and he didn't want to be cruel but it seemed a little creepy. He thought back to what MASAL said earlier; that he could alter himself to be any size he wanted to be. He willed himself to grow larger and it became true. Soon he towered over the people, the creatures and MASAL. The things that were contacting him shied away. After they were gone, Aason returned back to his original size.

Standing in front of him was an older woman and two young girls.

"Aason Bierak," the woman said. "It is so good to see you again."

Aason stared at her. He thought he recognized her but he didn't know who she was.

As the woman observed his confusion, she laughed. "I *was* Reema," she said. "I was Queen of the Onsiras for a while."

"Oh, yes," Aason nodded. Reema had kidnapped him when he was only four years old and tried to make him lure his parents into a trap. Her face came into sharp focus and the days leading up to her death flashed back to him. He frowned at the thought. He looked down at the little girls. "Who are they?"

"I was Sussen," the one girl said. "It was because of you and your parents that I died in the battle of SoCal."

"I remember that. Are you angry at me?" Aason asked, a bit apprehensively.

"Oh no," replied the little girl. "We don't do that around here. Everything happens for a reason. We just don't always know what that reason is." She shrugged her shoulders. "I am happy now. The only thing I regret is I was responsible for my Reema's death."

"It is quite all right, dear," Reema said, stroking her head. "We were all going to end up here eventually."

Sussen turned her head up to Reema and smiled.

"And I was Estar," the other little girl said. "Your mother killed me in a fight underneath the volcano."

Aason sighed. "She told me," he said sympathetically. "And you're not angry either?"

"Heavens no," Estar said. "I am glad I got to meet you. It is funny, though. My death was so preventable. I had your mother trapped and demanded she tell me the truth and she did. She told me about you but I just chose not to believe her and that disbelief got me killed. It was my own fault."

Aason cocked his head. "How come you two look like little girls to me?" he asked. "You were a lot older as I understood these things."

The girls looked at each other and laughed. Sussen spoke up. "On Earth, the Onsira phenotype ages twice as fast as a regular human being, Vuduri or otherwise. Both of us were only 12 years old when we died. We just looked like adults to you and the others."

"And I was only in my 20s," Reema said. "My phenotype made me look so much older as well."

Aason nodded. It sort of made sense to him. As much as anything did around here. He pointed to the little red man standing next to him. "MASAL says you might be able to help me find my sister and maybe my cousin. My sister was kidnapped and brought here against her will."

Reema looked down at MASAL then off in the distance.

"We cannot help you but there is a group around here who can. They call themselves the Suduri…"

As soon as she said it, MASAL hissed then slapped his hand against his face. "I have to stop doing that," he muttered to himself.

"I know about the Suduri," Aason offered. "I led an expedition on Deucado looking for them," he said. "We never found them."

"That is because they moved to another world," Reema said. "But there is a whole group of them here. They'll know what to do."

"Where are they? How do I find them?"

Reema pointed to a direction that Aason had arbitrarily thought to himself as the east.

"Do you see that set of hills off in the distance with the mountain set in the middle?"

Aason activated his telescopic vision and looked where Reema was pointing. Way off in the distance was a low standing set of hills with one fairly prominent mountain, right in the middle.

"Yes," Aason said. "I see them."

"That is usually where they gather. Go there. If you do not find them there, ask someone. You will find them eventually." She looked up and down Aason's white-clothed body. "I saw that you can change your size. You might want to make yourself larger. You will get there quicker."

"Thank you," Aason said. With that, Reema reached out with her hands and the two girls took them. "Goodbye," she said over her shoulder and started walking away. Sussen turned around to wave at him and he waved back at her. Then they were gone.

"OK," Aason announced. He reached down and picked up MASAL. He started growing larger and larger until he towered over the cluster of buildings in front of him. He placed MASAL on his shoulder.

"Are you secure?" he asked him.

"Yes," MASAL replied grasping Aason's collar. "I'll be OK."

Now that he was much larger, from his new-found perspective, Aason could see the rivers of flowing ground much more easily using a combination of all his Vuduri senses. He picked out one that was flowing in the direction that Reema had indicated and hopped aboard. Soon they were traveling at a comfortable speed.

"Why did you make that hissing sound when Reema mentioned the Suduri?" Aason asked.

"I have a bunch of issues I have to work out," MASAL said obliquely. "My feelings toward the Suduri are one of them. When I was alive, they were quite a thorn in my side."

"Why?"

MASAL looked up Aason and shrugged sheepishly. "When I released the 24th chromosome into the Vuduri population, I expected it to eventually convert mankind into an army of living robots answering to me."

"I know that," Aason growled. "That was beyond wrong."

"I know that now," answered MASAL. "But I didn't back then. Anyway, when I first released it, not all humans chose to accept my 'gift' and they became the mandasurte. Your Grandbeo's family were among them. That was why I set up the prison world of Deucado."

"I knew that part," Aason said. "What's that got to do with the Suduri?"

"There was another group that did choose to receive my gift. However, once the 24th chromosome was released, the Overmind did not spring up overnight. In fact, life on Earth the day after its release was very similar to the day before. It took a while for the Overmind to organize itself. I had to wait several generations until it was fully in control before I could take over."

"So what's this got to do with the Suduri?"

"As the Overmind began to exert its control, not all the Vuduri were happy about that. It was not a problem with later generations since they were born into that world, but for that first generation, at least for some, it was a serious issue."

"And?"

"The Suduri, they had no interest in surrendering their sense of self. They wanted to retain their autonomy. It got to the point where tensions between the Overmind and the Suduri became heightened, almost to the point of violence."

"They never came to blows, otherwise I would have heard about it," Aason offered.

"No," replied MASAL. "They were very spiritual and used their mind-connection to become more so. The entire group built an armada and left Earth. They went off to find their own planet but where they went, I surely don't know."

"Their own planet or up here?"

"No, they don't live here," MASAL answered. "Although when they die, their souls come here, just like every other human being. The way I understand it, the Suduri, they found a portal here so that the living could come and go as they please. To visit with their departed loved ones. To learn from them. That sort of thing. But I'm sure the dead, the souls, eventually, they join the crowd up top." MASAL pointed straight up.

Aason looked up but there was nothing but featureless sky. He shrugged his titanic shoulders.

"Hey," MASAL shouted out, grabbing on for dear life.

"Sorry," Aason replied. The hills they sought were rapidly coming into view. The moving portion of the surface transporting them veered off to the left up ahead. Figuring they were as close as the ground was going to take them, Aason stepped off the flowing earth right at the base of the mountain. There was a deep split starting way at the top and coming all the way down to the base. In between the two halves of the split, they could see a crevice and a little light shined through it.

Aason decided to shrink back down to what he now considered his "normal" size so that he and MASAL could squeeze through it. They made their way along the rocky passage and when they emerged, they found a whole crowd of white-robed humanoids, gathered together, chanting in unison. Aason knew in his heart that these were the Suduri.

Aason and MASAL walked up to one of the Suduri standing near the edge. The man turned and looked at the boy as if he had seen a ghost. He shook his head violently and called out to the crowd. A younger man with a scraggly beard strode forward and the crowd parted as he made his way through.

"Aason Bierak," the man said. "Welcome." He held out his hand.

Aason reached forward and the man grabbed hold of his forearm. Aason did the same. They shook arms for a moment then the man released him.

"Thanks," Aason said. "I'm looking for my sister. Do you know where they might be keeping her?"

"Probably. How is it that you came here? You certainly aren't dead."

"A god named Molokai built us a starship that was fast enough to punch through."

"Interesting. And your sister?"

"Molokai said his brothers had reached down from above and grabbed her and brought her here. Or wherever."

The man stroked his thin beard thoughtfully. "Your sister is very powerful, isn't she?" he asked.

"I suppose," Aason replied. "What's that got to do with anything?"

"They all felt it," he said, pointing back to the group. "Even all the way down here. When she first arrived, that is. They couldn't stop talking about it."

"So where is she now?"

"Someone like that, they'd probably take her topside." The man pointed up. "I'm sure you've already been told but everybody calls it Heaven for lack of a better word. I imagine there'd be quite a tussle over that one."

"Is she safe?" Aason asked."What do you mean by tussle?"

"I've never been there myself," the man said. "It's too dangerous for an ordinary soul like me. I'd get eaten up right away. I prefer to remain here and greet new souls as they arrive. But from what I hear, they have an architecture. They'd put her in the center of...I don't know what you'd call it. They'd make her accessible to all."

"For what?" Aason asked, his throat constricting slightly. "What would they do to her?"

"Again, I don't know," the man said. "The Suduri, they just come here to commune with their lost relatives and then they return home. None of the living souls venture out there. It's too dangerous."

Aason cocked his head. "You mean you can travel between our world and this one?"

"I can't but they can," the man replied, nodding over his shoulder.

"How?" Aason asked. "We had to build a spaceship the size of a planet and accelerate to an incalculable speed to get here."

"Not every portal requires such brute force," the man said. "There are an infinite number of ways to get here, if you know how. Your way is one. Dying is another. The Suduri use yet another way. You might call it a back door. Those who can communicate with the dead, yet another."

"So does that mean there are an infinite number of ways to get back?"

"Of course. The Suduri just use the way that works best for them. For other species, it would be completely different."

"Hmmm," Aason said. This was good information but right now he had to focus on the task at hand. "So if they're keeping her topside and they'd swallow me up if I go after her, how am I going to get her back?"

The man laughed. "If you don't want to get swallowed up, the answer is very simple. You must become a god yourself."

"Become a god?" Aason asked incredulously. "How would I do that?"

The helpful man looked at Aason thoughtfully. "Do you understand the purpose of life?"

Aason shook his head. "I didn't know there was a purpose of life."

"Of course there is. Surely you didn't think life was merely a random series of births and deaths. Evolution just there to amuse itself?"

Aason shook his head.

The man opened his arms wide, trying to indicate the vast expanse of the land before them. "Since the beginning of time, men, and other creatures, have asked themselves the purpose of life. While each culture may have different specific goals and priorities, the purpose of life itself is and always has been to achieve a mass-mind that can transcend the physical body and remain self-aware. This has happened countless times in the past, both in our galaxy and uncounted others throughout the universe." The man pointed straight up. "Up there is the place is where they all go once they achieve that state. Your mother's people, the Vuduri were headed down that path." The man shook his finger at MASAL. "Their Overmind is merely a detour. Eventually, humans will achieve an Over-mankind and rise up to take their rightful place among the gods above without fear of dilution or absorption."

"You still haven't told me," Aason fired back. "How does that help me here? Now?"

"Everyone here is waiting for something. Maybe enlightenment. Maybe they just grow tired of being bored. But every soul that has self-worth would want to know that they could retain their autonomy. Ask for volunteers and make that your offer. You'd be surprised how many are ready to go up if they only knew how. Just tell them you are a living soul, you are going topside and you'll take them along."

Chapter 21

THE HELPFUL MAN ATTEMPTED TO PROVIDE AASON WITH instructions
on how to accomplish his goal but in the end, Aason felt the process
itself was very simple. He and MASAL left the Suduri compound
and hopped aboard another region of the flowing ground, navigating
their way back to what Aason called the south. They passed the
village where Sussen, Reema and Estar lived. They passed through
the woods where Aason had encountered Skodla. Eventually, the pair
returned to the opening Aason used when he first arrived in
Purgatory. The golden light from the other world came streaming in.
Aason turned his back to it and looked out upon the strange silver,
gray and white world of Purgatory.

"The man seemed to think that all I had to do was shout,"
Aason muttered out loud. "That seems pretty mundane for such a
final act."

"They'll hear you and they'll come," MASAL replied.
"Every soul here is looking for resolution. And that's what you'll
offer to them. Look, I'll start so you see what it's like."

"How do you do that?" Aason asked. "I really didn't
understand his explanation about all the ins and outs."

"I agree he made it overly complex. It really is very simple. I
glom onto you and our two bodies will merge. We'll be ourselves but
we will reside in one body. As soon as the others see that, especially
those who have already accomplished their afterlife's goals, they'll
get the idea."

MASAL placed his two hands upon Aason's leg. They began
to lose their substance and flowed into Aason's being.

"Wait," Aason said. "Stop."

MASAL pulled back. His hands were stuck on Aason's leg.
Aason reached down and grabbed them and it took a bit of doing but
eventually he was able to pull them free.

"Why did you do that?" MASAL asked.

The boy looked down at him. "Are you sure you want to do
this? You said you had some issues you needed to resolve. What are
you going to do if this is a one way trip?"

MASAL nodded thoughtfully. "I have come to see that you
are my redemption. If I help you do this, I will have done sufficient

penitence to earn my way topside. At least that's the way I feel. I've spent enough time here." The little mechanical man looked up at Aason. "What I'm saying is that I am ready to go."

"Oh." Aason nodded. "OK." He cupped his hands around his mouth and shouted as loud as he could. "I'm going topside," he called out. His voice boomed unnaturally along the valleys and the mountains. "Anybody who is ready to go up, I promise you'll retain your individuality."

The ground started shaking and off in the distance, a cloud of dust rose up that quickly resolved itself into a thunderous herd of beings rumbling toward them.

"Let me get on board before they get here," MASAL said, pressing his hands against Aason's leg. I can help you manage things."

"OK," Aason said, "go ahead."

MASAL reached forward and hugged Aason's leg with his stubby arms. His body became more fluid and melted inward until his entire substance flowed through Aason's body. While he could no longer see MASAL, he could feel him as if he were still present. He closed his eyes and the faint shape of MASAL was in his imagination.

"Are you still there?" Aason asked, looking down and all around.

"Yes," answered MASAL. *"We are one, now. Brace yourself. They are coming."*

The crowd of creatures and people moved ever closer. At the front, zombie-like, a few entities shuffled forward. They reached out for him and soon some were brave enough to melt inward. Aason shivered with the first one or two. As each soul became part of Aason's being, he could feel their individuality inside. It was a peculiar sensation. It was like being in a crowded room except this room had no walls. This first wave was the people or beings that were ready to go but did not have a vehicle.

The next wave was a mixture of creatures and people that had a different agenda. They were the ones who were waiting for an assurance that they would not be lost. As more and more beings merged with him, Aason felt himself grow a little more in size. He looked down at his body and noted that it was becoming slightly more transparent. The effect was somewhat the same as when Starship OMCOM was nearing escape velocity. The more souls that merged with him, the larger he grew. At the rate he was growing, Aason realized he had to get outside before he became too large to fit through the opening.

He squeezed his bulk through the entrance and straightened up, bathed now in the golden light of topside. With the continuous influx of souls, it didn't take long until he was nearly as tall as entry pool. The torrent of merging souls at his rear did not show any signs of slowing down. Each soul was fighting to force Aason's body to resemble their own form. The end result was that he was becoming more and more teardrop shaped, just like the creatures he had observed when he had first arrived here. The only way Aason could explain it was that this shape would be the lowest common denominator. More and more beings joined him and his physical form continued to swell. Finally, he became so large that his top part, you could no longer call it his head, poked up above the pool so that the other upside down teardrop-shaped beings could see him. Some of the beings who were plucking the shrimp-like creatures from the pool stopped what they were doing. Aason did not know how he knew but he knew they were turning their attention to him.

From underneath, the never-ending flow of souls continued to increase Aason's volume and strength. It was not long before he was the same size as the other blobs standing around the pool but his swelling did not stop. Aason knew he had to get out of where he was or soon he'd be too large to even exit the structure housing the pool. Like a liquid snake, he slithered past the other creatures which he could only assume were gods until he exited the structure and found himself in the open air. His far end, the one that had remained within Purgatory, finally snapped free and he was now as large as he would get. To look at him, you would have thought he was a gigantic upside-down rain drop or teardrop. The bulk of his being was on top. The bottom was just a tiny, translucent stalk.

The being that had been Aason looked all around. The majesty and beauty of the realm before him was indescribable. The cloudless sky was a brilliant gold, uniformly illuminated by an unseen source. To his left and his right were uncounted thousands upon thousands of rows of teardrop-shaped creatures stretching off to the horizon and beyond. They were swaying back and forth as if they were being blown by an unfelt breeze. The ground itself was a glittering gold made all the more spectacular by reflecting the golden sky. The only deviation from this scene was a thick black stripe that extended before him to way beyond the horizon. It seemed out of character for this most perfect of places.

Even though it was not necessary, Aason turned his being to the left. The teardrops spoke to him in his very soul.

"Join us," they intoned. *"Revel in the mystery of all of creation. Luxuriate in true faith. Come sing with us."*

Their pull was very powerful; their incantations were like a siren's song. However, from behind him another chorus arose, much different in tone.

"Join us," the other group called out, *"Revel in the glory of all knowledge and reason. Come sing with us."*

It couldn't be this simple. Aason only had to choose between faith and reason? The offer of knowledge was too strong. Wasn't that why he was here? Aason shuffled his tiny bottom past the black stripe to the other side and planted himself into the golden ground. Without conscious thought, he began swaying in time to a distant song. He could feel the souls that he had accumulated absorbing the ethereal music as well. He turned the bubbly top part of his mass upward and soaked in the golden rays from whatever made the sky glow. It was an exquisite feeling. All the voices within him were singing the same glorious song in perfect harmony. He did not know how he knew but slowly their individuality, the one thing they prized, was dissolving away. None of them cared. He knew he didn't care.

Never had anything been more clear to him. Where he was now, what he was doing, this was, in fact, the point of all existence. To gather together like this and sing the song of Species Zero Prime. The edges of his person, his being, his soul began to erode. He was letting himself dissolve as well. He wanted it to dissolve. He wanted to become part of the all. It was so beautiful. If only Lupe...

Lupe! Aason's mind snapped back into place. She was the reason he was here. Trapped as he was, he could never find her. He could never help her in this form. He would have to break free but then what? How would he even find her? He didn't know where she was. He needed help and help he got.

"You can use your computing engine to ask Species Zero," a silent voice echoed in his mind. *"He will know where your sister is."*

Aason's bubble self twisted around trying to see who was addressing him. The millions upon millions of teardrops all the looked the same. All were swaying in time to the heavenly music gnawing at his mind. No, wait! There was one upside-down teardrop that pushed its way forward, parting the crowd until it was standing directly on the black stripe. The bubble shape narrowed and shrank and became more opaque. Soon, in its place, stood a man of indeterminate age, clothed in a traditional white Vuduri jumpsuit.

"Who are you?" Aason asked silently.

The man opened his mouth and spoke out loud, "You called me Molokai back in your universe. That will do for now."

"Molokai!" Aason exclaimed. He looked down. His body had extricated itself from its former teardrop shape and he was now standing on the black stripe next to the human-looking being that had once been a creature made only of light. The boy had somehow grown so that he was nearly as large as the teardrops.

"Come back," called the nameless, faceless blob that had previously housed his spirit. *"We need you. We want you. Come sing with us."*

"No," Aason said and he closed them out of his mind. He turned to Molokai. "Who is Species Zero? And what computing engine were you talking about?"

"Species Zero is the collective consciousness of a certain group of…"

"You mean like our Overmind?"

"Conceptually you would find it similar."

"And the computing engine?"

Molokai replied, "The computing engine is the one we brought with us. You called him OMCOM."

"OMCOM? Where do we find him?" Aason asked, looking all around.

"We need only follow the lines of battle to the central dais." Molokai pointed down at the black stripe to illustrate. "He will be there."

"What do you mean lines of battle? Battle as in fighting?"

Molokai nodded solemnly. "Yes, there has been a war here dating back to the beginning of time itself. Up until now, the two sides have been evenly balanced, tempered by Species Zero Prime. But the arrival of your OMCOM will give the side of knowledge the upper hand."

"I don't understand," Aason replied.

"You do not need to," Molokai said. "Come. Let us find your sister." With that, he turned and walked away from where Aason was standing, careful to always remain on the black stripe. Aason hurried to catch up.

"Please explain to me," Aason called out. "This is Heaven. It's supposed to be all peace and harmony."

"Shhh," Molokai said. "Keep your voice down. You do not want to attract the attention of my brothers." Molokai swept his arm indicating the sea of upside-down teardrops stretching to the horizon and beyond. "If one of them gets a hold of you, they may decide to absorb you. They are slow but they are not infinitely slow."

With that, Molokai turned and continued on the path, picking up his pace. Aason fell in line behind him, checking to his left and right on a regular basis and occasionally behind him. The landscape never varied. It was filled as far as he could see with swaying teardrop-shaped entities. If you had pressed him before he arrived here, Aason would have guessed that Heaven was a pretty interesting place. The reality, such as it was, was that it was rather monotonous. He and Molokai were moving along the path too quickly for him to calculate areal density and therefore estimate how many gods he was seeing but it was a lot. He hurried a bit more and tapped the other being with his finger.

"Who are all these gods?" Aason whispered toward Molokai. "I thought we humans were Species 927. There are millions and millions of them. And you said each represented a different species?"

Molokai stopped for a moment and looked around. "Your species designation is prefixed by your galaxy number. Your designation of 927 simply means you are the 927th sentient species discovered in what you call the Milky Way. What you and I would call Species Zero is the collective consciousness of all the species of that particular galaxy. However, there are more than one hundred billion galaxies in your universe. That is their origin. Species Zero

Prime is the collective consciousness of all that you see here, all the Species Zeroes. But do not concern yourself with it." Molokai jerked his thumb toward the stripe in front of them. "Let us hurry. The central dais is in sight."

Looking past Molokai, Aason spotted a structure right in the middle of the path. It was a wide platform raised up into the air. There were banks of stairs mounted on each of the four sides however it was too high for Aason to see what was on top of it. The only features he could make out were two columns, one gray and one white on each end of the far side.

Molokai moved even faster and Aason broke into a jog to keep up. At last they came to the golden steps leading to the top. Aason went dashing past Molokai to the top of the stairs and what he saw there made his heart stop, if he had a heart that is.

It was Lupe!

Chapter 22

"LUPE!" AASON CALLED OUT AND HE RAN ACROSS THE PLATFORM TO his sister. She was seated on a very ornate chair, reminiscent of a throne, strapped down by bonds made up only of glowing lights, sparkling and twinkling with every color of the rainbow. Some of the tubes, pulsating with indescribable colors were entering and exiting her body carrying what could only be her life-force within them.

"Lupe, Lupe," Aason said. He clawed at the shimmering tubes passing through her body but he could not gain a purchase. His hands went through the tubes of light as if they were just made of light. Aason reached in and lightly grabbed her chin, turning her expressionless face up toward him. Her eyes were open but they were completely white, devoid of irises, only reflecting the golden glow of the sky above. He could not tell if she saw him or not but there was certainly no reaction.

Aason let go of her head and tried pulling on her arms but while the tubes and bonds were made of light, they were perfectly effective in keeping her locked in place. He could not get her limbs to budge.

"Help me," Aason called out to Molokai. "I have to get her free."

"She belongs to us now," shouted a different voice. Another man, dressed all in white, holding a tall golden staff, came strolling up the steps to Aason's right. As he approached, Aason could see the man looked much older than Molokai's incarnation, with a long flowing beard, also snow white. He was dressed in a white caftan covered by a pure white robe.

"She doesn't belong to you," Aason protested. "Why do you need her? Why won't you let her go?"

"We are using her power to increase the efficiency of the computing engines," the man said, pointing. Aason followed his finger and saw a thicker, glowing tube leading from Lupe to the base of the white column. He stared at it. Fused to the column was an all-white livetar. It was OMCOM, frozen in place. Aason ran over and shook the former livetar. "OMCOM, OMCOM, wake up," he said.

Three slits formed on the bullet-shaped head, which had previously been featureless. The eye slits opened up and regarded

Aason. "I see you made it," OMCOM said finally. "I knew that you would. Give me a moment to get unbound."

With that, OMCOM wrenched his arms and legs free and then his torso. With a jerking motion, he fully extricated himself from the column. The glowing tube which had been attached to the bottom of the column quickly retracted itself back within Lupe's throne. OMCOM shook himself then pointed toward the slate gray column.

Aason looked over at the other column and realized that it was Junior, attached in the same way as OMCOM. He ran over and shook his cousin. As with OMCOM before, two eyeholes and a mouth-hole formed on the featureless head.

"Cuz!" Junior said. He swiveled his head around, looking from side to side. "Where are we?"

"We're in Heaven," Aason said. "Pull yourself free. I need your help."

"Can do," Junior replied and he began to disentangle himself.

Aason didn't wait for him. He went back to the older man and demanded, "Let my sister go."

"I told you no. She stays here."

"The boy has arrived," OMCOM offered. "It is time to release the girl."

The being with the long white hair shook his head. He bent his staff forward to point to Lupe. "We have come to realize she serves us a great benefit. Her strength is nearly infinite. We have decided we are going to keep her for all time."

OMCOM stepped even closer. "That was not the bargain," he insisted. "The boy only had to bring me here. You said if he showed up, you would let her go."

Aason cocked his head. "What do you mean not the bargain? You knew they were going to take her?"

OMCOM nodded.

"You amoral, selfish, arrogant bastard," Aason shouted angrily. "You got Lupe kidnapped? Look at what they've done to her."

OMCOM held his hands out. "Aason, I do not expect you to understand."

"What's to understand?" The boy shook his fist at the former livetar. "You were working with them all along. That makes you responsible."

"It is not like that," OMCOM said. He turned to the young man. "Way back when, I created my mutations for the sole purpose of discovering the nature of the universe and to see if there was anything beyond our existence. Some of them found this place. When they returned, they told me about the war here. They told me it was slowly coming to a head and the end result could be destruction beyond comprehension. The residents on this side," OMCOM pointed to his left, "felt I could help them win the dispute and possibly put an end to the war for all time. It seemed a worthy venture to me and certainly more fulfilling that just spinning in orbit around Tabit. In this place, I would be serving a greater goal. But the only way to do this was to get you to go fetch Molokai and convince him to bring me here."

"So you used us. You manipulated us. Like we were just some sort of tools or puppets?" Aason cried out. "Did you ever once consider our safety?" Staring at OMCOM's impassive face, he suddenly stopped his rant, seeing that it served no purpose. He looked over at Lupe then asked, "Why did you pick me anyway? And why Lupe? Why didn't you just come yourself?"

Molokai answered on his behalf. "Aason, by now you have come to see that between your world and ours, there are an infinite number of dimensions and qualities far outside of your experience. Yes?"

"Yes," Aason answered glumly.

"As I explained to OMCOM some time ago, beyond your world, there are dimensions that can be accessed only by possessing the proper qualities. It was your desire to save your sister that allowed us to come here. Without that desire, we would have wandered aimlessly forever looking for this place. It was a necessary condition."

"Well it was wrong," Aason said, pounding his hand into his fist. "We were not created to serve your needs. We're human beings. You may be a god but you're not our God. You had no right."

Aason turned to the older man. "Let her go. Now!" he commanded.

"I agree with the boy," said Molokai. "The presence of the computing engine is enough. Adding her power is only causing an unneeded escalation."

The man in white scoffed at Molokai's statement. "You are descended from a trivial pacifist species. You always thought you were above the fray. Your taming of your holy Stareaters. Giving them a purpose. Finding a way to extend the life of the universe does not make you any better than the rest of us."

"I am just as important as you," Molokai said angrily.

"No. I took a stand. We all did," said the white-bearded man. "You refused to take sides. We banished you until you agreed to see it our way. Are you reneging on our offer to redeem yourself? Do you wish to be branded a traitor again?"

Molokai pounded his chest. "My redemption was complete by bringing the computing engine here. And your escalation of the war could result in the destruction of Heaven and of all of existence including the real universe."

"You are no one to pontificate. I am the appointed representative of Species Zero Prime and…"

Molokai interrupted him. "Self-appointed representative," he said sharply

The white bearded man continued, "Nonetheless, Species Zero Prime has decreed that there can never be eternal harmony until there is a resolution to the conflict. And we have figured out a way to resolve it. Him." He pointed at OMCOM.

"At what cost, though? The disenfranchisement of spirituality? The end of faith?" Molokai offered.

Aason sighed in frustration over their argument. He couldn't help himself. He had to speak up. "What kind of war can gods have anyway?" he asked bitterly. "You already have everything you need. You live in Heaven. You live forever. Why do you even need a computer? What could you possibly do with him?" He pointed at OMCOM.

The white bearded man replied, "Since the beginning of time, there has been a fundamental disagreement regarding the nature of knowledge. The first few who arrived here were content to revel in the mystery of creation and they had no desire to learn all things. However, soon the more curious species, myself included arrived and we began to question the nature of bliss itself. One side, that side," the man pointed to the uncounted row after row of teardrop shapes swaying to the north. "They believe that knowledge is beyond infinite and we cannot know all things. Our side…" The man pointed to the south. "We believe that all things can be known. We brought the computing engine here to collate our knowledge and prove once and for all that all things are knowable."

Aason shook his head. "That's the stupidest thing I've ever heard in my life. What possible difference could it make which side is right? Why go to war over it?"

"You are merely a human, a living soul," the entity said. "There is no way for you to understand."

"Of course I understand," Aason said. "But you've missed the point totally. You have a hypothesis. You ask the question are all things knowable? The only way to find out the answer is to perform an experiment. The results of the experiment will confirm or discredit your hypothesis. In other words, you'll determine if you can know all things or you can't. So your side, their side, it doesn't matter. You'll know when you know. Why fight about it? You'd find out a lot faster if both sides worked together."

The white bearded man started to speak and then stopped. He turned to look at Molokai who nodded.

"The boy is right," Molokai said. "This has been discussed before. Why not all work together? We will know when we know. His analysis is correct. There is no need for war."

The long-bearded entity crossed his arms across his chest and bent his head down. At last he lifted it up and said firmly, "The concept of a truce was rejected eons ago because we had no neutral third party to compile the information without bias. War was inevitable."

"What about him?" Aason asked, pointing at OMCOM.

The older man squinted as if he was unable to focus then he opened his eyes wide. "You would be able to do this?" he asked. "Collate information collected by both sides fairly and impartially?"

"It would be my honor," OMCOM replied.

The man tugged at his beard. "It appears that perhaps it *is* time to revisit this issue again," he said. "It certainly would be more efficient for all of us to work together."

"Then we have a truce?" Molokai offered.

The man nodded once. "There is no harm in trying."

"So now you'll let my sister go?" Aason asked.

"No!" commanded the white bearded man. He slammed the end of his staff into the platform and the top end began to glow. Sparks started shooting out it. "She stays. Regardless of the outcome, we can still use her. Her power."

Aason formed his hand into a fist and raised it in a threatening manner. "I want her back," he said grimly.

The older man looked right at Aason and pointed his glowing staff at him. "Do not test me, boy. You are not even a molecule in our world, you are simply an atom. No, I am overstating it. You are not even an atom. You are a subatomic particle. You are meant to build us, to allow us to achieve glory. You, yourself, are insignificant. You can still die and return here as a tasty morsel for one of my brothers."

Molokai walked up and put himself between the staff and Aason, shielding him. "The boy has earned her freedom. The time has come to let her go."

The white-bearded one thrust his staff past Molokai's side and violently tried to sweep him out of the way. Molokai grabbed the staff and raised it up. The older man grasped Molokai with his free hand and tried to fling him off to the side. All around them, the uniform swaying of the million, million teardrop shapes became more disjointed on both sides of the platform. A low thrumming noise washed over them as the disturbance on the platform interfered with their singing of the perfect song.

Molokai held out his right arm and a huge teardrop-shaped being from beyond came flying in, sinking into his body. Molokai swelled up to more than twice the size of his opponent.

"Those were the nine billion souls from the Earth," Molokai said, "Aason's father's birth world. They believe you should let the girl go."

The white bearded man held out his right arm and another teardrop-shaped being came flying in from the other side, merging with him and swelling him up until he matched Molokai's new size.

"And those are the three *trillion* souls of Bandalarea who died as a species trying to prove our original thesis. I know they disagree."

210

Molokai leaped forward and locked the man in bear hug and they twisted each other toward the right. Molokai swung the man the opposite way, to his left and the man responded. It was a violent dance. Round and round they went, ever faster. As their spinning increased, their shapes mutated. Their forms became grayer, more diffuse. Soon they had darkened and swelled so much that they formed a vortex, a mini-tornado spinning right in front of OMCOM, Aason and Junior.

Aason turned away from them and walked over to where Lupe was being held captive. He looked at his poor, tortured sister and sank to his knees. There had to be another way and he was going to find it. He closed his eyes, held his arms straight up and beseeched the higher powers for help. He kicked in whatever passed for his EM transmitters and PPT transceivers for extra measure.

"Oh Lord, Species Zero Prime, whoever you are, whatever your name is," he intoned wordlessly, *"This is not how it is meant to be. Lupe should be allowed to live her life. You don't need her now. She'll be back here soon enough. Give me the strength to release her so that we can sing your song of glory back where we belong."*

A hot white flash of knowledge entered his mind, exploding into an epiphany regarding the fundamental nature of existence. This place called Heaven was just one infinitesimal part of a much larger, infinite Cosmos, a hyper-universe. There were uncounted such Heavens stretching from here to eternity. The ultimate power reaching down to Aason transcended all of it. It told him the conflict playing out in front of him was as insignificant to the grander universe as the emotions a single grain of sand would be to the ocean. For one brief moment, Aason understood not only the nature of the universe but its connectedness. He understood his role and Lupe's role. He understood the purpose of their lives and life in general. He couldn't help it. The higher power had seared it into his brain. Things were far simpler than he had ever dreamed and he now knew it was within his abilities to make the situation right. All he had to do was to *truly* perceive the unreality of it all.

"Aason, look," Junior shouted, pointing at Lupe.

Aason opened his eyes and saw the bonds restraining his sister shimmer and disappear. With nothing binding her to her chair, Lupe pitched forward. Aason lunged toward her and caught her before she could fall over. He stood up and lifted the limp body of his sister in his arms, rocking her back and forth. He kissed her forehead gently.

Meanwhile, the tornado swirling around behind him reached ever upward toward the sky. Lightning bolts were flashing from within. An ethereal wind buffeted them but Aason was more than up to holding steady for the time being.

"Go, now," OMCOM whispered harshly. "I will guard you." The livetar moved quickly to Aason's left, spreading his arms to give the boy a corridor between the spinning gods and the edge of the platform.

"Come on, Junior," Aason said. His cousin joined him and they raced across the floor with OMCOM providing protection from the wind and lightning. Aason ducked down as a lightning bolt sailed over his head. He dashed down the steps with Junior only a step or two behind. Ahead of him, the transparent bubbles were closing ranks across the battle line to block his way.

"Stand back," Junior shouted and he raced ahead of Aason, crouched so that he was using his right shoulder to block the beings like a fullback tearing through some lightweight linebackers. Aason followed behind in his wake. The slow-moving bubbles were no match for the livetar. More likely, they just didn't care very much. On and on they went, Aason cradling Lupe as tightly as he could until they came upon the structure in which Aason appeared when he first arrived here. Aason pushed past Junior, past the remaining upside-down teardrops, around the vast pool to the far side where the platform stood.

"We have to go there," he said, using his knee to indicate the silvery glowing gap between the platform and the floor.

"It's too narrow. How do we fit in there?" Junior asked, fighting off more teardrops that seemed intent on glomming onto him. As long as it was limited to just one or two, Junior was fine but more were piling in through the door during their exchange.

"I'll show you," Aason said. "In this place, you can be anything you want to be. You just have to imagine it."

With that, Aason embraced his unconscious sister as tight as he could and made himself smaller and smaller until he was small enough to fit inside. He dashed under the overhang and stopped. He turned in place and looked up. To his dismay, he saw that a gigantic Junior was being overwhelmed by a tsunami of teardrop-shaped creatures flooding into the building.

"Come on!" Aason shouted. "Make yourself small!"

"I don't know how," Junior replied. Where his arms were caught between the bubble creatures, they were beginning to dissolve. "You go," Junior said. "I'll never make it. I'll buy you the time you need." He shook his arms violently but most of them were gone.

"Junior!" Aason cried out. "You can do it. You told me you don't have an imagination but we know you do. Use it. You just have to imagine how you want things to be. It doesn't have to compute. Everything in this place is what you think it is."

"I'm still a machine," Junior said resignedly, his legs were beginning to dissolve now. "This is the only way I can imagine I am."

It was clear to Aason that Junior was losing the battle. He fought off the sadness that was washing over him trying to think of a different way to approach it.

"Junior, if you were just a machine, you could run a simulation of what a human being would do," he shouted. "You could emulate what I would do. But you're so much more than just a machine. You're a living soul. Otherwise you wouldn't be here in the first place. You're my cousin." Aason took a step forward, exposing himself once again. "You need to think outside your machine programming. We're blood. You said it yourself. Be my blood. Use our bond to imagine yourself otherwise."

Junior cocked his head and stared down at the diminutive Aason. "Emulate imagination? Of course! I know what to do. Simulation initiated…" he pronounced. In the blink of an eye, the livetar disappeared completely.

Aason lowered his arms in defeat, still grasping the unconscious Lupe as tightly as he could. His beloved cousin was gone. But then he felt something crawling over his foot. He looked down and saw that it was a tiny, tiny slate gray livetar who waved at him and squeaked, "Let's go home."

Chapter 23

AASON SHRUNK DOWN A LITTLE FURTHER AND JUNIOR GREW A BIT until they were roughly the same size. Together, they passed through the gap between the platform and Purgatory and entered the other world. They only went a short distance when Junior stopped to look around. He turned in place to confirm that the entrance was still behind them. He turned back and looked from left to right then he looked up, staring at the featureless sky.

"I find the geometry of this place rather confusing," the livetar observed.

"You haven't seen anything yet," Aason said, continuing forward. "The whole ground is like a bunch of rivers. You just need to step on the proper stream and it'll take you anywhere you want to go."

"Where *do* we want to go?" Junior asked.

"We have to find the Suduri. They know how to get back to our world without a spaceship the size of a planet. Follow me."

Aason stepped ahead and used his senses to visualize the stream that would carry them off to the mountains to the east. Junior was right behind him. As before, a herd of fuzzy creatures came up the rub against him. This time, it didn't bother Aason at all. Some of the creatures took the opportunity to rub up against Junior. The livetar reached down and picked one up. He turned it left and right but couldn't make out any structural details. He placed it back on the ground and they continued. Aason skipped over to another stream and yet another and they were soon moving at a decent pace. The flow of the ground was not insensitive to him. It seemed to understand where he needed to go and cooperated.

Off in the distance, huddled around some outcroppings, a few human-like figures waved at them.

"I can't wave," Aason said, lifting Lupe up slightly. "Wave back for me."

"Do you know who they are?" Junior asked while he was returning the greeting.

"No," Aason replied, "but it doesn't matter. Everybody that was ever alive ends up here as some point. Life and death are just part of the same continuum."

Junior said, "As a machine, I have always treasured facts above beliefs but being in this place has taught me that humans may have had it right all along."

"What do you mean?"

"I will give you an example. I have heard many stories about things called ghosts. I had previously dismissed such stories as just so much superstitious nonsense. But I now realize that the phenomenon is probably real. The apparitions reported are simply souls that have temporarily found their way back from this place to our normal plane of existence."

"I guess you're right," Aason said. "Now that you mention it, a lot of people who have had near-death experiences always report seeing the same thing. I always found that too odd to be a coincidence but I had nothing to base it on."

"What do they say?"

"They all say they see a bright light and a tunnel and at the other end of the tunnel are their loved ones, beckoning to them. The living souls who are near death are probably just creating a temporary portal and looking up here."

"Fascinating," Junior said. "I will have to consider more of these stories and see if they fit with what we now know after we get back."

The ground beneath them seemed to approve of Junior's pronouncement because the flow picked up its pace even more. Ahead loomed the hills and mountain Aason had seen when he first encountered the Suduri. They were stretched out with higher and lower peaks but still recognizable.

When they finally arrived at the base of the mountain, Aason stepped off the ground flow and headed toward the crevice he had seen earlier. Junior followed him. It was much wider now which worried Aason a little bit but as soon as they were through, he was pleased to see he was not wrong. The Suduri were still gathered there, milling about as before. Having gained much more experience with the denizens of this odd place, Aason was able to see clearly there were living souls intermingling with the ghostly presence of those that had died before. The same bearded young man who had greeted them earlier in the day came up to them.

"I see you were successful," he said, stroking Lupe's head gently.

"I don't know," Aason said, looking down at his sister. "She won't wake up."

"She will but she needs to get out of this place," the man replied. "I can see they have drained her of much of her strength. You must take her back to the living world. She needs to be surrounded by her loved ones to recover. Their love for her will nurture her and bring her back to health."

"In that case, can you help us?" Aason asked. "You said you had a way to get back to our universe. You called it a portal."

"The Suduri have discovered many such portals," he replied. "I can show you the one they use to go back and forth to their home world." The man cocked his head at Junior and pointed. "He is not human, is he?"

Aason turned and looked at his cousin. "No. Does that matter?"

The man shook his head sadly but thoughtfully. "The way of the Suduri, their portal, it will work for you and your sister. But it would not work for him, unfortunately."

"Why not?" Aason asked.

"The Suduri are human. They are very spiritual, but they are human nonetheless. It was their very humanity mixed with that spirituality that allowed them to climb the ladder, so to speak, and find this place. Their method of going back and forth depends upon those qualities. A machine just cannot resonate with those requirements."

Aason shook his head violently. "I refuse to believe it," he said. "His soul is just as valid as mine and yours. He's my blood."

"You may love him as if he was your brother but it doesn't change the fact that he isn't human," the man said sadly. "It's not an indictment. Just a fact. You have to understand how they built the portal. They used their absolute belief that Heaven was real to devote themselves toward reaching upward. The more they dedicated themselves to the pursuit, the closer they came to their goal. Once they broke through, they were thrilled to find not only their relatives but many, many souls who had preceded them. So the portal was built by the power of the human mind and spirit. It only goes between here and their home world. And only humans can travel along it. I'm sorry."

Junior reached over and put his hand on Aason's shoulder. "It's OK, Aason. You can go. You get Lupe home. I'll figure out something, somehow," he said.

"No!" Aason insisted. He furrowed his brow. "Find me another way. You told me there were infinite portals. Find me one where we all go back together."

The man stroked his thin beard thoughtfully. "I am aware of another portal that might work, not too far from here, but I do not know exactly where it leads."

"Does it take us back to our universe?" Aason asked. "Or somewhere else?"

"I am virtually certain it leads back to our original universe. While the spirits that have come here through it are like nothing we know about, their general makeup and experiences would seem to indicate so. They are a mix of the organic and cybernetic. It might work."

"OK, show us," Aason said.

The man sighed. "It is a risk," he said. "If you went back with the Suduri, while it would not take you to your home world, at least you would be safe. It would give your sister time to heal."

"Show us the other portal," Aason commanded, lifting his elbow.

"Very well," the man replied. He turned and walked slowly through the center of the group of living and dead. The crowd parted to let them pass. The man led Aason and Junior past an outcropping on the other side to a moving part of the ground which was very wide. It flowed in the general direction that Aason had decided to call the west. They hopped onto one particular section with ease. Aason realized that this piece was not like a river. It was more of a free-floating smallish plateau. Aason imagined the sensation of riding it must be something like a polar bear back on Earth might experience riding an ice floe through a sea except there was no water and no freezing cold temperatures. The section seemed to understand their needs. The man pointed ahead at a dark circle in the ground.

"We get off here," he said and he scampered off the large chunk of solid ground to another section. Aason and Junior followed.

In front of them was a yawning black hole, not unlike a PPT tunnel that was pointed to an unpopulated section of space. However, there were no points of light. There was nothing that indicated it led anywhere.

"Last chance," the man said pointing down. "That is the actual Suduri portal. Are you sure you don't want to go there? It is a known."

"I'm sure," Aason said, adjusting Lupe's weight. It seemed odd that she should be getting heavy since there was nothing real about this place but his human mind couldn't shed a lifetime's worth of experience.

"Very well. Beyond here, we must walk. The portals prevent much movement of the ground."

With that, they continued on until they came to a large field made up of a series of black circles. Some were small, some were fairly large.

"Be careful you don't fall into one of them," the man said. "We do not know where most of them end up. We believe some may actually go to other universes."

"Aason, stand behind me, just in case," Junior said and he charged ahead of Aason so that they walked in single file around the circles. At last they came to one hole that was at least twice the size of the others.

"There it is," the man said. "I am virtually certain that it leads back to your universe judging from the quality of the souls that emerge but that is all I can tell you."

"So what do we do?" Aason asked, coming up beside him. "We just jump in?"

"That is how I've seen the Suduri do it, at least within their own portal," the man replied, "but there is something else you must consider."

"What?"

"I cannot be sure that the other end will even take you to a planet. It might put you right in the middle of space. It would be a shame for you to go through all this trouble just to die in a vacuum and come right back here again. Even though you now know that Heaven is real, you still should not be in a rush to return."

"If it is protection from being in space, I can help with that. I'm going to use my imagination," Junior said with a wink of his eye hole. Aason laughed. He had never seen a livetar do that before.

Junior lay down on the ground in the prone position. He placed his hands along his side and they seemed to fuse to his trunk. He started stretching and growing, elongating, until he approximated a miniature version of his starship shape. He split open his humped dorsal surface, folding back the two edges so that there was room enough inside for Lupe and Aason.

"Hop in, Cuz," Junior said, his voice muffled somewhat. "I'll finish getting back to my old shape after you are inside."

Aason shrugged. "OK," he said and he laid Lupe's unconscious body on the floor of the tiny starship. He turned to face the man.

"Thank you," he said. "You've been very helpful. I..." The boy stopped speaking and looked the man, who appeared to be little older than himself. "You never told me your name."

The man rested his hand on Aason's shoulder. "When I was alive, I was known as Jack Henry but I believe your mother's people referred to me as Hanry Ta Jihn. I am your great, great, great, great, great...well, there would be too many greats. Let's just say you are my great, great grandson."

"G, G, Grandson?" Aason stuttered. "What?!" His jaw hung open.

The man smiled. "I have been looking down on your whole family tree for the last 800 years. My parents too until they decided to move on."

Aason had to use his hand to close his slack jaw. "Hanry Ta Jihn," he whispered.

"It's no big deal," the man said.

"How did you, how do you..." Aason couldn't even form the question.

"I had brief contact with your mother when you were maybe two years old. Your mother's mind has the ability to transcend time and space under the right circumstances. I'm sure she is aware of this. She reached back and touched me during a really hard time in my life. From your perspective, it would have been more than 800 years ago. I didn't actually know it was her until I came here. Your mother is really quite a remarkable woman."

This was almost too much for Aason to process. He just stared at Hanry Ta Jihn, tilting his head to the side as if that would help. This meant the stories his mother told him were true. She really had traveled in time or at least her mind did.

"My mother told me we were descended from you but I never really believed it. From what she told me, I thought you died before you ever had children. Something just didn't add up."

Jack Henry waved to another person far behind Aason. The boy turned and saw a young woman, quite beautiful in her own right, come over to join them. She bent over and gave Aason a quick kiss.

"I'm Lacy Henry," she said. Aason cocked his head. He had never heard of her. "I know," she continued as if she were reading his thoughts. "My name was kept very quiet for protection from the Ark Lords. Jackie and I were going to get married when he returned from his fight with the Ark Lords but he never came back. He died before our wedding could take place. But we were already committed to each other so in our hearts, we were already married," she said. "I was already pregnant with his son before Jackie went off to fight his final battle." She reached forward to stroke Aason's cheek. "Aason, I am your great, great, great grandmother."

While Aason was staring at her blankly, she knelt down and patted Lupe's head and gazed upon her lovingly. Then she stood back up again and faced the two men. "It pleases me no end to see how strong and smart and noble you've become."

Aason just shook his head. Even though he would have given anything to not let Lupe get taken and have to come to this place, just meeting these people was beyond extraordinary.

"As I said, my parents have since moved on," Jack Henry offered, interrupting Aason's reverie. "But I know they would have loved to send their regards. You'll do that for me and Lacy? You'll say hello to your mother for us? You'll tell her I am very much looking forward to meeting her some day?"

"Sure," Aason offered enthusiastically. "Of course."

"Just know that I have resisted moving along all these years because I wanted to meet her in person. After that, I will take my final journey."

"That's, that's, I don't know what to say…"

"You don't have to say anything. I'm glad we got to meet. Now get along. Your sister needs tending to."

"Thank you. Thank you for everything," Aason said.

Hanry Ta Jihn and his wife Lacy nodded. Aason stepped inside the little spaceship and lay down, taking his place right next to his sister. The couple waved to him as Junior closed the flaps of his miniature cargo bay and sealed Aason and Lupe within. Although there was no light, Aason assumed his i-rods could see by the warmth of his body and his assumption was rewarded by being able to make out Lupe's immobile form. She looked as comfortable as was possible given the circumstances so he shouted, "All set."

Aason heard a rumbling sound, reminiscent of a plasma thruster and he could feel them moving along the ground. He had to grab hold of Lupe as the whole thing tipped forward. It felt as if they were falling but then everything went from black to truly black.

Chapter 24

JUST AS HIS FATHER HAD EXPERIENCED SLEEPING 14 CENTURIES IN cryo-hibernation, there was no way for Aason to be aware of how much time had passed while he was unconscious. He opened his eyes and found himself buckled into the strong, supportive pilot's seat within Junior's spacious cockpit. Everything looked amazingly normal however his body didn't feel normal. He felt torpid, like he was drugged. He slowly turned his head to the left and saw his sister strapped into the co-pilot's chair wearing a traditional white Vuduri jumpsuit. Her eyes were closed and she appeared to be sleeping or even out cold.

"Lupe!" he whispered with relief. He knew he should be jumping up and down for joy but his body reacted like it was in slow motion. Aason tore at his X-harness, trying to get it unbuckled. Looking down, he realized he had two hands again. He was shocked and surprised but completely delighted. At least that was one benefit of going to Heaven and coming back again. He finally got himself unbuckled and stood up somewhat unsteadily. He felt dizzy. He gripped the armrest until the wave of vertigo passed.

"Hey Cuz," he said while staring at Lupe. "You there?"

"I sure am," replied the starship excitedly through the grille built within the front console. "We made it!"

"Where are we?" Aason asked groggily, moving around his chair so he could get to Lupe. He looked down at his body which was also dressed in all white. He patted his chest. The sensations felt odd, especially from the hand that had not been there when they left. If his hand was back, how could he be sure he was really himself after what happened? It was an absurd question but then everything he had just experienced was absurd.

"I don't know yet," Junior answered. "I'm getting my bearings now. From the preliminary evidence, I believe we've made it back to our own galaxy. I just launched some star-probes to help me map out the star field. I'll have results for you shortly."

Aason stepped past the center console to Lupe's slumped-over body and tilted her chin up slightly. Just to see her, to touch her, was a thrill for him. Her skin was warm but she didn't seem to notice. He carefully lifted an eyelid and was pleased to see that Lupe's eyes had returned to their normal color. Her pupil reacted to the light appropriately. Aason was not a doctor but that seemed to him to be a good sign. He let her eyelid go and leaned her head back gently against the headrest.

"Lupe, can you hear me?" Aason asked quietly. There was no response from the girl. "Lupe!" he barked much louder this time.

Lupe's eyelids fluttered and she opened her eyes all by herself. She looked up at Aason then around the cabin.

"Who are you?" she asked in a weak voice.

"It's me, Aason," her brother replied. "Don't you recognize me?"

A sad expression washed over her face. "No," was all she said. It seemed like the exertion of speaking just the one extra word drained her. She closed her eyes and leaned back in her chair as if her brother were nothing but a distraction.

"Uh oh," Junior said through the grille, interrupting Aason's examination.

The boy snapped his head around. "What do you mean uh oh?"

"Well, the good news is I can definitely confirm that we made it back to our own galaxy," Junior replied.

"You're saying there's bad news?"

"Do you see that bright star off to the starboard side?"

Aason looked out the cockpit window to the right. "Yeah," he said.

"It's called Deneb."

"I've never heard of it but if you know what its name is, that's a good thing."

"Not exactly. Deneb is over 3200 light years from Tabit. Even with the X-drive, it's going to takes us almost eight days to get back there."

Aason walked over and wearily sat back down in the pilot's chair. He glanced over at the body of his sister who looked as peaceful as an angel in repose then turned to face the front.

"Well, I suppose it's better than nothing. I'm worried about Lupe, though. We need to get her examined as soon as possible. She seems really out of it." Aason glanced out the window again at the star field. "Any way to speed things up?"

"I suppose I could find us a planet and manufacture more memrons. In theory, I would be able to achieve a higher velocity that way."

"How long will that take?"

"I don't know. We'd have to find a suitable planet or asteroid. Figure maybe a day or two to mine the ore that I need and manufacture more units."

"And how much will the extra memrons cut down on our travel time?"

"Perhaps a day or two?"

Aason held up his hands palms up, almost like they were part of an old-time balance scale. "Then that doesn't really seem like it's all that useful," the boy observed.

"I agree. I believe it is called diminishing returns."

Aason turned to look back at the bulkhead then he came back around to face forward. "You don't have to support OMCOM's matrix anymore. Doesn't that give you more computing power?"

"I already figured that it into my calculations," Junior answered with a hint of sadness in his voice.

"Oh."

Aason racked his brain. Nothing came to him. His head was still too fuzzy. "I suppose you better get started then," he said. "No sense in waiting around."

"Roger that. I'm on it."

The starship fired up the whining sound of the modified PPT projectors. A black hole appeared in front of them eclipsing the star field dead ahead. A muffled roar rumbled from the rear as Junior pulsed his plasma thrusters and as soon as he entered the tunnel, he activated the X-drive generators and the blacker-than-black of null space washed over the front.

"Do you want some virtual instruments?" Junior asked.

"Not right now," Aason said. He stood up and returned to Lupe, unbuckling her. He lifted his sister up out of her chair, cradling her head against the crook of his left arm and supporting her legs in the other arm. His right hand felt surprisingly strong.

"I'm going to go put Lupe to bed," he said. "I don't know exactly what's wrong with her but at least it'll be more comfortable than sitting in a pilot's chair."

"You got it," Junior said. "I'll be here."

With that, Aason carried his little sister out of the roomy cockpit and a short way down the corridor turning left into her cabin. He carefully laid her on her bed and covered her with a blanket then sat down next to her. He watched her for a long while. Her facial expression was completely relaxed. Her breath was slow but steady. Aason sighed and stood up. It didn't seem like staring at her was really helping all that much.

Just as he turned to leave her room, he heard Lupe's voice.

"You said your name was Aason, correct?" she asked softly. Her voice had an almost ethereal quality about it.

Aason turned in place. Her voice sounded like Lupe and yet it did not. It didn't matter to Aason. A broad smile came over his face. "Yes!" he answered as he sat back down on the bed next to her. "I'm Aason."

"The being known as Lupe. If you are Aason then you would be Lupe's brother."

Aason cocked his head. "Yes, I'm your brother. Wait. What? What do you mean the being known as Lupe? You're Lupe."

"I do not know," she said. "I am aware of her existence but I am not certain I am she."

"No!" Aason said, reaching forward. He stroked her long brown hair, flecked with gold, moving it off of her face. "You're Lupe. You're my sister. I brought you back. You're here with me now. You're safe."

Lupe shook her head. She closed her eyes and said, "I hear your words but I am having trouble associating them with what I know." She lifted her arm weakly and made an indistinct gesture. "Could you leave me now? Your presence is not... I must be alone to think."

"But, but..." then Aason stopped. The poor girl had been through so much. Arguing with her wasn't going to accomplish anything. Dejectedly, he left her room, taking one more moment to glance back at her before he returned to the cockpit. Junior's company is what he needed right now.

"How is she?" Junior inquired upon his arrival.

"Something's not right," Aason said, sitting down in the pilot's seat. "She says she doesn't know if she's really Lupe."

"How can that be?" Junior asked. There was genuine concern in the starship's voice.

"I don't know. How could anybody know? Look at me." Aason held up his hands. "I ended up with two hands again. How is that possible? And we don't know what they were doing to her up there. I mean we were dealing with people's souls. What if they kept her soul and just sent her body back?"

Junior didn't answer. He rotated the main display to its full upright position. The flat panel lit up and the starship projected an image of an ovoid shape, off-white in color. Red lines circled around it, emitting from one end and reentering in the middle. A second set of lines, this time green with a tight helical spiral interposed, flowed from one end to the other. A third set of lines, Day-Glo yellow, appeared with the spiral flowing in the opposite direction starting at the distal end, looping around and reentering where the green ones came from.

"What are you doing?" Aason asked.

"I have an idea," Junior replied. "It just came to me. Let me finish my simulation."

Aason just sat there quietly, watching the brightly lit display. After a few seconds, the colorful lines stopped and instantly, the display burst into a bright white light and then the image was gone.

"Just as I thought," Junior said.

"Thought what?" the boy asked, perplexed.

"You know how memrons operate, right?" Junior did not wait for Aason to answer. "Anyway, they use a steady stream of microwaves which are then converted into useful power by employing an ultra-efficient thermocouple. There is an oscillator inside synched to the frequency of the radiation. That means a memron's internal clock is determined by the density of the microwaves."

"OK..."

"So if I create an auxiliary power source, in this case a dual stream of polarized microwave radiation, I could triple the amount of power flowing through the memron pool by using circular polarization. One clockwise, one counter-clockwise."

Aason said nothing. He knew enough to wait for Junior to finish.

"In essence, I could over-clock the memrons and get probably three times the computing power out of them. Since the X-drive is driven by the power law, I'd be able to up our top-end speed by a factor of ten or maybe even a little more."

"You're kidding me," Aason said incredulously.

"No, I'm not. My simulations tell me that at the higher velocity, I could get us home in roughly 18 hours."

"That's fantastic," Aason replied excitedly. "Do it."

"Hold on. There's one slight problem."

"What?"

"Memrons really aren't designed to run that way. Once I put in that much power, they'll burn out as soon as I stop. It would be the end of me."

"No," Aason shouted emphatically. "You're talking about suicide. I can't let you do that."

"I'm not wild about the idea myself but we need to get Lupe home."

Aason folded his hands across his chest. After a moment, he snapped his head up. "Show me your dorsal surface."

Junior activated his topside cameras. The central display revealed the huge bulge running along the top of the starship that was the result of OMCOM's graft now what seemed so long ago.

"What if you, I don't know, just used the extra memrons that OMCOM gave you for the boost? Keep your regular complement the way it was before he added on?"

"That's a good idea," Junior said. "But to segregate them, I'd have to shield the ones that make me, well, me, and shut them down until we stopped. I couldn't have them exposed to the polarized microwaves."

"OK, so do that."

"You still need an on-board computer to manage the X-drive. I'd have to create a clone of at least part of my operating system on the outboard section. Once we got to our destination, it would burn out along with the rest of the memrons. I'd need you to reboot me after the all-clear."

"I can do that," Aason said, excitedly. "And you'd be your regular self, right?"

"Yes," Junior answered however, there was a wistful tone to his voice.

"What?"

"I kind of like all that extra computing power," Junior said. "I'll miss it."

"We'll get you more," Aason replied. Then he added, "At the store!" He was pleased with his rhyme.

"You're right. Memrons are cheap. Let's do this."

The shushing sound of the null fold generators faded away and they dropped into normal space. It was hard for Aason to make any sense of the star field around him being so far from home but it didn't really matter. As long as Junior knew where they were going.

There were some strange thunking noises and occasionally the cockpit jarred slightly. Odd sounds emitted from Junior's grill from time to time. After a little while, Junior spoke up.

"It's ready," he said. "Aason, I want you to meet Junior, Jr."

"`Hello,`" emitted a tinny voice from the same front console. "`Pleased to meet you, Aason, sir.`"

"He sounds like your Dad," Aason observed, laughing.

"I thought that would amuse you," the starship replied. "I'm going to go to sleep now. Don't forget to wake me up on the other side."

"Are you kidding me?" Aason said. Then he realized Junior really was kidding. "You're my best friend. I don't know what I'd ever do without you."

"`We aim to please,`" replied Junior, Jr.

"Junior?" Aason said. "The real Junior? Is he still there?"

"`His matrix has been shut down. Mine is ready. Course laid in. I am prepared to begin upon your order.`"

That Junior would just wink out without saying a formal goodbye surprised him. But then, he knew he shouldn't be surprised. The computers had a different take on such things. Much of the time, they seemed like people but in the end, they were still computers or at least not organic. Junior had showed him he was so much more but at the same time, it was also very clear that he was not human.

Aason shrugged. "OK, go!" he commanded.

With that, the PPT generators began ramping up. Once again, a yawning black hole appeared in front of them, occluding the star field. The plasma thrusters pulsed on and as soon as they were through, the null fold generators kicked in. Their sound was slightly different, deeper maybe. The entire cabin shook as the starship picked up speed.

"Virtuals?" Aason asked.

"**Roger**," replied the replacement voice.

On the main display of Aason's wraparound console, the familiar four quadrants appeared. Of highest interest to Aason was the virtual speedometer. It started at 150 Kc then jumped up to 350 Kc and continued climbing fast. It quickly passed 1000 Kc but then the rate of increase started slowing down. It settled in around 1530 Kc, just as Junior had predicted.

"Sleek," Aason muttered to himself then he had a sudden moment of panic. He looked all around the cockpit, worried that a waving set of translucent multi-colored tentacles might appear out of nowhere. He scanned the cockpit from top to bottom and back and forth but nothing unusual happened. After a while, he shrugged, got up and went to check on Lupe again.

Chapter 25

THE FEW REMAINING DIGITS ON THE ETA COUNTER INDICATED THEY were nearing the end of this phase of their journey. Besides the occasional bathroom break and grabbing a snack, mostly Aason spent the bulk of his time alternating between staring at the virtual instruments, dozing off in the pilot's chair and checking in on Lupe. She just did not want to get up. Aason was able to awaken her several times to make her take some water, which she accepted, usually without a word. He occasionally tried to offer her some food which she steadfastly refused. One time, she allowed Aason to guide her to the refresher. Luckily, she seemed to know what she was doing in there by herself. Even though the trip was made in silence, Aason was relieved to know she wasn't totally dehydrated.

Given their proximity, this was going to be his last visit to her before they arrived at Tabit. He entered her room and sat down on her bed.

"We're nearly there, Sis" he said. "Don't you want to come up to the cockpit and watch?" he asked hopefully.

Lupe opened her eyes and stared at Aason for a long time. At least she took the trouble to shake her head no.

"Do you want to wait in the sitting room?"

"I prefer to remain here," she said quietly but firmly.

"Well, is there anything at all I can do for you? Can I get you anything?" he asked.

"No thank you," she said and she closed her eyes again.

"OK," Aason answered gently. "I'll let you know when we're there." Having done it enough times, he was pretty sure he had gotten as much conversation out of her as he was likely to get. This troubled him more than anything but he wasn't going to push her. He tucked her in one final time but as he was about to leave, he heard Lupe's voice.

"Aason, will your mother be there?" she asked.

He turned in place. It almost sounded like the old Lupe. "Mom? Of course," he said, smiling, although he was confused at the odd way she phrased it.

Lupe mumbled something but Aason couldn't make out what she said. She rolled over to face away from him. He knew this visit, like all his previous visits, was at an end so he went forward to await the end of their transit.

"**Three minutes to arrival,**" announced Junior, Jr. echoing what the ETA ticker told the young man. Aason didn't bother to point out to the simulation of his cousin that its statement was redundant. He was used to dealing with ultra-intelligent computers with real personalities. It made him realize that the old-fashioned kind were really nothing more than exotic interfaces to equipment and computations. Despite all of that, Aason felt compelled to try one more time to engage it in what was probably going to be their last interaction.

He stared at his wraparound instrument panel, focusing on the fluttering simulated dials, meters and counters. Finally, he asked, "What happens to you when we shut down the drive?"

"**I cease to function.**"

Aason chewed on his lip before speaking. "That's a rather cold assessment. Doesn't that bother you?" he asked.

"**No. I cannot find any algorithmic module that would even equate to your expression. Bother serves no purpose.**"

"Well it would certainly bother me," the boy replied.

"**That may well be true for a human but not for a heuristic, algorithmic entity.**" The voice paused then continued. "**Allow me to clarify. I am merely a copy of an operating system. I serve a function. When that function is complete, I am no longer necessary. Therefore, my existence should be and will be extinguished. It is completely efficient and what my programming dictates.**"

Aason shrugged. "Whatever you say." He could see he was getting nowhere so he decided to change the subject. "Let's go over the shutdown sequence one more time."

"**When the ETA counter displays all zeroes, you press the 'Off' icon. It will resemble a button. I will position it in the center of your main display screen. As soon as you press it, your action will cut off the power supply to my computational core.**"

"Then what happens?"

"**Without power, my computing structure will cease to function. However, from your perspective, the ship will be without a controlling computer for the duration. You will then need to reactivate the original Junior** operating system using the interlock located beneath your instrument cluster."

"And that's it?"

"Affirmative."

"OK," Aason answered, shaking his head. Junior hadn't bothered to give the simulation a personality module so that made easier to look at it as just a machine. There was no element of this thing's being that would be making the trip to Heaven, any more than an air car or molecular sequencer.

"One minute to arrival."

Aason shrugged. He reached behind him and grabbed the straps of the X-harness and buckled them in place just in case. The display changed from a minutes counter to a seconds counter. Aason focused on it as the seconds ticked their way down toward zero. He started fidgeting in his seat. Even though he knew what it represented, he tried to temper his excitement by concentrating on the task at hand. As soon as the ETA counter hit single digits, a large yellow circle appeared in the middle of the display with the word 'OFF' in the center in large letters.

"Well, Junior, er, junior, it's been fun."

"If that is your observation, so be it," replied the pseudo-computer. "Goodbye."

With that, the digits hit all zeroes. Aason reached forward and tapped the icon for OFF.

A thunderous explosion rocked the cockpit, forcing Aason to grab the armrests even though he was firmly buckled in. The shushing sound of the null fold generators shut down immediately. As soon as the vibrations stopped, Aason unclasped the X-harness and leaped up, looking all around the cabin. His eardrums felt full then started popping meaning there was a dramatic loss of atmospheric pressure. The front display faded and the entire cockpit was plunged into inky darkness.

"Junior?" Aason called out tentatively, finding it somewhat hard to breath. There was no response. "Junior!" he called out again, louder this time and again there was no reply.

Aason forced himself to suppress his panic. He looked out the front of the cockpit and saw a normal star-field. His inability to draw in a breath and the pressure behind his eyeballs told him that the atmosphere was getting very thin. There had to be hull breach but there would be no time to repair it before he passed out.

Aason used his i-rods and body heat to survey the cockpit immediately in front of him. Following the plan they had set forth; Aason bent over and removed a panel built into the underside of the control console. He felt around until he found the interlock that Junior had prepared for him. He pulled it out and pressed it back in to force a system reset. The cabin lights came back on which meant that part of the maneuver was successful.

Aason quickly climbed out from underneath the console and stood up. The main display screen activated and showed a steady march of diagnostic symbols indicating startup.

After a moment, Junior spoke up in his normal voice as if nothing had ever happened. "Are we there yet?" the starship asked.

"Cuz, Cuz," Aason shouted breathlessly. "Hull breach."

"Oh, yes, I can see that. Let me do a quick survey," Junior replied calmly. He activated his dorsal camera's view of the top of the ship. Most of the hump which had been grafted onto his airframe had blown off leaving Junior's top end superstructure exposed without a stealth shield and light emanating from a variety of pinpoint holes.

"Hang in there, Cuz," Junior said reassuringly through the rapidly thinning air. With a rat-a-tat-tat, Junior flew clumps of constructors to the affected areas, plugging the holes one by one. Eventually, the rate of tapping sounds decreased and Aason found it easier to breath as Junior restored the atmosphere to an adequate pressure. Finally, the sounds stopped and once again, the roomy cabin assumed its normal, comforting silence which was the hallmark of the starship under regular conditions.

"Well, that was close," Junior observed finally.

"You got that right," Aason said, taking a deep breath and letting it out slowly. His head snapped up. "I better go check on Lupe," he said.

He darted out of the cockpit and raced back to Lupe's room but he needn't have bothered. She appeared to be asleep, seemingly unaware of the near disaster that had almost taken place. Aason reached over and touched her shoulder gently. Lupe made a tiny sound and shifted around slightly but didn't appear to wake up.

Convinced she was alright, he returned to the cockpit and sat down in the pilot's chair.

"Cuz, you sort of gave me a scare there. It sounded like a bomb went off."

"It kind of was," Junior replied sheepishly. "My simulations told me the over-clocked units would shut down as soon as we withdrew their direct irradiation. I think I overlooked the fact that the residual microwave radiation stored within the memrons would have to dissipate somewhere."

"Boy," Aason said. "Maybe next time you could work that out in advance."

"I suppose that would have been more prudent," Junior replied churlishly.

"So where are we?" Aason asked looking out the windshield at the star field in front of him. Without the help of a star chart, the sky before him was pretty but didn't really have any meaning. He cocked his head trying to make sense of it all, scouring the skies for a constellation he might recognize.

Junior made a clicking noise from deep inside his grille. "Uh oh," Junior said ominously.

"What?" the boy asked anxiously.

"More bad news…" the starship replied, his tone dropping off.

"Come on," Aason said with exasperation in his voice. "Now what?"

"Based upon my star charts, we missed our mark."

"Missed our mark? Dammit! By how much?"

"By an entire tenth of a light year." There was clearly mirth in the starship's voice.

Aason did a double-take then laughed with relief. In cosmic terms, that was a blink of an eye. "Buddy, you are too much. How long to get back?"

"My computing infrastructure is pretty messed up right at the moment so I'd say the Null Fold Drive is gone for now. However, I still have our old-fashioned force projection PPT drive but that means it's going to take old slowpoke here almost an hour to make it back."

"Puh," Aason exclaimed. "Junior, you are absolutely the best!"

"As I programmed Junior, Jr. to say, we aim to please."

"Let's get going, buddy. I've got to get Lupe back." He sat back down in the pilot's chair and buckled in the X-harness.

"You got it, Cuz," the starship replied. "Next stop, Tabit."

Junior pulsed his trim jets laterally so that they rotated roughly 180 degrees about the vertical axis. The starship then activated the opposing trim jets to bring them to a dead stop relative to the nearest gravitational well. A whining noise from the rear indicated the regular PPT generators were ramping up to speed. A yawning black hole appeared with the tiny remnants of Tabit centered in the middle. The plasma thrusters ignited and they entered the tunnel to begin the final leg of their journey.

One hour later, as soon as they dropped into normal space, Aason felt the familiar tickle of a PPT connection taking hold. It was his mother reaching out to him. After he gave her a brief overview assuring her that he, Lupe and Junior were back safe, Aason cut the conversation short by telling her it would be better if they discussed the events that had transpired in person. Rome agreed and instructed him to return to the spot where Planet OMCOM would have been before the gigantic computer left this universe. Aason passed on these instructions to Junior and they now found themselves floating in space with the nearest celestial body only the remains of the star that had once been known as Tabit.

Junior's MIDAR tracked the approach of his father, the starship called MINIMCOM, and as soon as they were close enough, Aason made his way back to the cargo bay where he anxiously awaited his parents' arrival.

With a whoosh and a pop, Rome, Rei and Aroline appeared at the back of Junior's cargo compartment in a huddled mass. Aroline immediately broke free and ran up to Aason, grabbing him and kissing him passionately, molding herself against his frame.

"I've missed you so much," she sighed.

The touch of her body against his was a feeling that Aason warmly received. "I missed you, too," Aason whispered. "More than I can even tell you."

With that, Aroline squeezed him even tighter. Finally, after she released him, he held up his hands, flipping them back and forth showing them to her, smiling the whole while.

"All healed," he said.

"I see," Aroline observed happily. She stroked his hands lovingly then concentrated on running her fingers up and down the valleys between each of the fingers of his previously missing right hand. "You could never tell it was ever gone," she said.

"Yup," Aason responded proudly.

In the mean time, Rome had come up next to Aason with Rei right behind her. Aroline stepped aside so that Rome could hug her son. "I'm so glad you're safe," she said. "I was so worried."

Rei put his hand on his son's shoulder and added, "I'm very proud of you, son."

Rome pushed herself away from Aason and asked, "Now where is she?"

Aason's smile dimmed a little bit. "I'll take you to her but, well, this is what I wanted to tell you in person. I don't think she's exactly right just yet."

"What do you mean?" Rome asked with a horrified expression.

"Well...she says she isn't sure she's Lupe," he replied. "She talks about herself like she's somebody else."

"What? Take us to her. Now!" his mother commanded.

Aason led the group up the corridor and into the little bedroom. Rome sat down on the bed while Rei stood looking over her shoulder. She tugged on the girl's arm and Lupe cooperated by moving around so that she was flat on her back. Rome brushed her hair from her face and her daughter opened her eyes.

"Lupe," Rome said softly and she bent down to kiss her. The teenager blinked several times.

"I know who you are. Your name is Rome. You are Lupe's mother. Correct?" the girl in the bed said. Even from across the room, Aason could tell that her voice was definitely stronger than before.

"Yes, Lupe," Rome said, smiling affectionately. "I'm your mother."

Lupe moved her neck around and looked up at Rei's face. "And you are Reinard Bierak, Lupe's father? You have saved mankind many times over."

"Yes, sweetheart," Rei said, chuckling. "I'm your father, little Lupe."

"You all keep saying that name as if I am she," Lupe said a little miffed then her tone softened a bit. "I'm so confused." She searched the eyes of her parents and said, "I'm sorry but I don't know exactly where Lupe is. I think it's possible that I may have left her behind."

"What?" Rome gasped. She quickly placed her hand on Lupe's forehead. There was no fever. She activated her telepathic powers to search around inside Lupe's mind, trying to find a vestige of her daughter's personality. A tidal wave of images washed over her and those images were staggering, simultaneously overwhelming and incomprehensible. She was dazzled by a brilliant golden light, more pure than was imaginable. She saw an unending sea of gigantic upside-down teardrops swaying slowly back and forth in time with a music that could not be described. Rome tried to grasp the enormity of the visions in Lupe's mind but it was like looking down the barrel of infinity.

Even as Rome continued to probe deeper, her breath was becoming shallow and rapid. Her heart was racing. There was something happening to her physically. It was as if her very being was transferring from within her to her daughter. She could tell that it was nourishing to Lupe, making her stronger but it was draining her completely. She felt like her soul was being sucked out of her body.

Finally, Rome became too faint. She knew she had to break free otherwise she would pass out. Reluctantly, she pulled her hand away from Lupe and leaned back. With slightly unfocused eyes, she glanced down at her daughter. Lupe was gazing back at her and there was definitely more color in her face.

Rome took several deep breaths, trying to slow her heart rate down. After she had recovered somewhat, she spoke up, forcing herself to sound positive. "Lupe, my baby. I know you've been through a lot but you'll be all right. You just need time to heal."

Lupe looked so innocent lying there. Rome needed to comfort her more but feeding her all of her psychic energy was too much for her system. Then it came to her. "Lupe, do you remember when you were a baby, when I used to sing to you? To help you sleep?"

The girl stared back with a quizzical expression on her face. Rome placed her hand lightly on her daughter's cheek and with her beautiful, lilting voice she sang quietly, "Lupe, Lupe, flies through the air. She loves to feel the wind in her hair." Rome sang the verse twice more, looking for signs of recognition on her daughter's face.

"That does seem very familiar," the teenager said thoughtfully when Rome was done. After a moment, she took her eyes off of her mother and searched the room. She peeked between her parents to where Aason and Aroline were standing. She pointed at Aroline who was positioned just behind Aason in the doorway. "Who is that girl?" she asked with just a hint of disdain.

Aason put his arm around Aroline and guided her forward into the room. "This is Aroline," he said proudly. "She's my, my girlfriend." Aroline's face lit up when he uttered those words. She waved a tiny wave at the girl lying in the bed and smiled at her.

"Hmpf," Lupe said, wrinkling her nose. She rolled over and faced away from her family. "I can tell you all mean something to me. Something important," she said. "But having so many people in this room makes it difficult to absorb. Could you leave me alone for a bit so that I can think?"

Rome tried very hard to keep a stiff upper lip. "All right, my baby," she said. "We'll be here when you're ready to get up." She stood up then she stepped aside as Rei bent over to give his daughter a kiss on the back of her head.

"We'll be back later, sweetheart," he said gently. He activated the "cell-phone" in his head and asked her, *"You'll be OK by yourself?"* He thought he heard her reply, *"Yes, Daddy,"* but he wasn't sure. He couldn't ask anybody because no one would have been listening in. He shrugged.

Lupe's mother couldn't hold it in anymore. Tears started rolling down her cheeks. Rei put his arms around his wife and Rome pressed her head against his broad chest, sighing deeply. She shook her head slowly then looked up into his eyes. He cocked his head toward the door and Rome nodded. Her husband led her out of the room, leaving only Aason and Aroline standing there.

After they were gone, Aroline looked up at Aason. Her psychic connection with him was still very strong and she could see he was near tears himself. She lifted her hand up to caress the boy's cheek. "She'll be OK," she whispered. "I know she will. It's like your mom said. She just needs more time." She kissed him tenderly and stepped back into the corridor.

"Maybe," Aason muttered. He tried to make himself believe it but they didn't know what he knew. They hadn't seen what he had seen. He couldn't shake his memory of her blank expression, her colorless eyes, her motionless body with the glowing tubes draining her of her life force. He could only hope there was something left of her soul in the body that he brought back with him from the heavens. He drew in a breath and held it for a moment then let it out slowly. Staring at his sister, he shook his head. Aroline was right. There was nothing more they could do but wait.

He turned to leave but just as he did, he heard a voice in his head using their private EM transmission channel. It was Lupe's voice!

"You and your girlfriends. Now I remember!" she said laughing. Her mental tone changed to more of a sing-song. *"Aason and Aroline sitting in a tree, K, I, S, S, I, N, G."*

Aason whipped his head around just in time to see Lupe sticking her tongue out at him. A huge smile broke out on his face.

At long last, Lupe, his Lupe, was back.

Epilogue
Year 3505 AD (1424 PR)
(29 years later)

ROME SAT QUIETLY IN HER STUDIO, DAYDREAMING, STARING OUT the window. She had just completed the background for her latest still life painting and she was waiting a little while for the oils to dry. Rei was off attending a Union conference in Central City and would not be home until late in the day.

Life had been very peaceful these last few years. The X-drive had opened up contact with many, many species within the Milky Way galaxy. Deucado had long since eclipsed Earth as the central hub of human activity and was selected to house the headquarters for the Galactic Union. Rome had retired from her job as librarian and teacher choosing instead to spend her golden years perfecting her art. Her once beautiful long brown hair had turned completely silver and Rome had cut it short as her mother had done near the end of her life.

Rome's reverie was interrupted by a loud knock originating from the main entrance to the house. She looked out across the U-shaped courtyard and saw a tall man, dressed all in white, standing at the front door. This in itself was strange because her studio overlooked the path leading to their home and she would have noticed if someone had come up the walkway. Shrugging, Rome arose and walked around the house to the front door and opened it wide.

Standing there, in front of her, was a handsome young man. He was about two meters tall, with broad shoulders, dressed in a standard white Vuduri jumpsuit. Oddly, he was also wearing a somewhat incongruous white cape. It was clear he was not Vuduri, not only because of his height and build but because his hair was completely white as well.

"Can I help you?" Rome asked.

"I take it you do not recognize me," the young man said.

"No," Rome replied. "Should I?"

"Would it help if I spoke like this?" the man said, his voice changing to a deep, metallic sounding rumble.

"OMCOM?" Rome asked, confused. "You are an OMCOM?"

The young man's face appeared to melt and for just a moment, his eyes and mouth changed to slits before returning to their previous humanoid shape.

"At your service," the man replied.

"I don't understand," Rome said. "Are you a livetar? From the Library? From the clone ships?"

"No, it is truly me," OMCOM said. "The one you used to call Planet OMCOM. I have returned in this form from the place Aason called Heaven. I needed to speak to you."

Rome stood there, just blinking. She finally composed herself long enough to stand to the side.

"Come in," she said. "Come in." She waved her arm toward the inside of the house. The former computer stepped through the doorway. Rome closed the door behind him and led the being into the living quarters. OMCOM sat down on one sofa, Rome sat on another.

"How are you?" OMCOM asked.

"I am doing well," Rome said smiling as the absurdity of the situation started to wear off. "I retired several years ago. I am an artist now!" Rome waved her hand in the direction of her studio.

"Excellent. And Rei? How is he?"

"Rei is also doing very well. He is emeritus coordinator of the Union. It's an advisory role but it keeps him very busy. Our one rule is that when he is on-planet, he always comes home for dinner."

"And our children?" OMCOM asked. "How are they?"

"They are wonderful," Rome said, beaming with pride. "They run the First Contact Academy. Aason is the administrator. He married Aroline many years ago and they had two beautiful children of their own. All grown up now. In fact, I am a great-grandmea!"

"That is wonderful. And Lupe? Did she marry also?"

Rome chuckled to herself.

"After what she went through, I don't think one man could ever have handled her. It's just as well. She dedicated herself to the Academy. She teaches First Contact skills. Several years ago, she and my grandson Rory played a large role in ending a Shell War with one of the alien Unions we came across. Right now, she's out in deep space overseeing a field exercise for the latest graduating class from the Academy."

"That is admirable," OMCOM said. He folded his hands across his lap.

Rome stared at him. Now that she studied his face, she could see it had a slightly artificial quality about it. His skin was too smooth. But beyond that, it was an incredible simulation of humanity.

"How are you doing?" Rome asked, not really sure why she posed the question.

"The intervening years since I last saw you have been spent most productively," OMCOM said. "Once the two sides agreed to cooperate, I have been helping the gods themselves collect and collate information. We have built a series of n-dimensional living memory banks to extend the information storage capacity. It is a remarkable endeavor."

OMCOM's description of his duties made Rome frown. "At what cost?" she asked. "You know what you did to my children."

"I am sorry if I caused them any discomfort," OMCOM replied. "I had a grand calling and using them was the only way to achieve that."

"You made me a promise, so many years ago, that you wouldn't ever do that again." The irritation was growing in Rome's voice. "You said you would not manipulate people without their knowledge or permission," she said stridently.

OMCOM nodded gravely. "I broke that promise, I know. But it sounds to me that Aason and Lupe have fully recovered. You, yourself, alluded to the fact that perhaps they benefited from the experience."

Rome made a growling noise and shook her head. "Let's stop talking about it. I assume you have been enjoying your new role."

"It has been extremely satisfying," OMCOM replied, "As I look back, I believe this was the very purpose for which I was created. I believe it was why you created me. And for that I will be forever grateful."

OMCOM leaned forward and stared at Rome intently. After a few moments, he said, "Please do not misunderstand me, you look very well preserved for your age but nonetheless you do look old."

"I am old," Rome replied. "I am seventy five. That is getting on in human years."

"Why is it that the Vuduri have never extended the length of the human life? It seems well within their scientific capability."

Rome cocked her head to the side. "I don't understand," she said. "What has that got to do with anything?"

"It is just a question," OMCOM said. "Why can you not stay youthful for longer?"

Rome sat back. "I can explain," she said, "but I don't know if it will make sense to you."

"Please try," OMCOM requested.

"OK," Rome replied. "You are correct. It's well within the scientific capability of the Vuduri to extend life. They've already demonstrated proof of concept with lab animals. But they've made the conscious decision not to do so. They want each person to grow old and die."

"But why?" OMCOM inquired insistently. "A person such as yourself has much to contribute. It seems so short-sighted that you have a limited number of years in which to do so."

"The Vuduri believe that every tree must give way to the seedling," Rome said. "They believe that death is a part of life so each generation must yield to the next."

"Do you agree?"

Rome sighed a deep sigh. "I don't know," she answered finally. "I know that it pains me to see my children growing older."

"Just as I thought," OMCOM affirmed. He closed his eyes for a moment then opened them again. "It is done," he said.

"What is done?" Rome asked, confused. Something about her did not feel right. Or maybe it was the other way around, that is, everything felt right for a change. Her normal aches and pains that were a constant part of her life disappeared. She looked down at her hands. Her skin was smooth and free of the mottling that she had gotten used to. She put her hands up to her face. It, too, felt abnormally smooth.

"What is happening?" she asked, the breath going out of her. She stood up and sprinted over to the mirror in the foyer. A beautiful young face was staring back at her, the face of her youth. The only difference was that her hair was still silvery gray instead of brown with the occasional strand of gold.

"What have you done to me?" she screamed. "OMCOM!" She turned to face the robot/computer/livetar/human simulation.

"You will recall the yellow pill that you took some fifty years ago. It did not just change your genetics. It also took, to use the vernacular, a snapshot of your genetic structure at the time. I simply invoked that structure and restored your DNA to the state it was in on that day."

"Oh no!" Rome said, staggering back. "You cannot."

"It is already done," OMCOM said. "I activated it on Rei as well. When he returns, you will see that he looks just as the day you met him."

Rome shook her head. The implications were staggering. She had been through so much with OMCOM that nothing, not even this, was beyond imagination. She just had no way to prepare. She returned to where OMCOM was sitting. She fell back onto the sofa heavily.

"What would possess you to do such a thing?" Rome asked, putting her hands up to her face. "Why have you come? Why are you here?"

OMCOM took a deep breath. He was taking the representation of a living human being to a very realistic level.

"I have come to enlist your aid. And Rei's. And all of mankind. And I needed you at your fullest capacity mentally and physically."

"For what?" Rome asked plaintively. "Why? Why did you have to do this to me?"

OMCOM looked down at his hands then back up to Rome. He leaned forward.

"Rome, we must destroy the Stareaters," OMCOM said gravely. "All of them."

Despite Rome's renewed, youthful vigor, her shoulders sagged. "Why, OMCOM," she asked wearily. "Why do we have to destroy the Stareaters?"

"Because they represent the wrong end to the universe."

Rome looked at him askance. "I don't understand, I thought they ate stars to delay the end of the universe."

"They do and that is the problem. When we used them to help Molokai return to Heaven, they learned about the X-drive from us.

They have adapted it to their own use and now several of them have already made the leap to other galaxies. Soon they will be spread everywhere."

"So that's a good thing. It means they will be even more effective."

"No!" OMCOM insisted. "The Stareaters are a disease, an infection. And like any infection, as long as it is limited to one cell, in this case our galaxy, it was not an issue. But once the infection learns to jump from cell to cell, eventually it can destroy the entire body which in your case would be the entire universe."

"I thought they were extending the life of the universe, not destroying it."

"What you see is not all there is. There is also Heaven to consider. Think of the two together as the cosmos," OMCOM replied. "The cosmos must go on. Everything must live and die according to the natural order. And the Stareaters are not the natural order of things. Even Species Twenty Two, the ones who charged the Stareaters with their mission, even they now agree. They sent me here specifically to explain this because you cannot perceive them."

"So what is the natural order of things?" Rome asked with a wistful tone.

"It means…" OMCOM stopped as Rome held up her hand, palm forward. She closed her eyes to concentrate.

"Rome!" Rei shouted into Rome's head using the EM transmitter which Rei called the cell-phone built into their heads. *"Something's happened to me."*

"I know," Rome replied mentally. *"It happened to me, too."*

"Where are you?"

"I'm at home."

"Then wait there. Don't even move," Rei barked back. *"MINIMCOM, can you send me home right now? It's an emergency."*

"`Of course,`" MINIMCOM replied from off in the distance.

There was a whoosh and a pop right outside the door. "ROME!" Rei yelled, barging into the house. "What the hell has happened to us?"

Rome met him in the hallway and pressed her finger to his lips. Rei's eyes widened. He could not believe what he was seeing.

The woman in front of him was the stunning, beautiful Rome of his youth although her hair was still pure silver.

"I, I…" Rei said in a muffled tone.

"Come with me," Rome offered, reaching down and pulling the speechless Rei's hand. She led him into the living area.

The white-clothed man there stood up. His head had reformed into a bullet-like shape. The face showed only slits where the eyes and mouth should be.

"Rei," Rome said. "This is OMCOM. The real one."

OMCOM took a step forward.

"Of course he is," Rei said. He turned to his wife. He looked at her and it was as if it were 50 years in the past. Except for the color of her hair, this was the very Rome he first fell in love with. The woman of the future with the glowing eyes. The one who quested for knowledge and broke free of the Overmind's grip, all on her own. "What has he done now?" Rei asked.

"Hello, Rei," OMCOM said. "You are looking very well."

"What did you do to us?" Rei shot at him. He brushed his hand along his own cheek, marveling at its smoothness.

"I merely restored your DNA to the day you first swallowed the yellow pill," OMCOM said. "Physically, you are now a snapshot of the day that I met you."

Rei looked at OMCOM. Then he looked at Rome. Then he looked back at OMCOM again. "Why?" he asked. "Why did you do this to us?"

OMCOM took another step forward. "Because I need you," he said. "I need your help."

"Help doing what?" Rei asked. He turned to Rome.

"OMCOM wants to us to destroy the Stareaters," Rome said unenthusiastically. "All of them. They have begun to spread to other galaxies."

Rei turned back to OMCOM. He laughed.

"You're crazy," he said. "There's no way. It's mathematically impossible."

"No," OMCOM offered. "It is not impossible, merely difficult.

"Difficult?" Rei scoffed. "Forgetting about the fact that they are noble creatures dedicated to the preservation of the universe, how would we find them all? Even with the X-drive, it would take an infinite number of humans an infinite number of years just to get there, let alone track each and every one down. And kill them."

"Not infinite," OMCOM said quietly. "It will take roughly 4 billion years and millions upon millions of human lives. But it can be done."

"Why?" Rome directed to the livetar. "Why do we have to destroy the Stareaters? You never finished explaining yourself."

OMCOM looked down at his feet then up to Rome. "As you know, the Stareaters are dedicated to restricting the expansion of the universe," the former computer stated. "If they succeed, your universe will reach steady state and would never contract upon itself."

"So what?" Rei interjected. "That sounds like a good thing."

"As I told Rome, this is not the natural order of things. This universe must be allowed to reach the end of expansion and contract again. Your scientists refer to the contraction as the Big Crunch. Once it reaches its climax, a singularity, it will explode again in a new Big Bang and create its own successor."

"And if the Stareaters succeed?" Rome asked.

"If they succeed, the universe will chill down to absolute zero in some 17 billion years and remain that way for all of eternity."

"So what happens if we do as you ask and stop them?" Rei inquired.

"Roughly 13 billion years after we stop the Stareaters, the universe would contract to sufficient density where it would erupt into the next Big Bang which would in turn start the next cycle."

"So…" Rei said in a level voice, "Our choice is to spend the next 4 billion years sacrificing our entire lives, dedicated to tracking down high-minded, noble creatures. You haven't even accounted for the possibility that they might fight back. But say we kill them all. We then get to spend the next 13 billion years waiting until our universe collapses and anything that is still alive dies anyway. That versus just waiting the same total of 17 billion years to die during the long dark night?"

"Yes," OMCOM said. "That is essentially it."

"If those are our two choices, then we respectfully decline," Rome said. "The time frame is the same and the net result is the same.

Death to our universe. Death to all of life. What difference does it make to us how the universe dies?"

OMCOM formed his hands into fists. "It makes a great difference," he said gripping them tighter. "You cannot take this lightly. Heaven cares about this very deeply. It is the only way to create a new source of life to sustain them and grow."

"Why should we be worried about what happens in Heaven?" Rei asked.

OMCOM unclenched his hands. "You do know you will end up there someday, right?" he asked.

Rei nodded, "That is what Aason told us."

"Then if you want your lives to have value, your children's lives, you must see to it that the cycle repeats to sustain your legacy."

OMCOM lowered himself to his knees. He took Rome's hand and bent his forehead toward it, touching it gently. "Mother," he whispered. "We must do this so that your life and the lives of your children are not in vain."

"Our lives are not in vain," Rome said lovingly. She pulled on OMCOM's hand so that he stood up. She looked into his eye slits. "It is a matter of perspective. The purpose of life lies within life itself. The purpose of life is to evolve into a mass-mind and then have that mass consciousness transcend into Heaven. At least that is how Aason told us the residents up there view it."

"That is correct. They view life in general from a species perspective. It is the sole purpose of evolution."

"But what you are missing is the *meaning* of life."

OMCOM cocked his head. "I do not understand. What is the difference?"

"The meaning of life lies within the individual. How each being lives his or her own life determines its value. What you are asking us to do negates that therefore we must refuse."

"What is the meaning of *your* life? Or of Rei's for that matter?"

Rome smiled and looked over at Rei. "The meaning of my life, of Rei's life, of our children's lives, is to live, to love and to be loyal. That's all. And that's enough."

"That cannot be all there is," OMCOM protested weakly. "You have to consider the greater good."

"No we don't," Rome said firmly. "Our lives are short and all we can wish for our children and our grandchildren and all their successors is to live good lives as well."

"But the grand plan?" OMCOM asked. "To be so short-sighted."

Rome put her hand on OMCOM's shoulder. "You are a computer. What is your job supposed to be in Heaven?"

"To help them collate all facts. To quantify everything."

"Aason told me that our universe is not all that there is," Rome said knowingly, "Just as we are made of particles too small to see, so too, our universe, everything we perceive, is but a particle of something greater, a hyper-universe, Aason didn't really have a name for it. Whatever it is, it encompasses all that we are and an infinity more. OMCOM, surely you could have deduced this. The place you call Heaven is just one of an uncountable number that sit somewhere in between all of these other universes. It's not infinity times two. It isn't even infinity squared. It is infinity to the infinite power."

"Then, then," OMCOM actually stammered appearing to be momentarily confused by the influx of information. "I can never know all of it. I am doomed to fail."

"You won't fail," Rome said kindly. "You can know *our* entire universe if you let it die. After every atom has stopped its motion, there will be no more information to be had. You will have all of eternity to do your job secure in the knowledge that there will be a finite end to the data you must compile. To reach beyond that would be impossible for anyone or anything."

OMCOM started to speak and then stopped. He looked off into the distance. After a moment, he turned back to Rome.

"The gods never told me any of this," OMCOM said quietly. "Who created this hyper-universe? This infinity of infinities?"

"It was created by God with a capital G," Rome replied.

"You are talking about Species Zero Prime?" OMCOM inquired. "You are saying it is responsible for all things?"

"Wait! What?" Rei coughed, trying to speak, "God is just a species? Species Zero Prime?" He stopped as his mind tried to grasp the gravity of his own words.

"No," Rome answered patiently. "Species Zero Prime only extends to our universe. The one true God is beyond all things. God is not a species. He is not the end result of evolution. He has no beginning. He has no end. He is responsible for all of creation and the manifestations of His glory are reflected in our universe and the next and the next and the next."

By now, Rei had recovered enough to speak again. "I didn't think the Vuduri even believed in God," he stated.

"This is not belief," Rome said, her eyes glistening. "This information was passed on to Aason by his brief contact with a power beyond knowing."

Rei rubbed his chin. "Yeah," he said. "From an engineering perspective, it's the only thing that makes sense. Like looking at mirror within a mirror except this is an infinity of infinities."

"Yes," Rome said. "It is all the sense." She turned back to OMCOM. "OMCOM, whether this universe disappears into the cold dark night or collapses down to make a copy of itself, it does not change the whole, the hyper-universe. If ours leaves a hole in its wake, another will come along to replace it."

"So... you are saying it does not matter if our particular universe dies properly?" OMCOM offered.

"I am saying every universe dies properly no matter how the end occurs."

OMCOM started to speak but Rei held his hand up to stop him. "Look, OMCOM, let the Stareaters be. Let us live our life and whether they succeed or fail, the only thing that matters to us is that we live *our* lives well. And we leave a better world to the next generation. And they try to do the same. Anything beyond that, we have no control. Infinity is just too big for us to take on."

OMCOM closed his mouth slit and turned back to the living area. He trudged over and sat down on the sofa. He lowered his bullet-shaped head and held it in his hands. Whether the gesture was required or simply for the sake of the humans, it was totally effective. Hand-in-hand, Rei and Rome walked over to where OMCOM was sitting. After a time, the livetar looked up at them.

"You are right, of course," OMCOM said. "It was silly of me to analyze the problem of cataloging everything in our universe as if it were the totality. I limited my consideration of the issues to that which the gods of Heaven lay down to me despite the fact that that is not my nature. I was intoxicated by their reliance on my cognitive abilities. They are wrong. The very nature of God is as you said. That He is beyond knowing. And from your perspective, each life is a universe unto itself. I now agree with you. I can succeed in my specific task only if the Stareaters succeed. And you *should* be allowed to live your lives the way you wish."

OMCOM stood up abruptly. "I am sorry to have bothered you. As I told you once so very long ago, you have both been very civil toward me. I am sorry for all the harm that I have caused. I will not disrupt your lives any further." The livetar turned his head upward. "I will leave now," he said.

"Wait!" Rome shouted. "The changes you made to us. Can they be reversed?"

OMCOM turned back to her. "No," he said quietly, "they cannot be reversed."

"Are we going to live forever?" Rei asked with trepidation.

OMCOM made a sound that could have been a chuckle. "No," he replied. "This was a one-time procedure. From here on in, I believe you will age normally. You will die someday. It just will not be for a great many years. I will see you again. Up there." OMCOM pointed toward the ceiling.

Rei looked down at Rome, trying to gauge her reaction. He couldn't read her face. He shrugged. "Well, thank you then. I guess," he said. "I know I'll enjoy the break from my arthritis, anyway."

OMCOM nodded once. He raised his arms up as if he was beseeching the heavens. His form began to glow, shimmering with all the colors of the rainbow rushing back and forth through his body in swirling waves. Abruptly, the livetar disappeared, leaving only speckles in its wake.

"Well," Rei said as the last speckle vanished. "You certainly put him in his place." He patted down his chest and his legs. "I have to tell you, I feel absolutely great but, like, what are we supposed to do now that our bodies are so young again?"

Rome continued to stare at where OMCOM had stood. "I don't know what to think," she said quietly. "I suppose we should tell Aason about OMCOM's appearance. He would want to know. Do you agree?"

Rei didn't answer her. Instead, Rome felt him put his arms around her waist and draw her in. "Honey," Rei murmured into her

251

neck, "Aason can wait an hour or two. Please don't take this the wrong way but the way you look now…"

Rome turned in his arms and smiled up at his youthful face. She was able to read Rei's mind without even reading his mind. She kissed him lightly on the cheek, drew her hand down to Rei's hand and grasped it firmly. Then, with a yank, she tugged him toward the bedroom.

NOT THE END

www.ingramcontent.com/pod-product-compliance
Lightning Source LLC
Chambersburg PA
CBHW050025180626
46810CB00002B/574